ZANE PRESENTS

Daddy Long Stroke

A NOVEL

Dear Reader:

It is once again my pleasure to present a novel by Cairo, one of the latest and hottest editions to the Strebor Books family. His first book, *The Kat Trap*, was so intriguing that it became an instant classic. His follow-up, *The Man Handler*, was equally a classic; both featured female lead characters. Now Cairo delivers a novel depicting the lifestyle of a womanizer.

Alexander Maples, aka Daddy Long Stroke, is a sex-crazed gigolo who has an insatiable desire to bed down as many women as possible. The story is told in raw, gritty language as we discover what whets the appetite of this outrageous character who seeks satisfaction from women coast to coast. Daddy Long Stroke successfully lures females into his tricky web not considering the pain and heartache it causes.

Hopefully, after you read this book, you will walk away analyzing your own sexual behavior, the decisions that you make in the name of love and lust, and how everything has its consequences. Cairo has once again penned a wonderful novel and we are all highly anticipating his future works. Stay tuned for his next adventure, *Deep Throat Diva*.

Thanks for supporting the authors in the Strebor family and for the continuous love and support that you have shown me over the past decade. I love and appreciate each and every one of you. To find me on the web, please go to eroticanoir.com or my social networking site at planetzane.org. You can find me on Twitter as PlanetZane, on Facebook as Zane Strebor and on Myspace as Zaneland.

Blessings,

Zane

Zane
Publisher
Strebor Books International
www.simonandschuster.com/streborbooks

ALSO BY CAIRO

The Manhandler

The Kat Trap

ZANE PRESENTS

Daddy Long Stroke

A NOVEL

CAIRO

SBI

STREBOR BOOKS

NEW YORK LONDON TORONTO SYDNEY

Strebor Books
P.O. Box 6505
Largo, MD 20792
http://www.streborbooks.com

ISBN 978-1-59309-278-8
LCCN 2010925105

First Strebor Books trade paperback edition August 2010

Cover design: www.mariondesigns.com
Cover photograph: © Keith Saunders/Marion Designs

10 9 8 7 6 5 4 3 2 1

Manufactured in the United States of America

DEDICATION

This book is dedicated to the women who crave thick chocolate,
and the bad boys who serve it.
Open wide…this one's for you!

ACKNOWLEDGMENTS

With each passing day, I remain encouraged, determined and steadfast. I am progressing, evolving, growing, and learning to be better than the day before. I owe all that I am to the One who continues to guide me along my journey. I am truly blessed!

To all those who continue to believe in me, thank you for the never-ending love, support and encouragement.

To the growing fans, thank you, thank you, thank you! Please continue to spread the word. And be on the lookout for *Deep Throat Diva* coming at ya in 2011!

To all the reviewers, I appreciate all of your feedback/comments: good, bad and/or indifferent.

To the sexually liberated and the open-minded, I hope you get pleasure from reading *Daddy Long Stroke* just as much as I took pleasure in writing it. Sit back, relax, and enjoy the ride!

One luv—

Cairo

1

Damn, I love eatin' pussy! 'Specially when a broad got that sweet 'n tangy, saucy-type pussy that sticks on the tip of my tongue. Or that juicy, gushy, peach-type pussy that squirts into my mouth, then drips down my chin as I slurp it all up. Man, listen…there's nuthin' like havin' a chick squattin' up over my face, sittin' her pussy down on this long tongue, or havin' her on her back wit' her legs up over my shoulders and my face buried deep between them smooth thighs while I'm tongue-drillin' her. Or havin' her bent over a chair wit' her ass spread open and my tongue deep-strokin' her from her asshole to the back of her slit—while I'm beatin' my dick, or got her throatin' it.

Mmmph, mmmph, mmmph…I love the way it tastes, and smells—well, provided the ho isn't a walkin' fish market, smellin' like sewage, or leakin' a buncha shit that looks like snot or cottage cheese, feel me? A smelly bitch, forget it…no tongue, no dick, nada—it's a muthafuckin' wrap! But a chick who keeps that box right…mmmph, man, listen…finger-lickin' good! There's nuthin' more intoxicatin' than the savorin' scent of a clean, excited pussy oozin' wit' hot, sticky juices. Gotdaaaaamn, talkin' 'bout gobblin' up a pussy got my dick bricked like a muhfucka, word up. And, on some real shit, I love eatin' it almost as much as I love fuckin' it.

See. Pussy eatin' is an art. It's like paintin' the perfect portrait, feel me? It's all in the brushstroke—or, in this case, the tongue-stroke. See, it's all 'bout technique. When a muhfucka like me has his head between a bitch's legs, I'm puttin' in work. I'm aimin' to bring her the greatest, most intense orgasm she's ever experienced. And I do it by usin' my mouth, tongue and fingers—simultaneously and alternately. The first ten minutes, or so, I'm teasin' her. I'm kissin' and lickin' her hips, her legs, her inner thighs. Then I slowly begin lickin' her pussy lips—right side, left side...mmmph, damn. Then I lick her clit, flickin' it wit' my wet, long tongue before circlin' my tongue 'round the edges of her asshole. Seein' that sweet brown eye pucker up in excitement turns me the fuck on, word up. And the more turned on I am, the more turned on she's gonna be.

Fuck what ya heard. Tongue-fuckin' is sumthin' a muhfucka should take pride in when doin' it. Just like I expect a broad to handle this dick like she loves it, I expect the same shit from myself when it comes to eatin' her pussy. I make love to that shit wit' my mouth, lips, and tongue, eatin' it like there's a chocolate-covered cherry stuck dead in the center of her pussy. And the only way to get to that sweet muhfucka is by mountin' ya wet mouth 'round it, then plungin' ya tongue deep in it, lickin', lappin' stickin', and flickin' that hole 'til she starts buckin' them hips up. See. A nigga like me is a greedy pussy eater, real talk. I ain't tryna stop 'til a bitch's walls start to shake, her asshole starts to ache, and she's chantin' to a higher power. That's when I slowly slip these big-ass fingers in her, swirlin' 'em 'round the inside of her cunt, pressin' up on that G-spot while I'm suckin' on her clit. I don't care how long it takes, I'ma make sure she gets hers. And when her breath quickens, her body quivers, and her moans escalate, I start wildin' out on the pussy—suckin' and lickin' her clit like a frantic, crazed-ass muhfucka 'til she nuts all over my tongue, hard. Then I ease up over top of her, slip my tongue in her mouth so she can taste her creamy juice on it, while I'm slidin' this dick up in her. And by the time I'm done slayin' her wit' this wood, nine-times-outta ten, the bitch done forgot her name and address, done tossed me the keys to her whip, or done begged me to move in. So be clear. If a muhfucka like me is tongue-fuckin' you, you best believe it's 'cause you either got sumthin' I want, there's sumthin' I need for you to do, or there's sumthin' I know I'ma get from you in the future. Otherwise, no extras are comin' at ya. I'm straight-dickin' you and that's it.

So, to my niggas who eat pussy: keep ya tongues wet, playas. And to those lame cats who act like they scared to taste the pussy, or who can't eat no pussy: You'se some whack-ass muhfuckas, word up! Get ya minds right, my niggas, and step ya tongue game up 'fore another muhfucka takes ya spot, real talk.

Nah, hol' up! I ain't sayin' e'ery ho deserves to have her pussy eaten 'cause some of these broads out here are straight nasty. That's why a muhfucka gotta use some discretion. But for the ones who keep that pussy lookin' right and feelin' right, a muh-fucka gotta learn to let it do what it do, feel me? 'Cause trust me. I've had plenty of bitches drop major paper, or lace a muhfucka wit' some wears, after I done served 'em a night of tongue lickin', followed up wit' a pussy beatdown wit' this long-ass dick.

Like this trick I got holed up in my room right now. Shakeeta's her name; a brown-skinned cutie from Irvington—wit' a lil' waist and one hundred and forty pounds of ass 'n titties. And, of course, she's a ho I met offa Myspace. We been fuckin' off and on for 'bout three months now, and she's already sucked down my dick and swallowed my nut 'bout eight times. And I've fucked her 'bout three. Now, she's actin' like she's in love wit' a muhfucka. But tonight's the first time I'm givin' her this tongue treatment. And the only reason she's gettin' it *now* is 'cause she laced a muhfucka wit' four pairs of 7 For All Mankind jeans and two pair of Gucci loafers for my birthday. Well, it ain't my actual born day, but she doesn't know that shit. Yo, relax. Sit tight. I'll explain later.

Shit, hol' up…let me introduce myself to ya'll, first, before I start suckin' the nut outta this broad's fuck-box. Aiight, check it. I'ma six-foot-four, 215-pound—lean and solid, for the record—slightly bow-legged cat with dark-brown eyes, thick full lips, a chiseled chest, strong muscular back, and big hands. My government name is Alexander Maples. But my mans 'n 'em call me Alley Cat, 'cause a nigga like me is always prowlin' 'round for some new pussy. However, on some real shit, I shoulda been named Hershey 'cause I'ma dark-chocolate nigga that melts in ya mouth and all up in ya guts. Yeah, that's right. I'm ya sweetest, most dangerous addiction. And I'm here to feed ya cravin's—one stroke, one slurp, at a muthafuckin' time.

So I'ma let you know from the gate. I'm the type a cat who loves to fuck—all day, e'eryday. Just like the U.S. Postal Service, I'm always ready to deliver. Rain, snow or sleet—I don't care if it's in ya face, ya mouth, or ya muthafuckin' ass—I'm ready to skeet. That's not to say that e'ery chick I get at is willin' to give up the pussy after seein' all this beef hangin'. 'Cause eight outta ten times, the ho's gonna run scared. But, for the hoes who do try, it definitely doesn't mean that they can actually handle all this dick. It only means they done bit off more dick than they can chew—or fuck, I should say. So they usually grin 'n bear, beg 'n pray, or cry 'n scream, hopin' their well-fucked, overstretched pussies snap back for them average-dicked niggas they fuck wit'.

However, for those ambitious freaks wit' them bottomless, un-latchable pussies, the ones who take e'ery inch of this dick, they call me Daddy Long Stroke 'cause I gotta long, thick, chocolate stick that heats up and beats up the pussy. Nice 'n slow, long 'n deep, fast 'n hard, all muthafuckin' night long—anyway, anywhere, anyhow you want it, I give it. Ya heard? You want it rough, you want it rugged. I'ma slay ya muthafuckin' ass 'til ya shit-hole starts to smoke. You want it slow, you want it gentle. I'ma rock ya box 'til ya eyes cross, real talk. Fuck wit' this dick if ya want, a nigga like me'll have ya ass crawlin' 'round tryna find ya way home. Have ya soakin' ya swollen pussy lips overnight. So, I'ma tell ya some real shit. Fuck at ya own risk. And be prepared to get rocked inside out 'cause I'ma slam it, grind it, and wind it, all up in ya. Deeply, savagely, tenderly—whatever, this dick is made for stretchin' that sweet, tight, wet pussy to the limit. And there you have it.

Anyway, back to the bitch I got in front of me. I have her legs up over my shoulders, my face is buried between her thighs, and I'm tongue-fuckin' the shit outta her pussy, alternatin' between eatin' her pussy and lickin' her asshole while jerkin' my dick. I got her wrigglin' and squirmin' and moanin'. "Oh, yes...ah...ah... oh, yes...ohmyGod, you gonna make me cum...aaaah...aaaaah... oh, shit...I'm cuuuuu—" Now guess what the fuck she does while she's creamin' on my muthafuckin' tongue?

This nasty bitch lets out a loud, hot-ass fart! And it's one of them rotten-ass, lingerin' kind. Now I don't know 'bout you, but this kinda shit ain't acceptable. Keepin' shit real, a few times I've had a chick fart while suckin' on my dick. But, I have never—and I mean muthafuckin' *never*—had no shit like this happen. It feels and tastes like I've just sucked in a mouthful of horse shit. This bitch is lucky I'm not into smackin' up a chick, 'cause if I was... man, listen, I'd peel her muthafuckin' skull back. I can tell she's embarrassed. But...I. Don't. Give. A. Fuck. I'm sorry, it's a wrap. Game over! This bitch has to go!

"Yo, what the fuck?!" I snap, yankin' my head back and jumpin' up. "You'se one nasty-ass bitch for real, yo. How you gonna bust off in my muthafuckin' face like that?"

"I'm so sorry," she says apologetically. "Sometimes I cum real hard and, when I do, I pass gas unexpectedly. I tried to hold it in, but it crept out. You had me feeling so good. I really didn't mean for it to happen."

Crept out? Nah, fuck that. Who the fuck she think she's talkin' to? I done fucked her pussy inside out, makin' her nut 'til she shakes on more than one occasion. And not once did this bitch ever bust outta her ass. But, okay, maybe she does cum hard and farts at the same time from time to time. Yeah, whatever! If that's the case, then why the fuck didn't the slut warn a muhfucka? Crept out, my ass! This bitch is literally full of shit—word up. The way that fart roared the fuck out, the bitch pushed it out purposefully, feel me?

"Well, why the fuck didn't you tell me to move outta the way, or somethin', instead of havin' a nigga's face all pressed up in your ass like that, suckin' in ya funky-ass fumes?"

"I got caught up in the moment," she offers, sittin' up. "And wasn't thinkin'.'"

"You wasn't thinkin'?" I repeat. She tries to keep from laughin'. But, a muhfucka like me don't find shit amusin' 'bout someone bustin' they ass in ya muthafuckin' grill. Stupid bitch! "Well, guess what? You not thinkin' done got ya funky ass put the fuck out. So, get ya shit on, and get ta steppin'.'"

She looks at me like I have boogers 'n snot hangin' outta my nose or some shit. But fuck what ya heard. I ain't the one. She frowns. "Are you serious? I said it was an accident."

"Yo, I'm dead-ass. Get the fuck out." I walk over and start pickin' up her clothes and tossin' 'em at her.

She gets up offa the bed and starts snatchin' her shit up. "That's real fucked up. You know that, right?"

"Bitch, I don't give a fuck," I hear myself sayin' in my head. But I igg the ho instead; stare at her as she puts back on her bra. I pick up my cell, scroll through my address book 'til I get to Carla's number. I hit the call button, then wait for her to pick up.

"Hey, boo," she answers. "You finally got around to calling me."

"Hey, baby, what's good?"

"You," she coos.

I cut my eye over at Shakeeta. She got the nerve to be ice-grillin' me while gettin' dressed. I keep my eyes locked on hers. Stare her down. Stupid bitch! Who the fuck names their child Shakeeta any damn way? Fuckin' ghetto-ass bird.

"That's wassup, baby. Yo, you feel like suckin' this dick tonight?"

"Always," she responds. "Just let me know when."

"Bet. I'ma swing through as soon as I toss out this trash."

Shakeeta slams her hand up on her hip. Her neck starts rollin'. "Nigga, I know your black ass is not tryna call me trash. And how the fuck you gonna call another bitch up and I'm standing right here…"

"Who's that in the background?" Carla asks. "Sounds like—"

"I'll see you in a half-hour," I say, cuttin' her off and snappin' my phone shut.

"…That's some real foul shit, nigga, for you to disrespect me like that," she continues as she puts on the rest of her shit. "But, not to worry, muhfucka, I ain't hard-pressed for no nigga, or his dick, especially yours. Trust me."

I laugh at her ass. "Mighty funny ya ass is always blowin' up my line talkin' 'bout how much you need this dick, how much you love this dick, how much you don't wanna stop gettin' this dick. But now you ain't pressed. Yeah, okay. That's what ya mouth says."

"Fuck you!" she yells, swingin' open the bedroom door, and stormin' down the stairs. I follow behind her, holdin' my breath, hopin' like hell Pops ain't here to hear this shit. That's all I need right now. "You ain't shit, nigga, for real." She gets to the front door, swings it open, then stops before walkin' out. She turns to face me. "I shoulda shitted in ya motherfuckin' mouth."

"Ho, get ya stankin' bum-ass on up outta here."

She gives me the finger. "Fuck you, nigga! I've been thrown outta better places." She storms out, leavin' the front door wide open.

I walk over and shut the door, lockin' it. Then stand in the middle of the livin' room for a minute, listenin' to see if I hear Pops stirrin' 'round up in this piece. I can't front, a nigga's relieved that it's quiet. Pops done warned me hundreds of times 'bout bringin' this kinda shit up in his spot, and the last thing I need is for him to walk in on it. Dude would be up in here snappin' for sure. *Nigga, you know you shoulda handled that bitch better than that,* I think, headin' back up the stairs to slip on some sweats and a T-shirt. *What if she woulda started bustin' shit up in here? How the fuck would you 'splain that?*

I take the steps two at a time, goin' upstairs to the bathroom. I brush my teeth and tongue, starin' into the mirror. Even after I've scrubbed my gums 'n shit, I still taste her rotten ass in my mouth. I brush my tongue again, then rinse my mouth out wit' Listerine. *Fuck that nasty, skank-ass bitch,* I think, shakin' my head. I rinse my mouth, again, then shut off the lights. *She mad 'cause I tossed her ho-ass out wit' a throbbin' pussy, and gypped her outta a nut.* I grab my cell, then redial Carla's number as I'm headin' back down the stairs to let her know I'm on my way. Of course she wants me to eat her pussy. Fuck outta here. I let the bitch know that's not 'bout to happen, not tonight. Especially not after the shit that just went down with Shakeeta's triflin' ass.

She sucks her teeth. "Are you gonna at least stay the night?"

I think for a minute. I got a lotta shit to do early tomorrow so this bird is gonna haveta settle for a drive-by. "Nah," I tell her. "I got shit to do in the mornin', but I can swing back through later on to hit you up wit' a dose of this heavy dick, aiight?"

Silence. The bitch knows if she doesn't wet this dick tonight it's a wrap. I'm cuttin' her supply off. And I know like she does, that's the last thing she wants. "When you leaving?"

I laugh to myself. "Now. So have them dick suckas wet 'n ready."

Two hours later, I'm back home, steppin' outta the shower. I'm refreshed, relaxed, and ready to take it down for the night when my cell rings. I glance at the screen. It's this broad I'm 'posed to get up wit' tomorrow. I met her up on BlackPlanet, another spot where I meet most of these broads I'm smashin'. She had hit my Daddy Long Stroke page up a few months back after peepin' my body flicks on it. Then she started visitin' my page e'ery damn day, leavin' me comments on my guestbook, and hittin' me with notes, and gifts 'n shit—like all the other broads I meet on there. Word up, it be live and poppin' on that site. Alotta them Black-Planet hoes be some real thirsty asses. Fuck what ya heard. The economy may be all fucked up, but trust and believe, there's a surplus of pussy out here, and a nigga wit' a good stroke game will never go broke.

I look over at the digital clock. It's 1:22 a.m. *What the fuck she want this time of night?* I think, pressin' the TALK button. "Yo," I say into the phone.

"You still coming up here tomorrow?" she asks.

"We still fuckin', right?"

She sucks her teeth. "Is that the only thing you interested in?"

"Hell yeah. You gotta problem wit' that?"

"Well," she says, pausin', "I was hopin' we could grab a bite to eat, then maybe catch a movie or something, first."

I frown. For the last few weeks, fuckin' is *all* we been talkin' 'bout. Now all of a sudden this ho wanna be on some let's-grab-a-bite-to-eat bull, like she tryna go out on a muthafuckin' date. Fuck outta here! I think, *do I tell this ho what she wants to hear, or do I keep shit real?* I decide to give it to her straight, no chaser.

"I'm tryna get this dick wet, baby. That's it. You can save the extras for some other cat."

Silence.

"Yo, you still there?"

"Yeah," she says, soundin' annoyed. "I'm still here."

I feel myself 'bout to spaze out on her dizzy ass for callin' here this time of night wit' this stupid shit. I take a deep breath, spark up the half-smoked blunt layin' in the ashtray on my nightstand, then take two long, deep pulls, holdin' the smoke in my lungs 'til I calm myself down. I blow it out. "So, what's good? We fuckin' or not?"

"Yeah."

"Oh, aiight, then. That's what it is. What, you done talked all that shit over the phone and now you gettin' scared 'n shit?"

"I'm not scared."

"Then why you call here tryna front on a muhfucka?"

"I told you. I was hoping we could go out somewhere, first."

I take another pull offa my blunt, then slowly blow it out. "Nah, baby, it ain't that kinda party. You been talkin' a lotta good shit, now it's time to show 'n prove. Let a muhfucka see if you really know howta throw that pussy up on a dick. 'Cause, on some real shit, I'm tryna snap ya spine."

She starts laughin'. "OhmyGod, you real funny."

Funny hell. Ho, I'ma rip ya muthafuckin' back open. "Yeah, go on and get ya laugh on, baby," I warn. "I'ma be up there tomorrow. Let's see if you gonna be laughin' then." She giggles some more, then gets quiet after I tell her she betta take her ass to bed 'cause she's gonna need all the rest she can get. 'Cause on some real shit, after I'm done wit' her she's gonna need the paramedics. A muhfucka's comin' through to dig her ass out.

2

"Yeah, that's right, baby. Spread them pretty-ass legs, and pull open ya pussy," I say, strokin' my dick while watchin' my fuck for the night play in her juicy fur burger. Don't get shit twisted, though. This honey-dipped ho with her wavy black hair and mesmerizin' eyes is bad as hell. Her skin is fuckin' flawless, too—soft and smooth like silk. And her body...whew! Man, listen, pictures do her no justice. This bitch's body is the fuckin' truth. Little waist, flat stomach, big-ass cantaloupe titties with inch-long pierced nipples—yeah, and a nigga like me gotta thing for a chick with long nipples. I like to lightly pinch, twist, pull and tease 'em with my fingers, then nibble on 'em with my lips and teeth. Oh, damn...I done got sidetracked thinkin' 'bout suckin' all over them thing-things. So, dig. Like I was sayin' 'n shit, this chick gotta ass you can bury ya face up in. A muhfucka can get lost for months up in them cakes. It's the kinda ass you can bounce up and down on all night. But, on the real, yo, how the fuck a bitch gonna drop her muthafuckin' drawers and not have her bush trimmed? I don't mind hair, but gotdamn...this shit right here is unreal. Don't get it twisted. I don't discriminate. I love all types of pussy. Fat pussy, tight pussy, loose pussy— bald, trimmed, and covered with hair. I don't give a fuck. Just make sure that shit is hot 'n wet. 'Cause at the end of the day, it's all fuckable as long as it's clean. But, man, listen...this chick's snatch is like a fuckin' rainforest. And on some real shit, it better be as wet as one, or I'ma ram this thick dick straight up in her Neanderthal ass.

"Stick them fingers deep in that pussy and get that pink hole wet and ready for me."

She moans, lookin' over at me. "Oh...uh...uh...mmm...I'm soooo horny. I want some of that dick..."

"Not until you get that pussy nice 'n slippery," I tell her, tossin' my left leg up over the arm of the chair in her bedroom. Her eyes stay locked on me the whole time as she plays in her twat, watchin' me beat my dick. "That's right, baby. Fuck that pussy for me. Yeah, get that shit ready for big daddy."

"I want you to fuuuuuck me...oooh, give me that dick..."

She thrusts her hips up at me, tryna offer up the pussy. I decline, knowin' she ain't ready for none of this black anaconda. "Hell, nah," I say. "I wanna see steamy juice bubblin' outta ya slit before you get any of this dick, you dig?" She moans again, throwin' her head back, bitin' down on her bottom lip, and massagin' her clit with one hand, while fuckin' herself with the other. "Yo, answer me when I'm talkin' to you. I said I wanna see ya fingers all cummy 'n shit before I fuck you, ya heard?"

"Yesssssssssss!" she shouts, windin' and humpin' her hips and twistin' and pumpin' her fingers into her hungry pussy. I grin when I see her pink hole glisten, then drip. I continue strokin' my dick in and outta my hand watchin' her get off.

On some real shit, I love sittin' back and watchin' a fly-ass chick I'm 'bout to fuck play in her hole. That shit is like havin' my own up-front and personal peepshow, feel me? Damn, you see that shit? She got some big-ass pussy lips. I lick my lips. If the bitch didn't have so much damn hair between her fuckin' legs, I'd be on my knees right now lickin' the folds of her pussy, and suckin' the juice offa them pretty-ass lips. But fuck that, I ain't tryna have a bunch of cunt hair lodged down in my muthafuckin' throat—not tonight. So, she's assed out. I'ma serve her this dick, then dip. Yep, I'm lookin' to bang, bust 'n bounce. Damn, what the fuck is this bitch's name? Shit. I can't think. Fuck! It's some exotic-soundin' shit. Fioni…Falasha…FuFu…oh, yeah, Falani, that's it.

She moans again. Her body shakes. Yeah, baby girl's nuttin' all over herself.

I swear I hope she got some good pussy. 'Cause if not, a nigga's gonna be hot. I drove two-and-a-half muthafuckin' hours to get it in wit' this ho when I could be laid up with Maleeka right now, gettin' fucked down. Now that bitch got that sweet gushy shit. Word up. E'ery time I slide my dick in her, her hot pussy melts all over it. And the bitch is a true champion of ridin' this long dick. Then again, her pussy is 'bout as wide as a parkin' garage 'cause all she likes is super-sized dick. That ho will never be able to fuck wit' an average size, or lil' dick, nigga. It'd be like drivin' through a car wash and stickin' ya dick outta the window, fuckin' a bunch of wet air. But a nigga like me parks this dick up in that big hole and fills it the fuck up, lettin' her slosh her juices all over it.

I get up and slowly start walkin' toward her holdin' a handful of dick. "You ready to fuck?"

"Yessss," she whispers. "Fuck me…"

"Yeah, that's right, beg for this cock," I say, swingin' my semi-hard dick from side to side. "You want me to split ya guts open, don't ya?"

"Yesssss."

I smirk, knowin' this ho ain't really ready. See. Over the years, I've learned that there are a lotta chicks stuck on the size of a nigga's dick. It's what these dumb hoes crave, even obsess over. And some of 'em are constantly talkin' reckless 'bout what they can do wit' a big dick. They front like they really 'bout it—'bout it when it comes to takin' dick. But then a nigga steps outta his drawers and shows 'em what's really good, and these same dick-hungry bitches start stutterin' and babblin' 'n shit, tryna back outta the room.

By the time I get to her bed, my dick is now thick 'n full to maximum capacity, achin' to fuck. I can feel my nut bubblin' up in my balls. I crawl up between her thighs, liftin' her hips up. She takes my body in, then blinks. Her eyes almost pop outta her head. "OhmyGod, your dick's bigger than I thought," she says, leanin' up on her forearms. Truth is, the hornier I get, the longer and thicker my dick gets. So what a chick might initially see when my shit gets hard ain't really what she's gonna get when it really bricks up, feel me?

I pull her down toward the edge of the bed so I can lift her up off the bed and plunge this dick in her nice 'n' easy. Tell her she can handle it, as I roll the magnum XL down on this dick, but I know she's not built for a dick like this. Still, I boost her up. "I'ma tear this pretty pussy up, you know that, right?" She moans, but I can see the fear in her eyes. "You remember all that nasty shit you was talkin' on the phone, right? Well, here's ya chance to fuck this dick down into the mattress. Here's ya chance to fuck my dick into a sling; you remember all that slick shit, right?"

As soon as I push the head in, she gasps. "Aah, oh shit...OhmyfuckingGawwwd! Aaah, oh shit. It's hurting." *What the fuck?!*

I frown at her, pullin' out. "Yo, you want this dick or not?"

"Yes," she says, clutchin' the sheets as I slap the head of my dick 'cross her clit and pussy hole; rapidly beat her lips open wit' my shit. I press the head up against her wet slit, then slowly push in. "Mmmph...oh..." She bites down on her bottom lip, then pulls it in and squeezes her eyes shut.

"I see you ain't all giggles now," I say, pushin' another inch in. "Laugh now, baby."

I push a little more dick up in her.

"Aaaaaaaaah…ohmyGaaawd…stop…take it out. It's too big."

"What the fuck!" I flip, pullin' out. Yeah, a nigga pulls out. The bitch said stop, and that's what it is. You ain't tryna get me hemmed up. Fuck that! A bitch don't want no dick, then that's what it is. I ain't beat for no bullshit-ass rape charges, feel me? I suck my teeth. "Check it. You knew I had a big-ass dick. I told you that shit from gate, and you saw my flicks, so you already knew what it was. And you been playin' in ya muthafuckin' pussy watchin' me jerk the shit off for the last thirty-five minutes. So what the fuck did you think; it was gonna shrink up or some shit?"

"No, I didn't think that. But I've never fucked a nigga with a dick *that*—" she points at my long, swollen dick—"big before. So, you gonna have to go easy on me until I can get used to it, then once I am, I promise you I'll handle it."

I bite down on my lip. But on some real shit, I'm ready to slap her in the muthafuckin' face wit' this heavy-ass dick, then black on her dizzy ass.

I breathe easy. Decide that this ho—fine or not, can't be recruited for the team. She's just another one of them "fuck 'n go" hoes I can hit off a few times, then dismiss. 'Cause on some real shit, if a bitch can't take dick, I have no real use for her ass unless she can deep throat a dick wit'out gaggin', and even then it ain't no guarantees that I'ma keep lacin' her wit' this dick unless she's a cum-guzzler. Now a cum-guzzler…man, listen. A broad who gulps down buckets of cum like it's vanilla puddin' can almost definitely stay on my squad. And if she ain't throatin' dick, then she had better be lacin' a nigga like me wit' some major paper, or some other shit, real talk.

"Kiss my dick," I whisper, pressin' the tip of my dick up to her lips. The way she's lookin' at it, I know she ain't lyin' 'bout not havin' a dick this big in her life or up in her guts before. I smirk.

"C'mon, it ain't gonna bite you." I lean in, and start playin' with her swollen clit. Lightly twist her pussy lips. "C'mon, kiss it." She places gentle kisses all over the head, then takes my shaft in her soft hand, holdin' it at the base, then slowly licks it like a Blow Pop. I slip one finger, then two, into her pussy. Press on her clit with my thumb. She moans, wrappin' her other hand 'round my dick, then starts lappin' the head with her warm, pierced tongue. "Yeah, just like that. Lick daddy's dick up, baby."

She opens her mouth, then wraps her lips around the head of my dick. She starts suckin' all over it, makin' poppin' noises, gulpin' in air as she sucks. I don't pump my hips or grab her by the back of the neck like I do most chicks. I'ma let her guide my dick down in her tight throat, then when she's relaxed, I'll slowly start swabbin' the back of her throat.

"Yeah, baby…suck that dick…ah, shit…that's what I'm talkin' 'bout."

I'm lookin' down at her while she's caressin' my balls and slurpin' my dick. On some real shit, she could be a real dime-piece, but like wit' e'erythin' else affected by this muthafuckin' recession we're in, her ass went down in value the minute she posted her ass and titties up on BlackPlanet.

She starts to gag, then pulls back a little. She licks my dick a few more times, then stops, lookin' up at me all teary-eyed 'n shit.

"Yo, what the fuck's wrong wit' you? You was on the phone talkin' a buncha shit 'bout how you was gonna wet this dick 'n shit. Now you got the muhfucka in ya hands to do what you want wit' it, and ya ass's suckin' the shit like you a muthafuckin' stroke victim or some shit."

"Nothing," she replies, placin' more kisses on my dick. "I just think I might need some help to handle all this. And I know just the person." She jumps off the bed actin' all excited 'n shit. "Hold up. I'ma call my girl Lydia and tell her to come right over."

I let out a disgusted grunt. "Well, I hope she can take dick, 'cause you killin' me, ma. Word up. And I'm really tryna be nice about it." She flips open her cell, promises to make it up to me. Claims her girl is gonna rock this cock; serve me up proper.

I sit on the edge of the bed, leanin' back on my forearm, playin' wit' my rock-hard dick. *Yeah, ya ass gonna make it up to me alright.* I start calculatin' in my head: gas, travel time, wasted time, loss of gettin' good pussy 'n head somewhere else. "Well, hurry ya ass up and get whoever you gonna get, 'cause I'm ready to nut. But in the meantime, you need to wet this dick up and suck it like you mean it."

She walks back over to the bed, drops down to her knees, grabs my dick wit' both hands, licks her lips, then stuffs it into her wet mouth. I roll my eyes up in my head as she strokes and sucks my dick at the same time. Finally, the bitch acts like she's got some dick-suckin' sense. Now this is the fuck what I'm talkin' 'bout. Suck my dick like you want it, like you love it. Don't suck my shit like it's some borin'-ass job. Suck it like it's ya favorite sport. Get on ya muthafuckin' knees and worship this long, black dick like it's ya muthafuckin' idol, you dig?

I am standin' wit' my legs spread apart, and my hands on my hips, watchin' her slide her lips up and down my shaft, before pullin' my balls into her mouth one at time, making loud slurpin' sounds. Her thick saliva lathers up my nuts. *That's right, tea bag them muhfuckas.* "Yeah, baby, wet them balls up."

She greedily keeps suckin' 'til I bust a hot, thick nut in her mouth. She tries to swallow, but it's more than she can handle. She gags, lettin' my cream overflow outta her mouth. I grin when she smears most of it across her lips, then licks 'em. *That's right, you nasty bitch, lick them dick suckas.* I feel myself 'bout to spit another round. This time I back up and shoot my nut in her face barely missin' her eye, then flick the last bit of it into the air.

"Aah, shit," I grunt, slappin' the head of my dick against her lips, then smearin' the rest of my nut all over her face.

"Damn, you got some good nut," she says, lickin' her lips again. "I ain't never sucked a nigga whose cum was as thick and sweet as yours."

Then why the fuck you waste all my shit, bitch? I glance over at her clock again: 1:36 A.M. Shit! "And you never will, baby. Believe that. Now where's ya peoples at?"

She gets up offa her knees. Goes over to get her phone, and calls the bitch back. There's no answer. It figures. Bitches ain't really 'bout it. "I don't know where she is. She shoulda been here by now. Forget her. After sucking your dick, you got me so fuck-ing horny. I think I'm ready to take that dick myself." *This lyin' bitch!* I roll my eyes up in my head. Just a few minutes ago the bitch was actin' like she was scared of the shit; now she tryna play super ho talkin' 'bout she ready to handle this dick. I laugh at her ass. "Why you laughing?"

"'Cause I wanna fuck, and I ain't got time playin' games wit' you. Either you gonna let me stroke ya insides or you not. But, I ain't beat for no bullshit. So, what's good? We fuckin' or not?"

She nods her head. "All night if you want. Just go slow until I can get used to it." She climbs up on the bed, arches her back, then pulls open her ass cheeks. *'Bout muthafukin' time!* "Just don't knock my uterus off the hinges."

I lean down and start lickin' the back of her pussy, dartin' my tongue in and outta her to relax her. She wiggles her ass, lets out a soft moan. Damn, she got some sweet-tastin' pussy. Tastes like duck sauce. I eat that shit up, gobble the back of it for a few min-utes, forgettin' 'bout the jungle of hair that's wet and plastered 'round the back of her pussy, then straighten my body. "Now, you ready," I say, pressin' down on the small of her back, then pushin' the head of my dick in. "And when I'm finished wit' you, baby, you ain't ever gonna wanna fuck with another lil'-dick nigga again." She moans. And inch by inch, I slowly feed her pussy wit' my cock 'til I have it all in. I slap her on the ass. Keep strokin' her pussy hole, slow. Deep grind into that shit, grabbin' her by the hips and slayin' her. The bitch starts to stutter, then holler, and scream, and beg for me to stop one minute; then the next minute she wants me to keep fuckin' her. *I wish this confused bitch make up her mind*, I think, windin' my hips up into her.

"What's my name?"

"Uh…uh…Alley Cat…"

I ram her deep, slappin' her ass. She screams like she's bein' slaughtered. "No, bitch, what's my muthafuckin' name?"

"Uh…aaaaaah…ohsweetmercifulGaaaaaaaaaawd…aaaaaaaaah…"

I quicken my thrusts.

She's clutchin' and clawin' at the sheets. "Uh…uh…uh… Daaaaaaaady…Loooooong…Strooooooooooke," she groans.

"I can't hear you," I say, slappin' her on the ass again. I slow my rhythm, stroke her deep, then pick up speed.

"Daddy Loooooooong Strooooooooooke," she repeats louder, tryna inch up from this dick. But, I got my hands locked on her shoulders, rapidly slammin' my hips into her. "Aaaaah…aaaaaah… oooh….oooh…"

And for another twenty-five minutes I beat her pussy the hell up for wastin' all my muthafuckin' time. And when I'm ready to bust, I pull out, snatch off the condom—tossin' it next to her, then tell her to pull open her ass cheeks, aimin' my dick straight in the center of her ass. I rapidly slap my dick on her asshole, then stroke it. "Oh, shit…I'm cummin', baby." I rapidly start jerkin', then shoot my load in her crack and on her back, smearin' my nut all 'round her asshole. When I'm done nuttin', she rolls over onto her back, rubbin' her titties, tryna catch her breath. She lies there in a daze for a minute or two, then says, "OhmyGod, you got my pussy so sore, it feels like it's on fire. But, you fucked me soooo good."

I smile, leanin' over to kiss her on her cum-crusted lips. "Well, if you wanna keep gettin' this good dick, then you gonna need to learn how to handle it. And not be wastin' a buncha time."

"So, what you saying? You wanna start spending time together?"

Spendin' time together? What the fuck? "Yo, ma, on some real shit. I ain't checkin' for you like that. And I'm definitely not lookin' for nuthin' serious; just some stress-free pussy from time to time, that's it."

"What, you got a girl or something?"

Hear we go with this shit, I think, grabbin' the edge of her sheet and wipin' my cum-slick dick off on it. She looks at me, frownin'. But I act like I don't peep the shit. "Nah, I'm solo," I say, pickin' up my boxers that were tossed over in the corner of the room, then slippin' them on. "But I gotta whole lotta friends." I pull on my white tee, then reach into the front pocket of my True Religions and pull out my cell. I have forty-seven missed calls. The message envelope flashes, lettin' me know I have voicemail. I stuff the phone back into my pocket.

"What's a whole lot of friends?"

"Enough to keep my dick soaked," I say, tryna keep from spazzin' on her muthafuckin' ass for bein' so fuckin' nosey. I can't stand a bitch who yaks her fuckin' jaws, askin' me a bunch of dizzy-ass questions after I just finished servin' her this dick.

"Hmmm," she says, pausin'. I'm sure to try 'n figure out how many broads it's takin' to keep this pipe wet. She keeps her eyes on me, tiltin' her head. "Well, if you so single, what's your rush? Why you gotta leave?"

I stop what I'm doin' and stare at her, long and hard. "Yo, I just gave you some good-ass dick. Don't fuck it up by askin' me a bunch of stupid-ass questions. I ain't ya muthafuckin' man. You dig what I'm sayin'?"

"I was just asking. I mean, I was hoping you would stay the night."

"Well, listen, baby. If you want me to stay the night, then say it. But don't come at me wit' a buncha shit. Now, if you want me to keep servin' you this dick, then you gonna have to make it worth my while. 'Cause time is money, and money is time."

She blinks, takes in what I just said. I start puttin' on my jeans. "How much you need?" she asks, lyin' back on the bed, then pullin' her legs up, and bendin' 'em at the knees. "Give me another round of that dick, and I'll make it worth your while." I glance at her opened pussy—wet, wide and invitin', then over at the clock: 3:14 A.M.

I pull off my shirt, kick off my jeans, step outta my boxers, then walk back over to the bed. "How much cash you got on you?" I ask, rollin' another condom over my dick, then pullin' her legs up over my shoulders. I slide my dick back in her.

She gasps, then whispers, "Oh, shit...goddamn...how much you need, baby?"

I grin, pumpin' this dick deeper into her. I stick my tongue in her ear, then whisper, "I need five hunnid, ma."

She squeezes my ass, pullin' me into her. "Mmmph...aaah... ooooh...oh, shit...ohhhkaaaay, baby . . ."

3

I can't believe it's almost seven in the fuckin' mornin', and I'm racin' down the Turnpike tryna get back to Jersey so I can take a long, hot shower, then jump my ass in the bed. A nigga's beat. Word up. I yawn, flippin' open my cell. *Ah, shit.* Sixty-two missed calls, ten messages—all from Tamera's nutty-ass. I retrieve my messages, deletin' 'em wit'out listenin' to them shits. I know I need to call this ho. But I gotta have my mind right, first, before fuckin' wit' her dramatic ass. I can't stand a bitch who gotta make a production outta e'ery goddamn thing—yellin' 'n screamin' and cursin' 'bout stupid shit, feel me? And that's exactly how Tamera gets down.

I reach into my ashtray and pull out a half-smoked Dutch. I spark it, take a hit, then hold the smoke in my lungs before slowly blowin' it out. I switch the cell's ringer from QUIET to NORMAL, tossin' the phone over on the passenger seat. On some real shit, though, I had no intentions of keepin' this bitch's Acura coupe out all night. I just planned to run up to Connecticut, fuck ole girl real quick, then swing back through and hit Tamera off wit' some of this good lovin'. But shit didn't go down like that. On the way, I stopped off in Brooklyn to give my peoples Electra— this little Dominican and black chick—her weekly feedin', and scoop up a few dollars from her ass. Yo, this sexy-ass broad is a true dick washer. I swear this ho gotta clit in her throat. I never seen a chick nut the way she does by just suckin' a nigga's dick.

Her throat game is wicked. I ended up stayin' almost two hours with her, lettin' her spit shine this nozzle, and gargle up these balls. And as an extra treat, I dicked her down nice 'n slow—after she hit me off wit' some paper, of course—wit' eight inches of this dick 'cause that's all she can take. But she loves this good shit. And she has no problem linin' a nigga's pockets wit' paper she gets from some other nigga she's fuckin'. By the time I bounced from her spot—wit' three Benjamins in pocket—it was already three o'clock.

I finish my blunt, then spark another one, takin' three hits before reachin' for my cell. I flip it open. Take a deep breath, and dial, knowin' this ho is 'bout to fuck up my high. Watch.

"Hello?!" she snaps, soundin' all wired up 'n shit.

"Yo, what's good?" I ask all cool, calm and collected.

"*Yo, what's good?!?* Motherfucker, WHERE THE FUCK IS MY GODDAMN CAR?! I've been calling you all motherfucking day and night. You got me running around all over town looking for your black ass, calling hospitals 'n shit, thinking your goddamn ass was somewhere dead. And you got the fucking nerve to call here all nonchalant like shit's good. Nigga, you really fucked up! You knew I had to go to fucking work yesterday. You lucky I didn't call the police on ya black ass. That was a real bullshit-ass stunt you pulled, nigga. But trust and believe. You will never get your ass behind my motherfucking steering wheel again."

"Aye, yo, what the fuck? Why the hell you spazzin' 'n shit?

"Nigga, I'm spazzin' 'cause you had my goddamn, motherfucking car out all fucking night. And didn't even have the motherfucking decency to call me or answer your goddamn phone."

I sigh. "You know I was gonna bring ya shit back to you, so why the fuck you actin' like I was tryna house you for it?"

"Motherfucker, you was *supposed* to bring me my shit back yesterday afternoon, not the next MOTHERFUCKING morning! And why didn't you answer your goddamn phone?"

I frown. "Aye, yo, don't fuckin' question me. I didn't answer it, 'cause I didn't fuckin' want to—"

"Nigga, I know you not tryna get cocky. I'll question you all the fuck I want when you out with *my* goddamn car, all *fucking* night. Bitch-ass nigga, you done bumped your motherfucking head, talking that 'don't question me' bullshit. You got the wrong one."

And this is exactly why I ain't beat for bein' in no relationship, especially wit' no loud, mouthy-ass bitch. I sigh, takin' a long, deep pull from my blunt, then blowin' it out. This ugly bitch actin' like I put a gun to her skull, then strong-armed her for her keys. No. What a nigga did was slam this dick up in her guts, stick a finger in her asshole and suck all over them big-ass titties of hers. And when I was done, she practically tossed them muthafuckas at me.

"...And I know you didn't have no other bitch in my mother-fucking shit, either. I knew I shoulda never fucked with your sorry, black ass. You ain't shit, nigga. For real! I want my fucking car, NOW! And you better bring my shit back to me with a full tank of gas."

"Or what?"

"Nigga, you'll see."

"Yeah, yeah, yeah," I say, takin' another big-ass pull to the head. Who the fuck this bitch think she is tellin' me what the fuck I *better* do? Now, you already know she done fucked up, right? I pull the phone away from my ear, allow her to continue her bullshit-ass tirade. She's talkin' so fast that she starts to sound like one of the muthafuckin' chipmunks. But, on some real shit, I...DON'T... GIVE. A. FUCK. I press END, then flip my phone shut. She calls back. I let it go into voicemail. And now, the bitch is gettin' real belligerent wit' it, callin' back to back to back. I turn the shit off.

When I finally get to exit 136 off the Garden State Parkway, I open my cell, turn the shit back on, then hit Akina up. She's this half-Japanese, half-black hottie I've been fuckin' for a minute. And the chick's sittin' on paper from money her grandparents left her when they died. Plus, her moms is a big-time criminal lawyer and her pops is a doctor, so chick wants for nuthin', feel me? Man, listen...this bitch is fiyah, fo' sho. And the best thing is she's a certified ass-lickin', ball-suckin', cum-gulpin' freak wit' one of them basketball booties you can palm and smack 'round all night. She's flat-chested as hell, but the ho gotta deep, wet pussy that slurps up the dick and gushes like a waterfall.

"Heeey, baby," she coos into the phone.

"What's good, ma?"

"You, and all that pretty dick. When am I gonna see you? We miss you, boo."

"Oh, word? And who's we?"

"Me and this wet pussy." She giggles. "Where you been? I called you three times yesterday."

I take another toke from my blunt. "I had a family emergency. Why, you need some dick?"

"And you already know," she says, soundin' all sexy 'n shit. "Is everything okay with your family?"

I sigh into the phone, frontin' like a nigga's all down and whatnot. "Yeah, I hope so. But, I don't really wanna talk about it, right now."

"Baby, I understand. Just know I'm here for you if you need me."

"Thanks, I 'preciate that. Listen, I do need you to do me a favor, though."

"Just tell me what it is, you know I got you."

I grin, makin' a left onto Raritan Avenue. "I need you to pick me up in Linden, then drop me off home."

"Just tell me when and where, and I'm there." I tell her where to pick me up, and what time to be there, then hang up. Fifteen minutes later, I finish smokin' the rest of my blunt, turnin' up into Tamera's apartment complex. I make sure I don't leave anything in her shit before puttin' her keys in the glove compartment. I get out, lockin' the fuckin' doors. *That's for talkin' shit, bitch,* I think, slammin' the door shut. I walk to the corner, and ten minutes later, Akina whips around the block in her forest-green 2007 745i, lookin' fly as hell in her fresh Versace shades.

She unlocks the doors, and I slide in. "What's the deal, baby girl?" I ask, closin' the door, then leanin' over and givin' her some tongue action. "You ready to fuck?"

"All damn day," she says, runnin' her hand along my thigh, then grabbin' at my dick.

"Then let's roll," I say, flippin' open my cell, and callin' Tamera's ass back. When she picks up, I say, "Aye, yo, I parked ya shit."

"Where, motherfucker?"

"In ya muthafuckin' parkin' lot."

"Well, where are my goddamn keys, nigga?"

"I put 'em in ya glove compartment."

"Nigga, are you serious? Why the fuck would you leave my motherfuckin' keys in the car, with my doors unlocked so mother-fuckers can be all up in my shit?"

"I locked the doors, ya dumb-ass," I snap, shuttin' the power off, then flippin' my phone shut. "Stupid bitch."

Akina glances over at me. "You aiight, baby?"

"Yeah, I'm good," I answer, adjustin' my seat, then reclinin' it all the way back. "But, I'll be even better"—I unzip my pants, then fish out my Johnson—"when you get on this dick."

She grins, reachin' over and grabbin' it. She licks her lips. "Oooh, damn, daddy, it feels good in my hand."

"And it's gonna feel even better in ya mouth."

She laughs, puttin' her hand back on the steerin' wheel. "You so conceited and nasty, it's a damn shame."

"Yeah, whatever." I laugh, strokin' my dick. "Yo, you had breakfast, yet?"

She shakes her head. "Nope. Why, you wanna stop and get something?'

"Nah, I wanna bust this nut real quick. Pull over somewhere and let me feed you ya mornin' shake."

A cat like me loves gettin' his top spun in public. It's just sumthin' 'bout fuckin' and gettin' brain when you know you might get busted. And this fine-ass broad bein' the good little freak she is does what the fuck she's asked, pullin' into Aviation Plaza. She parks, shuts off the engine, leavin' the radio on. Then she leans over and takes my chocolate pole in her tiny soft hands, unlatchin' her jaws, then mountin' her hot mouth over the head of my dick, glidin' her pierced tongue all over it, slowly swallowin' it in inch-by-inch. When she gets half of it in, she starts to gag, but stops, steadies her breathin', then takes in more. I reach over and palm her ass, then slap it. It bounces and shakes. "Yeah, daddy gonna tear this ass up. You want daddy to beat this ass up?"

She moans, slurpin' and gulpin' down this pipe, cuppin' my balls. She pulls seven inches of my dick outta her throat, then starts jerkin' it off while suckin' my balls. Her nose is all up in my pubic hairs. She sniffs, sniffs again, then yanks her head up, frownin'.

"Aye, yo, why you stop?"

She twists her lips up and says, "It smells like pussy around your balls."

"Yeah, okay, and?"

"Were you fuckin'?"

I frown. *What the fuck?! If this bitch starts that 'I ain't suckin' ya dick' shit, I'ma scream on her ass.* "Yeah, earlier this mornin'. But what the fuck that got to do wit' you handlin' ya business, now?" I squeeze my throbbin' dick at the base, grabbin' her by the back of the neck and pullin' her back down toward the mic. "You know you like pussy, so clock back in, and clean them balls up."

She rolls her eyes, pushin' me offa her. "Yeah, I like pussy, nigga. But that doesn't mean I wanna smell another bitch's dried-up scent on your dick, and I damn sure don't wanna have to be the one to suck it off. That's real foul, nigga."

I glare at her. "So you wanna beef, or you gonna finish suckin' this dick 'n balls? 'Cause if not, you can just drop me the fuck off at the crib, real talk." She stares me down. I raise my brow, ice-grillin' her. My patience for bullshit is short, 'specially when it comes to me tryna get this dick wet. I'll cut a bitch off real quick if she starts frontin' on this dick. "Yo, real talk, ma. You wastin' my muthafuckin' time. So what's it gonna be?"

"You make me sick, nigga," she says, suckin' her teeth and leanin' back over to finish cleanin' my balls.

I grin. "Yeah, that's what the fuck I thought. I make you sick, aiight. But you ain't sick of this good dick, are you?" She ignores me, twirlin' her tongue 'round the head of my dick before pullin' my cum-funky, pussy-stained balls back into her mouth, one at a time. I lean my head back and allow her to let it do what it do. "There you go, baby, suck that cunt juice up offa them balls… yeah, that's it…you daddy's freak-nasty girl."

Twenty minutes later, I shoot a load of gooey custard down in her throat. She swallows, then allows some to dribble outta her mouth and slide along the sides of my dick, then greedily slurps and laps up the rest of my nut. *Gobble, gobble*, I think, runnin' my hands through her hair. *Mmmm-hmmm, good.* "That's right, baby, drink up ya mornin' shake."

4

Three hours later, the air in my room is hot, sweaty, and filled with the scent of intense fuckin'. Akina and I are sweaty and lay up in my bed, catchin' our breaths. Her head is on my chest and I am lightly brushin' my fingers over her soft skin. Yeah, a nigga like me likes to cuddle…uh, don't get shit twisted—only when I'm gonna benefit from it. Otherwise ya ass is beat. I'ma bust this nut, and be out.

"Why you so quiet?" she asks, liftin' her head up and lookin' at me.

I shake my head. "I'm thinkin'."

"About what?"

I take my time before answerin', then sigh. "It's nuthin'."

She lightly strokes my face, then traces my lips with her fingertips. "Alex, baby, don't do me like that. I told you, I'm here for you. I can tell something's on your mind. You can talk to me about anything. I got your back."

I grab the side of my head, pressin' my eyes shut, actin' like I'm tryna fight back tears. "Yo, why you so good to me?"

"'Cause I love you."

Awwww, damn! He we go wit' this love shit. The word makes a nigga like me cringe, but I keep it together. "But I ain't ya man. And I most likely never will be."

"Yeah, I know. But it still doesn't change how I feel about you. I know you out there doin' you. Hell, don't think I'm not gettin' it in, but none of them niggas compare to you."

I know that's right, I think, holdin' back a grin, *'cause most of them niggas' dick game is whack*. "And that's how I feel 'bout you when it comes to them other broads I fuck. But don't let that shit go to ya pretty-ass head 'cause a nigga ain't tryna be put on lock."

Although I just fed her a bunch of bullshit, Akina's still good peoples, and she's the type of broad a nigga like me needs on his team. But the bitch still ain't the type of broad I'd wanna wife. Any bitch who sucks the nut outta me, then swallows it on the first night ain't wifey material in my book. I don't give a fuck how fine ya ass is, or how good ya brain game is, you played ya'self. And you a damn freak-nasty bitch only good for fuckin' and suckin' on this dick. And that's what it is.

"Well, don't get gassed, nigga. The dick is good and all, but I ain't tryna put a lock 'n chain on it."

Yeah, right. "Oh, aiight, if you say so."

She laughs. "Nigga, it is what it is." She rests her chin up on my chest, keepin' her eyes locked on me. "So why you fucking all them other bitches if they don't compare to me?"

I grin. "I thought you didn't care."

"I don't. I just wanna know."

Yeah, okay. "'Cause I can," I say, keepin' it real wit' her ass. For as long as a nigga can remember, bitches have always thrown the pussy at me. Growin' up, I wasn't like most cats who had to hound a ho for some ass; bitches pressed me for a taste of this chocolate. And since bitches loved to talk 'bout the size of a nigga's dick, almost e'ery bitch in Essex, Union, Hudson, and Pasaaic counties knew 'bout my dick game. And they all wanted to see—and feel, for themselves. And they still do. "And as long as they're willin' to throw me the ass," I tell her, kissin' her on the lips, "I'ma keep catchin' it. I love pussy, and I love to fuck."

She rolls her eyes. "Well, you fuck all the bitches you want.

But you make sure you don't catch nothing else besides pussy 'cause I'm not tryna catch nothing I can't get rid of."

"Aye, yo, don't play me. I might fuck alotta pussy, but I keep my man strapped up at all times, real talk."

"Mmm-hmm," she says, twistin' her lips up like she ain't believin' it, "if you say so."

"It's what it is, baby. I might be many things, but reckless ain't one of 'em."

She looks at me. "Well, maybe not. But like I said, as long as you got me wetting ya dick, you make sure you keep it strapped. I don't wanna have to shut shit down."

I laugh. "Yeah, right."

She mushes me. "I ain't laughing, nigga. As long as I'm fucking you, don't bring me no extras."

I grin. "Oh, so you think you gonna keep gettin' this dick?" I ask, rollin' up on top of her. I reach for a Magnum, placin' it beside me on the bed.

"Yep," she says, spreadin' open her legs. I allow my tongue to travel over her invisible titties, 'cause she's all big-ass nipples. I lightly pull 'em wit' my teeth while fingerin' her already wet pussy. She moans. I plant soft kisses down the center of her chest, kiss her stomach, dip my tongue into her belly button, then journey down to the triangular trimmed patch of hair, coverin' her pussy. Now this is the fuck how a bitch's pubic hair is 'posed to look. She has hers shaved and dyed platinum. I flick my tongue 'cross her pierced clit, then start lappin' it. She moans louder. Tells me how good I make her feel. I cover her pussy wit' my mouth and eat her inside out, causin' her to buck her hips, and snap her thighs around my head. I wet my middle finger with her pussy juice, then stick it in her ass and finger fuck her hole nice 'n slow while tongue fuckin' her pussy. She palms my head, then grinds her hips into my mouth. "I'm cumming…aaaaaah…I'm cuuuuuumming…" She squirts her nut into my mouth and I swallow her sweet sauce, lickin' all around her clit 'n shit, while rollin' the condom on. I pull her legs up over my head, then slid my dick in. "Aaaaaaaaaah…oh, yessssss…whatever you do, don't ever stop fucking me…" She holds onto me, clutchin' my dick wit' her snapper.

I don't bust this nut 'til she cums again. And when she finishes, I pull out, snatch off the condom and pump this dick. I watch my nut shoot all over her stomach, her titties and up under her chin. Then I flop over on the bed exhausted as fuck.

Thirty minutes later, she's steppin' outta the shower wit' a white towel wrapped 'round her body. I'm lyin' 'cross the bed, watchin' her as she drops the towel, then starts oilin' her body up. Admirin' her toned body, I feel my dick startin' to get hard again, but I try to will the shit still. Unfortunately, it has a mind of its own, so I let the shit swell up. She slips back on her pink g-string, then pulls her Juicy Couture jeans up over her curves. Them muthafuckas wrap around her plump ass like a glove. *Damn, I wanna fuck this ho in that big ass*, I think, puttin' my hand up to my nose and smellin' her ass scent on my fingertips.

"Aye, yo," I say, gettin' up and walkin' over to her. I pull her into me, and start kissin' her. "I really 'preciate you wantin' to be here for me." She looks up at me, stares me in the eyes.

"Alex, I told you. I got you. Whatever you need, I got you, baby."

I bite down on my bottom lip. "My moms' real sick, babe. And I'm stressed the hell out, for real for real. I don't know if she's gonna make it. And I need to get out there to see her. But money's real tight for me, you feel me?"

"Wow," she says, runnin' her hand through her hair, "sorry to hear that." She looks at me, like she done figured some shit out. "Wait a minute. I thought your mom lived in Jersey."

"Yeah, my biological mom does, but she didn't raise me. My grandmother did, so she's who I consider my moms, feel me?"

She nods. "Yeah, I feel you. So, where is she?"

"Atlanta," I tell her.

"Is she in the hospital, or something?"

I slowly nod. "Yeah, she's in ICU." I pause for a minute, then hit her wit', "In a coma."

She gasps, holdin' her hand up to her mouth. "OhmyGod, Alex, why didn't you tell me this earlier. I'm so sorry, baby."

"I 'preciate that," I say, reachin' for her hand. I take it in my mind, then kiss it. "My head's been all fucked up over it. I need to get out there, but my paper ain't right. And I can't ask my pops to spot me 'cause he's already carrin' my black ass, feel me? And my moms is caught up in her own world."

"Don't stress ya'self, baby. I got you. How much you need?"

I look her in the eyes. "Just a little sumthin' to get a plane ticket and have a few dollas in my pocket."

"Done. When you tryna go?"

"ASAP," I tell her. She thinks for a moment, walkin' over to my leather chair in the corner, then rummagin' through her Louis knapsack. I can see her calculatin' in her head. I sit on the edge of the bed, watchin' her. As she turns, I quickly hold my head in my hands, then slowly look up at her, sighin'. "Umm, you know what. Don't sweat it, baby. I don't wanna put a strain on ya pockets. I'ma see if I can get it from one of my niggas, but I hate fuckin' wit' them cats like that."

"Oh, you know it ain't no sweat off of me. I told you I'ma hold you down. I'm just tryna figure out how to do this." She pauses, pullin' in her bottom lip, then pulls her cell outta her bag. "I tell you what. I'ma call the airline, and book your flight. Is tomorrow too soon?"

I think for a moment. "Nah, tomorrow's good." She calls the airline, and makes a reservation wit' Continental. She writes down all the information, then hangs up.

"It's settled. You're leaving on flight eighty-five, at one thirty-five. It's an open ticket so you can come back anytime." As she's lookin' in her wallet, I peep her pullin' out bills. My dick starts to brick up. "I can give you five hundred; is that cool?"

Well, damn. Maybe next time I'll hit her up for a few gees. I get up and walk toward her, then pull her into me and give her another tongue-probin' kiss. "Good lookin' out, baby. I'ma definitely get it back to you."

She presses her body up against mine, strokes my Johnson. "Take your time, baby. I'm not going anywhere."

Of course you not, I think, grabbin' her ass. *You wanna keep gettin' this black dick*. "Well, as long as you keep wettin' up this dick"— *and linin' my pockets*—"I might keep ya fine ass 'round for a while."

She punches me in the chest playfully, suckin' her teeth. "Yeah, whatever, nigga."

I grab a pair of navy blue gym shorts from outta my dresser drawer, then slip 'em on. I open the bedroom door. "C'mon, baby. Let me walk you out." When we get downstairs, I lean in and give her another tongue dance, then open the front door. "Don't be suckin' no other nigga's dick while I'm gone, either."

She smirks. "You're not my man, remember?"

"Yeah, aiight. You just make sure *you* remember that."

She flips me the finger as she walks out, switchin' her juicy ass. "Whatever!" I watch her get into her whip and back outta the driveway before closin' the door.

5

"Okay, so which one outta your harem is she?" the deep voice in back of me asks, spookin' the fuck outta me. It almost makes a nigga jump outta his skin.

"Oh, shit," I say, quickly turnin' 'round to face my pops, an older version of me—tall, bow-legged, worked-out, and dark chocolate. No, homo…but the nigga's got real flava. And at fifty-two, Pops looks like he's still in his early forties, hands down. A nigga can't front. I'm glad he gave up all that drinkin' and feelin' sorry for his ass. It was startin' to make him look real weak 'n shit. And it got way outta hand when he started wakin' up and hittin' the bottle first thing in the muthafuckin' mornin'. Man, listen. All he did was drink, curse, complain and keep an army of bitches runnin' in and outta here when he wasn't passed the fuck out. It's surprisin' he held down a job wit' all that drinkn' 'n shit. But he got his ass up and went to work e'ery damn day, hung over or not. And get this. He worked as a plant foreman for the Budweiser distillery in Newark. Ain't that some shit? A mutha-fuckin' alcoholic workin' at a damn beer company! And his ass didn't even drink the shit.

I guess livin' in a house wit' a drunk wasn't all bad, though. For one, Pops didn't stress me 'bout no bullshit-ass rules like my moms did. As long as I followed my curfew and took my ass to school, it was all gravy. I could bring chicks to the house and crack this nut up in 'em anytime I wanted. I played varsity ball in high school—all four years, which kept the bitches on my dick. And I even got offered scholarships to play at St. John's, Syracuse, Howard, Norfolk State, and Hampton. Of course a nigga went to Hampton, and flunked out after two years 'cause I was too busy tryna major in pussy, instead of takin' my ass to class. But don't get it fucked up; a nigga ain't stupid.

"When'd you get in?" I ask. "I didn't hear the alarm chirp."

He's standin' in front of me wearin' a white Norfolk State University T-shirt with the green and gold emblem on the front, faded blue jeans and a crisp pair of white-on-white Air Force Ones. I can tell he's been to the barber today. He's sportin' a fresh shape-up, and his mustache and goatee are neatly trimmed. The one carat in his left ear is blingin'. He even got on some smell-good. I bet he got some pussy lined up for tonight.

"Of course you didn't. You were too busy up there tryna rip that gal's guts out. I'm surprised she didn't shatter all my windows with all that damn yelling and screaming she was doing." He stares at me, shakin' his head. "I thought you were up there playing opera at first with all that damn ear-splitting screeching going on."

I laugh, ploppin' down onto the leather sofa. "Pops, you crazy."

"Boy, I ain't laughin'. You gonna have to stop bringing all them screeching-ass women up in my house, like this is some damn cathouse."

"But what 'bout all them broads you used to have runnin' through here?"

He tilts his head, raisin' a brow. "Nigga, the last time I checked, I paid the bills here, so I can have as much pussy as I want comin' in and outta here. But, you, on the other hand, can't. Besides, that was then. And this is now. And right now, I'm not on it like that. At some point, a man needs to grow up, get anchored, and decide what he wants outta life, then live by it."

I scratch my head, lookin' at Pops like he has three heads or some shit. He's soundin' like a black Doctor Phil. "Pops, you sound like you ready to turn in ya playa card."

"The day your mother put me out, my card had already expired. I was just holding on to it to keep from crying."

"I hear you. But you were the one always tellin' me that a man should always have more than one bit...uh, woman on his team."

"Yeah, fool," he says, walkin' over to me and playfully poppin' me upside the head, "but I didn't say bring 'em up in here. You got your own place; fuck 'em there. Besides, that was my belief back then when I was young, dumb and ignorant."

I pretend like I'm hurt, rubbin' the side of my head. "Owww," I say, jokin'. "You know I ain't down for havin' none of these broads knowin' where I rest." And that was on some real shit. I'm not beat for havin' a bunch of bitches bringin' drama to my door-step. And I ain't wit' that cop shit either. I copped me a slick two-bedroom condo in Pier Village down by the beach in Monmouth County. And since I only fuck wit' chicks from up the way, I don't havta worry 'bout none of 'em drivin' way down there tryna bring the bullshit. I can sit out on my balcony at night, smoke a blunt, stroke my dick—if I want, and stare out into the ocean on some chill-out shit wit'out a bitch all up in my ear. Dig what I'm sayin'?

"Well, you need to make some other kinda arrangements 'cause all that sticking and moving gotta stop. I don't want another repeat of what happened over at your mother's happenin' here, and at the rate you going..."

I nod, knowin' exactly what he's talkin' 'bout. I was fifteen—a young hard-headed cat wit' a hard, hot, horny dick, and was con-stantly sneakin' bitches up in my room when my moms wasn't home. Moms was cool 'n all, but she didn't play that fuckin'-in-her-house shit. But a nigga like me wasn't beat to follow house rules, so I was gettin' it in e'ery chance I got, havin' them dick-hungry hoes climb through my window 'n shit. So, dig, I'm up in my room diggin' this eighteen-year-old Spanish *mami*'s guts out when this bitch, Jasmine—who was like twenty, comes 'round to the back of my house, and lifts up my bedroom window for a dose of this dick.

Had a muhfucka been on point I woulda heard her ass openin' the window and climbin' in, but I had my eyes closed enjoyin' my lil' hot tamale ridin' my dick. And her horny ass was makin' so much fuckin' noise that I didn't even know the chick was in my room 'til I popped open my eyes. She had the Spanish chick's hair wrapped around her hand, and was yankin' her offa my dick, swingin' her 'round the room. The next thing I know, they tearin' shit up, knockin' my TV and stereo to the floor, swingin' each other into walls 'n shit. Then when I tried to break 'em up, Jasmine's retarded ass jumped on me, and started fuckin' me up. I had to manhandle her lil' ass, and drag her ass through the house, then shove her out the door, slammin' the shit in her face. I went back to finish bustin' my nut, thinkin' that was the end of it.

Twenty minutes later, this crazy smut comes back and starts bustin' my mom's front windows out with a baseball bat. Now, you know a nigga was wrecked when I heard glass smashin' 'n shit. I slipped on my boxers and ran through the house, swingin' open the door, goin' outside to see what the fuck was goin' on. This nutty bitch started chasin' me around the yard with the bat, tryna swing off on me, word up. She had my dick bouncin' and swingin' all 'round the yard tryna keep her ass from smashin' my lights out. And the Spanish bitch snuck outta the bedroom window, then climbed over our backyard fence, bouncin' on a nigga. A neighbor called the cops. And Jasmine's psycho ass got locked the fuck up.

Needless to say, when Moms pulled up and saw her shit all busted out, she went noodles on a nigga, cursin' and screamin'. She beat my ass so bad I thought she was gonna peel the skin offa me.

"I told your black ass about bringing all them nasty, trampy, hot-in-the-ass bitches up in my motherfucking house, didn't I?..." *Slash! Slash! Slash!* She had a nigga runnin' 'round yellin' and screamin' like a lil' bitch. "...I told your motherfucking ass... No"—*Slash*—"bitches"—*Slash*—"in"—*Slash*—"my"—*Slash*—"mother"—*Slash*—"fucking"—*Slash*—"house..."

"Aaaaaah, Ma...I'm sorry...aaah ...owww..."

"You just like your goddamn father, sneaky..." *Slash!*

"Owwww...I won't do it again, I promise...ooooow."

Seems like the more I apologized, and promised to not let it happen again, the angrier she got. She wasn't tryna hear nothin' a nigga had to say. For some reason, it felt like Moms was beatin' my ass on the strength of all her anger toward Pops. She just snapped, it seems like. For e'ery wrong thing he ever did, it felt like she took that shit out on my ass. I know she was hurt. Hell, I would hear her cryin' in her room sometimes. And that used to fuck me up, for real. Moms had married Pops when she was like eighteen, then had me three years later. They had been fuckin' all through high school, and thought they were in love. They probably were. But Pops loved fuckin' other bitches. I guess I got that shit honest. Anyway, moms knew how Pops got down before she married him. But like so many other broads, she thought she could change him, or that maybe he would change on his own. Well, he didn't. And eventually, she got tired of beggin', and cryin' and arguin' 'bout his cheatin'. She just gave up, and started creepin' on his ass, too. They woulda probably still been together, fuckin' behind each other's backs if one of Pops' hoes didn't come to the house tryna get shit poppin'. That's when Moms flipped the script and lit chick's ass up, then packed Pops' shit and put his ass out. I was thirteen.

Slash! "Nigga, 'don't oww, Ma' me. You wanna fuck. You wanna get that black dick of yours sucked; then, nigga, you can't stay up in this house. Anything your black ass wants, I get. I work two motherfucking jobs to make sure your black ass has a roof over your head, food in your stomach and high-priced clothes on your motherfucking, ungrateful-ass back, and you can't even follow my rules. Instead, you FUCK in my house. SNEAK bitches through your window. LET one of your dizzy, whorish, hot-in-the-ass little bitches bust out SIX of my motherfucking windows."

"I'm sorry, Ma. I'ma…"

Man, listen, I don't know how long she was beatin' my ass. But what I do know is, when she finally stopped, a nigga's arms, ass 'n back was on fire, and there was blood e'erywhere. She stood in the middle of the room, heavin' and sweatin', and waitin'. But I was scared as fuck to move.

"Get the fuck up," she said, walkin' over to my window, then pullin' it up. She swung it up so hard I thought it was gonna shatter. "And get the fuck out!" I crawled my way over to the bed and pulled myself up. She was starin' a nigga down so hard I thought she was gonna drop the cord, then pull out a burner, and start blastin' holes in my ass. I kept my eyes on her, though. "Just like you been sneaking them fast-ass girls in and outta my goddamn window, you gonna climb your sneaky, black ass outta here the same way you let them bitches in. And you ain't taking *shit* I paid for. Now, get. OUT!" And then she had the nerve to start beatin' my ass while I was climbin' outta the window, word up. I couldn't believe it. My own moms put me out in my motherfuckin' drawers all bloody 'n shit. And she wouldn't let me back up in her spot— not even to visit—until I had paid her for e'ery damn window.

I shake the thought, shiftin' in my seat. The memory of that ass whoopin' causes a nigga to wince. I look over at Pops. "Nah, it ain't goin' down like that," I say.

He squints at me, unconvinced, then stands. "You make sure it doesn't."

My cell rings. I ignore it, gettin' up, too. I step in to give him some love. "I got you, Pops."

"Nigga," he says, backin' up and scrunchin' his nose up, "what you got is a bad case of funk. Go wash your stankin' ass, and brush your tongue. It smells like you been fuckin' 'n suckin' a bushel of rotten crabs."

I bust out laughin'. "You crazy, Pops. Word up."

"Crazy my ass."

"Aiight, Pops," I say, chucklin'. "I'll holla atcha lata. I'ma hit the shower, then catch a few zees."

"Yeah, you do that." He grabs his keys from off the table. "Listen, I gotta make a run. If I'm not here when you get up, lock up when you leave."

"Bet."

"Oh, and one more thing," he says, openin' the door.

"What's that?"

"Invest in a muzzle."

I tilt my head, givin' him a confused look. "A muzzle?"

"Yeah, fool. To keep them gals from making so much damn noise when you're up there stretching their insides out."

I burst out laughin'. "Oh, shit. Pops, you one funny dude— word up!"

"Funny hell," he says, walkin' out and shuttin' the door behind him.

6

I finish my shower, dry myself off, then walk back into the room I grew up in as a teenager. Although I painted and piped the shit out wit' a king-size bed, Bose sound system and a Toshiba flat-screen TV, it's still a lil'-ass room for a grown-ass man. But, it is what it is. 'Cause like I said, ain't no bitch comin' up in my spot tryna bring da noise. And I ain't payin' for no muthafuckin' motel room. I reach into my pants pocket and pull out the five hunnid I got from Falani's ass last night—well, early this mornin', then the three hunnid Electra laced me wit', puttin' it wit' the paper Akina hit me wit'. *Thirteen hunnid tax-free dollas in less than twenty-four hours*, I think, ploppin' 'cross the bed. *Not bad for a nigga.* "Oh, shit," I snap, reachin' over and grabbin' my cell off the nightstand. "I betta call this bitch and let her know I'ma be comin' through tomorrow." I glance at the digital clock: 12:30 P.M. "Her lil' ass betta pick up." I dial the number. And after five rings, she answers.

"Hello?" she says in her squeaky-ass voice, soundin' like she's been suckin' on helium or some shit. The shit's fuckin' annoyin' as hell. But based on the flicks she's been sendin', she's finer than a muhfucka; pretty cocoa-brown skin, big brown eyes, thick hips, and a nice phatty. And, yes, a nigga tryna bury his dick all up in that shit, real talk. She claims she used to be a dancer at some titty spot in downtown Atlanta, so I'm expectin' this bitch to give me more than one front-row viewin', feel me?

"Yo, what's good, ma?"

"Who's this?"

Now I know this dumb ho has caller ID, so why the fuck is she askin' who it is? *Alexander the Great, Bitch!* "Alley Cat."

"Who?"

I suck my teeth. "Daddy Long Stroke from offa Myspace."

"Oh, heeeeey, baby." I roll my eyes up in my head. *What a fuckin' reject!*

"Did you get my note? I left you one last night, asking you to call me 'cause I lost all the numbers I had in my phone."

"Nah, I ain't get that shit. I haven't been on that piece in a few days."

"Yeah, I know. I saw when I went to your page."

Nosey, bitch! She was probably checkin' to see what other bitches hit my page up 'n shit.

"So, dig, baby, why you wanted a nigga to holla atcha?"

"I don't know," she says, tryna act all shy 'n shit. "I was just thinking about you, that's all."

"Yeah, right. You thinkin' 'bout how you can get some of this hard dick. Keep it gully. You wanna fuck. You ain't gotta front wit' a nigga like me, baby. You want some of this chocolate stick, don't ya?"

"Damn, you make it sound like I'ma ho or something."

'Cause you are. I hear Betty Wright's old joint, "You're A Hoe" playin' in my head. I shake my head, rememberin' my Moms playin' the hell outta that shit. Sometimes she'd leave it on one of Pops' jump-offs' answerin' machines. Other times, she'd call one of his chicks up, and start singin' the shit to 'em, then hang up. I laugh, thinkin' 'bout some of the other crazy shit Moms used to do to get at some of Pops' chicks. Like drivin' 'round lookin' for his car. Then when she found it, she'd knock on all

the doors or ring the doorbells, askin' to speak to her husband. If she found exactly where he was, which was usually nine outta ten times, she'd leave a message for him to get home before his clothes were packed. Other times, she'd drag the chick outta her house and fight her. Or she'd sit on the hood of Pops' ride, blastin' her tape player to songs like, "I'm His Wife, You're Just a Friend" or "Homewrecker," waitin' for him to come out. And she'd always drag my lil' ass out wit' her. Yo, real talk, Moms was a certified mess, back then, word up. But, on some real shit, them singers back 'n the day used to get wit' each other real quick on vinyl like it wasn't nuthin', 'specially them chicks Shirley Brown and Barbara Mason. Them broads would go at it.

"Nah, baby," I say, lowerin' my voice, tryna get my sexy on. "I ain't on it like that. I'm just sayin'. After our last phone epp 'n shit, you had a nigga ready to beat sumthin' up the other night, feel me? You was talkin' like you really 'bout it. Like you was ready to put some work in. You tryna give me some of that goodie-goodie or what?"

The dumb bitch giggles. "Yeah. I'm about it. I already told you what it is. It's whatever."

"That's what it is, then. I'ma be down there tomorrow afternoon. So I'ma see what's really good wit' you."

"For real?" her squealin' ass asks, soundin' all excited 'n shit. "How long you gonna be down here?"

"A few days, maybe a week. It depends."

"Who you staying with?"

"I gotta room," I lie. But, if I know her like I think I do, before we hang up, she'll be beggin' a nigga to squat at her spot. I always like to let a chick think she's the one comin' up wit' the ideas, when it's really me pullin' the strings, manipulatin' her puppet-ass into givin' me what I want.

"A room?"

"Yeah, baby. It's not like I know anyone there. I'm comin' to chill to see how I'ma like it if I decide to move out there, feel me? Besides it's my birthday weekend, so I'm tryna get into sumthin' different, and let it do what it do."

"Wow. I thought you were only talking when you said you might move out here. What day is your birthday on?"

"It's Saturday, baby," I tell her, slippin' my hand over my dick, then massagin' my balls. A nigga's ready for some more pussy, real talk. "Why, you tryna throw me a party, or sumthin'?"

She laughs. "Maybe, you never know. It'll be a surprise."

"Well, just so you know, baby. A nigga like me loves surprises. So, you got all weekend to amaze me."

"OhmyGaaaawd, I really thought you were joking."

"Nah, baby. A nigga like me keeps shit real. If I say I'ma do sumthin', then that's what it is. And I'm hopin' to dig that back out while I'm out there, you feel me?"

Silence. The dick-hungry bitch's thinkin'.

"Yo, you still there?"

"Yeah, I'm here. Um, I was just thinking."

I smirk. "'Bout what, baby?"

"About you staying here instead of a hotel."

"So, whatchu sayin'?"

"Why don't you stay here? You don't need to be up in some hotel all by yourself."

I grin. "Damn, baby, I'm sayin'. I can't do you like that. I don't wanna put you out, feel me?"

"No, it's cool. I'm off the rest of the week, so we could spend the whole week together, and do something really nice for your birthday. I can even take you sightseeing, or we can just chill or whatever. Besides, I know this really nice restaurant we could go to for your birthday."

Yeah, the "whatever" bein' me showin' ya ass howta spend ya checks. "Well, check this out. The only sights I'm tryna see while I'm there is that big, fluffy ass of yours bent over wit' this dick goin' in and outta ya pussy. Then I wanna see you down on ya knees wit' my balls smackin' ya chin while you suckin' on this dick, real talk, ya heard?"

"Ooh, that sounds good to me."

"Then that's what it is."

"What time does your flight get in tomorrow?" I give her the flight details. "Okay, I'm gonna pick you up at the airport, so cancel your rental."

Hell, I didn't even have one, but I go along wit' it anyway. "You sure? 'Cause I can just drive out to you?"

"Yeah, I'm sure. I told you I'm off, so it's not a problem."

"Aiight, then, bet. I hope you ain't gonna front on a nigga."

"Hell no," she says. I can tell she's grinnin' and all happy 'n shit 'cause she's 'bout to get her ass some thick, juicy Jersey dick. "I been thinking about you every since we started kicking it on Myspace and on the phone. I'ma be there before the plane hits the ground, waiting for you. You just don't know how you made my day. OhmyGaaaawd. I'm so excited." Sounds like the chick is salivatin'. *Them country-ass, bama niggas down there must not be slingin' no real dick.*

"Aiight, then, baby girl. I'ma see ya fine-ass tomorrow. And when you come through, don't wear no panties. I wanna play in ya pussy on the way back to ya spot."

"Okay," she says. "Can't wait to finally see you in the flesh."

"I can dig it. One more day, and it's fuck city, baby. So, brace ya'self 'cause you 'bout to get the muthafuckin' ride of ya life. See ya tomorrow."

"Umm," she says, clearin' her throat. "I need to tell you something before you get here."

"Aiight. I'm listenin'," I say, rollin' over on my side, starin' at the wall.

"Uh…" The bitch pauses. And I start thinkin', *Awwww, shit. This ho is 'bout to tell me she looks like Fiona in Shrek.*

"Yo, you still there?"

"Yes."

"Aiight, then. So what's good? What you gotta tell me?"

"Well…uh, those pictures I sent…well, they don't really look like me."

I frown. *I knew it! The bitch gotta face like a groundhog.* "So, what you sayin'? Ya ass is ugly or sumthin'? 'Cause the chick in those flicks look good as hell, word up."

"No, no, I look good."

"You got that fat ass, right?"

"Yes.

"Okay, then, you still fuckable. So what's the problem?"

"Well, I'm much shorter, and a bit lighter, in person."

I let out a sigh, chucklin'. "That's it? Shit. I thought you was 'bout to hit a nigga wit' some shit like you was a burn victim wit' no teeth and legs."

She laughs. "No, nothing like that. I have all of my teeth. And I'm definitely not a burn victim. I just didn't want you to be caught off guard when we met."

"Check this shit out," I say. "As long as you gotta fat ass, ya pussy is clean, and you tryna eat this nut outta my dick, we cool. You dig what I'm sayin'?"

"Oh, good. That's a big relief. Most guys start tripping once they meet me."

Trippin' 'bout what? "Yo, you ain't no muthafuckin' nigga, are you?"

"Huh?"

"Yo, don't 'huh' me. Do you have a muthafuckin' dick hangin' between ya legs? A muhfucka like me ain't on it like that, real talk. 'Cause you tryna get ya muthafuckin' biscuit pushed in if so."

She laughs. "OhmyGod, nooooo. I'm all woman."

"Oh, aiight then. I was 'bout to say. Fuck 'round and have me catcha case. As long as you were born wit' a *real* pussy and some *real* titties, it's all good."

"I promise you, I was born female."

"Then we cool. Just make sure you got ya fine ass at the airport to pick me up."

"I will." We bullshit for a few extra minutes, then hang up. I let out a loud-ass yawn, then close my eyes, thinkin' 'bout all that juicy Georgia Peach ass I'ma get up in while I'm down there. I think 'bout callin' Keisha to come through and suck on this dick, but decide to jerk my shit instead. Yeah, I know I just finished fuckin' a few hours ago. And? Fuck what ya heard. A muhfucka likes to beat his shit, too, which is what I contribute my great dick and nut control to. Some days when I'm jackin' off I wanna slow-bleed this nut, which is where I'm jerkin' my dick, then I stop strokin' it, and just let my nut flow out by itself. Other times, I wanna gusher-type nut where I keep beatin' my dick 'til I'm 'bout to nut, then stop, let my nut roll back down into my balls, then start beatin' my dick again. I keep doin' it over and over again, bringin' me closer and closer to the edge. Then when I'm finally ready to bust, I pump my dick hard and fast and let my nut fly out all over the place. Whew! That shit be good as hell, word up. Some niggas think jackin' off when you got a steady flow of pussy is whack, but them dumb-ass muhfuckas got it twisted. Beatin' ya dick can teach you a lot 'bout ya body.

And 'cause of all my years of beatin' this dick, a muhfucka can fuck for almost two hours straight before bustin' a nut if I want.

But that usually depends on how good the pussy or head is, and the type of ho servin' it up. If she's broke, she could end up gettin' slayed wit' three to thirty minutes' worth of dick. But, if she's a ho lacin' a nigga and handlin' a muhfucka real proper, then I'ma most likely run an all-nighter on her.

Anyway, today, I'ma make this a quick nut. I glance at the clock: 1:47 p.m. I grab the baby oil offa the nightstand, then let it do what it do. Ten minutes later, I spit this nut, then roll over and fall off to sleep, 'cause a nigga's beat.

7

It's almost seven-thirty in the evenin'. I decide to swing past my moms to see how she's doin' 'n shit since I'ma be outta town for a minute. Besides, I haven't seen her in a week or so. The minute my phone rings, I suck my teeth. Tamera's blowin' the shit up, again. I ignore the bitch. Now she's textin' me. And a nigga like me ain't beat for this textin' bullshit. I read the message: *Nigga, that's real fucked up how you locked my motherfucking keys in my car. And now your black ass avoiding my goddamn calls. But it's all good, nigga.* I delete the shit. Dumb bitch!

"I don't believe this shit," I say, shocked to see my pops' car up in my moms' driveway as I pull up alongside the front of her spot, then park. From where I'm sitttin', it looks dark as hell up in that piece. Not one damn light is on. *What the fuck is he doin' over here,* I think, takin' a hit off my Dutch. *And why the fuck are all the lights out? I know they ain't up in there fuckin'. Mom can't stand his ass.*

Okay, on some real shit. I was kinda fucked up for a minute when Moms and Pops split up. I mean, I was like one of the few cats on my block who had both parents—who worked—under the same roof, feel me? Even if they hardly spoke, unless it was to yell or scream at the other; even if they were both fuckin' on the side—they were still together. And we were a family. You dig what I'm sayin'?

I lay my head back on the headrest, then turn my head toward the house I grew up in—the same house Moms tossed my ass outta—and stare. Moms' voice rings in my head. It's 1988, and I'm ten again.

"Alexander Maples, do you hear me calling you, boy? I told you I had somewhere to be, now hurry your ass on."

I sucked my teeth. "I'm comin', Ma," I yelled down the stairs. I walked back into my room, shuttin' the door, then finished dressin'. "Dang, I don't know why I can't stay home," I complained, checkin' myself out in my mirror. "I'm almost eleven. And Daddy said I'm almost a man." I slipped on my jean shorts, pulled my white tee over my head, then put on my black high-top Chucks.

"*Now*, Alex," she yelled. "Not tomorrow." She was already at the front door wit' her keys in her hand, tappin' her foot when I finally came down the stairs, frownin'. "Boy, bring your ass on. And fix your damn face. I didn't give birth to no ugly-ass child."

"I don't wanna go," I whined.

She squinted her eyes at me. "Alex, I'm telling you right now. *Don't* start, okay?"

I stuck my bottom lip out, poutin'. "I'ma tell Daddy," I snapped, stompin' past her. Before I could get outta the door, she yanked me by the arm, swingin' me 'round to face her. She dug her nails into my skin. "Owww," I winced. "You hurtin' me."

"In a minute, I'ma do more than hurt you. Do you want them new sneakers today?"

I quickly nodded my head. I wanted the fresh Air Jordans that had just hit the shelves. They were like a hunnid 'n shit. And I woulda done any muthafuckin' thing Moms told me to do to rock them shits before e'eryone else got 'em.

"Then what the hell do you *think* you gonna tell him, huh?" she snapped through clenched teeth. "Half the time his black ass ain't here, and the other half of the time when he is here it's like him not being here any damn way 'cause he's too busy fucking

God knows who or what. If he can be out wetting his dick, then damn it, I can be out wetting one, too. I have needs. And you will not have me choose between you or them. So what the fuck are you gonna tell him?" She dug her nails deeper into my arm.

"Owww, Mom, I'm not gonna tell him nuthin'."

"Just what the fuck I thought." She let go of my arm, then started fussin' in my head of curls. "I don't know why you make me have to get ugly. But I know one damn thing, you had better be glad I love you as much as I do 'cause I swear I feel like smacking the shit outta your fresh ass sometimes. But I promise you this, if you dare open your motherfucking mouth to tell anything on me, I'ma beat the skin off your black ass. You understand me?" I nodded, rubbin' my arm. She yanked me by the shirt. "Now let's go."

For some reason, thinkin' back on that shit, now, is funny as hell to me. Moms spoiled the hell outta me, mostly to keep my mouth shut. But, Pops pulled the same shit when he took me off wit' him while he went to get his top spun. E'ery Saturday, he broke his neck to get to the barbershop, and when we were done gettin' our cuts, Pops would make a pit stop over to some chick's spot to get his dick wet. And he'd leave me sittin' out in the livin' room watchin' TV or some shit while he did his thing. Then he'd buy me the latest video game for my Nintendo Entertainment system, like the *Super Mario Brothers 2* joint that had just come out. Yo, that was my shit back in the day, word up. Mario and Luigi were my niggas. Thinkin' back the shit has me crackin' the fuck up.

But on the real, growin' up and bein' the only child 'n shit, I stayed laced wit' all the hot shit—Atari 2600, Sega Genesis, Game Boy, you name it…I had it. And my good fortune was always at the expense of Moms' and Pops' lyin' 'n cheatin'. And I bet they were both fucked up wit' guilt 'n shit, too.

I remember sumthin' Pops once said to me when I was like eleven: "They're all a bunch of conniving, scheming-ass bitches. So, make sure you ram your dick in their asses first, before one of 'em tries to ram you in yours. Men aren't meant to be chained at the hip to one woman. Men need variety. It's in our nature to fuck. Bitches! They ain't good for nothin' 'cept suckin' dick and fuckin', any damn way. So make sure you get as much pussy as you can. You hear me, boy?"

Mouth open, eyes wide in shock, I nodded. "Yes."

The whole time he was talkin' to me he was slurrin' his words 'n shit 'cause his ass was lit the fuck up. I watched him unscrew the cap offa his bottle of E & J whiskey as he kept babblin' on 'bout bitches and how fucked up they were. He downed his drink, poured himself another round, then put his glass up to his lips and tossed his head back, gulpin' down the dark elixir. Then he poured another. He stared at his glass, then at me; his large hand clutchin' his drink as if his life depended on it. And in some way, I guess it did.

As soon as we heard jinglin' of keys at the backdoor that lead into the kitchen, we both waited and watched as the door opened. On some real shit, Moms was a real looker back then—shapely, smooth cocoa-brown-skinned, big doe-like eyes, and deep dimples. And Pops was a real jealous-type cat; probably 'cause his ass was out doin' him. The minute she stepped through the door, Pops started his shit. I held my breath.

"Where the hell you been?"

She set her pocketbook on the counter, then removed her coat. "Out," she calmly replied, not looking at him. She glanced over at me. "Alex, go to your room."

"No, you sit right there," Pops warned, pointin' at me. I stayed put, didn't blink a muthafuckin' eye. Moms shot me this evil-ass look, but I wasn't beat to have my ass beat by Pops. I lowered my eyes. "He needs to see firsthand what a bitch is."

She blinked, blinked again. Her nose flared, but she kept her composure. On some real shit, I don't know how she was able to keep it together after bein' referred to as a *bitch* in front of me, but she did. "Well, since I'm such a bitch," she said, walkin' over to where we were sittin'. "Then this is from the bitch across town you've got sucking your gotdamn dick"—she slapped his face— "And this is from the bitch around the corner you've been fucking…" She slapped him again.

Pops jumped up from the table, almost losing his balance while grabbing her arm. "Woman, you're fuckin' crazy. Ain't nobody cheatin' on you. Now, where the fuck you been?"

She yanked her arm from his grip, pushin' him backward. He tumbled over the chair, fallin' to the floor. "You're full of shit!" Moms snapped, snatchin' his drink from off the table and tossin' it in his face. "And this is from *me*. The bitch you keep lying to and fucking over." She looked over at me, before stormin' outta the room, and said, "Learn to keep your dick in your pants, or you're going to end up being just like your cheating, lying-ass father."

The ironic thing is her ass was doin' the same thing. So, go figure. And this is probably why a nigga like me ain't beat for fallin' for a broad. Muthafuckin' bitches cheat just as much as niggas. They just slick 'nough to not get caught. I take another deep pull of my blunt, then blow out a cloud of confused smoke, before puttin' the shit out. I glance back up at the house, shakin' my head. It's not 'til I peep the light flick on in Moms' bedroom, that it hits me. "Oh, shit," I snap. "These two are fuckin'."

I get outta my whip—yeah, a nigga gots his own shit. What, ya asses thought I was one of them bum-ass niggas that borrowed chicks' rides 'cause I didn't have my own wheels? Nah, I ain't that nigga. I just don't let e'ery bitch I'm smashin' know how I'm doin' it. When I'm on the prowl, I either ride another broad's ride to get my creep on, or I push a hoopty, feel me? After Racquel— some ho I was fuckin' from Pasaaic—keyed up my shit, smeared dog shit on my windshield, and flattened all four of my mutha- fuckin' tires two summers ago, a nigga like me isn't gonna let another broad get the opportunity to put in work on my shit again; I put that on e'erything I love.

Shit. I had to file a complaint on her nutty ass, word up. Lucky for her, I was lookin' to get some hot shit any-damn-way, so she did me a favor. Otherwise, a nigga woulda probably choked her ass out. Yo, hol' up! Not that I would ever push a ho's biscuit in (unless she puts her hands on me—*first*), but I damn sure woulda choked her to sleep. And now wit' that Jazmine Sullivan chick poppin' shit 'bout bustin' windows 'n shit, I really ain't beat. Fuck that. These silly hoes can fuck each other's cars up if they want. But they ain't fuckin' wit' mine.

What the fuck! Tamera texts me again. *Why you fuckin' iggin' me nigga?* I sigh, decide to text back. *Suck my dick!* I slip my phone back in its holder, then shut and lock my door, makin' my way up the stairs to Moms' house. I ring the doorbell, since my key privileges are still revoked. Moms still doesn't trust me to not bring hoes up in her spot when she's not home. That shit cracks me the hell up. But, hey, it's her spot, her rules.

I reach for the bell again, but the door opens up before I can press down on it. I smirk. I'm standin' face to face with Pops. His eyes widen. I can tell gettin' busted wasn't on tonight's agenda. But it's all good. "What's poppin', playboy?" I ask jokin'ly.

He lets out a nervous-ass chuckle. "Oh, hey…uh, what are you doin' here?" he asks, fumblin' wit' his keys, and steppin' back so I can come in.

"Raynard, who's that at the door?" Moms asks. She's in the dinin' room area.

"It's ya son," I say, grinnin'. I wink at Pops, brushin' past him.

Moms comes into the livin' room, tryna cover herself. She's wearin' a flimsy-ass robe, probably buck-ass naked underneath. Her hair is all over her head. *Yeah, they been gettin' it in, fuckin' hard,* I think, smilin'.

"Oh, hey, baby. Glad to see you." She runs her hand through her tangled hair.

I smirk. "I bet you are," I tease, lookin' over at Pops, then at her.

She rolls her eyes. Pops grins. "Your father stopped by to bring me something."

I tilt my head. Give her one of those "come again" looks. "Unh-huh, I'm sure he did. Sumthin' hard and dark, right?" Pops shakes his head, chucklin'. I walk over and give her a hug. I sniff her, then the air.

"Oh, boy, stop," she says, swattin' at me.

Pops opens the door. "Alice, I'ma get going. Alex, I'll talk to you later."

"Aiight, playa," I joke. "I'll holla."

"Get home safe," Moms says, watchin' him walk out the door. She smiles at him. He smiles back, then shuts the door behind him.

I plop down on the sofa. "Damn, Ma, you 'n Pops really up in here gettin' it in, hunh?"

She laughs, flickin' her hand at me. "Oh, please."

"*Oh please* nuthin'," I mock, grinnin'. "Ya'll up here gettin' buck wild 'n nasty. You got Pops wide open, Ma. So, spill it. How long Pops been fuc...uh, makin' it clap?"

She raises her arched brow at me. "Makin' it clap? What in the world? Your father hasn't been making shit clap over here."

I stare at her, not believin' her. "C'mon, Ma, keep it gee. How long you been lettin' Pops rock ya box?"

She rolls her eyes and laughs. "I'm not lettin' your father rock nothing. And I don't kiss and tell."

"Lies," I kid, shakin' a finger at her. "But, it's all good. If you wanna keep secrets from ya only child, then so be it."

"Secrets, hell," she says, wavin' me on. "You just too busy tryna be all up in my Kool-Aid. What me and your father do or don't do behind closed doors ain't none of your business."

I laugh, knowin' she's gonna spill the beans, anyway. "Yeah, aiight. I see ya work. But, it's all good. Um, I thought you couldn't stand him."

She bucks her eyes. "I can't…" she says, tryna sound all indignant 'n shit. But it's all a front. She has that fresh "I-just-got-my-fuck-on" glow, and the way her eyes are twinklin' 'n shit I already know what it is. Pops served her up a dish of stiff dick. She pulls her belt tight 'round her waist, "…outside of the bedroom. But, in between the sheets…" she pauses, fannin' herself.

I cover my ears, gettin' up from my seat. "Aiight, aiight. I get the picture. Pops does his thing-thing, and got you strung out, huh?"

She laughs. "What can I say, Good sex is hard to let go of. And your father got…"

"Okay, Ma, chill. I got you."

"Well, you asked. So be prepared for what you hear." This is one of the things I've always loved 'bout Moms. She keeps shit real. Ain't no sugarcoatin' shit with her. That's probably why we have such a close bond. We've always had that kinda vibe where we can keep shit real wit' each other. Growin' up she was always more like a friend—nah, scratch that, a chill-ass older sister— than a mom to me. Yo, but don't get shit twisted. She got in my ass 'n shit, and didn't play that disrespectful shit, but at the end of the day she was mad cool.

"Yeah, I asked. But that doesn't mean I wanna hear all the details."

"Well, then stay outta grown folks' business."

I suck my teeth, smirkin'. "Yeah, aiight. But you still haven't told me how long this been goin' on."

She sits in the chair 'cross from me, crossin' her legs. Tells me they've been fuckin' for almost six months.

"Six months?" I repeat, lowerin' my voice. I shake my head in disbelief. "So, ya'll datin'?"

Moms clucks her tongue. Leans forward in her seat. I can tell she's 'bout to give it to me raw. "No. We're fucking. Big difference."

I shift in my seat. "But the two of you are thinkin' 'bout gettin' back together, right?"

She loses her smile, raisin' her brow. "Hell no. I divorced him for a reason. Your father was a lousy husband. But he was a good provider, and a damn good lover. I'm open to a dinner here, a movie there. But, getting back together in the traditional sense is not an option for me. He can come by twice, maybe three, times a week and scratch my itch. Other than that, he can keep his ass right where he's at."

I laugh at her. "Yo, Ma, you real funny. You know that, right?"

"Mmm-hmm," she says, gettin' up from her seat, headin' toward the stairs. "Let me go put something else on. I'll be right back."

"Whew!" I joke. "Thank Gawd! 'Cause for a minute there, I thought I was gonna hafta start tossin' dollars atcha."

She stops, slams her hand on her hip, pretendin' she's 'bout to bring it to me. "You must want me to whoop your ass up in here. I taught you better than that. You better try twenties and up."

I laugh. "Ma, you crazy for real, word up." She waves me on. And I smile, shakin' my head as she heads up the stairs. *Pops got his hands full wit' her*, I think.

8

Moms comes back down wearin' a pair of powder-blue Baby Phat sweats that cling to her hips and a white Baby Phat T-shirt. I blink, tiltin' my head. Now, either Moms been hittin' the gym e'ery day doin' squats 'n shit, or she's been hidin' her body. 'Cause on some real shit, I didn't know she was stackin' cakes like that. I shake my head.

"You hungry?" she asks, switchin' past me.

I jump up from my seat. She doesn't hafta say another word. After all the fuckin' and tree smokin' I did earlier, I'm starvin'. And Pops didn't have shit up in his spot to tie me over. I started to hit St. Georges Avenue and swing by that US Fried Chicken spot over in Linden on my way here to pick up a chicken snack. I'm glad I didn't.

"You already know," I say, followin' her through the dinin' room into the kitchen. "What you cook?"

"I made some barbecue chicken, mac 'n cheese and fried cabbage," she says, openin' up the cabinet and pullin' down a plate. I take a seat and watch her as she shuffles 'round the kitchen fixin' my plate. She sticks it in the microwave. "You want something to drink?"

"Yeah, I'll get it," I say, gettin' up.

She waves me on. "Sit. What do you want? Cranberry or grape juice, Sprite or water?"

"Cranberry juice."

She grabs a glass, then pours the juice to the rim. I smile. I don't care how old I get, Moms still waits on me. The only thing she won't do is my laundry. Once I started havin' wet dreams and nuttin' in my drawers, she said I was on my own.

When the microwave stops, she brings me my drink and plate, then pulls out a chair and sits 'cross from me. She watches me as I bite into one of the chicken breasts. Damn! I lick my fingers and lips, then shovel a mouthful of cabbage in my mouth. "Mmmmmm. This is good as hell. You really did your thing, Ma, word up."

She playfully swats at me. "What I tell you about talking with your mouth full." She leans forward, placin' her elbows on the table, restin' her chin on her closed fists. "So, tell me. Besides chasing skirts, what else have you been up to? Have you found a job yet?"

I shake my head. "I'm not lookin," I calmly answer, takin' a sip of my drink. I set the glass down, then finish eatin'.

"Why not? Don't you think you should be? I know you're not paying for all of those designer clothes, expensive shoes, and that car note and mortgage with just your looks."

Nah, these looks get me in the door. It's this big ole dick that gets me in them wallets.

She shakes her head as if she read my thoughts. "Hmmph. Don't you think it's time you grow up, and start taking life serious? The world can't always be your playground. And whatever little money you have left in the bank isn't gonna last you forever."

I sigh. I knew this was comin'. She thinks a grown man should be responsible enough to find a job and keep a job. And make his own paper. I agree, if that's ya thing. But, a nigga like me ain't beat for slavin' for someone else. And I ain't interested in lettin' the shiesty-ass government dig into my pockets tryna get their cut either, real talk. I tried that nine-to-five shit once, and it just wasn't me. A cat like me ain't built for takin' orders, or havin' someone constantly over my shoulder sweatin' me. I don't need no muthafuckin' babysitter watchin' what the fuck I do, or clockin' my moves. Fuck that. I felt like I was bein' chained to a desk and time clock. The only bright side of goin' to work was gettin' off. Oh, and fuckin' my supervisor. She was married and miserable, and needed some young dick in her life, so I was more than happy to put in the overtime to work her pussy over.

But then she started gettin' on her bullshit when she found out I was smashin' another supervisor in another department, too. Shit started gettin' real hectic, so a nigga bounced. And I haven't worked since. Well, not in the traditional sense.

A few years back I was what they call an exotic dancer. Aiiight, aiight, shit…I shook my dick for a livin'. But a nigga made a muthafuckin' killin'; especially doin' the private party thing. Broads paid out the ass. And a muhfucka like me gave 'em their money's worth. I had bitches literally beggin' to see, feel, taste, and fuck this dick. I ain't gonna front, slingin' this dick and gettin' paid to be on display was aiight for a minute. But, even that shit started gettin' hectic. Bitches fightin' 'n shit tryna get ya attention; hoes stalkin' ya ass. Man, listen. Some of them chicks got real reckless when it came to 'em tryna get at this chocolate cock. Like lyin' to their niggas 'bout where they been, spendin' up their rent money, jumpin' up on stage lettin' me do any-and-e'ery-mutha-fuckin' thing to 'em, bouncin' state to state to follow this dick, neglectin' their damn kids. They were some real live groupie bitches, straight birds. And a nigga had no problem takin' that paper—still don't. But at the same time, I was lookin' at a lotta them bitches sideways for how muthafuckin' stupid they were.

After awhile, the whole scene got really played. And I wasn't beat for a buncha bitches pawin' and clawin' to get at me. So after three years of swingin' this dick up in a buncha nameless faces, I split. But, don't get shit twisted. I had a trail of hoes—well, I still do—in almost e'ery state from here to Cali. And e'ery last one of 'em paid to get slayed, feel me? And many of 'em still do.

Kickin' some real shit to you, I got broads thinkin' I don't own my own shit—that I'm practically homeless 'n shit, and they'll flat out tell me I can move in wit' 'em. And I don't have to pay for shit. They'll keep me laced in the hottest shit, pay my bills, and keep a nigga's pockets lined. The only thing they want is a muhfucka to come home to, someone to make 'em feel good 'bout themselves, someone to fuck 'em down real good. They'll work all muthafuckin' day, then come home and cook me a full-course meal, then drop down on their knees and worship this big, black dick like I'm king Ding-a-Ling. So, hell no, I ain't lookin' for no muthafuckin' job! I already got one.

"Well, what can I say, Ma. The hoes got it bad for me."

She glares at me. "What I tell you about referring to women as *hoes.* You really need to stop it." I almost wanna laugh. I lost count the number of times growin' up I heard her usin' the word. She musta forgot that she used to refer to Pops' jumpoffs as *hoes* and *bitches.* And how many times she ran up in one of his hoes' spots draggin' 'em out by the hair callin' 'em e'ery type of bitch there is. I decide not to remind her.

"Ma, on the real, in my opinion and based on what I've experienced, that's exactly what most of 'em are. And you know it."

She shakes her head, dismissin' my comment. "You and that fat, black dick of yours…"

I choke. "Oh, shit! Ma, you buggin', word up."

"Bugging, hell. I'm your mother. I changed your pissy Pampers, wiped your ass, and saw you walking around in your drawers growing up, so I know what's hanging between your legs. You're a Maples. And the one thing I learned, and overheard, about the Maples men, they are *all* holding—every last one of 'em, including your hot, sex-crazed ass. So, don't 'Ma' me. Now like I was saying, that big dick of yours is going to be your downfall. You can't keep fucking over all these women and not expect one, if not two, of 'em to snap."

I put my fork down. "Ma, it's not like that. These broads know what it is. I'm not tryna wife none of 'em. It's strictly sex."

"And you're using them for whatever you can get out of 'em."

I laugh at her. "Ma, I'm single. I have no kids. And I'm not lookin' for a relationship. I'm just chillin'. I'm not hurtin' anyone. As far as I see it, it's a mutually satisfyin' arrangement wit' any broad I get wit'. They want sumthin' from me and, nine-times-out-of-ten, I'm gonna deliver it—for a price, of course."

"Oh, please. Any woman dumb enough to accept that damn shit is a stone-cold fool."

"Well, most of 'em are."

She sucks her teeth, rollin' her eyes, knowin' what I say is truth. "Well, that may be so. But, your ass is still asking for trouble. You're using these women and it isn't right."

I take a deep breath. On some real shit, I wanna bring it to her raw. Let her know that I. Don't. Give. A. Hot. Fuck…'bout none of these silly-ass broads out here, 'specially the ones who care 'bout dumb shit like the size of a nigga's dick, or the size of a muhfucka's feet and hands. And believe me. Any bitch who comes outta her grill askin' if I gotta big dick gets dragged through the muthafuckin' mud, real talk. These bitches will know that I'm fuckin' other chicks and still give me the keys to their cars, their cribs, bank cards, Family First cards, and e'ery muthafuckin' thing else. It's all because I gotta long, thick, black dick loaded wit' a buncha hot, creamy nut for that ass 'n throat. But keepin' shit real, all a big dick does is make an already dumb-ass bitch dumber. So if anything, a dumb, low-self-esteem-havin' bitch should be tryna stay far the fuck away from a nigga like me. 'Cause if she doesn't, then her muthafuckin' ass is gonna get slayed and played, real talk. I'ma fuck her silly-ass into a muthafuckin' coma. And if I see any sign of weakness, I'ma take her retarded ass straight to the cleaners. And that's what it is.

My cell rings. I pull it from offa my hip, glancin' at the screen. Fuckin' Tamera's nutty-ass, again. I sigh, hittin' IGNORE. It rings again. This is that bullshit, word up. I answer. "Yo, what the fuck?!"

Mom raises her brow, squints her eyes. I shrug.

"Oh, so I see you on some funny-style shit, now. But it's all good."

"Ain't nuthin' funny-style 'bout not bein' beat for *you*. So what the fuck you want? " Moms glares at me. I put my hands up, and mouth, "My bad, Ma." She gets up and starts puttin' the food away.

"Oh, so you ain't beat for me now."

"Isn't that what I just said?"

"You real fucked up; you know that, right?" she says, smackin' in my ear.

"And you a real bird, so what's ya point?"

"Fuck you, nigga!"

"Choke on my nut," I say, snappin' the phone shut. *Fuckin' smut!*

Moms turns to look at me. "You must really want me to slap the shit outta you."

I wanna laugh, knowin' she's only poppin' shit. "My bad, Ma."

She narrows her eyes and twists her lips, but says nuthin'. She goes back to flittin' 'round the kitchen, finishes puttin' e'erything in the 'fridge, then sits back down. She allows me to finish eatin' in peace. Patiently waits for me to gulp down the last bit of my juice before she starts in on me. She folds her hands on top of the table.

"Alex, listen. You're playing a very dangerous game messing over these women the way you do. No matter how fucked up you think a woman is, she still has feelings. And when you play with a woman's emotions..."

"C'mon, Ma, keep it gee. Is it my fault that they play themselves?"

"No, but it's your fault for taking advantage of 'em. No matter what a woman thinks of herself, you are still responsible for how *you* treat 'em."

Oh, well. If it's not me draggin' 'em, then it'll be some other muh-fucka. So it might as well be me. I shrug, glancin' down at my watch. It's almost nine. I get up from my seat, then walk over and kiss Moms on her forehead. "I love you, Ma. But, whether it's right or wrong, I'ma do what I do no matter what you think about it. I'ma be outta town for a minute, but I'll hit you up when I get back."

She gets up, takes my empty plate and places it in the sink. "And I love you, too. But that doesn't mean I'ma stop doing what I do. And that's being your mother, worrying about you, confronting you on your irresponsible choices, and cussing ya ass out when need be."

"Yeah, yeah, yeah," I say, smilin'. "But just remember, they're my choices. And I like it when you cuss." I walk up and grab her in a big bear hug, then pick her up. "I don't want no problems, Ma."

She laughs. "Boy, put me down." I do. She gives me a hug, then looks up at me. "I don't wanna see anything happen to you that coulda been prevented by being honest."

I kiss her on the forehead. "Ma, I am bein' honest wit' these chicks." I grin, shruggin'. "Well, okay, 'bout most things. Still whatever heartache or drama they feel, it's shit they brought on themselves, real talk."

She shakes her head, followin' me toward the front door. "I love you."

I flash her my mega-watt smile, givin' her another hug and kiss. "I love you, too, Ma."

She closes the door behind me as I walk to my car, shakin' my head and smilin'. I disarm the alarm, then slide behind the wheel, crankin' the engine and sparkin' a blunt, makin' my way toward the parkway, headin' south to my spot.

9

I'm tired as fuck! My muthafuckin' flight to ATL was delayed two hours. Then they kept a muhfucka cooped up and bunched up on that biotch for almost forty minutes before finally takin' the fuck off. A nigga needed a damn blunt bad, still do—straight to the dome. Lucky for me, I don't fuck wit' alcohol, otherwise, a muhfucka woulda got right. The one good thing outta the whole fucked-up flight is that I was posted up next to this bad-ass bitch from Stone Mountain. Whew...man, listen. Chick is a real beauty. Model-fine type wit' long, sexy legs, nice bubble ass, lil' waist and slanted gray eyes. Then she got the nerve to have a sexy-ass mole over her lip, and a muthafuckin' Gabrielle Union smile. Man, listen. You know I had to put my thing down on her fine ass. And yeah, a nigga got the digits.

So, here I am walkin' and talkin', just straight kickin' it wit' her fine-ass. I'm diggin' her vibe, and I can tell she's diggin' mine. And on some real shit, I almost forget the bitch I got waitin' on me. I sigh when we get off the tram and make our way to baggage claim. I make a promise to get at this cutie before I bounce; not even on some fuck-type shit—well, not unless she's tryna step outta them drawers, but on some straight chill shit.

"Make sure you do that," she says, smilin'. She shifts her brown Dolce & Gabbana handbag from one arm to the other.

"No doubt," I say, lickin' my lips. "I'm definitely tryna holla."

"You got the number. Use it or lose it."

I laugh. "I can show you better than I can tell you."

"So, who you out here staying with?" she asks, starin' me in the eyes and grinnin'.

"My peoples," I state. "But I'm tryna spend some time—"

"Alex, over here," I hear. I cringe. *Fuck!* I know who it is the minute I hear that squeaky-ass voice. I turn around, lookin' for… uh, damn, what's this bitch's name? Vita, yeah, that's it. I don't see her, so I go back to talkin' to my Stone Mountain beauty.

"…with you, ma," I continue. "So, make sure you pick up ya phone when you see a nine-seven-three area code comin' through. It's gonna be me tryna get at ya."

She smiles. "Well, if I'm not busy, I'll pick up. If I don't, leave a message. Oh, there's my bag," she says, pointin' to a black Louis travel bag. I reach over and grab it before it goes by, then hand it to her. "Thanks, she says.

I glance 'round, lookin' for Vita's stupid ass, but I still don't see her. "So dig, baby, I'ma hit you up in a few days."

"Well, if you don't, that's on you." She grins.

I grin back. "And if I do?" I ask, lickin' my lips, steppin' into her space.

She locks her eyes on mine. "Then that's on you, too."

I smile wider. And just as I'm 'bout to scoop this beauty up in my arms, I see this lil' bow-legged chick, wobblin' up on me, wavin' me down. *Who the fuck is this lil' bitch?* At first I think it's some fresh-ass, hot-in-the-pussy shorty tryna holla. But then I notice her face got some age on it, and realize she's a grown-ass woman.

"Heeeeeeey, Alex," she says, grinnin' from ear to ear, showin' the gap between her teeth, like she just hit the Lotto.

I ice-grill the bitch. "Yo, what's good? Do I know you?"

She keeps her smile plastered on her face as she walks up to where we're standin'. She looks up at my Stone Mountain beauty, then up at me and says, "Yeah, boo, it's Vita."

My jaw drops. A nigga is ready to pass the fuck out! Ole girl looks at me, then down at this chick, and smirks. I can tell she's thinkin', *You fuckin' that? Oh, I see your work.* She looks me in the eye and says, "It was nice talking to you. Enjoy your stay in the ATL."

"Most def. I'ma hit you up." I watch her walk off, then return my attention to this ho. *Vita?* A nigga tries to keep his composure. *What the fuck?!* I look down at this lil' Munchkin bitch. Vita? Oh, hell naw. The chick in those flicks is brown-skinned wit' thick hips and lips, and has big brown eyes and a sexy-ass smile. Not some muthafuckin' light-bright, high-yellow bitch wit' big, pink lips and burgundy hair.

I frown, scratchin' the side of my head. "Hol' up," I say, shakin' my head in disbelief. "You're ATL Rough Rider Cutie, Vita, from offa Myspace?"

"Yeah, boo," she says, laughin' "You so crazy. Who else? I was calling you for a minute, but I guess you didn't hear me."

Nah, bitch, I heard you. I just didn't see ya ass. And now I know why. I pull in my bottom lip, and bite the fuck down on it before I blast her ass right here in the middle of the muthafuckin' airport. *Rough Rider Cutie my muthafuckin' ass!* "Nah, I didn't hear you," I say, grittin' my teeth.

"You want me to wait here with you until your bag comes?"

I see muhfuckas eye-ballin' us and I'm startin' to feel some kinda way 'bout it. "Nah, I'm good," I say not lookin' down at her.

"Oh, okay. Well, I'ma be sitting over there waiting for you then." She points over to a metal bench by a set of payphones.

I take a deep breath. "Aiight, you do that." I watch this broad waddle in her tiny-ass heels, lookin' like muthafuckin' Minnie

Mouse 'n shit. All the ho needs is a big-ass bow in her hair. I shake my head. The ho got little feet, little hands, little mouth, and little body. E'ery muthafuckin' thing on this bitch is little, 'cept for her big-ass head—and that fat ass of hers. I lock my eyes on her phatty, shakin' my head. I need a muthafuckin' blunt, *now!* The ho said her ass was short, not some toddler-sized adult. She shoulda kept shit real wit' me. At least prepare a nigga first; dig what I'm sayin'?

I let out a deep, disgusted sigh. All that good shit she been talkin' over the phone 'bout how deep her pussy is, 'bout how much she loves to fuck, 'bout how she's gonna rock this dick, had a nigga ready to beat her guts up. And this is the shit I end up wit'—a damn pint-sized, freak-nasty ho. I shoulda known the shit was too muthafuckin' good to be true.

When my bag finally comes, I swagger over to where her ass is sittin'. She's on her cell, but disconnects her call when she sees me comin'. I'm lookin' at her, thinkin' how the fuck I'ma get outta this shit. I got like two grand on me, so I know I can always cop me a hotel somewhere, and be out. Then I can maybe hook up wit' that Stone Mountain cutie. Fuck! I forgot her name, that quick. Shit!

She looks up at me. "You mad at me?"

I frown. Am I mad? This smut is the size of a fuckin' poodle standin' on its hind legs, and she got the muthafuckin' nerve to be askin' me some dumb shit like that. Damn straight, I'm heated. But since this ho gassed me up, it's gonna cost her extra. I smile, decidin' to milk this situation for e'ery muhfuckin' thing it's worth.

"Nah, baby, it's all good. Let's get outta here."

She smiles. "Whew! I was worried for a moment. I thought you was gonna tell a sista to beat it or something."

Oh, I'ma tell ya dick-thirsty ass to beat it aiight. "Nah, never that, baby. I ain't no shallow-type cat. I came to spend time wit' you. And get this dick wet. And that's what it is."

I stare at her, start to wonder if she got good pussy. I smirk at the thought of layin' back, proppin' her up on my dick, then spinnin' her ass 'round on it like a doll. My dick starts to jump. *Yeah, I'ma run this dick straight through her muthafuckin' back. Lyin'-ass ho!*

When we get to her shiny black customized Benz truck, I say, "Damn, I didn't know Benz made whips for midgets." I hear her suck her teeth as she disarms the alarm, unlockin' the doors. I toss my bag in the back, then get in. I watch her climb up and in. She looks over at me. And on some real shit, the bitch got the nerve to be aiight lookin' in a funny kinda way. Sorta like a chimpanzee.

"Please don't refer to me as a midget. It's offensive, and derogatory," she says, slammin' her door. "I might be many things, but a midget ain't one of 'em."

Bitch, please. I'll call you what the fuck I want. I feel like laughin' dead in her muthafuckin' face. "Well, then what are you?"

"Well, for starters, I'm a woman. My name is Vita. And I'm a little person. 'Little people' is the term used to refer to us. Calling little people *midgets* is no longer politically correct. I'm not part of some old circus freak show."

I can't tell. "Oh, aiight, my bad. So why didn't you just keep shit real and tell me what it was wit' you from the gate?"

She looks at me. "Do you want the truth?"

What the fuck you think, bitch? I nod. "Yeah."

"As fine as you are, would you still have come out here to see me if I told you the truth? And be honest."

I think, do I lie or keep it real? *For the right price, hell yeah, ho!* "Nah, I probably wouldn't." She looks at me, raises a brow. "Aiight, hell no."

She gives me a smile. "Exactly. Look, I apologize for not being up front with you. I was wrong for that. But I'm not gonna apologize for wanting to spend time with you, or for wanting to lie in your arms. I like you. I know I don't really know you, but after all of our phone conversations and email exchanges, I feel an emotional connection to you."

Lie in my arms? Emotional connection? What the fuck?! *Cuckoo-cuckoo-cuckoo*. This bitch talkin' like she's one screw from crazy. "Dig, baby, I don't know if you notice or not, but I'ma big man. Wouldn't you rather fuck wit' a little nigga instead of a cat who's almost three times ya height?"

She shakes her head. "Those aren't the kind of men I'm attracted to. I like a man I can climb up on and crawl all over, the taller the better. I like it when a man lifts me up and props me up on his dick. I might be a little woman, but I got a big sex drive."

Let me find out this bitch can fuck all night. "Oh, is that so? Well, that's what ya mouth says."

"That's what I know. So, do you have a problem with what you see, or do I need to drop you off somewhere else?"

Not at the moment. I lick my lips, lean over and kiss her, slippin' my tongue deep into her mouth. The bitch gotta mouth like a furnace, and I immediately imagine my dick up in it. She sucks on my tongue as I reach for her lil' right titty. Her nipple is hard as a pebble. I massage it over her shirt. She moans. I can smell her pussy juices simmerin'. And I wanna marinate this dick in it. "Nah," I say, lookin' her in the eyes. I kiss her again. "I'm right where I wanna be. Now let's hurry up and get to ya spot 'fore I end up fuckin' ya fine ass in the backseat of ya truck."

She giggles. *Silly-ass bitch*, I think, grinnin' at her. She backs outta her parkin' space, then heads east onto Interstate 285 toward Decatur. My cell rings. I pull it from my hip and peep the number. It's my nigga Mike. "Dig, ma. Excuse me for one minute, I say, pressin' TALK. "Yo, my nigga."

"Alley Cat, what's good, nigga?"

"Shit. What's good wit' you?"

"You already know. We rollin' out to Diva's Lounge in Montclair later tonight. You down?"

"Nah, my dude, can't. I'm outta town."

He laughs. "Prowlin'?"

"Nigga, you know how I do."

"Do you, my dude. When you comin' back?"

As soon as I run through this bitch's purse. I glance over at Minnie Mouse. When she looks over at me, I wink at her, lickin' my lips. She smiles. "In a week or so."

"Aiight. Hit me up when you get in."

"Most def."

"Oh, before I forget. You still down for All-Star in February?"

"Damn, I almost forgot about that shit. Where's it gonna be again?"

"Phoenix, nigga," he says, laughin'. "Ya ass can't remember shit."

"Whatever, nigga," I say, laughin' wit' him.

"Just let me know how much the shit's gonna run us."

"Aiight, lata."

"One," I say, endin' the call. I look over at Vita. Watch her maneuver her way through traffic. On some real shit, I'm impressed wit' her road skills. Still, she reminds me of Mrs. Potato Head. I unzip my jeans, then pull my dick through the slit of my Polo boxer briefs. She snaps her neck in my direction, and glances at my dick. "You think you can handle this?" I ask, slowly strokin' it.

She shifts her eyes from me to the road, then back to my dick, then back to the road in front of her. "Are you kidding? Of course I can handle that." She glances at this snake again. I grin, knowin' damn well she's gonna change her tune the minute this sleepin' giant awakens. She tries to keep her eyes on the road.

"You sure 'bout that?"

She doesn't answer the question. I smile, continue stretchin' my dick out. "Why you sitting there playing with your dick, teasing me?"

"'Cause I want you to see exactly what you gonna be gettin' all week before we get to ya spot." I continue to jerk it until it gets long and thick. She does a double-take, and her eyes pop open.

"Oh, shit," she says, swervin' from one lane to the other.

I laugh. "Damn, this dick got you tryna run off the road 'n shit. Relax, baby. Ain't no need to try 'n kill us. I ain't gonna hurt you wit' this pipe. But if you scared, say you scared."

"I'm not scared," she says. "Look at me. I've been faced with plenty of challenges all my life, and I've overcome all of them."

I laugh. "Oh, so you see takin' this dick as a challenge, huh?"

"No. I see it more as an adventure."

"Adventure, eh?" I grin. "Yo, I like that. So, you gonna handle this dick?"

She swallows hard. "Umm, I'm gonna sure do my best. It's been a long time. Just make sure you take it slow, and not try to ram it in me."

"Oh, not to worry, baby," I say, pumpin' my dick in my hand. *When I'm finished wit' ya dumb ass, you gonna be runnin' 'round in the middle of the day wit' a flashlight in ya hand, lookin' for some more of this dick.* I stop myself from spittin' all over her dashboard and windshield, wait for my dick to go down, then stuff it back in my boxers. I zip my pants up. "I got nuthin' but time. I'ma inch this long dick up in you nice 'n slow."

10

Yo, e'erything up in this chick's spot is top-of-the-line shit. Word up. I peep the Sony fifty-two-inch flat-screen wit' Bose surround sound and the Italian leather sofa set. Her spot is clean and smells fresh. I guess I expected her ass to live in a dollhouse wit' a buncha tiny-ass furniture 'n shit. But, I gotta give it to her, chick got some flava.

After she takes her shoes off at the door, she gives me the grand tour of the downstairs, then upstairs. I take it all in, really impressed. When she's done showin' me around, I follow her back down the stairs, watchin' how she maneuvers herself down each step, slidin' down one step at a time. For some reason, I feel like scoopin' her up under my arm like a puppy and walkin' her ass down, but I check myself. "Can I get you something to drink? Water, juice, or I have something a little stronger, if you like."

I hear Jamie Foxx's "Blame It" in my head. A nigga like me ain't never had to blame shit I do on alcohol, feel me? Fuck that "I was drunk" shit. If I fuck a bitch, I'm dickin' her knowin' exactly what I'm doin' and who I'm doin' it to. "I don't drink," I say, takin' a seat on the sofa. "You got any bottled water?"

"Sure. Make yourself comfortable while I get it. I hope you don't mind if I fix myself a cocktail. It's my vacation, and I like to get nice whenever I can."

"Do you, baby," I say, sittin' back on the sofa. She goes off into the kitchen, and I hear cabinets openin' and closin' and a buncha stirrin' 'round. My cell rings. It's Shavron. Another Myspace freak I met 'bout six months ago. The last time I hit her wit' some dick was a few weeks ago, and the bitch's been sweatin' me for another fix. "Yo, baby, what's good wit' you?" I ask, lowerin' my voice so Minnie Mouse doesn't hear.

"When I'ma see you?" she asks, soundin' like she got a lil' attitude or some shit. "Seems like you tryna avoid me or something." I grin. *Yeah, this bitch's real tight wit' a muhfucka.*

"Why you say that?"

"'Cause ever since I gave you some pussy, you acting like you ain't beat."

Uh, that's'cause I ain't. The bitch's pussy don't stay wet 'nough for me. I mean, the shit's big and can fit this dick up in it, but it's not gushy. A muhfucka like me likes a real juicy pussy sloshin' my dick up when I'm strokin' it. Not that dry shit she be servin' up. The last time I fucked her, it felt like I had my dick wrapped in sandpaper. Had my shit raw for two days. But I know her dumb ass is feenin' for some more of this dick. And I know if I slay her ass just right, she's gonna be comin' up offa them child support checks. The ho got four kids by three different muhfuckas. And I bet the bitch think I'ma be her next baby daddy. She already actin' like she wanna get this dick naked. "Nah, baby, it ain't nuthin' like that. I been kinda stressed lately. Gotta lot on my plate 'n shit."

"Well, I still wanna see you."

Damn, I tell this ho that I been kinda stressed, and her selfish ass ain't even ask if a muhfucka's okay 'n shit. Didn't think to ask if there's anything her dumb-ass can do. All she worried 'bout is how she can get at this dick. And then muhfuckas wonder why I drag these bitches. "Oh, you miss me, huh?"

"Something like that."

I laugh. "Yeah, whatever." On some real shit, I can never understand why bitches gotta play. Hell, if you miss a muhfucka, just say it. What's so hard 'bout that? Geesh! "You know you miss this dick," I tell her.

She sucks her teeth. "And so what if I do?"

"Then say the shit. If you miss this dick, say you miss it, baby. It's all good. Daddy ain't goin' nowhere, you dig? I'ma come through and feed you this Snickers bar real soon. And it's loaded wit' a buncha hot creamy nuts just for you, aiight?"

"When?"

See. Wit' a ho like Shavron I gotta ration out this dick to keep her ass from gettin' sprung the fuck out. So when I finally break this dick off in her sandbag pussy again, she'll 'preciate it. Otherwise, she could become a fuckin' headache, real quick. Besides, I never give a ho this dick when she wants it. It's when I think she deserves it. You want this good nut, then you need to earn it, feel me?

"Well," I say, glancin' over my shoulder to make sure Vita isn't comin' back into the room. "I'm outta town 'til next week. And when I get back, you know it's my birthday the followin' week so I'm tryna get right."

"I know. And I wanna spend it with you. I'm not gonna have the kids, so make sure you make some time to get right with me, too. I got something for you."

Aye, yo, I know I just told this bitch my birthday's in two weeks. And I know I told Vita my birthday was on Saturday. Well, peep this shit out. A nigga like me has about fifty different birthdays throughout the year. Hell, I can barely keep up wit' 'em. But they damn sure keep the gifts flowin'; dig what I'm sayin'?

"Oh, word? You copped me that new Xbox 360 joint?"

"Yeah, I got you that, and something else."

I grin. "Oh, yeah? And does that sumthin' else come wit' a side dish of hot pussy?"

She laughs. I roll my eyes up in my head. "Yep, and a slow, wet dick suck."

"That's wassup," I say, openin' and closin' my legs. I feel my dick startin' to come alive. "Tell big daddy how you gonna wet this dick."

"Well..." Vita steps up in my space carryin' a tray wit' a bottle of Dannon water, and a drink for herself. I take the water, then put my finga up for her to give me a minute. She sits 'cross from me, sippin' her drink, waitin'. "...I'ma kiss the head of it, twirl my tongue all around it, then I'ma suck and lick all over your balls, one at a time, then slowly pull 'em both into my mouth while jerking you off."

I cut my eye over at Vita. Slowly open and close my legs, tryna pinch down the swellin' in my boxers. She's actin' like she's busy goin' through CDs, frontin' like she's not listenin' to my conversation. She downs her drink, then goes back into the kitchen.

Shavron makes slurpin' noises into the phone, bringin' me back to the conversation. She got my shit slowly brickin' up. And listenin' to this ho got me ready to beat sumthin' up. But before I ever consider givin' this bitch another dose of this dick, I make a mental note to buy her some K-Y Jelly lubricant, Wet, Astroglide, or some other shit to help wet her ass up. I pull my cell from my ear and glance at the time. *Damn. I've been bullshittin' wit' this freak for almost fifteen minutes.* I guess it's kinda fucked up that I'm still talkin' wit' this chick instead of vibin' wit' Minnie Mouse.

Vita returns wit' a bottle of Patrón and a small bowl of sliced limes. I watch her pour herself another drink, squeeze in one of the limes, then downs it. She pours another one, downs it. *Oh, shit*, I think. *This lil' bitch's a real lush.* I peep her eyein' me as she walks by goin' into her sittin' room-slash-office. She closes the door, then a few minutes later comes back out, and goes into the kitchen.

"Listen, baby. I gotta bounce. I'll hit you up when I get home."

She sucks her teeth. "That's real fucked up. I wasn't fin—"

I hang up, cuttin' her off as Vita wobbles back into the room, then sits down. She's fumblin' through CDs again. The bitch can't seem to sit her ass still. She acts like she got an assful of bugs crawlin' and bitin' up in her. She keeps gettin' up and goin' from one room to the other. I frown, wonderin' if this ho is ADHD or some shit.

"Dig, baby," I say, lookin' at her as she sits back in the chair 'cross from me. "Sorry 'bout that."

She shrugs, twistin' her face up. "It musta been pretty important for you to stay on the phone for almost twenty minutes when you supposed to be chilling with me."

Oh, shit. This bitch got the nerve to be actin' jealous. I raise my brow, but say nuthin'. *Yo, fuck her!* Aiight, aiight…yeah, I know it was straight-up rude. Oh, muthafuckin' well. She stares at me. Picks up her drink, then gulps it down. "The way you were whispering I thought it mighta been somebody else, like your girl or something. It sounded like you were having a very intimate conversation. Is she somebody you deal with?"

I think. Catch myself from gettin' at her neck for tryna check for me. *Nigga, stay focused.* I open my water and take a long drink. *I need a muthafuckin' blunt!*

"Why?"

She shrugs, pourin' herself another drink. "Just asking."

"Yo, check this out," I say, leanin' forward in my seat. "I'm solo, all day, e'ery day. I don't have a girl. And I don't answer to one. So I fuck who I wanna fuck, smell me? But if I did have a chick, make no mistake, I wouldn't be sittin' here wit' you. Dig what I'm sayin'?"

She nods. "I hear you. So, have you ever cheated?"

I frown. "Why?"

She shrugs again. "Just curious."

Now, on some real shit, a nigga ain't really ever been in a serious relationship, so technically, I've never cheated. But fuckin' a string a bitches? You already know! "Nah, can't say that I have."

"That's good. I hate men who cheat."

And I hate bitches who can't suck a dick. She goes to pour herself another drink. *Damn, that's like her fourth drink in less than an hour.* "Damn, ma, what you tryna do, get drunk or sumthin'?"

"No. Not really. I just wanna enjoy my vacation and get nice. I hope you don't mind."

As long as ya ass don't start stumblin' and throwin' up, I don't give a fuck. "Nah, baby, do you." I take her in. She has big-ass brown eyes that kinda make her look like a ladybug. Other than that, she ain't really a bad-lookin' chick. I mean, I can fuck her face forward. Hol' up, don't get shit twisted. She ain't ever gonna be Halle Berry, or a Beyoncé, but she's a far cry from bein' an orangutan. And, although she ain't no beauty queen, she can still get fucked wit' the lights on. And I'll even give her ass some tongue. Besides, the bitch got some big, juicy dick suckas I'm dyin' to feel wrapped 'round this dick.

I lean all the way back in my seat, stretchin' my arm out over the top of the sofa. "Yo, baby doll, why you sittin' way over there? Come sit closer to me so we can get better acquainted."

She grins, gettin' up like she's happy to finally get some attention from a nigga. She puts a few CDs in the CD player, then presses PLAY. I watch her waddle back over wit' her drink in her hand as Usher's "Trading Places" plays. Her tiny nipples poke out like Skittles in her pink and white T-shirt. She slows her steps, and sways her hips to the beat. I smirk. Wait for her to take her seat beside me. I lean in. Sniff, sniff again. She smells like vanilla and cinnamon. I take another whiff. I don't remember smellin' perfume on her earlier. Then again, I wasn't beat. But, now…on some real shit, the bitch smells delicious. And if her pussy smells anything like this scent she has on, I'ma tear her the fuck up all night. There's just sumthin' 'bout a chick who smells good that turns me the fuck on.

"Damn, baby, what's that perfume you have on? It smells sexy as hell."

"It's *de Lolita Lempicka*," she says, smilin'.

I lean in closer. "Yo, that shit is bangin'."

"Thank you. It's one of my favorites."

"Oh, word," I say, eyein' her and lickin' my lips. "Yo, that shit can get a nigga in some serious trouble, word up. Have me wantin' to eat you up all night."

She giggles. "I like the sound of that."

Yeah, I bet you do.

11

"So when's the last time you had some dick in ya life?" I ask as she puts her glass to her lips. She coughs, chokin'. It takes her a minute to catch her breath. "Yo, you aiight, ma?" She nods, holdin' her chest. "OhmyGod, you real direct, I see."

"That's the only way to be, don't you think?"

"Yeah, I guess. But I think in most situations using tact is best."

Tact? I almost wanna laugh in her big-ass face. This trick got a muhfucka she met for the first time offa Myspace stayin' at her spot, and she talkin' 'bout usin' some muthafuckin' tact. Not to mention, the bitch *lied* to a nigga; got me out here under false pretenses. What the fuck? Fraudulent bitch! I'ma give her tact aiight, when I tack this dick down in her tight-ass throat.

"Well, check this out. I don't know nuthin' 'bout tact, so answer the question. When's the last time you swallowed a dick?"

She gulps down her drink, almost chokin'. "Six months ago."

I smirk. This ho done forgot she told me online she hadn't had dick in over a year. Now she sayin' "six months ago." On some real shit, I don't give a fuck one way or the other. I just love catchin' these bitches in lies. I let it go. "Oh, word. I bet that pussy extra tight, too." She nods, sippin' her drink. "So, did he fuck you good?"

"It was okay, I guess. I don't really remember."

Now how the fuck a bitch gonna let a nigga run up in her and she don't remember if the muhfucka hit that shit right? Either this ho was blitzed outta her mind, or the nigga's dick game was mad whack. She catches how I'm lookin' at her and laughs.

"We were both so drunk. That whole night was one big blur."

"So you let 'im bust that shit down raw?" I ask.

She rapidly shakes her head. "Hell no! I don't play that."

"Well, you were fucked up, so how you know if he did or didn't?" I wait for this ho's response. 'Cause you know as well as I do that if ya ass is ripped the fuck up 'n horny, neither one of ya asses is thinkin' 'bout wrappin' the hell up. You just tryna get it off. So nine times outta ten, a nigga goin' in that pussy straight naked and she's spreadin' them legs takin' it all in. Then, when the shit is all said and done, muhfuckas start stressin' hopin' they didn't catch shit they can't get rid of.

"You right," is all the bitch says. And it's all I need to hear.

"So why you don't have a man?"

She shrugs. "I really haven't been looking, besides most men seem to have a complex being seen out in public with me. They'll be okay with coming by late at night for a booty call, but that's it. Sometimes I want more than just sex."

As fucked up as it is, I can relate how them other muhfuckas mighta been feelin'. 'Cause on some real shit, I don't know if I wanna be out in public wit' her ass either. I know it's fucked up, but I'm keepin' shit real. I mean, she seems cool 'n all, but I ain't really beat to be out 'n about wit' her like that. Not tonight, anyway. But tomorrow I might feel differently after I done fucked her down a few times. Or better yet, after I've blazed a few trees.

"So, you want a man?"

"I want companionship. Sometimes I get lonely and just want someone to hold me, and to know that I can count on him to always have my back and be real with me."

I shake my head, thinkin', *Here we go wit' this shit*. I glance at my watch. It's almost seven-thirty. I take a deep breath. Allow Usher's "Love You Gently" to fill the room. Under different circumstances and wit' a different type of chick, a nigga's dick would already be brick and I'd be dickin' her down. "I feel you, ma. Some niggas just gonna play you out. Take what they can from you, then bounce. You need to be careful who you open ya heart and legs to, that's all. You just gotta keep ya head up, baby. And know all muhfuckas ain't fucked up like that."

"I know." She takes another sip of her drink, starin' at me. She tilts her head. "Are you fucked up like that?"

Hell yeah, bitch! Fall for a nigga like me, I'ma become ya worse muthafuckin' nightmare. I shake my head. "Nah, pretty baby, I ain't the one. I'ma real nigga."

"So, what are you lookin' for?"

"You mean now?"

"Yeah," she says, sippin' her drink, then sittin' it down on the coffee table, "now and in the future."

I look her dead in the eyes. "On some real shit, I ain't lookin' for no extras right now. Just some good, hot, wet pussy. And a nice, slow dick suck wit' no strings, and no muthafuckin' stress."

"And what about later?"

"Some more pussy."

She nods. "I appreciate your honesty."

"It's what I do, baby girl. And, just so you know. I may not be ya man, but while I'm here chillin' wit' ya, I'ma fuck you like I am."

She smiles, gettin' up. "Excuse me for one minute." I watch her walk back into her office, then shut the door. For a split second, I start thinkin' the lonely bitch went in there to cry. But I don't put too much energy into it. I check my cell for any messages instead. There are ten.

"Hey, baby, it's Akina. I didn't want nothin'. Was just thinkin' 'bout you, and wanted to make sure everything was okay with ya grandmother. Give me a call when you can."

Delete.

"Alley Cat, you ain't shit, nigga. You can't even be man enough to tell a bitch to her face you ain't beat no more. That's real fucked up, nigga. But, it's all good. And in case you don't know who the fuck this is. It's Sherria. You know. The bitch who gave you her heart and you just fucked it over. I want my fuckin' house keys back." *Bitch, change ya muthafuckin' locks.*

Delete.

"What's good with you, sexy? This's Rachel. When you comin' back down to Tampa? I could definitely use another hit of that good stuff. Give me a call when you get a chance." I press seven to save.

"Hey, big daaaaady, it's Cherry. I miss you, baby. It's been three months toooooo long. When you comin' back to L.A.? My pussy is achin' for you. I wanna see you, soon. Give me a call so we can make it happen."

Save. Now, this bitch right here, is a real live dick rider. I smile, rememberin' my last visit wit' her freaky ass. She had a nigga out there for almost a week, fuckin' me e'ery which way. Damn, she got some good-ass pussy. The bitch can't suck dick for shit, but she ain't scared of takin' it. And she even likes it in that big ass of hers. Man, listen...this bitch's asshole is as wide as the Grand Canyon, and handles a dick better than most pussies. Whew! When I finally bounced from her spot, I left up outta there wit' a certified bank check for ten grand. Yeah, a nigga's definitely tryna check for her, again.

"Hey, big daddy. It's Ramona. I miss you soooo much, baby. I can't take this shit. I want some more of that good dick, baby. It's killing me not being with you. Pleeeeeeaaaaase call me as soon as you get this." She leaves two more messages.

Delete. Delete. Delete. This bitch is too clingy. And a potential hazard. I fucked her—three months ago—e'ery day for a week, and the bitch talkin' 'bout she's in love wit' a muhfucka. Bitch, is you serious?!? I told this ho from dip not to go there, and she does anyway. So, hell no! No more dick for her nutty-ass.

"Hey, Alex. It's Falani. Call me when you get a chance. My night with you had me in the hospital for two days in pain. You knocked my uterus off its hinges"—she laughs—"I'm laughing, but I'm serious. The doctors said my uterus has been bruised. Now I'm on bedrest and medicine. Anywaaay, I hope all is well. Give me a call when you can. I'd like to see you again for another dose."

Delete. I shake my head. *That stupid bitch is crazy.* I done gouged up her uterus and she still tryna get at me. Man, listen. She can keep fuckin' wit' me if she wants. But, I ain't tryna be responsible when her greedy ass ends up havin' her insides pulled out for fuckin' this big dick.

"Hey, baby, it's Carla. I'm ready to suck that big-ass dick 'til I choke. Holla atcha girl when you can. I'm horny as fuck. A bitch tryna ride that dick and fuck ya fine-ass to sleep."

I laugh at her cum-thirsty ass, then listen to the last message from Tamia's nut-ass. The bitch is still screamin' 'bout me iggin' her retarded ass. *Delete.*

Vita walks back into the room. I squint, tryna see what the fuck she got on. The bitch changed her clothes, and is now wearin' a lil' sheer slip dress. She looks like a dressed-up Cabbage Patch doll. I shake my head. For some reason, her eyes are wide as saucers and make her look like a fly, nah…fuck that, a prayin' mantis. I frown, watchin' her as she pours another shot of Patròn, then tosses it back.

"Aaaaah," she says, shakin' her head. She sits on the floor. "Whew, this stuff here gets me right."

"Mmmph." I'm feelin' myself gettin' restless. I'm ready to get this dick wet. "So, dig, what else you like to do besides drink?"

"Well, I like to just chill out and listen to music. And every now and then I like to get my high on."

Trees? Oh, shit. That's the fuck what I'm talkin' 'bout. Now, the bitch's talkin' my language. I grin. "Oh, word. You get lit?"

"Sometimes. But not that often because of my job, why? You indulge?"

Oh, aiight. This bitch might not be half bad after all, I think. "Hell muthafuckin' yeah," I say excitedly.

She smiles. "Oh, cool. I got some. You wanna do a little something?"

"As long as you got that good shit, no doubt."

"I only buy the best. I woulda asked you earlier, but I didn't know how you rolled."

I laugh. "Oh, I roll 'em thick, baby. So, wassup? We blazin' or what?"

It almost looks like this bitch is startin' to salivate. She jumps up outta her seat. And on some real shit, I'm practically feenin' myself. "Follow me," she says.

I get up and follow her into her office. It's laced wit' a computer, sofa, stereo and another flat-screen TV. I take a seat on the sofa, watchin' her go into the closet, then roll out some type of mini servin' cart. She rolls the shit over to where I'm sittin'. There are two wooden boxes on it. She lifts the lids up offa 'em.

"Whatever your pleasure; help yourself, baby."

A nigga looks, then blinks. *Oh, shit!* This bitch got weed *and* coke. Now, I'll smoke all muthafuckin' day and night, but a muhfucka ain't fuckin' wit' nuthin' else. And I ain't really beat to fuck wit' no bitch who does either. But, I'm here now. And a muhfucka ain't bouncin' 'til she breaks me off some paper, or laces me wit' some wears. And that's what it is.

"Yo, I don't fuck wit' no coke, baby. But, I'll smoke ya trees up, real talk."

"You can smoke all you want. I only sniff."

I only sniff? *Yeah, right. Lyin'-ass bitch.* "Do you, baby," I say, grabbin' a fat-ass blunt already rolled tighter than a buffalo's ass. I take the lighter from offa the cart, then spark up. As I pull in smoke, I watch this ho take a razor, make a neat line of coke, then snort the shit up in one long-ass sniff. *Oh, hell yeah. I'ma take this coke-snortin' bird straight through the wringer. Word is bond. This ho is a real live junkie bitch.*

I blow out weed smoke, then take another hit straight to the head. It ain't the kinda top-of-the- line shit I'm used to, but it'll do. This lil' pumpkin-head ho does another line, then goes out into the livin' room and comes back wit' the bottle of Patròn. She sits on the floor and stares at me. Her eyes start dartin' 'round the room, and she's sniffin' like she's got a bucket of snot rammed up in her nose. The bitch is skeed the fuck up.

"I'm so glad you came here to spend time with me," she says, gettin' up to do another line. "Ever since our first phone conversation, I have wanted to meet you...It's been so long since I've spent time with a real man who's comfortable in his skin. And who's not just tryna fuck me 'cause they think I'm some kinda science project..."

Bitch, you are! I sigh. On some real shit, I ain't beat for this yip-yappin'. A muhfucka's ready to get aggressive wit' this trick. "Yo, cock open them legs," I snap, "and let me see you make that pussy pop."

She opens her mouth like she's shocked. "Excuse me?"

"You heard me. I ain't stutter. Let me see you get that pussy wet. So take them fuckin' drawers off, and let me see you make it do what it do."

I take another pull offa my blunt, hold the shit in my lungs, then blow a cloud of smoke at her. She leans back, and I smile. The bitch already doesn't have on any drawers. And as soon as she spreads open her legs, her fat pussy lips poke out. "Damn, look at that pretty pink cunt...get that shit wet for big daddy." She strokes her clit, then sticks a finger in her hole and moans.

I lick my lips watchin' her tight pussy glisten. I feel my dick start to stiffen. "Yeah, baby. I like that shit. Suck ya fingers for me." She licks her fingers, then continues playin' in her hole for another five minutes or so. Then she stops, gets up and goes back over to the cart to snort up more coke. She hoovers up halfa line, pauses, then starts back up. I watch and start to get disgusted lookin' at her fiend ass.

She looks over at me all bug-eyed 'n shit. "You the kinda man I could really get into. I'm so sick of niggas trying to use me, or think I'm some lonely charity case that has to pay them to fuck me. Yes, I get lonely for companionship sometimes. But, I'm far from desperate. Yes, I'm a sexual woman with needs. But I'm also a woman with standards. I'm a woman who wants to be loved. I hope you not going to try to hurt me like everybody else."

I frown. What the hell is this ramblin' fuck-box talkin' 'bout? "You know what," I say, standin' up and removin' my jeans, then pullin' my dick outta my boxers. "I'm not tryna hear all that dumb-shit comin' outta ya dick washer. Drop down and get on ya knees and crawl over to this dick. I didn't fly all the way out this bitch to listen to a buncha babblin' 'bout how lonely and fucked up ya life is. I came to get this dick slobbed; so punch in, and get to work."

She opens her dick sucka to say sumthin' else, but catches how I'm starin' her down wit' my shit swingin' in my hand. She knows what it is. She drops down low, makin' her way over to this horny, hard-ass dick. She stands up, stretches open her trap, then wraps her lips 'round my dick and greedily sucks on it. "Wet that shit up, baby...spit on it...there you go...suck that dick like you own it..."

12

I glance over at the clock: Six A.M. Gotdamn! A nigga can't even get any fuckin' sleep up in this muhfucka. I'm dead-ass tired from fuckin' all night. And I wanna get some zees. But I got this lil' piglet bitch here snorin' and droolin'. And to make matters worse, she got the muthafuckin' nerve to have her heavy ass body up on top of me like she's a damn infant, like I'm her damn daddy 'n shit. Hol' up…I bet you nosey muhfuckas wanna know how the pussy was, right? Yeah, I knew it. Well, keepin' it real, the shit wasn't half bad. The bitch wasn't servin' up no five-star pussy, but it definitely gets nice 'n wet. And a nigga can't even front, this ho got some super-dupa tight pussy. And hell yeah, I'ma fuck her lil' ass again. As a matter of fact, I'ma beat that hole up as soon as I wake her growlin' ass up.

I shake her. "Yo, ma, wake up." She doesn't budge. "Yo, Vita." *This bitch is in a coma*, I think, shakin' her again. She still doesn't move. And if the bitch wasn't snorin' so fuckin' loud, I'd think I fucked her to death. I shake her again. And this time when she doesn't move, I swing her up offa me, causin' her to roll offa the bed.

Thump! She hits the floor, hard. "Aaaaah…owwww…ouch!"

"Oh, shit. My bad," I say, tryna keep from laughin' at her ass. "You aiight?"

"I guess," she says, scramblin' to her feet and rubbin' her right arm, then her head. "Why'd you push me off the bed like that?"

Damn, I almost feel bad. "I was tryna wake you so I could take a piss. When you didn't budge, I tried to roll you offa me so I could use the bathroom, but you just rolled off the bed. C'mon back up here, and let me take care of ya pain, baby."

"What you gonna do to make it feel better?" She pouts, tryna be sexy 'n shit.

I get outta bed. "Ugh, shit," I say, steppin' on four cum-filled condoms. "Let me drain this hose and I'ma show you." I walk over to her, lift her up and kiss her on the lips. "When I come outta the bathroom I wanna see you on ya back wit' ya thick legs up and wide open, ya dig?"

She nods. I kiss her on the lips again, then pull her bottom lip into my mouth, slowly suckin' on it. I slide my tongue into her hot mouth. Twirl my tongue around hers. Taste her dick breath, then stare at her naked body. Take in her bite-size titties. Gaze down at the trimmed patch of hair coverin' her pussy. She spreads open her legs, allows me to stick my hand between her thighs. I wet my fingers wit' my spit, then play wit' her clit. Get her worked up, then slide a finger into her slick pussy, then another. She arches her back, buries the back of her head into her pillow, and lets out a deep moan, placin' her small hands on top of mine, grindin' her hips. "Oh...oh...ooooh..."

Her body starts to shake, and her eyes roll up in the back of her head. She snaps her head from side to side, then nuts all over my fingers and hand. I pull 'em out and slip 'em into her mouth. "Yeah, suck that creamy shit..." The bitch greedily sucks and moans. "Good girl. You like that shit, don't you?"

She moans again, noddin' her head, tryna catch her breath. She lies still for a few minutes, blinkin'. I guess a muhfucka musta finger-fucked her into a daze or sumthin'. She gazes at me and asks, "What are you trying to do to me, baby?" *Get ya pathetic ass to spend ya paper*, I think, grinnin'. "I ain't never cum like this before."

"Just tryna make you feel good, baby. That's all." I lean in and give her another kiss on her pussy-stained lips. "Just lay back and enjoy the ride, 'cause you ain't seen nuthin' yet."

I walk away from the bed. "Oooh, don't leave me like this."

"I'll be right back," I say over my shoulder. "I need to drain the snake."

"Hurry."

I take my piss, then wash my hands, starin' at myself in the mirror. *Nigga, you a real trip*, I think, smirkin' at my reflection. *You gonna fuck 'round and have this bitch givin' you the keys to her spot*. I smile, walkin' back into the bedroom. Vita's lyin' in the middle of the bed wit' her legs up and bent at the knees wit' her tight, puffy pussy smilin' at me. I lick my lips, decidin' I'ma eat her pussy. Hell, what the fuck. Even midget hoes need good dick and tongue in their life, right? And, this bitch ain't had either, so I'ma give her the Daddy Long Strong deluxe. After I tongue-fuck her pussy and asshole wit' deep, long, wet strokes and then make slow, sweet love to her clit, this bitch'll be beggin' me to move in.

I stroll back over to the bed. Don't say shit to her; just get between her legs, kiss the center of her pussy, then pull her lips apart and slowly start lickin' up 'n down and all 'round 'em. I stick my tongue up under her clit, rapidly flicking it. She moans, restin' her legs over my shoulders. I push them back up wit' my hands, bury my face between her thighs some more. And continue givin' her what she's been lackin'. I hold her legs back wit' one hand, then slip three fingers deep into her pussy as I suck on her clit. I hear her gasp. I think I hear gurglin' noises comin' from the back of her throat. I lift my head up. Smile. "You like that shit?" She bucks her hips.

"Yeah, that's it, baby. Make that pussy skeet...cum all over my tongue...give me that sweet cream, boo." I wrap my whole mouth around her pussy and suck 'n slurp. Five minutes later, her nut squirts out into my mouth and onto my tongue. A nigga can't front; this pint-size ho got some sweet, creamy pussy. I swallow. Finish suckin' her hole clean, then flip her over onto her stomach like a rag doll. And eat her ass out from the back 'til she passes out.

Two hours later, I got her wrapped up in my arms. "Damn, boo," she coos. "You really know how to fuck and eat pussy. Oh-myGod, I never knew a tongue could feel so good." She reaches for my dick, wraps both her hands 'round it, then slowly strokes it. "And this dick, mmmmm…it's so addictive. You got my pussy pulsing, and aching and so sore, but it felt so good. I wish I could keep this beautiful dick right here with me when you leave."

I chuckle. "Sorry, babe, when I go, I take Long Dong wit' me. But, while I'm here you can get as much of it as you like. And since you already got it in ya hand, tryna wake it, you might as well wet it wit' ya tongue so I can spit another round." She smiles, shiftin' her body. She presses her lips to the tip and starts plantin' soft, wet kisses all over it. "Yeah, that's right, baby. Kiss daddy's dick." She swirls her tongue around the head, then wraps her mouth 'round it. I pull in my bottom lip, then lick my lips. "Yeah, suck that shit," I say, claspin' my hands, then placin' 'em in the back of my head. "Cup them balls." She tries to use one hand, but my balls are too big for her lil'-ass hand. She's gonna need both of 'em to get me off. She grabs 'em wit' both hands, but has a hard time tryna handle suckin' my dick wit'out holdin' onto it. So I help the ho out. I lift up and hold my dick at the base, steady this rock-hard cock for her so she can squeeze the nut outta my balls.

After she finishes suckin' my dick, and gulpin' down this nut, I check my voice messages, again, while she's in the shower. She's in there butcherin' up Brandy's "1st and Love." I shake my head, tryna block out her screechin' while listenin' to all my messages.

Tamera left four messages—crazy bitch! Akina left two. Falani left one, and Electra left three. I call Electra first. And of course, she wants some dick. So I tell her I'ma swing through one day next week and bless her. Next I call Falani. The ho states she's still limpin' from the last dose I served her ass, but she's on that "I can't stop thinkin' 'bout you" shit. I tell her dumb-ass that the next time I come through I wanna threesome; that I wanna watch her eat another bitch's pussy while I'm beatin' that hole up from the back. She laughs, but then says she'll think 'bout it. So, you already know.

I decide to call Tamera's nutty-ass. "Damn, it took you long enough," she says, soundin' all tight and whatnot. "I done left you mad messages 'n shit."

"Aye, yo, what's fuckin' good wit' you, yo?" I already know what it is. This slew-footed ho misses the dick! I wanna hear her say it, though, feel me?

"Nigga, why the fuck you coming at my neck 'n shit?"

"'Cause I ain't beat for the bullshit."

She sucks her teeth. "Nigga, you acting like I shitted on you or something. If anything, I'm the one who should be heated with you for locking my fucking keys in the car. That was some real foul shit you pulled."

"Oh well. You shouldna came at me sideways and it woulda been all good. But, you tried to be on some ole rah-rah-type shit. So it is what it is."

"Muhfucka, you had my car out all damn night, then didn't wanna answer your phone. Puhleeeze, I had a right to spazz out on ya black ass."

"Listen, the shit is done. I ain't beat to keep goin' back 'n forth wit' you. So why the fuck is you constantly blowin' up my line, huh? You got ya shit back, so what the fuck else you want, *now*?"

"I wanna know why the fuck you avoiding me 'n shit."

I let out a deep breath. "I told you, I'm not beat."

"So what you sayin'? You ain't fucking with me now?" she asks, soundin' all pitiful 'n shit. It just amazes me how a bitch will be on some tough-girl-type shit, but the minute she knows she 'bout to lose out on some good dick, she wanna be on some ole other shit.

"Basically."

"Hmmph. So you gonna let that one incident come between us?"

Come between us? Obviously, this fuckin' hood-rat bitch really thinks I give a fuck 'bout her spazzin' out 'n shit. Truth of the matter is her dick time expired. Anytime a bitch is talkin' more shit than she's puttin' out pussy and loot, it's time to revoke her dick-ridin' card. And that's what it is. "You still haven't said why you keep callin' me," I say, dismissin' her question.

"'Cause I wanna see you, nigga. That's why. But you acting like a real bitch 'n shit."

I laugh. "Go 'head wit' that dumb shit."

"Whatever, muhfucka. When you comin' through?"

I laugh, knowin' this ho's pussy's achin' for this thick chocolate to melt up in it. "So, you tryna suck on this dick? Fuck, what?"

"Yeah, nigga. All the above. Ain't nothing changed."

"Whatever, yo."

"Oh, shit's changed with us?"

"Check this out," I say, sighin'. "There is no *us*. Never was, never will be. What part of the memo don't you get? I ain't fuckin' wit' ya smart ass. You always comin' outta ya neck crooked 'n shit. So 'til you know howta talk to a muhfucka, you gets no more of this dick. Ya ass is on punishment."

She laughs. "Punishment? Are you fucking serious? Nigga, please! Don't think your dick is the only dick out here."

What a fuckin' smut! "Yeah, you right. It ain't the only dick out there. And it's probably not the only dick you got ya dick suckas wrapped 'round. But it's the only dick ya dumb-ass keeps callin' for. It's the only dick that's got you cryin' e'erytime I finish beatin' that pussy up."

"*What*ever."

"Oh, so what you sayin'; this dick didn't have you shakin' and cryin' the last time I fucked you?"

She sucks her teeth. "I hate ya black ass, nigga. You are so full of yourself."

I laugh. "Yeah, yeah, yeah…Keep it gee, baby. You ain't gotta front wit' me. It is what it is." I hear the shower stop. Hear Vita swing back the shower curtain. "Look, I gotta bounce."

"Whatever. Am I gonna see you, or what? Damn."

I grin, knowin' if I decide to slay her ghetto ass, again, I'ma shred her muthafuckin' hole to pieces for bein' such a fucked-up bitch. "Maybe, maybe not. I—"

"Nigga, kiss my ass then," she snaps, cuttin' me off. "I'm not gonna beg ya black ass. You got the game fucked up, if you think I'm *that* pressed for some dick."

I bust out laughin'.

"What the fuck's so funny?"

"Your trick-ass," I say, still crackin' the hell up. "You talkin' like you a real dime; like you gotta line of niggas pressin' *you* for some of that raggedy-ass pussy. Fuck outta here!"

"Nigga, please. Your black ass can think what you want. But know this: I was getting it in *before* you, and I'll be getting it in *after* you. So having a muhfucka come through and serve me some dick will never be a problem."

I continue laughin'. "Whatever, ho. We both know ya ass'll be blowin' my muthafuckin' line up again, tryna get ya back split 'cause ya dizzy ass can't get enough of this long, black dick."

"Fuck you, nigga."

"Nah, baby, fuck you!" I press END. What a pigeon, word up! I don't know why these bitches gotta play themselves. If a muh-fucka ain't beat to fuck wit' ya ass, then take ya retarded ass on. But, noooo, its thirsty-ass hoes like her that'll start stalkin' a muh-fucka 'cause he done shut off her cum supply. I shake my head. Fuckin' pathetic!

When Vita finally comes outta the bathroom, I go in. Take my shower, then get dressed. Thirty minutes later, we're out 'n about. She takes me to this Italian spot, Brio Tuscan Grille, down in Buckhead. And I can't front; the food was bangin'. Bein' out wit' Vita wasn't as bad as I thought it would be. I mean, yeah, there were a few chicks and a couple a cats who were kinda lookin' at us sideways 'n shit—well, at least in my head they were. But I didn't really give a fuck. Keepin' shit real, she ain't half-bad.

After we grub, she shows me around Atlanta. We drive down to Piedmont Park and walk around for a while. Then we check out the Coca-Cola spot, The Underground, and the Aquarium. I guess I fuck her head up when I tell her I wanna check out the Martin Luther King Jr. Memorial site. This silly bitch didn't think a nigga like me would be interested in history. And I guess I fuck her head up even more when I look at her ass like she's crazy when she says she's lived in Georgia all her muthafuckin' life and has never been there. And when I hear she's never traveled outta the South, I'm really amazed. How the fuck can anyone be okay wit' not ever explorin' the world? Wow...that's all I could think.

Eight A.M., Saturday mornin', Vita comes skippin' up into the bedroom singin', "Happy birthday to you, happeeeee birthdaaaay to you! Haaaaaaaaaaaaappeeeeeeee birthdaaaaaaaaaay, Dear Alley Cat...Happeeeeeeeeeeeeeee birthday to youuuuuuuuuuuuuu..."

I stretch and yawn, then lean over the side of the bed so I can see her. "Thanks, baby."

I get up and sit on the edge of the bed, rubbin' the sleep outta my eyes and grabbin' the plush rug wit' my toes. "Why don't you climb ya sexy-ass back up on the bed?" She grins, climbin' back up in bed. "Let me go drain this snake, then I'ma take care of ya."

I get up and take a leak, wash my hands, then come back into the room. She's sittin' up in the middle of the bed wit' two king-size pillows propped up in back of her. She smiles. "What, why you smilin'?" I ask, gettin' back in bed.

"I'm happy," she says.

"'Bout what?"

"All this, you holding me, making love to me, spending time with me…" *I need to check my phone for any messages,* I think. *And see 'bout gettin' at that Stone Mountain beauty before I bounce. I bet she got some good pussy, too.* "…I've never met anyone like you. Or had a man treat me the way you have."

And ya ass never will. "Oh, word?" She nods. I reach over and lightly kiss her on the lips. "I just want you to know how special you are. That's all, feel me?"

She blinks. Her eyes start gettin' all watery 'n shit. *Fuck, here we go wit' this teary-eyed shit!* A muhfucka like me has no patience for a cryin'-ass ho. "You really think I'm special?"

Yep, you'se an extra special ho. Meep, meep…the short, yellow bus kind. I keep myself from laughin'. "No doubt, baby," I say, liftin' her chin up and lookin' her in the eyes. "Don't ever let anyone tell you anything different, ya heard?"

She nods. She smiles, gazin' at me like she's all in love 'n shit. "I wanna take you out to Phipps Plaza and buy you something really nice for your birthday."

Now that's what the fuck I'm talkin' 'bout. "Awww, baby, you don't have to do all that. Just bein' here wit' you is nice enough."

"That's sweet of you, but this is your day. And I want to make it very special. So I'ma take you shopping, then out to eat."

"Yo, on some real shit," I say, pullin' her into me and kissin' her on the lips. I slip my tongue in her mouth. We kiss for a few minutes before I pull back. "You really tryna fuck a nigga's head up, baby."

"I think you're a really special man. And you deserve a woman who knows how to treat a man like you. A woman who can let you be the man you need to be; yet, still encourage and inspire you to be the best you can be..."

This broad sounds like she's preparin' for a muthafuckin' campaign or some shit. Why can't these hoes just enjoy a muhfucka wit'out tryna bring in all the extras. Damn! I wanna put the brakes on it, but decide to let it ride, for now.

"...I know I don't really know you, but I've never felt this way about any man. And trust me. I've had my share of them to know what I'm talking about. I wish I could put what I'm feeling into words that made sense. Hell, I'm still trying to make sense out of it. All I know is you're the type of a man I could fall in love with..."

Alrighty then! The whole time this chick is talkin' I'm hearin' cash registers and cuckoo clocks in my head. The shit's hilarious to me. And I'm 'bout to bust out laughin'. But I fight to hold it in.

"...Do you believe in love at first sight?" I hear her ask.

Cuckoo-cuckoo-cuckoo! "Nah, baby, not really."

"Well, I hope I don't sound crazy or anything, but I do. I knew the first time we spoke on the phone that I was going to fall for you. And when I picked you up at the airport, seeing you confirmed what I already was feeling in my heart."

Cuckoo-cuckoo-cuckoo!

"Listen, baby," I warn. "Don't do it to ya'self. A nigga like me ain't ready for nuthin' more than some pussy."

"I know, I know. Don't worry. I don't have any expectations from you. I'm a big girl. And I'm responsible for what I allow to happen. I don't expect you to feel the same way about me. But who knows. Maybe one day you will. If not, it's cool. No matter what, I'm glad I had the opportunity to experience this feeling with you." Her eyes start to well up. "I just want you to know how happy you've made me feel."

Cuckoo-cuckoo-cuckoo! I wanna tell this ho that a nigga should never be what makes her happy. That no matter how good a muhfucka fucks her guts out, it doesn't mean he's gonna be good for her. That niggas like me can smell a vulnerable, lonely bitch a mile away and will prey on her ass, and take her for e'ery muth-afuckin' thing she's worth. I wanna tell her all this, but I don't. Why the fuck should I? Hell, I'm tryna get all I can outta her ass. I pull her into my arms, kiss her on the forehead and then say, "I'm glad I could bring a lil' joy in ya life." I give her a few tongue-probin' kisses, then slide my fingers into her pussy, slow stroke her insides, 'til she nuts all over my hand. I suck her juices off my fingers, then slide my tongue back into her mouth.

Thirty minutes later, we're showered, dressed and out the door on our way to pick out my "birthday" gifts. And when we return, four hours later, I'm horny as hell from all the shoppin' she's done on a muhfucka. Well, aiight, aiight, that's not the only reason why my dick is brick. Akina's been textin' me all muhfuckin' afternoon talkin' 'bout how she misses me and wants me to eat her pussy, then beat it up like it stole a nut from me; 'bout how she wants to lick my balls and asshole, then suck my dick 'til I nut down in her throat; 'bout how she wants me to fuck her 'til her pussy burns. And of course I texted her back, lettin' her know exactly how I was gonna tear her ass out the frame when I get home. In the meantime, I'ma rock Vita's box.

"Thanks, baby, for makin' today real special," I tell her, droppin' six shoppin' bags by the side of the sofa. "This is one of my best birthdays."

"Awwww, it was my pleasure. And knowing that you appreciate the gesture makes it even more special."

Yeah, she's a keeper, for sure. Crazy or not, she's a generous, thoughtful ho. And, in today's economic climate, that's what really counts. I hit her wit' one of my award-winnin' smiles, then lift her up into my arms, carry her upstairs, remove her clothes, then remove mine. I suck and lick her tits, plant soft kisses all over her body, then fuck e'ery inch of her tiny pussy 'til her body shakes and she breaks down and cries. And by the time I finally pack my shit to bounce, I got her walkin' more gap-legged than she already is. And her pussy's stretched open wide enough to fit eight inches of this dick.

13

I'm finally home—chillin', kicked back watchin' CNN Live, tryna get caught up wit' what's poppin' wit' my dude Barack and his whack-ass opponent. I'm tellin' you, dude got this presidential shit in the bag—hands down! He's been waxin' that old-ass dude's ass in e'ery debate. That cracker can't rock wit' Barack, real talk. Dude might as well throw his ass in a ditch and let 'em toss the dirt down on him 'cause it's already over for 'im. Hell, the coffin was sealed on this election the minute dude announced that Gidget look-alike as his vice president—like that was gonna help him. Fuck outta here! Obama got swagger. And it's 'bout to be on up in the muthafuckin' White House, ya heard?

Anyway, a nigga can't front, it's good to be home—word up. That lil' stint in ATL wit' Minnie Mouse, nah...let me stop— wit' Vita, was aiight. I ain't even gonna style. She's cool peeps. Like I said before, she isn't the hottest chick on the block, but she ain't the ugliest either. And she ain't broke. So what she lacks in looks, she makes up in dollars, feel me? True, she can't handle the dick, *yet*. But she did try her damndest to serve up the pussy wit' enthusiasm and greed. And, for me, an enthusiastic, greedy bitch tryna bounce the pussy up 'n down on this dick gets mad props from me. Still a muhfucka's horny as hell and ready to fuck—*now!*

Who can I call? At least three dozen bitches, but I ain't feelin' none of 'em. I want some new pussy. That Stone Mountain cutie comes to mind. I curse under my breath for not gettin' at her while I was in ATL. I woulda loved slidin' up between them hips, word up. I scroll through my phone, find her number, and call. When she doesn't pick up, I decide to leave a message—this time, then get up from the sofa and run upstairs to get my laptop from outta my office-slash-guestroom. I come back down wit' it, ploppin' back down on the sofa. I kick my feet up on my leather coffee table, then call Maleeka while waitin' for the PC to boot up. I leave a message, lettin' her know big daddy wants some pussy. My dick starts to thicken thinkin' 'bout her big, wet pussy slurpin' in this dick. I pull my dick outta the slit of my boxers, and stroke. I close my eyes. Imagine her ridin' this dick bronco-style wit' her perky titties bouncin' up 'n down. *Damn, I wanna fuck.* I deepen my strokes on my dick, cup my balls wit' my free hand, then lighty squeeze on 'em. I'm on the brink of bustin' a quick nut when my cell rings, disruptin' my flow. It's Shavron. I let go of my dick. Let my nut ooze out.

What the fuck this lame bitch want? "What's good, baby?" I say, grabbin' a T-shirt and wipin' my nut off my stomach and from 'round my dick and balls. I log onto BlackPlanet. I click on my NOTES page. Damn, there's seventy-eight notes. I go through 'em, deletin' the ones I ain't beat for. I click on the pages of the ones that pique my interest. I wanna see who these hoes are before I respond.

"You," she says in a low voice. I'm not sure if the bitch is sad, or tryna sound sexy. "You still outta town?"

"Nah, I'm back."

"Oh, for real? When you get back?"

"Yesterday," I lie. Yeah, I coulda kept shit real and told this ho I got back last week, but what the fuck for? Bitches be straight lyin' all the time. Besides, it's none of her muthafuckin' business when I touched the fuck down.

"Then why didn't you call me? I thought you said you was gonna hit me up when you got back."

Is this bitch fuckin' serious? "Aye, yo, bit…"—I catch myself before I rip into her ass—"Listen, don't muthafuckin' question me. I had mad shit to handle when I got back. I got sidetracked. Shit happens. But you know I was gonna hit you up sooner or later, damn—relax, baby."

She softens her tone. "I didn't mean to come off like I was questioning you…" *Yes the fuck you did.* "It's just that I've been anxious to see you, and I wanted to make sure we were still on for your birthday."

Damn, I almost forgot I had another birthday weekend comin' up, which means more gifts. I grin, rememberin' the Xbox she copped me. A muhfucka changes his tone, quick. "Oh, no doubt, baby." *I need to make sure I scoop up some lube before I get at her, though. There's no muthafuckin' way I'ma stick my dick back up in that desert of a pussy. I might as well just go out and fuck a box of sand.* "You remember all that slick shit you was talkin' 'bout how you tryna suck this dick, right?"

"Yeah, I know what I told you. And I meant it."

"That's what ya mouth says," I tease. "But we know you ain't ready to put in no real work."

"I was born ready," she states, laughin'. "I don't ever gotta get ready; thought you knew."

Same script, different ho, I think, shakin' my head. "Yeah, yeah, yeah…I've heard that before."

"And now you're hearing it again. Only difference is, I bet them other chicks don't love giving you head as much as I do."

"Oh, word? What you love 'bout suckin' on this dick?"

"Everything."

"E'erything like what? Tell me." She tells me how she loves

the way it tastes; how big, black and beautiful it is; how strong and heavy it is; how she loves the way it pulses in her mouth and stretches her jaws and mouth open. Then she tells me how she wants my baby batter on her tongue and smeared all over her lips.

As I'm listenin' to her, I'm readin' and deletin' notes, and clickin' on members' pages that catch my attention. I come 'cross DrSweetPussy's page. It's done in red and black and there's a flick of a chick wit' her face blacked out wearin' a black-lace bodysuit and a pair of red stilettos. The shit is sexy as hell. Her profile says she's fifty-five—*goddamn, this bitch gotta a body like a twenty-year-old. I bet she got some good pussy, too*—lives in Jersey, married and seekin' sumthin' on the side. I peep the outline of her nipples, then zoom in on the imprint of her pussy. She got one of them phatties fo' sure. I imagine slidin' this dick up in that shit. It's been a minute since I had some seasoned, old-school pussy. Shit, the last time I fucked some aged-pussy was like eight years ago when I fucked one of my man's moms. Yeah, I know I shoulda felt bad for rockin' his moms' box. But, man, listen…that old-ass ho knew how to make that shit pop, word up.

At fifty-six, Ms. Carson was one sexy-ass woman with a juicy, apple-bottom ass and big double-D titties. My dick used to feel good as hell beween them two cock knockers, word up. She had a few jelly rolls around her waist and stomach area, but she had some bangin' pussy. She'd hit me up late at night, like 'round two or three in the mornin' for some of this dick. I'd park my car 'round the corner, then sneak through her backyard and meet her out in the shed. She'd suck and fuck this dick for 'bout an hour or so, then stumble her hot-ass back into her house and climb back into bed wit' her husband. I ended up smashin' her walls for three more months before I deaded it. That greedy bitch wanted to keep guzzlin' this dick, but she wasn't tryna come up offa no paper. So you already know she had to go.

Damn, I bet that pussy is better now at sixty-four. *Okay, DrSweet-Pussy, I'ma give you exactly what that fat-ass pussy needs*, I think, starin' at her page and grabbin' at my dick. I hit her up wit' a note, leavin' her my email addy to holla back.

I bring my attention back to this broad I got on the phone. "So how many other niggas' tops you spinnin'?" Not that I gotta right to be askin', but I know she's gonna give me an answer, anyway—even if it's some half-truth bullshit.

"What?"

"Yo, you heard me. I asked you how many other niggas' dicks you washin'?"

"OhmyGod, I can't believe you'd ask me some crazy shit like that. Don't play me, nigga. I'm many things, but a ho ain't one of 'em. I don't go around sucking a bunch of dicks. The only nigga's top I'm poppin' is yours."

Yeah, right. Tell me any-fuckin'-thing. This bitch musta forgot who she's talkin' to. I know her work. She's the same cum-guzzlin' slut who piped out my man's 'n 'em two summers ago after a barbecue at Mountainside Park. And she's the same nut-catchin' ho who had some cat from Hillside stretchin' her throat a few months back. But she don't know I'm up on it. Not that it matters. She can slurp down as many babies as she wants. I ain't tryna wife the bitch, feel me?

"Yo, whatever! Fuck all that ying-yang you talkin'. You tryna wet this dick up, or what?"

"You already know."

"Aiight, that's wassup. And I want that shit real nasty, too. A whole lotta slob and spit all over this dick. I want that shit drippin' down my balls."

"I got you. You know I know how to serve you up proper."

Yeah, you just oughta know how! Cause you ain't servin' shit else wit' that sandbox pussy. I feel my dick startin' to brick thinkin' 'bout her wrappin' them big-ass dick suckas 'round my joint and me chokin' the shit outta her wit' it. On some real shit, I ain't beat for no head tonight, I wanna fuck a wet hole. But, unless I snatch up some pussy in the next twenty minutes, a wet throat will tie me over 'til I do.

"Alley Cat, I don't know why you be tryna play me. You already know what it is…" I text Lahney while this ho babbles on: Yo, what's good? U fuckin' 2 nite?

"…The only nigga I'm fuckin' with is you."

"Oh, word?"

"Word. I'm not interested in any other nigga."

I shake my head. "Listen…I hope you keepin' shit in perspective between us. Don't start tryna padlock a nigga down like he's ya man 'n shit 'cause I told you from dip what it is—"

"Nigga, please. Don't trip. I already know."

Lahney texts back: Not tonight. Unless you up for a bloody Mary.

Fuck, this bitch stays on her muthafuckin' period, I think textin' back: That's aiight. I'm good. Hit me up when u ready 2 get that hole stretched.

Lol, nigga, u a trip! I will, she replies.

I decide to swab Shavron's throat, then swing by Akina's spot to have her ride down on this dick when I'm done. "Yo, I'm ready to come through wit' this hard-ass dick."

"Oh, so you really tryna get it wet?"

Duh, didn't I just say that shit? What the fuck else this dumb bitch think I'm tryna do wit' a stiff damn dick? Sit and watch movies wit' her simple-ass. "No doubt, baby. I only want a drop 'n go, though. No extras tonight, feel me?"

She sucks her teeth. "Yeah, I got you. But be clear. Just because you coming through tonight doesn't mean I don't wanna still see you on your birthday. This is just a little pre-birthday treat."

This bitch. "Don't worry, ma. We still gonna chill. And I'ma rock the snot outta ya."

"Mmmm," she moans. "And you gotta stay the night."

I smile, knowin' her thirsty ass is gonna be tryna gobble up these nuts all night. And, lucky for her, a nigga like me comes fully loaded wit' a full sack of cream. "You got that. But, in the meantime, get that dick washer ready for round one 'cause big daddy's comin' to dump a double load in it."

"I'll be ready," she says, laughin'.

"Bet." After we hang up, I jump up and run upstairs to take a quick shower, throw on a sweat shirt and pair of Polo sweats wit'out any drawers. My dick 'n balls can bounce freely, and give this ho quick access. So when I walk up in her spot, all she gotta do is drop down on her knees, yank these sweats down 'round my ankles, then let it do what it do.

I hop in my other hoopty—a blue four-door Chevy Impala, drive up Ocean Avenue, and make a left onto Broadway to get to the parkway. Livin' down here by the shore is cool 'n all, but it's nights like this when I wish I had some local broads to kick it wit' instead of havin' to drive all the way up to North Jersey for some throat 'n pussy action. I spark the half blunt in my ashtray, call Akina and tell her what time I'ma come through. Then I call Cherry in L.A., but leave a message when she doesn't pick up.

My cell rings. It's Maleeka hittin' me back. "Yo, what's good, ma?"

"Shit," she says. "I got your message."

"So, what's good, then? You feel like fuckin', or what?"

"When you tryna come through?"

"Now," I tell her.

She laughs. "Damn, nigga, you sound real pressed for some of this gushy shit."

Bitch, don't get it twisted, I think, laughin', *a muhfucka like me ain't never gonna be pressed for one bitch's pussy.* "Pressed? Nah, baby... never that. But a muhfucka's horny as hell."

"Nigga, you stay horny."

"You already know. So what's good? Can I come through and fuck, or what?" She pauses. I'm sure to think 'bout how I deep stroked that pussy the last time we were together. Nonstop, for two hours, I pumped her insides. By the time I finished, this dick had her ass shakin' and beggin' for some more. And, after the second round, a muhfucka walked up outta there wit' a quick four hunnid.

"Hell yeah, you can come through," she finally says. "But not right now. I got three heads to braid, and I probably won't get done 'til about eight, or nine o'clock."

"Nah, baby, that's too late. Can't you push those shits back and let me come through now?"

"Nigga, please, not today. Your stroke game is tight, but a bitch ain't about to let a nigga and his dick get in the way of me makin' my paper. You know how I am about getting that money."

On some real shit, I had to respect her hustle. With all of her regulars, chick pulls in anywhere from one-to-two thousand a week braidin' hair—straight cash. This bitch be rapin' the shit outta the IRS. I laugh to myself. *That's right, baby, get them snake-ass muhfuckas before they try 'n get you.*

"Yo, I can dig it, baby; can't knock a muhfucka for tryin', though. Make ya ends," I say bearin' off toward exit 145. I pay the thirty-five-cent toll, then drive toward South Orange Avenue. "I'm on my way to get my dick sucked, anyway. So it's all good."

She laughs. "Nigga, you're funny as hell. You comin' at me for some pussy and you already got some throat lined up. You stay tryna keep ya dick stuck in somethin' wet."

I burst out laughin'. "Yo, ma, why you think they call me Alley Cat?"

"'Cause ya nasty ass is always prowlin'," she answers, chucklin'. "Come through tonight, if you can."

"I might. If not, I'ma hit you up in a few days, aiight?"

"Make sure you do so I can smoke that dick."

And gargle my nut while ya at it, wit' ya cum-guzzlin' ass. "That's what it is," I say before endin' the call. I make a left, then several more turns before finally ridin' down Shavron's block. When I get to her spot, I park my ride, then make my way up to her buildin'. Before I can even knock on her door, it swings it open. She snatches my hand and pulls me in. As soon as the door shuts, she has me backed up against it, yankin' my sweats down 'round my ankles. She takes my dick into her soft hands, then mounts her lips 'round the head while squuezin' my shit at the base. She removes her lips from offa my dick, then starts greedily lickin' and suckin' on my balls.

She stops what she's doin' then stands up and opens her robe. She lets it fall off her shoulders and onto the floor, then drops back down to her knees, slippin' my dick back into her mouth. The way she licks and kisses all over this pipe tells me all I need to know. She's in love wit' a muhfucka's dick. I close my eyes and wind my hips, slow. Allow her to control the amount of dick she takes into her mouth wit' her hands. The head of my dick hits the back of her throat. I stand still; let her feed on the dick. She gags, but keeps on suckin', spittin' all over it, coatin' it wit' a glob of slob.

I open my eyes. Look down at her as she dutifully sucks on this dick, then glance 'round her spot. Clothes 'n shit all over the livin' room. I spot a pair of panties that look like they mighta been worn tossed up on the coffee table. Nasty bitch! This ho keeps a junkie spot, but what the fuck I care. She's suckin' my shit so damn good she got me openin' and closin' my toes in my Timbs. I moan. Decide that after I bust this first nut, I'ma reward her wit' an extra dose of cum. Hell, I might as well let her suck and swallow this baby batter. 'Cause on some real shit, this ho's runnin' the best damn all-night abortion clinic in town. Right down in her mutha-fuckin' throat!

14

Sunday mornin', I'm sleep on my back, and feel lips on my eyelids, then my nose, then my lips. "Wake up, Birthday Man," I hear. I slowly open my eyes, and see Shavron starin' down on me, naked and grinnin' ear to ear carryin' a breakfast tray.

I yawn, and stretch, then rub my eyes. "What's good, babe?"

"You," she says, smilin'. "And I bring you breakfast in bed to finish up last night's celebration." I sit up in bed as she hands me the tray. She has my favorite three-cheese and vegetable omelet, hash browns, turkey bacon, sliced strawberries, and a blueberry muffin wit' a lit candle on it. She starts singin' Stevie Wonder's version of "Happy Birthday"—again, clappin' and jumpin' up and down. I watch her titties bounce for joy. Feel my dick start to rise. I'm glad I bought that large bottle of Astroglide and tube of KY 'cause yesterday I used almost all of it on her ass tryna keep her pussy extra wet and slippery. And today I plan on usin' the rest, stretchin' her cunt to the limit. I fucked her practically all afternoon yesterday, then most of last night which surprises me that's she's already up, bouncin' 'round like a lil' Energizer bunny.

I yawn again, this time coverin' my mouth. "Damn, I thought *you* was gonna be breakfast," I say, frontin' like I'm mad.

She giggles. "No, baby...I'm brunch." She licks her lips, leans in, then slips her tongue into my mouth. I grab her fat ass. She pulls back. "Make a wish, and blow out your candle."

I close my eyes, smirkin'. *I wish this bitch had a wet pussy*, I think, openin' my eyes and blowin' out the candle.

"What did you wish for?" she asks, eyein' me all seductive 'n shit.

"For some of that hot pussy," I lie, pullin' the covers back and grabbin' my dick.

She sucks her teeth, grinnin'. "Fool, you get that anyway. What else you wish for?"

"You," I lie again.

She sighs. "Yeah right, try again."

I grin, swingin' 'n shakin' my dick side to side. "For you to suck on this dick."

She rolls her eyes. "I shoulda known that was coming."

"Well, then c'mere and put them pretty-ass lips to work."

She sucks her teeth. "You lucky it's your birthday weekend," she says as she leans in and takes my dick in her soft hands. She licks and kisses the head, then wraps her lips 'round it as she cups my heavy balls.

"C'mon, baby, suck that dick. Stop fuckin' wit' me." She licks and sucks for a few more minutes, then abruptly stops her mini slurp session. "Awww, shit. Why you stop?"

"We got all day for this."

What the fuck?! This is the same ball gargler who's always talkin' 'bout how much she loves suckin' my muthafuckin' dick, how much she loves swallowin' this nut. And now the cum-breath bitch actin' like she ain't wit' it. "Are you serious? You do know that's fucked up, right?" I stroke my shit. Let it thicken in my hand. "Stop playin' and c'mon and wet this dick."

She sucks her teeth, plantin' a hand on her hip. "Is gettin' ya dick sucked all you think about?"

"Nah. I think 'bout fuckin', too. You already know. So what's good? You tryna put work in or what?"

"Nope."

A muhfucka's tryna be nice, I swear I am. But this ho don't know. I'm a split second from blastin' her ass. I take a deep breath. "Damn, baby, how you gonna leave me layin' here wit' all this hard dick?"

She laughs. "Easy." She leans over and lightly kisses me on the lips again, grabbin' my dick. She squeezes it, then licks the head of it before lettin' go. I watch her ass bounce 'n shake as she goes into the bathroom. I'm smilin', but on the inside I'm thinkin', *As soon as I finish eatin', she had better be ready to hop up on this dick, or I'm dippin' on this bitch.* As far as I'm concerned, she's served her purpose. And we've both gotten what we've wanted from the other. Now I'm ready to be laid up somewhere wit' a big-lipped, wet-pussied bitch who knows howta swallow a muthafuckin' dick!

I glance 'round her bedroom, shakin' my head tryna figure out how e'ery other room in her spot looks like a muthafuckin' pigsty, yet this is the cleanest room in her whole spot. Wit' the exception of my clothes tossed on the floor over in the corner, and the blankets tossed on the floor, e'erything's neat and in its place. Still, in my head, she's a nasty housekeeper, and a lazy-ass, dick-swallowin' bitch. Defintely not the type of chick I'd wanna wife up.

I scoot over to the center of the bed, then frown. *Ugh, what the fuck!* My ass is in something wet. A reminder of all the fuckin' we've done. I move back over to my side of the bed, take a sip of my drink, bite into a piece of bacon, then cut into my omelet and start eatin'. I can't front, she did her thing. This omelet is bangin'.

My cell rings. *Fuck*, I think, placin' the tray of food on the bed beside me. *Let me get this shit to see who the hell is tryna get at me.* I get up to get my phone from outta my pants pocket.

She yells from her bathroom, "Tell them other bitches I said to beat it! You with me, and I'm the one you servin' the dick to all weekend."

I shake my head. *This stupid bitch*. "Well, you better act like you ready to put some more work in," I warn her as I retrieve my phone, "or one of 'em will be takin' ya spot before the day is over."

She walks back into the room wit' Noxema smeared all over her face, lookin' like a porcelain doll. "Excuse me?"

"You heard what I said. I want you wettin' this dick."

She sucks her teeth, goin' back into the bathroom. "Whatever."

"Whatever nuthin'. You already know what it is. Don't have me smack you wit' it." I see I have eight missed calls, and twenty text messages. I scroll through 'em, shakin' my head. Tamera's bird-ass is still at it. Eleven of the text messages are from her. There're two texts from Maleeka. I read 'em. My pussy's on E, nigga. Come thru and fill it up…I'm waitin' for you to hit me back. I wanna fuck…

She laughs.

I text Maleeka back. I'll be thru in an hr.

"Oh, aiight," I say, deletin' the rest of my texts, then puttin' the phone back into my pants pocket. "You think that shit's funny. It's all good, though, baby. You know I ain't one to keep sweatin' a broad for no brain or ass."

"Yeah, yeah, yeah," she says. "I'll keep it in mind."

My phone *dings* again, then starts ringin'. *Shit, I forgot to put the shit on vibrate.* It beeps to let me know I have a message. Five minutes later, it rings again. I have a call comin' in from Ramona's crazy ass. I press IGNORE.

Maleeka texts back: Don't have me waiting all day.

"I see you a real busy man. Whoever it is, they are blowin' ya phone up like it's a state of emergency."

I laugh. "Baby, any time someone's tryna get at this sexy-chocolate nigga and they can't, that's exactly what it is. Thought you knew."

I text back: Whatever. See u when I get there.

Shavron sucks her teeth. "Finish eatin'."

Don't tell me what the fuck to do! I take a deep breath. "I'm tryna get you to eat this dick, but you wanna be on some dumb shit." I put my phone back into my pants pocket, then walk into the bathroom and grab her from behind, wrappin' my arms around her, and pressin' my rock-hard body into her back. "I want some head."

She wiggles herself outta my embrace. "Not now." She turns on the shower, waits for it to steam up, then steps in. "You joinin' me in here?"

I wanna bust a quick nut in her mouth, and this ho tryna be on some ole other shit. I stare at her. Take another deep breath. I'ma ask her one more time. "You suckin'?"

She sucks her teeth, sighin'. "I told you, not now."

"Nah, I'm good, then," I tell her, takin' a piss. I flush the toilet, hopin' the water turns cold on her ass.

"Oh, so what, now you gotta attitude?"

"Nah, baby, never that," I say back, washin' and dryin' my hands, then walkin' back into the bedroom. I glance over at the clock: 10:16 A.M. *Let me get the fuck up outta here.* I start slippin' on my clothes. Instead of straight dissin' her, I go back into the bathroom to tell her I'm out. "Yo, I'ma get at you later."

"What?" she asks, stickin' her head outta the shower curtain. She looks me up and down, realizin' what I've said when she sees me wit' all my shit on. "Where you goin'?"

"To get my dick sucked."

"Excuse you?"

"I got shit to do," I say.

"Oh, hell no," she snaps, shuttin' the water off and pullin' back the curtain. "All of sudden you got shit to do, and you out. But just a few minutes ago you were prancin' around here naked wanting me to spin ya top. Now you all dressed and shit. That's real fucked up."

I stare at her naked body, watch droplets of water and suds roll down her breasts. Her nipples are hard. I lick my lips. Think 'bout suckin' her tits. Imagine throwin' her up against the shower wall and fuckin' her dry-ass pussy 'til it burns and turns raw. I decide against it. Instead, I tell her I enjoyed chillin' wit' her; that I appreciate the gift; that it's time to bounce; that I'll holla at her later. But the bitch isn't havin' it.

"Why, because I wouldn't suck ya damn dick when you wanted me to?"

"Basically, but it's all good. I found another willin' throat to plant this nut in."

She stares me down. Then the theatrics begin. Hand on hip. Finger pointin'. Neck rollin'. "Whaaaat? Nigga, are you serious? You leaving up outta here to go lay up with some other bitch after I fucked and sucked you practically all damn day yesterday and again last night. And you got the fucking audacity to stand here and tell me that shit."

"Yep," I say, shruggin'. Hell, she should be glad I'm keepin' shit real.

She huffs, puttin' her hand up. "You know what? You're an arrogant, selfish-ass motherfucker, for real. Just get the fuck out. I ain't begging your ass to stay."

"And I ain't askin' you to," I flatly state. "I shoulda just dipped on ya ass."

"Yeah, nigga maybe you shoulda. But you didn't, so dip now, muhfucka."

"Peace out," I tell her, walkin' outta the bathroom. She follows behind me, naked and wet. The bitch tells me to dip, but still trailin' behind me into the livin' room, poppin' shit. What the fuck?!

"So you really gonna fucking leave, right? You gonna dis me for some other bitch, right? Is that how you doin' yours? You gonna just straight play me like that?"

"Yep."

"Fuck you then. You ain't shit, nigga for real. I don't even know why I ever fucked with your broke ass, anyway. All you good for is fucking 'cause ya broke ass can't even afford a Happy Meal."

I slip on my Gores. Let her run her dick suckas. Yeah, I'm broke aiight. But, I'm the same muhfucka sittin' on close to a hunnid grand, collectin' interest. Money left over from a settlement I got when a drunk driver—a judge's wife, no less—in broad daylight, ran a stop sign, jumped a curb, then hit me as I was ridin' my bike on the sidewalk. I was like eight. And lucky for me I didn't have parents who tried to run through my paper, which is how I eventually bought my spot—paid in full, and copped me a slick-ass whip. But, this bitch wouldn't know all that. Keepin' shit real, a muhfucka like me gotta save for an unexpected drought. You never know when my wells are gonna start dryin' up, feel me? So I milk these hoes for as long as I can. Bottom line, a nigga like me—who ain't tryna work—ain't beat to be broke. And a hunnid grand these days ain't shit, feel me?

I grab the rest of my shit and head toward the door. "Oh, nooooo, nigga. You ain't taking that up outta here."

I turn to face her. "Are you serious?" I ask as if I really give a fuck. I love lettin' these dizzy-ass broads think I'm some kinda charity case.

"Yeah, motherfucker, I'm dead-ass. Since you on some other shit, let that bitch you getting ready to fuck buy you one. Since she's all eager to wet your dick, let her come outta her pockets. 'Cause that right there"—she points at the Xbox—"ain't leaving up outta here. You not gonna fucking try 'n play me."

I almost wanna laugh at her ho-ass for soundin' so damn stupid. This dumb bitch let me fuck her e'ery which way, and had no problem gulpin' down this dick last night—or the other night, or the times before that—but now she wanna talk 'bout somebody tryna play her. Fuck outta here.

"Yo, check this shit out. I don't havta try 'n play your dumb ass. You did that all by ya'self, boo. E'ery time you let me run my dick up in ya dry-ass pussy and nut in ya raggedy-ass face, you played ya'self. So you can have it, baby. It ain't that serious, yo. There's plenty more where that came."

"Fuck you, motherfucker!"

I laugh, openin' the front door. "I already did."

"Just get the fuck out!" she snaps, chargin' toward the door. Before she can come at me, I slam it in her face. I hop in my car, making my way over to Maleeka's to get this dick slobbered and wet and spit all over—the way a greedy-cum guzzlin' bitch is supposed to suck a dick.

15

Instead of takin' that long-ass drive back down to my spot, I decide to crash—like I do most times—at Pops'. Hell, after fuckin' wit' Shavron's Indian-givin' ass on Saturday, then Maleeka's cum-thirsty ass yesterday—even if I wanted to, I wouldna been able to make it to my crib. I was too damn drained and exhausted from bustin' four rounds of nut down in her throat throughout the day. And then I finally gave in and fucked her deep in that fat ass of hers, even though I told her from the dip that it was gonna be a drive-by. But she got on her whinin'-ass bullshit, so I stayed the night and gutted her out. When it was time for a muhfucka to bounce, she hit me up wit' a quick five hunnid wit'out blinkin' an eye. Man, listen, I really don't understand these hoes.

Then as soon as I got ready to lay it down, my cell kept goin' off. First, it was Tamera's nutbush ass, callin' and textin' me. That bitch is relentless. On some real shit, I'm startin' to think she's blazin' more than trees. She's too damn erratic. I swear I wanna bend her over and split her asshole wide the fuck open wit' this dick for bein' such a shitty-ass ho.

Then Candace called pressin' me 'bout comin' through 'cause she hasn't seen me in a minute. She's one of them church-goin'-type hoes doin' Bible study on Thursdays, praisin' 'n singin' in the choir 'n shit on Sundays, then gulpin' down dick the rest of the week. Her heathen-ass got the nerve to have a BlackPlanet page talkin' 'bout she's a good, God-fearin' Christian woman in search of a good man. But turns 'round and sends me a buncha flicks wit' her ass 'n titties out. What a fuckin' hypocrite! On some real shit, I've fucked her three times. And let me tell you… whoever said, "If you wanna find a real freak, go to church," ain't never lied 'cause this freak-nasty, scripture-spewin' strumpet likes it all. Damn, talkin' 'bout her takes me back to the first time I was at her spot ready to put this dick to her.

"I'm looking for some hot piss play, baby," she'd told me, catchin' a nigga off guard.

"What the fuck you just say?" I'd asked disgusted. "Piss play?"

"Yeah, baby, piss play," she'd repeated, gettin' up off of the bed and walkin' toward me. She wrapped her arms 'round my waist, looked up at me, starin' into my eyes. "Every now and then I like to be pissed on; it's no biggie."

It's no biggie? "Yo, what in the hell you get outta a muhfucka pissin' on you?"

"There's something sexy about watching a man holding his dick in his hands, especially when it's long and thick, while he's unleashing a golden stream of hot piss. It really turns me on."

I'd frowned, steppin' outta her embrace, then movin' to the other side of the room. On some real shit, a muhfucka was thinkin' 'bout gettin' the fuck up outta there. But a nigga still wanted his dick wet. "Yo, I don't know what kinda shit you into, but that's outta my league, baby."

"At least give it a try before you knock it. You never know, you might like it."

Yo, this tramp has got to be kiddin' me, I'd thought to myself, starin' at this broad like she was two screws from crazy. "Oh, ohhhkaaaay," I'd said, lookin' at her ass sideways.

She'd walked back over to me, wrapped her arms 'round my

waist again and looked up at me. "Piss on me, daddy. Pleeeeease. Let me feel me your strong, steamy flow of hot, golden urine, then take my pussy and fuck it like you own it."

I'd scratched the side of my head. "Okay, so let me get this right. What you sayin' is, you want me to piss on you, then turn 'round and fuck you wit' my piss runnin' down ya body?"

She'd nodded, lickin' her lips. "Oh, yes. Just the thought of it is gettin' me hot. To be perfectly honest with you, I've actually been dying to have a man with a big dick to hose me down, then squat over me and shit on my stomach, while he's playing in my pussy, with his ass facing toward me. Then we could fuck in the delicious mess."

Delicious? I'd frowned. Ain't a muthafuckin' thing delicious 'bout a muhfucka takin' a dump on someone. *What a nasty bitch!* I'd thought. "Yo, you an extra-special type of freak, for real—for real. And on some real shit, I ain't sign up for this kinda kink."

"I thought you said you were open-minded. And like it nasty."

"I am. And I do like it nasty. But not *that* damn nasty. I'm open to a lotta thangs, baby, but smellin' a buncha shit and piss while I'm tryna fuck ain't one of 'em."

"Okay, then just piss all over my titties, then bend me over and fuck me from behind."

Did I end up bouncin' on her nasty ass? Nope. Long story short, a muhfucka ended up fuckin' her, anyway. I followed her into the master bathroom, waited for her to get into the glass-encased shower, then stepped in after her wearin' nuthin' but my boxers. As she dropped down to her knees, I pulled out my dick, then hosed her down wit' my hot piss—like she wanted it, hittin' her nasty ass in the face, mouth, and all over her chest while she played in her pussy. Then she turned 'round, grabbed the back of her ankles, and waited for me to run this dick up in her. I wrapped up, then Rambo-fucked her freaky ass. And the crazy shit is, after I finished fuckin' her, I realized I liked pissin' on her dumb ass.

Anyway, between the textin' and the callin' and the beggin' and whinin' 'bout dumb shit, sometimes a muhfucka gotta shut his phone off 'n shit just to get a moment of peace. And that's exactly what the fuck I did before I finally went to sleep 'round three A.M.

When I finally opened my eyes, 'round ten this mornin', I got up to see what was good wit' Pops but he had already bounced— probably over to Moms' to get his fuck on. I checked my cell and saw I had two texts and one message—all from Akina, spazzin' the fuck out 'cause I didn't come through to feed her this dick like I said I was. And I didn't call. Oh well. She'll get over it. Anyway, since I had the spot to myself, I fixed myself breakfast, then went to the gym. And, as soon as I got back, I took a nice, long, hot shower, then dozed off.

Three hours later, the ringin' of my cell wakes me up. I stretch and yawn, glancin' over at the clock: 4:13 P.M. *Damn, I was knocked the fuck out.* "Yo, what's good, ma?"

"You and that humongous dick of yours," Cherry says in a low, sexy voice. The sound of her voice, the way it purrs through the phone, makes my dick brick instantly. I close my eyes, rememberin' how good my dick felt inside that big, wet, gushy pussy, as well as in her deep asshole.

"Oh, word? I can't tell. It took ya sexy ass long 'nough to hit a nigga back. I called you almost two weeks ago."

"With this housing market the way it is, it's been a bit hectic here. But, you know I'll make it up to you."

"Yeah, baby, you always do."

"This fat pussy misses you like crazy."

And I miss them fat cheeks. This ho's paper is long as hell. She owns her own real estate company and the homes she sells are two million and up. "Damn, baby. And this heavy dick misses you, too, boo," I tell her. "I've been dreamin' 'bout suckin' on that sweet, juicy clit of yours, and stickin' this tongue deep in ya hot slit. Nobody rides this dick like you, baby."

"Mmmm," she moans into the phone. "You keep talking like that and you're gonna have me catching the next flight out of L.A. to Jersey. You got me wanting to play in my pussy."

I laugh, slippin' my hand down in my boxers. "I done beat you to it, baby. I'm already strokin' my shit, thinkin' 'bout you ridin' down on this dick. And it's loaded wit' thick, gooey cream—just for you."

See, e'ery now and then, you gotta stroke a ho's ego. Let her know what you think she wants to know. That you can't stop thinkin' 'bout her, that you miss her, that she has the best pussy you've had and you can't stop dreamin' 'bout it. Let her think she got ya ass hooked on that cock clamper of hers.

"When you coming to see me?"

I smile. "When *you* wanna see me?"

"Now," she says.

I laugh. "Damn, baby, you horny like that?"

"You have no idea. I need to be fucked, deep and hard by a long, thick black dick."

"That's what it is. I'd be there to feed you this dick, on the next muthafuckin' thing smokin', if I had the ends. But shit's real hectic, feel me? A muhfucka's still not workin'." I grin.

"Alex, baby, you know you don't have to ever worry about money. All you gotta do is say the word and I'ma have a ticket waiting for you, along with spending money. You know how we do. I wish you'd pack all your things and move out here. You know I know a lot of people here, and have plenty of connections. I know I can get you hired somewhere. As a matter of fact, an ex of mine owns a large construction company out here. I could put in a good word for you."

I frown. *Construction?* Is this ho serious? What the fuck a muhfucka like me look like doin' some muthafuckin' manual labor? The only work I'ma do that requires me to sweat is *fuck*. All that extra shit she talkin' is out.

"Listen, baby," I say. "I 'preciate you tryna look out. But what I look like workin' for another cat who used to run his dick up in you?"

She laughs. "Baby, that man hasn't had a taste of this in over fifteen years."

"Still a muhfucka like me ain't diggin' workin' for ya ex, or anyone's ex, for that matter. But I definitely 'preciate you havin' my back, that's wassup. Anyway, wit' my moms in a wheelchair 'n shit, I can't just up and bounce on her like that, smell me? She's not in the best of health, but I'm not 'bout to put her in no funky-ass nursin' home. She's always been there for me, and I gotta always be here for her, feel me?"

"I understand. But, you need a break, baby. You need some of Cherry's good pussy and TLC. I'm sure you can sneak away for a week or two. Let Cherry rub you down, lick up them big balls for you, suck down that dick, and serve you up a platter of this hot ass and juicy pussy—the way you like it, rough and nasty."

This bitch knows damn well she ain't suckin' down no dick, but I let her live in her fantasy. I squeeze my dick. Jerk it in long, deep strokes. I decide to gas her head up even more. "You ain't never lied, pretty baby. I need to get away in the worst way. I'm sick of bein' deprived. These lame chicks out here ain't ridin' this dick right, and they damn sure don't know howta treat a muhfucka. You got 'em all beat, baby—hands down."

I can see her smilin' through the phone. I can't front, though. The bitch is *right*—nice, thick body; pretty face; hot, fat pussy; deep ass. She's the total package. And, at thirty-five, she's makin' power moves and really doin' big things. The only problem is she got a forehead bigger than Vivica Fox's, and the bitch is baldin'. All she rocks are weaves and wigs. And a muhfucka like me ain't wit' all that extra shit. I mean, it's cool if you rockin' it from time to time, but then you rockin' ya own shit, feel me? You know, let ya muthafuckin' scalp air out. But a ho who lives and breathes a buncha fake-ass hair, all the time…hmmph, you only good for fuckin' 'cause I'd never wanna wife ya bald-headed ass. I don't give a fuck how fine you are. You better take ya ass down to the muthafuckin' Hair Club and get that shit grafted, or invest in a case of Rogaine.

"Good, that's what I wanna hear. I don't need to be trying to compete for any of your attention."

"Nah, baby, it's all you. There's no competition. When I'm wit' you, you have my undivided attention." *My focus is right on ya muthafuckin' bank book.* "I've been missin' you, Boo."

"You gotta sista over here blushing," she says. "I've been missing you, too. Baby, you just don't know. My whole body aches for you. I haven't been fucked right since the last time you were here."

"Me either, baby. I'm so ready to bust this nut," I tell her, pumpin' my dick in and outta my hand, fast and furious. "I wanna put this big dick all up in you bad, baby." I scoop some Vaseline into my hand, then smear it all over the head and shaft of my dick. I feel like nuttin' so I decide to speed jerk a hot one out.

She moans. "You're makin' my pussy wet talkin' like that."

"Yeah, baby, just how I like it. You got that big, wet pussy… mmmm."

"Why you teasing me? Do you know how horny I am?"

"Yeah, baby, I know…ah, shit…" I pinch my left nipple. "Aah, fuck, baby…"

She laughs. "OhmyGod, how you gonna jerk off and not let me get off, too?"

"Sorry, babe. I couldn't help myself. You know anytime I hear your voice, I brick up. You make me horny as hell. Oh, shit…I'm gettin' ready to spit this nut."

She moans again. "Oooh, I wish I was there, or you were here, so I could catch that hot, gooey cum in my mouth."

"Damn, baby…you gonna let me smear this nut on ya tongue?"

"Mmm-hmm…"

The head of my dick swells as my nut rises. "Open ya mouth, baby…catch daddy's nut…you ready?"

"Yesssssssssss, baaaaaby, yesssssssss…"

"Here it comes…mmmph…aaah, shit…I cummin'…Aaaah, aaaah…" I cup my heavy balls, pull 'em, then bust my nut. It spurts out, shoots up in the air, then lands all over my stomach and chest. I keep strokin' it, milkin' the rest of this nut outta it. "Aaah, fuck…mmmph …" I rub my nut into my skin, wishin' I woulda had someone here to feed it to instead of wastin' it all on me. I smell my fingers, gettin' up from the sofa to wash my hands in the bathroom. While at the sink, I stare at myself in the mirror, flexin' my chest and stomach muscles. *I gotta hit the gym later today*, I think, dryin' my hands. I shut off the water, then go into the kitchen, pullin' out a stool and takin' a seat at the counter. I shuffle through the stack of mail. Mostly junk, but a few bills. I make a note to pay my cable and water bills, then toss the shit back on the counter.

"I'm glad you got yours. Now when are you coming here so I can get mine? And how long can you stay? And, please don't tell me only for the weekend. I want you here for at least a week, two if possible. And you know I *always* make it worth your while."

Although I ain't really beat to be out there more than two days, three at the most, I know she's good for at least five or more gees, and a new wardrobe. And I'm guaranteed nonstop fuckin' and suckin'. I think and consider my options, knowin' there ain't any. None of the other broads I'm smashin' at the moment are passin' a muhfucka any major paper, so…fuck them peanuts they shellin' out; I'ma let it do what it do. Of course there's no guilt for nuthin' I do, but I decide to let her think there is. "You know this shit fucks me up, right?"

"What, big daddy?"

"Havin' to lean on you for plane tickets 'n shit like that. I wanna be able to handle wit'out you comin' outta ya wallet all the time, feel me? A muhfucka wants to be able to show you my 'preciation."

"Oh, please. I told you don't ever sweat stuff like that. I make enough money for the both of us, and I don't mind sharing any of it with you. Life is too short. I want what I want when I want it. And I don't care what the cost. And right, now, I want your fine, sexy, chocolatey-self and that long, black horse dick of yours here in my bed, between my legs, fucking this pussy inside out. I'm booking you a flight. It'll be an open ticket. You want to show me your appreciation, then be on that flight and come here and fuck me *down*."

I grin. "Book the flight, baby."

16

S o, here it is almost six o'clock in the evening, the house is quiet as hell and I'm up in my room, chillin'—kicked back in my boxers, blazin' a blunt and burnin' incense 'round the room—watchin' the flick *The Kinsley Report* when there's a knock on the door. Thinkin' it's Pops, I put out the blunt and get up to open the door. Although Pops has never cared 'bout me blazin' in the house, outta respect I don't do the shit 'round 'im. I swing the door open, and almost pass the fuck out. To my surprise—and muthafuckin' dismay—Sherria is standin' on the other side of the door, scowlin'.

Fuck! First of all, how the hell she know where to find me? And, second, how the hell she get in? I'm the only one up in this piece, so I know Pops couldna let her in. *Or did he?* Nah, dude wouldna let her come upstairs like that. I start buggin' and thinkin' this crazy-ass trick done broke in. That's the last thing I fuckin' need, word up. "What the fuck?"

"Oh, what, you thought it was one of ya other bitches? Well, surprise, surprise, nigga. It ain't."

"Yo, how the fuck you know where to find me?"

"Don't worry 'bout that," she snaps, foldin' her arms 'cross her juicy double-D's. Images of my dick in between 'em pop in my head, and I feel my dick startin' to awaken. I quickly shake the thought before I forget the reason I'm not fuckin' wit' her ass anymore. She's one of those controllin', miserable bitches who got wrapped up wit' a few muhfuckas that cheated on her, lied to her, and pushed her biscuit in one time too many in her life. So she's angry wit' e'ery livin', breathin' muhfucka on earth. "I told you I knew where you stayed. A bitch like me did her homework. I asked around and followed you. Now are you gonna let me in, or what?"

I clench my jaw, keepin' my body between her and the door. "I wanna know how you got in here, first." *Please tell me this nutty, stalkin'-ass bitch didn' break in.*

She rolls her eyes, suckin' her teeth. "No, I didn't break in," she says, readin' my mind. "I'm not that fuckin' crazy." I give her an "oh really" look. She glares at me. "Your father was on his way out and let me in. Nice-lookin' man, too, I might add. I hope he isn't as fucked up as you are."

I frown. Why the fuck would he do some dumb shit like that? *Man, Pops is really slippin',* I think, eyein' her. I make a mental note to check him on it. I feel myself gettin' agitated. "Yo, what the fuck you want?"

"First of all, don't come at me like that..."

"Yo, check this shit out. I'll come at you however I want when you standin' up in my muthafuckin' grill uninvited, unexpected, and unwanted. So, again, what the *fuck* do you want?"

She glares at me. Nostrils flare. "You've been fucking avoiding my calls for the last two months, and I wanna fucking know why. I opened myself up to you, let you into my heart and this is how you fuckin' treat me."

I sigh, starin' at her. I already know there's no fuckin' way I'ma let her up in this bedroom. I'll never get her outta here unless I fuck her to death, and that ain't 'bout to happen. Pops done let this nutcase in. Now I gotta be the one to try 'n figure out how I'ma get her ass the fuck up outta here wit'out her bustin' up shit, or tryna claw me up. Some bitches can't handle rejection, and she's definitely one of 'em. The last thing I need is to be hemmed up on some domestic violence-type shit, feel me?

Fuck what ya heard. You can pop all the shit you want. But don't get up in my space, talkin' wit' ya hands. And do *not* put ya muthafuckin' hands on me. And this Looney Tune has already proven the last time I was wit' her that she likes to get it in when shit ain't goin' her way—like when she threw an ashtray at my head for tellin' her not to fuckin' question me 'bout where I've been.

"Hol' up, let me get some clothes on," I tell her, shuttin' the door in her face, then lockin' it. She bangs on it.

"I'm not fucking goin' anywhere, so you might as well open up this door, *Alley Cat*. Otherwise, I'ma keep fucking banging until you do. I wanna talk to you."

I need a fuckin' blunt. I snatch up the half-smoked blunt in the ashtray, and spark up. I yell at her through the door. "I said I'll be out in a minute. So stop bangin' on my muthafuckin' door."

"Well, hurry up."

I finish gettin' my smoke on. Then when I'm done, I open the door—ten minutes later—and this pigeon is still standin' in the same spot wit' her arms folded. I lock the door, closin' it behind me. "Aiight, let's talk," I say to her, brushin' past her goin' toward the stairs. She follows behind me. Now, had I been thinkin', I woulda had her go down the stairs—first, just in case she had a weapon and tried to stab or shoot me in the back, feel me? The bitch is one screw from crazy so anything is possible wit' her. But I'm so pressed to get this ho outta the house in case she goes off and starts bustin' up shit that I jump dead in front of her and race down the stairs.

I open the front door. "Let's sit outside and talk."

"Why can't we talk in here?" she questions, stoppin' in the middle of the livin' room and puttin' her hand up on her hip.

'Cause I wanna talk to ya unstable ass outside on the muthafuckin'

porch in front of witnesses, that's why. "'Cause I need some fresh air," I tell her, double-checkin' my front pocket to make sure I have my cell on me. I stand wit' the door open, waitin' for her ass to walk out. I'm relieved when she does.

I step down from offa the porch, then take a seat. She decides to stand in front of me wit' her arms folded tight 'round her chest, like she's scared to let sumthin' go.

"Okay, so talk," I say, ice-grillin' her.

"I wanna know why you stopped calling and returning my calls?"

Umm, you dizzy-ass ding bat that should be obvious: 'Cause ya ass is muthafuckin' craaaaazy! I sigh. "It wasn't workin' out."

"Oh really, since when?"

What the fuck?! *Uh, duh, since I stopped callin' ya dumb, lazy, dick-suckin' ass.* "Look, like I said, it wasn't workin' out."

"Humph. Mighty funny it was workin' out when I was lettin' you ride around in my car and come in and outta my apartment, but the minute I check you on something, it's not 'working out.'"

"No, the minute you tried to get at me on some rah-rah type shit, throwin' ashtrays 'n shit. That's when it was no longer workin'. I ain't wit' all that extra ghetto bullshit."

"So, you just stop fucking with me, instead of talking it out."

I tilt my head. Stare at this fuckin' broad long and hard. "Are you serious? Talk what out? A muhfucka who's tryna build wit' ya ass is talkin' it out, not a nigga who is straight smashin' you."

I feel my cell vibratin' and pull it outta my pocket. Lahney texts me: Cum through and ram that big, black cock up in me.

"I let you into my heart and this is how you fucking treat me..."

I text back: LOL, you don't really want it. This dick'll have ya ass cryin' again.

She sucks her teeth. "I can't believe you'd pull out your fucking phone and start texting while I'm standing here trying to talk to you. How fucked up is that?"

Lahney texts: Whateva, punk! U cumming to beat this pussy up or what.

I shrug. "You tell me. You the one actin' like a desperate house-wife, huntin' a nigga down 'n shit."

She tsks me. "Desperate? Nigga, puhleeeze. I'm coming to you like a grown woman, trying to resolve whatever has gone wrong between us."

I text Lahney back: Yeah, I got ya punk, aiight. 11.5-inches worth. What time u want it?

I look at Sherria. "Yo, check this out. There's nuthin' to resolve. How many times I gotta tell you, there was no *us*. We was *fuckin'*, that's it. You wasn't my girl. I wasn't ya man. And I never promised you a future wit' a rose garden. It was straight dickin' you down. If you allowed ya'self to catch feelin's, then that shit's on you. So don't come at me wit' all the extras. If you wanna come at me like a woman, then take it for what it was, a fuck. And…step."

Lahney texts: NOW!

"I know all that. But still, I thought you were different."

I look out into the street, let what she's said linger in the air, while she's standin' in front of me lookin' all pathetic 'n shit. *I thought you were different.* I almost wanna laugh at her ass. Hell yeah, I'm muthafuckin' different! Let's see. I ain't ever spit on her, smack her up, or use her face and body as an ashtray, puttin' cigarettes 'n shit out on her. I ain't ever fuck her sister—not that I would 'cause the bitch looks handicapped to me. I know, I know, you think a muhfucka like me will fuck anything. Well, news-flash: A nigga got standards. I might fuck a buncha hoes, but a bitch who looks like she belongs in the Special Olympics ain't my flava, feel me?

So what if I took her whip and dipped off to get my dick piped out? The first time I did the shit and didn't come back 'til two hours later, she shoulda made it her business to not give me her keys again. And that goes for the three other times. But she didn't. And so what if I ran her wallet? She bought what she wanted to buy. I never pressed her for shit. She tried to buy my attention and she wanted to have this dick at whatever costs. No chick wit' an ounce of common sense is gonna keep lettin' a muhfucka keep takin' from her. But she did, so it is what it is.

I text back: Give me an hour. Then bring my attention back to Sherria. I can tell she's strugglin' to keep herself from blowin' her top. And, on some real shit, I'm glad as hell that I got her ass outside in broad daylight wit' neighbors 'n shit 'round to be witness to anything she might try 'n do. Don't get shit twisted. I'm not scared of *her*, but I am scared of what the fuck I'ma do if she does try to set it off.

Lahney texts: See u then. Oh, and bring da Magnums. I'm all out.

This trick-ass, I think, placin' my phone back in my pocket. *I'm not fuckin' wit' her today.*

I look her dead in her eyes, then finally say, "Well, I'm not."

She looks hurt, shiftin' from one foot to the other. "I hope you know you're real fucked up."

I stand up. Brush the back of my sweats off. "Okay, so now that you know that, there's no need to keep wastin' my time or yours." I reach into my pants pocket, pull out my keys, remove her house-key from 'round my key ring, then hand it to her. She stares at my hand before snatchin' it from my hand. I frown. "Is there sumthin' else?"

She glares at me. Starts breathin' heavy, fightin' back what looks to be tears in her eyes. Or a rageful fit. "Yeah, motherfucker," she snarls through clenched teeth, "You ain't shit, you arrogant bastard!"

Before I can catch myself, I snap, "Bitch, you snore, and you leave your muthafuckin' raggedy-ass panties in the middle of the fuckin' floor, but you tryna come at my neck. Fuck outta here."

"Fuck you! I hate your ass!"

I shrug, walkin' back inside the house. "You don't hate me, baby. You hate yourself," I say, shuttin' the door behind me, leavin' her standin' there lookin' wounded and lost.

Two hours later, I get back from smashin' Lahney out. Yeah, I know I said I wasn't fuckin' wit' her today, but a hard-ass dick will change a muhfucka's mind in a heartbeat. So I went over and served her up some dick, then dipped. Fuck all that layin' 'round, cuddlin' up shit wit' her ass. She wasn't hittin' a nigga wit' no paper, so there was definitely no need for any extended stays. Feel me? But, as I was leavin', she caught me off guard when she slid me a key to her spot.

"What's this for?" I asked her as she handed them to me.

"It's for here. I want you to be able to come through anytime you want."

"Oh, word? Why?"

"Because I'm hoping one day I walk through the door and you'll be standing here in the middle of the living room butt naked, holding your hard dick in your hand waiting for me."

I grinned, unzippin' my jeans and slippin' my hand down in my underwear. "Is that so?"—I pull out my dick and stroke it—"Well, how 'bout we get started now." Needless to say, she dropped down low and let it do what it do, milkin' my dick wit' her mouth, then finally gulpin' down a rich, creamy nut.

Anyway, I'm up in my room loungin' in a pair of black boxer briefs and a black wife beater, gettin' ready to watch *Alphabet Killer* when my cell rings. I think to ignore the shit, but decide to grab it off the nightstand and check to see who's tryna get at me.

"Oh, shit!" I snap, peepin' the caller ID, "I ain't heard from this cat in a minute." It's my boy, Red. Yo, this nigga right here's been my muthafuckin' dude since eighth grade, word up. Dude is one of the coolest cats I know. And the nigga bags almost as much pussy as me. That's 'cause he's one of them light, pretty-boy muhfuckas wit' all that wavy hair them bitches be fallin' over. And the nigga be pimpin' the shit outta 'em. He got bitches takin' numbers, and standin' in line, to get at his dick. Well, he used to. I'm not sure how the nigga's movin' now that he's all hugged up wit' his shorty.

Growin' up we'd blaze trees, and I'd watch him get bent offa forties 'n shit while we puffed L's. We'd call up a few hot-in-the-ass hoes and sneak 'em down into his basement, then fuck 'em all night. He'd be diggin' one bitch's back out on the plaid sofa, and I'd be on the other side of the room dickin' down the other on the twin mattress he'd pull out and put down on the floor. Then we'd switch hoes and start rockin' 'em all over again. Or we'd bang the same bitch after she sucked both our dicks. And the wild shit is, we'd go up in them hoes straight raw. Man, listen… we was like fourteen and was some wild, reckless, horny-ass muhfuckas back then. But, after we both got burned and crabbed out by this dirty bitch, LaTonya, we started strappin' up. And bein' more selective. That ho had the whole block on fire. Good pussy or not, that syphilis and crab scare was all we needed to fuck more responsibly, feel me? Fuck what ya heard. A drippin', itchy-ass dick ain't a good look!

"Yo, what's good wit' ya punk ass?"

"This dick in ya mom's throat, nigga," he says, laughin'. "What's poppin' wit' you?"

"My nut in ya aunt's eye, muhfucka," I joke back.

"Yo," he says, laughin'. "You stupid-as-hell nigga, word up. So, what's good? How you?"

"Chillin', chillin'. You know how I do. What's good wit' you? You still kickin' it wit' that honey down in Maryland?"

"Yeah, man. We still doin' the damn thang. Ole girl done got a nigga hangin' up his pimp shoes 'n shit."

"Get the fuck outta here. She got you on lock like that?"

"Word is bond. I tossed out my booty-call book and the bat phone for this one."

I almost drop my cell. I can't believe what the fuck I'm hearin'. Like me, this nigga has never been a one pussy-type of nigga. "Get the fuck outta here! Say word."

"On e'erything I love," he tells me.

"Awwww, damn," I say, pausin'. I'm still tryna absorb what he's said. "Nigga, you serious?"

"You heard me. I had my other phone line disconnected, shut down my BlackPlanet and Myspace pages, and closed all my porn site accounts."

"Damn, dude. Sounds like she put that cock clamper down on ya."

He laughs. "Yeah, I can't front. My baby shut shit down, son. Gotta nigga thinkin' 'bout the future 'n shit, something I never did before. Real talk, it's a wrap, son. A nigga's done fuckin' wit' all that pussy chasin'."

"Yo, son, you talkin' 'bout givin' up a smorgasbord of hot pussy at ya disposal. You sure you wanna walk away from it?"

"Yo, most def. On some real shit, man. I'd be thrashin' that ass and bustin' shit down and after I finished nuttin', I'd still want something more."

I laugh. "Like what, nigga, more pussy?"

"Nah, my dude," he says, pausin'. "Well, at first, yeah. I thought that's what it was. But, once a muhfucka took a hard look at himself and got honest, I realized it wasn't the pussy I wanted more of. It was more of someone; maybe not that particular someone. But definitely someone I could vibe with, and one day build with, feel me?"

Keepin' shit real, I couldn't relate to shit he was sayin'. Not that I didn't want to, I just wasn't able to. Wantin' sumthin' other than pussy, head and a ho's paper wasn't ever anything I gave thought to. Nor has it ever been sumthin' that consumed me. Fuckin' a broad, yeah; buildin' wit' her ass, nope!

I say, "I hear you. But, yo, man…I'm shocked as hell hearin' this shit come from outta ya mouth, for real, yo."

He chuckles. "Man, listen…I'm shocked my damn self. On some real shit, I never thought I'd ever feel this way 'bout a chick. But, Coletta's different. She holds a nigga down. She's loyal, and the best part is, I *know* she loves a nigga."

The way he talks, he sounds happy as hell. And on some real shit, I find myself smilin'—happy for my nigga, too. "That's wassup," I tell him. "I'm happy for you, man."

"'Preciate that, playa. Don't worry, your turns comin', dawg."

"Not if I can help it," I tell 'im. "I like my freedom too much."

"Yeah, aiight, muhfucka. Talk that shit now. You just haven't run up on the right one, yet."

"Yeah, yeah, yeah. Whatever, nigga. So what's next?" I ask, changin' the subject.

"Actually, that's the reason I was callin' you. I'ma ask my girl to marry me on Christmas Eve. And I want you as my best man when we tie the knot."

My mouth drops open. "Say word, nigga!"

"Word on e'erything I love."

"Damm," I say. "You go ghost 'n shit for months, then pop up outta nowhere full of surprises."

He laughs. "Whatever, muhfucka. You wit' me on this or what?"

"No doubt, dawg. I got you."

"That's what it is. I knew I could count on you."

"No doubt. You know how we do."

"Mos def. Listen, I gotta dip. I'ma hit you up in a couple of weeks."

"Yeah, yeah, yeah," I say jokin'ly. "Muhfucka, the last time you said that shit, I ain't hear from ya pussy-whipped ass for almost six months."

"Don't be jealous, baby," he says, laughin'. "You know you still my number one nigga. But I rather be pussy whipped than havta be stuck fuckin' with ya ugly, black ass."

"Fuck outta here wit' that bullshit," I say, crackin' up. "Let me borrow ya grandmother for a few days, then let's see how ugly and black she thinks this dick is."

"Yeah, muhfucka, right after you let me borrow yours." We laugh and bullshit a few more minutes, then hang up. I lay back 'cross my bed, dazin' up at the ceilin' wonderin' how the hell Red's girl got him to give up all his hoes. I mean, she's bad as hell… but, damn. She got that nigga talkin' 'bout marriage 'n shit. *She must got some good-ass pussy*, I think, shakin' my head, smilin'. *Or her muthafuckin' head game must be off the damn chain.* I think about it a few more minutes, wonderin' if a cat like me had it in him to be on some exclusive shit wit' a chick. *Nah, fuck that! Good pussy or not. A muhfucka like me ain't goin' out like that. I'ma always be long strokin' more than one ho.* I roll over onto my side, and before I know it, I'm knocked the fuck out.

17

Yo, I'm watchin' this flick *Cover*, wit' Vivica Fox and that cat Leon. For a straight-to-DVD joint it isn't bad, but... man, listen. This muhfucka is on some real extra shit, fuckin' another muhfucka and he's married. What kinda bullshit is that? I don't knock no one for doin' what they do, and bein' who they are, real talk. But a muhfucka suckin' and fuckin' another nigga—when you got a chick in ya life, is some straight bullshit, for real, yo. That shit is disrespectful, dangerous and grounds for a bullet straight to ya muthafuckin' dome for frontin' on her, and puttin' her life at risk, feel me? Shit like this gets a muhfucka hot, for real, yo.

Punk-ass nigga, I think, shakin' my head. I can't even finish watchin' this shit. I light a blunt, and turn it off, then hit the remote to my stereo, and turn on my computer. Plies' "Excuse My Hands" blares through the speakers as I wait for my PC to boot up. I click on Internet Explorer to surf the web, then hit up my BlackPlanet, Facebook and Myspace pages. When I'm done goin' through all the bullshit notes, I decide to check the emails on my AOL account. As soon as I log on, the IM's start poppin' up. I shake my head. These some real hungry-ass hoes tonight, I think, iggin' most of 'em. But the one who gets my attention tonight is the older chick from BlackPlanet. We've been emailin' back and forth a few times, but this is the first time she actually IM's me. I wanna fuck the shit outta her, word up.

DrSweetPussy: Hello

DaddyLongStroke: What's poppin', pretty baby?

DrSweetPussy: *blushing*

DaddyLongStroke: Come on, baby. Don't get shy on a nigga

DrSweetPussy: Not shy; just embarrassed

DaddyLongStroke: Embarrassed? Why?

DrSweetPussy: That I'm doing this

DaddyLongStroke: Doin' what?

DrSweetPussy: This. Talking to you. Thinking about cheating on my husband

DaddyLongstroke: Well, isn't that what u've been lookin' for? A little side action in ya life?

DrSweetPussy: Yeah

DaddyLongStroke: Well, don't get scared now, baby. I ain't gonna hurt ya.

DrSweetPussy: LOL. I'm not scared; just confused

I take two pulls from the blunt. Hold the shit in my lungs, then slowly blow it out. Confused? Give me a fuckin' break! Obviously, the bitch ain't gettin' what she needs at home 'cause if she was, she wouldn't be all up on BlackPlanet 'n shit prowlin' for dick. And she damn sure wouldn't be emailin' and IM-in' muhfuckas. Her ass ain't gettin' dicked right, and she wants a muhfucka wit' a strong back and long dick to beat that shit up for her. And I'm just the man for the job. So what the fuck she confused about?

DaddyLongStroke: What u confused about?

DrSweetPussy: Maybe confused is the wrong word. More anxious than confused

DaddyLongStroke: About?

DrSweetPussy: Meeting u

DaddyLongStroke: Meetin' me should be the least of your worries, I think. Whether or not you can handle a Mandigo stud should be. What kinda dr are u?

DrSweetPussy: A psychologist

DaddyLongStroke: Aaah shit. An educated freak

DrSweetPussy: LOL

DaddyLongStroke: I've slayed a lotta professional chicks, but a psychologist is gonna be my first

DrSweetPussy: *smiling* hopefully, it'll be a good experience for the both of us

DaddyLongStroke: I'm sure it will be. Tell daddy some of ya fantasies, baby

DrSweetPussy: Umm, well, I fantasize about having sex in public, like on a beach with everyone watching. Other times I fantasize about speeding down the turnpike being completely naked and masturbating in my convertible.

DaddyLongStroke: Damn, baby. Sounds hot! What else?

DrSweetPussy: Being in the middle of a circle with a group of men jerking off while I'm playing in my vagina and watching them all stroke their penises over me. Then when they are ready to ejaculate, they cum all over me.

Vagina? Penises? Ejaculate? What the fuck?!? I take two more pulls. Allow the weed smoke to fill my lungs. This bitch gonna haveta come better than this. A nigga like me ain't beat for all that proper shit. She's gonna haveta bring it wit' lil' more raunch and wit' a lil' more filth than this bullshit, if she wanna get this dick hard. I blow out smoke and continue typin'.

DaddyLongStroke: Dig, what's up wit' all the proper talk? Loosen up, baby. Give it to me raw! Give it to me nasty, baby! Tell me how u wanna get that pussy rocked. How u wanna have a bunch of muhfuckas nut all over u. I need it uncut, ma, feel me?

DrSweetPussy: lol, I think I do. I'm just not accustomed to talking like that

DaddyLongStroke: Well, do u at least think it?

DrSweetPussy: Sometimes

DaddyLongStroke: Then let ya'self go. U can be free wit' me, baby. Unleash the freak in u

DrSweetPussy: Letting go is kinda new to me. I've been with the same man for over twenty years

DaddyLongStroke: Sorry to hear that

DrSweetPussy: lol, don't be. It hasn't been that bad

DaddyLongStroke: Okay, if you say so. Yo, dig, baby. I ain't beat for all this IM shit. U need to hit me up on the phone so we can talk. 973-555-0011. I wanna hear that sexy voice of yours.

DrSweetpussy: And who should I ask for?

DaddyLongStroke: Daddy Long Stroke. Thought u knew.

I close out the IM screen before she can respond back and shut off my laptop, pickin' up my cell and callin' Akina. She answers on the fourth ring, soundin' all outta breath 'n shit. "Hey, stranger."

"What's poppin', baby? Why you all outta breath?"

"I was working out," she says, soundin' like she has an attitude.

"Oh, word. For a minute I thought you was somewhere gettin' ya fuck on."

She sucks her teeth. "Yeah, right. The only fucking going on is with these fingers 'cause you too busy avoiding a bitch for anything else to happen."

I laugh. "Oh, what, you upset?"

"Nigga, puhleeze, you wish. I'm horny as hell, and want some dick."

I laugh. Although she's always sayin' she's gettin' it in wit' other muhfuckas, if she is, I know they ain't puttin' in no real work. 'Cause if they were she wouldn't be pressed 'bout me standin' her ass up. But, no matter who else she's fuckin', Akina's the type of dick-hungry chick that'll keep my dick stuck up in her if I'd let her. "Oh, you want me to run this dick up in you?"

"What you think, nigga? I haven't seen you since you got back from Atlanta. Do you know how long ago that was?"

"Yeah, it's been a minute."

"Exaaactly. And then you straight played me last week when you had me up in here with a wet pussy waitin' for ya black ass to come through to serve me. Then ya ass never returned my fuckin' calls."

I hold back a laugh. "Yo, ma, on some real shit, I'm sorry 'bout that. The night I was 'posed to come through I ended up goin' to the gym. And by the time I got home, a nigga was beat. I took a hot shower, smoked a blunt, then knocked the hell out."

"Mmm-hmm, if you say so."

"Why you say it like that?"

"Like what?"

"Like you don't believe me or some shit."

"Humph. I know how you niggas do, especially your nasty ass."

Here this horny bitch goes. She's tight 'cause a nigga ain't banged her pussy up in a minute. And now her ass goin' through wit'drawals 'n shit. "Yo, go 'head wit' that dumb shit. You know my situation. A nigga's been busy. Since I got back, shit's been real hectic."

"Hmmm, you are so full of shit. Too hectic for you to at least pick up the phone and hit a bitch up? Hell, text or something. You sure you were in Atlanta with your grandmother and not some other bitch?"

"What?"

"You heard me," she snaps.

"Yo, hol' up," I say, gettin' defensive, "since when you start tryna check for a muhfucka?"

"I'm not checkin' for you. I'm askin' you a question."

"Well, why'd you ask me some shit like that?"

"'Cause I know you better than you think, *Alley Cat*." I sigh. "You sneaky as hell. And I'm hopin' you didn't have me foot the bill for you to be runnin' ya dick up in some other bitch. 'Cause if you did I'ma be pissed the fuck off."

"Yo, hol' the fuck up. I can't believe you comin' at me wit' that bullshit. What the fuck I gotta be sneaky about? You ain't my muthafuckin' girl 'n shit."

"That's already been established, nigga," she says, suckin' her teeth. "So you don't have to keep sayin' the shit. Nigga, you do you. But don't play me, either. You get pussy and throat anytime you want it; just keep shit real with me. Were you in Atlanta fucking some other bitch on my dime?"

"What kinda muhfucka would lie 'bout some shit like that?"

"A muthafucka who doesn't give a fuck about no one else but himself would. So answer the question. Were you out there fuckin' some bitch at my expense?"

I get silent. I'm thinkin', *this bitch is muthafuckin' crazy tryna check for me.*

"Oh, why you getting all quiet 'n shit on a bitch? You got something on ya mind?"

"Nah, yo. But you know what; it's all good. I'ma get ya money to you next week."

She sucks her teeth. I smile, knowin' that's not what she wants. As usual, I flip the script. "You're missing the point, Alex. I don't want the money. If you need something, I told you, I got you. I just don't want you lying to me, or taking money from me to sponsor any of ya excursions to fuck some other bitch, that's all."

"Yeah, yeah, yeah…I hear you."

"Yeah, yeah, yeah, nothing, nigga. I'm dead-ass."

"Listen, I'm not tryna hear all that, right now. I want some pussy."

"Then come get it, muhfucka."

I grin. "I'm on my way."

An hour later, I'm at Akina's spot. I have her on her back wit' her legs bent and spread open, and my face is buried between her silky, caramel-colored legs. I'm suckin' and lickin' and slurpin' the fuck outta her fat, juicy-ass pussy. On some real shit, if I was into bustin' down a bitch raw, I would paint my nut all up in her suga walls. When I tell you this ho gotta pretty pussy…man, listen, she got that goody-good-thang-thang, word up. She got the kinda pussy that should be molded and sold to muhfuckas. It's a perfect heart-shaped pussy wit' full, pouty outer lips. And her inner pussy lips don't droop or hang, like a buncha flappin' skin. I hate nuthin' more than lookin' at an ugly-ass pussy. All stretched and weathered and worn the fuck out, lookin' like it's been beat up and fisted by King Kong. That shit's disgustin', feel me?

She moans.

I rapidly wiggle my tongue from side to side, then flap it up and down against her clit before slidin' it into her juicy pussy. She arches her back, clutches the sheets. "Oh, yes…aaah…oooh…Alex, baby…mmmm…"

She squirms, thrusts her hips. "Oooh…ooooooh…Oh, God…uh…mmmmph…oh, yes…oooh. *Damn, this bitch got some good-ass pussy.* I stick my tongue in between the crevices of her lips and pussy, leavin' no part of its fleshiness untouched. Her breath quickens. She thrashes her head from side to side. "Oh, God…stop teasin' me…put your tongue in me….Eat my pussy, baby…"

I change the pressure my tongue delivers to her clit. Go from light, feathery tongue strokes to heavy, deep tongue strokes. I alternate from short tongue strokes to long, fast licks. I use the front of my tongue, then the backside of it. I slurp her, swallow her, then suck her. Allow her fountain to overflow into my mouth. I bring her different sensations by strokin' her wit' my tongue pointed out and curled at the tip to focus on one spot, then flatten it to stroke more area. I zig-zag my tongue, lickin' back 'n forth, then swirl it all 'round her pussy. My left hand wanders over her body, squeezin' and kneadin' her titties and nipples. Wit' my right hand, I slip two fingers into her bubblin' pussy, search for her hot spot. When I find it, I massage it, stokin' her fire. I take another finger, and slowly push it into her ass.

I continue suckin', lickin, slurpin' her 'til she nuts again. When her body finally stops shakin', I come up for air. Her eyes are closed, her hair tossed all over her head. She slowly opens her eyes, looks 'round the room as if she's dazed, then blinks. She blinks again. Lifts her head and looks down at me.

I grin, lickin' my pussy-stained lips. "You liked that shit, didn't you?"

She moans, spreadin' her legs wide as I roll on a Magnum, then climb up over her. I take her right titty in my mouth and suck; then her left, swirlin' my tongue over and 'round her nipples. I place soft kisses up and down her neck. "Well, baby," I tell her. "That was only the appetizer."

"Oh yeah," she says, grinnin'. "Then what's the main course?"

I lift her legs up over my shoulders. "This big-ass dick," I whisper into her ear while pushin' the head of it into her slippery slit, stretchin' the mouth of her pussy. She gasps, then lets out a series of moans as I pump this dick up in her. I slow-fuck her 'til her eyes roll up in the back of her head, her lips quiver, and the tears start to fall.

18

Yo, check this shit out. By now, it shouldn't be no mutha-fuckin' surprise to anyone, and it damn sure ain't no big secret—but for me, sex is what it is: sweaty, animalistic, no-strings fuckin'. There are no emotions, no expectations, and no muthafuckin' promises. My only mission is to give a broad exactly what she's been cravin': A nigga wit' good dick; a muh-fucka who knows howta heat the pussy up, and beat the pussy up. And nine-times-outta-ten, when I'm done deliverin', she's gonna be checkin' for a muhfucka like me to come through and rock her box all over again. But if her ass is silly enough to start dreamin' of some kinda happy-ever-after, where a muhfucka like me is gonna fall for her ass or make her wifey, then she's in for a damn night-mare full of heartache and disappointment. It ain't gonna happen.

And the only person any of these hoes can really be mad at is themselves, 'specially when a muhfucka tells 'em from the dip what it is. Hell, I let these chicks know that this thick, black dick comes wit' no money-back guarantees. So don't come scratchin' and kickin'at my door tryna get ya retarded ass a refund. So be clear. If I fuck you once, there's no assurance that you gonna get a second round. There's no declaration of some undyin'-love for ya ass, no commitment to be in ya life. Most of these tricks seem to get it—or at least act like they do. But e'ery so often there's a ho or two, or three, who fail to read the memo and try to get on some extra shit. Like Ramona's dizzy ass. Sumthin' told me to ignore the call, but me bein' the type of cat I am, I decide to officially let her know she's been dismissed from her dick-wettin' duties.

As soon as I answer, she whines into the phone. "Why haven't I heard from you? Didn't you get the messages I left?" I frown. There's nuthin' more annoyin' than a whinin', complainin', needy-ass bitch, which is what this trick is to me. I try to figure out why I even fucked wit' her ass for as long as I did—four damn months of nuttiness, to be exact. I mean, aside from lovin' to fuck all night and havin' a fat-ass, this ho really didn't come to the table wit' much 'cept a shitload of insecurities. And a muhfucka like me ain't beat for tryna reassure some emotionally bankrupt ho 'bout shit she should already know.

"Yeah, I got them shits. And?"

"And?" she repeats, soundin' heated. "And I called you mad times, *and* texted you. So obviously I needed to talk to you."

No, obviously ya ass is muthafuckin' obsessed. I sigh. "You needed to talk to me 'bout what, Ramona?"

"First, I need to know why you haven't returned any of my calls. I mean, damn. Common courtesy doesn't cost anything. Even if you didn't feel like talking, you could have at least replied to my texts."

Now, maybe it's me; but if you constantly hittin' a muhfucka up and the nigga don't get back at ya…uh, duh, the muhfucka ain't interested. *Meep, meep!* This bitch musta fell off the short bus, for real. "You want the truth?" I ask, knowin' most broads can't handle it, even when it's starin' them dead in the muthafuckin' eye. Like, the truth that he doesn't want you; that he's a liar and a cheater; that he's gonna keep beatin' your ass; that he's gonna keep fuckin' you over; that he doesn't respect you or your lil' fucked-up relationship; that he's smokin' crack, snortin' dope and stealin' all ya shit; that he's got ya moms suckin' his dick and ya sister's knocked up; that ya dumb ass is smotherin' him; that ya retarded ass is too damn unstable and too muthafuckin' needy. And the list goes on. Humph…man, listen. All I can do is shake my damn head. But the bitch says she wants it, so I smack her wit' it. "One, 'cause I ain't ya man," I tell her. "Two, you can't suck dick for shit; and three, you too muthafuckin' clingy. A nigga like me ain't beat for that shit. And you ain't worth the aggravation."

"Whaat?! Are you fucking serious? So fuck me, right? You got what you wanted, and now you just dip on a bitch. No phone call, no nothin'. That's real fucked up, Alley Cat."

"Hol' the fuck up. What is it you *think* I got from you?"

"Me!" she screams into my ear.

I laugh. "Baby, I didn't ask for *you*. And I didn't take nuthin' you didn't wanna give. *You* gave me you."

"And you took advantage of me! You took my pussy, my money and my heart with no fuckin' regard for me, or my feelings."

I laugh again.

"What the fuck is so funny?"

"You," I tell her, pausin'. See, a delusional ho needs to be hit wit' a dose of reality—hard. "Listen. I ran this dick up in ya raggedy-ass pussy 'cause you wanted me to. I ran ya wallet 'cause you wanted me to. I didn't take shit from you, boo. So don't get it twisted. *You* gave it 'cause that's what da fuck *you* wanted to do. And, as far as ya heart goes, I didn't ask for it, nor did I want it. I told you, 'Fuck wit' a nigga like me at ya own risk.' I told ya ass don't come at me lookin' for love 'cause I ain't givin' none of the shit out. But you still dropped ya mutherfuckin' drawers, snapped open ya wallet, and invited me in. So don't come at me sideways wit' no dumb-ass shit."

"Who the fuck you calling a dumb-ass *trick*?"

I don't bother correctin' her. 'Cause in all truth, her simple ass tricked up whatever common sense she mighta had the day she swallowed my nut.

"Boo, you a bona-fide fool, for real."

"Motherfucker, the only fool is you," she snaps, raisin' her voice. "And I don't appreciate you trying to dismiss me the way you did. I deserve more than you ignoring my goddamn calls."

I laugh. Listenin' to her belligerent ass makes me think of that flick *A Beautiful Mind*. Just like dude in that flick, this bitch is hearin' and seein' shit that ain't there. "You need meds, for real— for real 'cause you gotta real vivid imagination, baby. And the last thing I'ma do is keep goin' back 'n forth wit' a nutcase—"

"Who the fuck you calling a nutcase?!" she screams into the phone.

You, bitch! "Listen, boo-boo, it's obvious you have a buncha invisible friends tellin' you shit that only you believe. So let me spell this out for all of ya'll to comprehend. The only thing that was ever between us was F-U-C-K-I-N-G. Be clear. There are no attachments to you, your pussy, or any of ya muthafuckin' split personalities. You got me confused wit' some other nigga, real talk."

"No, I don't have you confused with anyone. I know who the hell I'm talking to. And I know what I'm talking about. I'm so fucking pissed…"

I frown. "Well, the only one you should be pissed at is ya'self."

"You fucking used me! Anytime you wanted, needed something, I gave it to you. Anything you asked for, I made sure you got it. Money, clothes, jewelry, whatever. I *never* said no to you. I've been fucking good to you, nigga. And this is the thanks I get! If you didn't wanna keep seeing me, you shoulda just said that, instead of leading me on. You didn't have to keep coming over here fucking me."

"And you didn't haveta keep openin' up ya ashy-ass legs lettin' me. But ya did. So, whose fault is that?"

"Yours," she states.

I shake my head, convinced this ho needs to invest in a bottle of self-esteem 'cause she's all out. "Yo, you got issues for real, yo."

Silence.

I get up from the counter, walk over to the pantry and pull out a tin canister. I open the lid, then pull out a large Ziploc bag of Purple Haze. I open the baggie, then smell. *Yeah, this that good shit right here*, I think, goin' into the laundry room for my pack of Phillies.

I go back over to the counter, pullin' open a drawer lookin' for my razor. *Where the fuck is that shit?*

"How can you be so fucking mean and selfish?"

"Easy. Whatever heartache you feel, you brought on ya'self."

"I…I can't believe you…" Fuck what ya heard. I am not moved by all that cryin' 'n shit. A nigga like me has no muthafuckin' sympathy for a ho who can't stick to the script. She starts wheezin' 'n shit, like she's havin' an asthma attack. "I'm…so …fucking… sick…and…tired of…niggas…using me…and fucking me over…"

"Look," I say, splittin' the blunt down the middle wit' my razor. "I'm sorry you feelin' some kinda way, but"—I pack it wit' weed, then roll it tight—"you got what you got 'cause that's what you allowed."

"You're a fuckin' liar!" she screams. I light the blunt, then take a deep, long pull.

I blow smoke outta the side of my mouth. "Yo, listen, the only muthafuckin' liar is you."

"I never fucking lied to you, you black motherfucker!"

I don't know if the ho's ever lied to me or not. And I don't care if she ever did. But the one thing I do know is the bitch has been

lyin' to herself from gate. E'ery muthafuckin' day this ho wakes
up and looks in the muthafuckin' mirror—tellin' herself she's gonna
have me to herself, tellin' herself she's gonna keep fuckin' 'n
suckin' this dick 'til she bags me—she's straight lyin'. So I'm not
the one the bitch shoulda been keepin' shit real wit'. Her dumb
ass shoulda been keepin' it one hunnid wit' herself 'cause if she
had, we wouldn't be havin' this whack-ass conversation.

"You know what?" she snaps. "I don't need you, and I definitely
don't need your no-good, lying ass to take care of my baby. I can
do the shit on my own."

I drop the blunt, pullin' the cell from my ear, then starin' at it.
What the fuck did this ho just say? Baby? I return it to my ear. "Yo,
run that shit by me again."

"You heard me, nigga. I said, *baby*. I'm pregnant."

Now I might be many things, but a sucka ain't one of 'em. This
ho is reachin' for sure if she thinks I'ma let her pin that shit on
me. "Okay, so you pregnant, and?"

"It's yours."

I bust out laughin'. "Yo, you funny as hell, word up. Nice try,
baby, but you'se a real clown. Unless you can get pregnant from
swallowin' a nut, you had better go back to the lab and find the
real donor, 'cause it ain't me. And on that note, don't call my
muthafuckin' phone wit' no more of ya nutty-ass bullshit."

I disconnect the call, then light another blunt. I inhale, hold
the smoke in my lungs 'til it starts to burn, then blow it up into
the air. "Bitch talkin' 'bout she pregnant. Fuck outta here," I say
to myself, shakin' my head. "These thirsty-ass broads will do and
say any-muthafuckin'-thing to get a muhfucka to stay wit' 'em."
My cell rings, again. I look at the screen, then press IGNORE.

Twenty minutes later, my cell rings again. I grin. This time it's
Moms. "Hey, beautiful, what it do?"

"*It* calls its mother, that's what the hell it do," she says, pretendin' to be annoyed. "But obviously, you done forgot who gave birth to *it*."

I chuckle, blowin' smoke outta my mouth. "You right, my bad. Didn't I tell you I was gonna be outta town?"

"Yeah, you told me all that. I'm just tryna figure out why you didn't return my call."

"You called? When?"

"I don't remember which day it was; maybe a week or so ago."

"Oh. Well, I don't remember seein' a call from you. Did you leave a message?"

"No, fool," she huffs, "I figured you'd see my number and have sense to call back."

"Is e'erything okay?"

"Everything's fine," she says, softenin' her tone. "The question is, is everything alright with you?"

"Oh, no doubt," I tell her.

"You sure?"

"Yep. I'm good, Ma, real talk."

She responds, "I'm cooking tomorrow. Dinner will be ready at six."

I shake my head and smile. Anytime she calls me and says she's 'cookin',' she wants to see me. And, more than likely to beat me in the head 'bout sumthin' she's heard, seen, or thought I've done. She's never been one to confront me over the phone; it's always face to face. However, no matter the reason, a muhfucka drops e'erything for Mom dukes, no questions asked—whether I want to hear it or not.

"I'll be there," I tell her, puttin' out my blunt.

"See you then."

19

"Idreamt of fish last week," Moms announces at the table as I'm bitin' into my second piece of her slammin' cornbread, then scooping up a forkful of her infamous three-cheese baked macaroni and cheese.

I cough, chokin'. Ramona's words sting my ears. *I'm pregnant.* Moms studies me as I continue coughin'. I finally stop, takin' a sip of my pomegranate and blueberry juice. I swallow, hard.

"You okay?" she asks, raisin' her brow.

"Yeah, I'm good."

"Hmmm, as soon as I told you I had a dream about fish, you practically choke to death," she says, givin' me the eye.

"Ohhhhkaaay, and?"

"Is there something you wanna tell me?"

I frown. "Nah, there's nuthin' to tell you."

"You sure?"

It's yours. "No doubt."

"You know everytime I have a dream about fish someone's pregnant."

I don't know what the hell fish has to do wit' some ho bein' knocked up? I shift in my seat. "Well, don't look at me. I'm not the one pregnant."

She doesn't crack a smile. "Then who is?"

All of sudden I've lost my appetite. I get up from my seat, takin' my half-eaten plate of food over to the counter. *You heard me, nigga…I'm pregnant.* I shake the thought. Ain't no way that bitch pregnant by me. "The hell if I know." I gulp down the rest of my drink, placin' the empty glass into the sink.

Moms remains seated, watchin' me. "Alex, you need to come back over here and have a seat." I sigh, knowin' she's 'bout to beat me in the head. I walk back over to the table and take a seat. She folds her hands. "When I was married to your father, I could always tell when he was lying, or keeping something from me. And the last time I dreamt of fish I confronted him and he looked me dead in my face and"—she catches herself, foldin' her arms 'cross her chest, realizin' she's 'bout to say sumthin' I'm not supposed to know. She shakes her head, swipin' hair outta her face— "Is one of them hot-in-the-ass girls you fucking pregnant?"

I shake my head. "Not by me."

"Mmm-hmm," she says, raisin' her brow. "The left side of your jaw twitches like your father's when you're lying," she calmly states.

"I'm not lying."

"Well, then, you must be keeping shit out 'cause you're definitely not telling me something."

"There's nuthin' to tell," I tell her again, feelin' a headache comin' on.

She tilts her head, stares at me. "Are you protecting yourself?"

"Ma, on some real shit, I'm many things, but reckless ain't one of 'em. I keep my pipe wrapped at all times. Well,"—I grin— "unless I'm gettin' topped."

She rolls her eyes. "Please, you better be wrappin' that dick of yours up for that, too. The last thing you need is a baby, or catching some shit you can't get rid of. Then again…maybe having a child might slow your ass down and make you more responsible. You know, force you to get a job, knowing you'd have someone depending on you."

I shake my head. "Nah, I'm good. I'll pass. The only thing havin' a baby would do is make me miserable, especially knowin' I'ma be stuck wit' its mother in my ear for eighteen or more years. No thanks, boo. I'd rather kill myself."

She sucks her teeth. "'Boo,' my ass. You're a damn mess."

I get up and kiss her on her forehead, then say, "Well, I'm your mess, beautiful woman." I decide to tell her 'bout my fucked-up convo wit' Ramona's nutty ass. She takes it all in, then wants to know why I didn't tell her from the rip. And I tell her 'cause I really didn't wanna get into it wit' her. She nods, asks me if there's any truth to what she's sayin'.

"Hell if I know. I mean, she could be pregnant. But it ain't mine. That much I know for sure. I put my life on that. Ma, that bit...I mean, broad is crazy."

She sighs. "I'm sure she's no crazier than she already was when you decided to stick your dick in her."

"Yeah, you gotta point," I admit, chucklin'. "But, actually, I think she got worse once she climbed up on this *Maple*wood."

She rolls her eyes, suckin' her teeth. "Hmmph. I'm telling you, you and that dick of yours"—she shakes her head—"You really need to cut out all this ho-ing around you do. Nothing good is gonna come out of it. It's only a matter of time before you find yourself lying up in a hospital bed, bandaged from feet to head." —she snaps her fingers—"Just that much...from being dead..."

I burst out laughin', peepin' how she hit me wit' a verse from that joint "A Thin Line between Love and Hate." "You funny as hell, Ma, word up."

"You can laugh if you want, but I'm being serious."

"Ma, stop worryin' 'bout me. I got this."

"Okay, Mr. I Got This. You've been warned." She sighs. "I wish you'd find yourself one, even two, nice girls to date. What the hell you need with a dozen or more women anyway?" I give her a blank look. "Besides for the obvious, you fool."

"Other than for variety, nuthin'.."

She shakes her head. "You know what,"—she raises her hand, pausing—"I'm gonna leave it alone."

I laugh. "Yeah, right, Ma. That's what you always say."

"I know. And as your mother, smart ass, I'm allowed to change my mind. But, this time I'm serious. You're a grown man."

My cell phone chirps, lettin' me know someone sent me a text. "I'm glad you finally realize that," I tease, smilin' at her.

"Obviously, I realize a whole lot more than you do."

"Ma, whatever happens, happens. I'm doin' me. Now, tell me. Why'd you ask Pops 'bout fish?" My phone chirps again. I ignore it, keepin' my eyes on her.

"Ask him yourself," she answers, gettin' up from the table. She walks over to the sink and starts washin' dishes.

I raise my brow. "Wait a minute, are you tryna say Pops got some other chick knocked up while ya'll were together?" She doesn't respond. I walk over to her, lean up against the counter.

"Let him be the one to tell you." I stare at her. Watch as she washes and rinses the dishes, then move about the kitchen puttin' away food.

"So you just gonna leave me hangin'?"

She stops what she's doin' and looks at me, movin' a strand of hair from her face. "Let me say this: Some women can be some real crafty bitches." I keep from smilin', surprised she's referrin' to women as *bitches* since she's always comin' at my neck for usin' the word. "Yes, I said it: bitches. And a desperate bitch will stop at nothing to get her claws in what she can't have, including…" she pauses, narrowin' her left eye and raisin' a brow, "…another woman's husband."

I blink, take in what she's said, then it becomes clear. "Wow," is the only thing I say.

"Yeah, 'wow' is right." The doorbell rings. I glance up at the wooden wall clock: 7:43 P.M. "Speaking of which, that's him now," she announces, wipin' the table. "Go open the door."

"Aiight." My cell chirps, again, as I'm goin' toward the front door. I finally pull it from off my waist. It's Tamera's ass. You still on ya bullshit?

The doorbell rings again as I text back. Nah. What's good? I open the door. "What's good, playboy?" I tease, givin' Pops a pound. Although I wanna feel some kinda way 'bout what Moms insinuated, I don't. That shit was between him and her. But I ain't gonna front. A muhfucka still wants the rundown on shit.

"Hey, son," he says, steppin' into the house, then shuttin' the door. "Where's ya mom?"

Tamera texts: When am I gonna see you, nigga?

"In the kitchen," I tell him as I'm textin back. Why, U cravin' for some of this cock and cum? Pops walks toward the kitchen.

What u think, she responds. My cell rings. It's my nigga Mike. "Yo?" I answer, takin' a seat on the sofa.

"What's poppin', nigga?"

"Chillin', dawg. What's good wit' you?"

"Shit. Sittin' here wit' Gee's punk ass," he says, laughin'. Gee's another one of my boys from back in the day. We actually played ball together in high school and fucked some of the same bitches.

"Ya'll niggas smokin'?"

"Yeah, a lil' sumthin'."

"I shoulda known ya fiend asses would be blazin'."

"Fuck outta here, muhfucka," he says, laughin'. "You burn more trees than a wildfire, nigga."

"Damn, straight," I agree, glancin' at my watch. It's almost eight. "So what ya'll niggas 'bout to get into tonight?"

"We were thinkin' 'bout hittin' up that titty spot Mr. Cheeks down in Mount Holly. They got some bad-ass bitches up in that piece, son."

"Nigga, you'se a real clown if you think I'ma trick my money up on a bunch of ass-shakin', pole-ridin' hoes. Not the kid, muh-fucka."

Tamera sends another text. *So, what's good wit' u, nigga?*

This nut in ya throat, I reply.

He laughs. "Man, listen, them hoes is fiyah, nigga. I'm tryna get this dick wet, feel me."

I frown. What the fuck! A nigga like me might get into a lotta things, but payin' to get my dick wet ain't one of 'em. I don't give a fuck how horny a muhfucka gets. I'll beat my shit first, real talk, before I dig in my muthafuckin' pockets to lace a bitch for some pussy or some muthafuckin' head. But if that's a nigga's shit, then do what ya do. I just ain't that dude."

"Ya'll niggas go 'head. I'ma sit this one out."

"Yo, muhfucka, ya ass is corny as hell."

"Whatever, nigga," I say, gettin' up and walkin' back into the kitchen. "I'll be corny, but I bet you I won't be trickin' my paper up on no ass. I'll leave that shit for you whack-ass cats who don't know howta game a bitch up offa her ends."

He laughs. "Yo, you'se a funny nigga, word up."

Moms and Pops are sittin' at the table. She's drinkin' a can of ginger ale watchin' him shove a forkful of food into his mouth. "Funny, hell. I'm keepin' shit real. Yo' dawg, hol' up..."

"Aiight," he says.

"Aiight, ya'll I'm out." I walk over to the table, then lean down and kiss Moms on the forehead.

She smiles. "You remember what I said."

"I got you, Ma."

"Mmm-hmm," she says, smirkin'. "Whatchu got is a hard-ass head."

I laugh at her. "And you love me to death, too."

She waves me on, rollin' her eyes. "Get on up outta here with that."

I look over at Pops. "Aiight, playboy, don't be out all night."

"Stay outta grown folk business," he says, wipin' his mouth wit' a napkin.

I laugh. "Yeah, yeah, yeah." Mom shakes her head, chucklin'. I give Pops a pound, then bounce. On my way out the door, I continue my convo wit' my boy. "Yo, sorry 'bout that, man."

"Nah, don't sweat it. So, what's good wit' ya peoples? They gettin' back together?"

"Man, listen...the hell if I know. Right now they just breakin' each other off, feel me?" I hop in my whip, then head toward the parkway.

He laughs. "I hear you. Oh, check it. I got the rooms for All-Star Weekend."

"Aiight, that's wassup. Where?"

"The W in Scottsdale. Looks like most of the shit's gonna be poppin' off 'round that area."

"Yo, how many muhfuckas you packin' in a room? 'Cause you know I ain't beat to be in a room wit' a buncha niggas."

He laughs. "Nigga, shut ya ass up. If you listen, I said *rooms*, plural as in more than one. So obviously, I got ya stinkin' ass ya own shit. Gee and Ron are the only two muhfuckas sharin' a room. Them some cheap-ass niggas, word up."

"That shit's on them," I say, sparkin' the blunt in my ashtray. I take a pull. "All I know is I'm tryna snap a few spines while I'm out there, and I ain't tryna have shit block a nigga's flow. You smell me?"

"No doubt, son. I'm tryna get up into sumthin' my damn self. Awww, shit, sounds like you blazin'?"

"You know me," I say, blowin' smoke out. "I'm tryna catch up to you, muhfucka." He laughs. I take another hit. "I just hope them bitches look good. 'Cause, on some real shit, the ones we saw down in New Orleans last year looked like pure cow shit. I think I mighta saw two, maybe three fly bitches that were on point from head to toe the whole time we were there—and that's stretchin' it. The rest of them fake-ass, wannabe divas were weave-wearin' dragons in cheap-ass skirts 'n heels."

He laughs. I blow out more smoke. "Yeah, but a lotta them hoes had some fat asses."

"Fuck a fat ass. Them raggedy-ass booga bears looked broke as hell. If I'ma fuck a dog-faced ho, then the bitch gonna haveta look like she's holdin' some paper, feel me? You saw some of that outdated shit they were rockin'."

"Yo, son. You gotta remember where we were. Most of them heads were from Florida, Mississippi, Texas and other parts of the Dirty South. They gotta different flava than us. And you know they kinda late on some shit."

"Whatever, man. All I know is, oh-nine's All-Star better have some dimepieces there. I don't mind givin' a pretty bitch some free dick. But…man, listen, I'm sorry. My dick don't get hard for a broke *and* ugly ho…she's gonna need to pay to ride up and down on this pole."

He starts laughin' hard. "Yo, nigga, I swear. You crack me the fuck up. Yo, but on some real shit, you can't front. The All-Star out in Vegas was fiyah."

"Oh, no doubt…Vegas was on point. Now *that's* how a mutha-fuckin' All-Star's 'posed to be like, packed wit' a buncha fly-ass, ballin' bitches. Shit, even some of them white hoes were gettin' it in. I shoulda fucked the shit outta that white chick from Cali just for the hell of it while I was out there. That ho was cravin' for some of this chocolate dick. I woulda had her ass pawnin' her ice, and that shiny Benz she was pushin'."

"Man, that broad was finer than a muhfucka, too. I still can't believe you've never fucked some white pussy. A lotta them are some real freaky bitches for some black dick. They'll let you do almost anything to 'em."

"Nah, son, never had the urge. I don't give a fuck if she chews shit and eats cum for snack. My dick only responds to two colors, muhfucka: green money and black pussy."

He laughs. "Nigga, you a fool."

Speakin' of good, black pussy, I want some tonight. I decide to go to Pops' spot instead. If I'm tryna get this nut off, then it makes no sense to drive all the way down to the shore when e'eryone I fuck wit' is up this way. "Yo, you can laugh if you want, nigga, but I'm dead-ass."

"Yeah, I know you are, muhfucka. That's why the shit's so damn funny."

"Whatever. Aiight, listen…I'm done fuckin' wit' you for one night. I'm prowlin' tonight, so hit me up when you niggas are tryna get into sumthin' other than trickin' ya paper up."

He laughs. "Then bounce, muhfucka."

"I'm out."

"Aiight, then…one." We disconnect. I scroll through my address book, then press the call button.

"Hello?"

"Yo, what's good, baby? You want this nut tonight?"

"What time you coming?"

"Now."

"See you when you get here."

"Aye, yo…"

"Yeah?"

"I'ma need to hold a few dollars, baby. You got me?"

She sucks her teeth.

Damn, this buck-tooth beaver suckin' her muthafuckin' gums

like a muhfucka's always hittin' her up for her paper. "Yo, if it's a problem, boo, let me know. 'Cause I can keep it movin'."

"Did I say it was?"

"Nah, but you came off like it is, suckin' ya teeth 'n shit."

She huffs. "How much you need?"

"Three hunnid," I tell her. "So you got me?"

She sighs. "Yeah, I guess."

"*You guess?* Whatchu mean? Either you do or you don't."

"Yeah, nigga. I got you. But this is the last time."

Yeah, yeah, yeah. That's what ya ass said the last time. I grin. "That's what it is, baby. Have that pussy wet and ready for me." *And ya money in ya hand.* I hang up, then spark another blunt. Yeah, big pimpin' ain't always easy, but someone's gotta do it. And it might as well be a muhfucka like me.

20

M an, listen, I'm tired as hell. Last night I ended up pullin' an all-nighter wit' Crystal's fat ass. This cute brown-skinned chick from Union I fuck on the low from time to time. She's a bit chunky, though, wit' a head like a Chow's—big. But she got some good pussy. And she swallows and hits a nigga up wit' paper—even when the ho don't want to, so you already know what time it was. I didn't leave up from outta her spot 'til almost four in the mornin'.

I close my eyes, replayin' the night in my head. I licked and kissed her skin startin' from her thick neck to her wide collar bone to her itty-bitty piggy tits, twirlin' my tongue 'round each nipple before nibblin' on 'em. She moaned. Then I planted a trail of kisses in the center of her chest down to her overflowin' gut and over her wide hips. The whole time I'm wit' this rhino I gotta remind myself that big girls need love, too; that big girls like to fuck, too; that big girls can suck a mean dick, too. And, they love spendin' money on a muhfucka like me, too.

"Yeah, baby. Let daddy make you feel good. You want daddy to long stroke this tight pussy?"

"Mmm-hmm…"

I continued explorin' her body. I raised her ham hocks and placed kisses on the inside of each thigh. My lips traveled to her cankles. But I stopped when I got to her biscuit heels. You know a nigga ain't fuckin' wit' no busted-ass feet. And that ho has fluffy-ass buttermilk biscuits on the back of her heels. You know what I'm talkin' about; them big, white puffy heels that look like they've been soaked in yeast. What the fuck?!

The last time I was wit' her ass I told her she needed to go to a foot surgeon to get them shits handled. I don't give a fuck how good the pussy is, or what kinda muthafuckin' gifts I'm bein' laced wit', or how much paper I'm tryna fuck outta her ass. Some things are off limits. And fuckin' wit' her raggedy feet is one of 'em. She even had the muthafuckin' nerve to be openin' and closin' her toes like I was 'bout to suck on them gorilla claws. *Not tonight, boo. Not to-muthafuckin'-night*, I thought, spreadin' her legs open, then puttin' my head between 'em. I sniffed the silky patch of hair coverin' her thick pussy, flickin' her clit wit' my tongue. She moaned. I continued dartin' my tongue in and outta her, slurpin' her pussy. Then I pressed a finger on her asshole, and put my whole mouth over her clit and sucked, then licked. Then I stuck two fingers into her hot slit. The bitch started shakin'. I used more force, suckin' her clit, finger-poppin' her hole, and pressin' on her asshole.

She let out a loud-ass moan, then started screamin' and buckin' her hips. Three minutes later, her nut oozed out into my mouth and onto my tongue. A nigga can't front, that fat ho got some sweet, creamy pussy. And it's hot, and muthafuckin' tight. I finished suckin' her hole clean, then flipped her over onto her stomach. "You ready for this big dick, bitch?" I asked, slappin' her on her ass. I tried not to frown at all the dents and craters in her ass.

"Yes, fuck me," she moaned, archin' her back and pumpin' her hips. "Stretch my pussy with that big-ass, black dick, nigga."

I grinned, slidin' on a condom, then pushin' the head of my dick into the back of her pussy. Biscuit Heels gasped as I slowly entered her. I fed her this dick nice 'n slow. Reached 'round her and started squeezin' her niblets—my term for teenie tits wit' lil' nipples. I fucked her wit' six inches of dick, then let her twist 'n wiggle up on it, takin' in the rest. And the whole time I was hittin' it from the back, I was thinkin', *Damn, this bitch needs a back bra for all this muthafuckin' back fat.*

But I gotta say big girl handled this dick. I had my hands on my hips watchin' her ass jiggle 'n bounce. The more she bounced and shook, the more dick she took in. By the time I finished rockin' her box, I walked up outta her spot wit' not only the paper she hit me wit', but wit' her beggin' me to come back through today to run up in her fat, low self-esteem-havin' ass again. Bless her chubby lil' heart!

I pull open my laptop, then turn it on. And the minute I log onto my email account. Several IM screens pop up. *Damn, these bitches are real thirsty*, I think.

ILoveSweetCum: Hey, baby. Haven't seen you online lately, where you been, boo?

DaddyLongStroke: Chillin', ma. What's good wit' you?

ILoveSweetCum: Missing u

Yeah, right! How the fuck this ho gonna miss me. The dumb bitch doesn't even know *me*. Hell, none of 'em do. And if I've fucked any of 'em, then the only thing they know is how I rock the box. Other than that, these bitches be straight bullshittin'. I shake my head.

Daddylongstroke: Bring me them pretty-ass dick suckas, and prove it

ILoveSweetCum: LMFAO. U a trip, nigga

Daddylongstroke: Nah, baby. I ain't trippin'. I got a bucket of thick, sweet cum for ya throat. Stop frontin' and cum get it

I switch to the next IM box, then alternate from one screen to the next, tryna keep up wit' these hoes tryna get at me.

ThicknDaHips: When you gonna stop frontin' and stroke me up?

DaddyLongStroke: Oh, so you think you ready for this dick?

ThicknDaHips: Baby, I was born ready

DaddyLongStroke: LOL, that's what ya mouth says. U can't take no real dick

ThicknDaHips: CTFU. Try me

Onmyknees2plez: Hey, big daddy; why u hiding from me? Stop acting like u scared of me, baby. I don't bite

DaddyLongStroke: lmfao. Baby, ain't no body hidin' from ya sexy ass. U da one runnin' from this dick. E'ery time we supposed to hook up you backin' out on a nigga

Onmyknees2plez: ROTFL. Nigga, u got me confused with one of them other chicks. U ain't said nothing but a word. What kinda condoms u use?

DaddyLongStroke: Magnums, baby. XL. U know what that means, right?

Onmyknees2plez: Yeah. That a big dick don't mean shit if u don't know how to use it

ThicknDaHips: Hello, u still there????????

DaddyLongStroke: Yeah, hol' up

ILoveSweetCum: U still there??

DaddyLongStroke: Yeah, baby. Hold up, BRB. Gotta take a leak

DaddyLongStroke: Well, I know howta use it. The ? is do u know howta take it?

Onmyknees2plez: Sure do

DaddyLongStroke: Yeah, yeah, yeah. That's what they all say. Stop frontin' and show 'n prove

Onmyknees2plez: Call me, TONIGHT

DaddyLongStroke: what's ya number again?

Onmyknees2plez: 908-444-5533

DaddyLongStroke: Aiiight, bet. I'ma get at u later tonight

Onmyknees2plez: U better

DaddyLongStroke: So, Thick, what's good? When we gonna meet up so I can split that back down the middle? A nigga tryna pop ya spine out

ThicknDaHips: Lmao@a nigga tryna pop ya spine out. U funny as hell

DaddyLongStroke: Nah, baby. I'm dead-ass. I wanna fuck. But, you da one frontin' n shit. Hol' up. Gotta piss. BRB

ThicknDaHips: Aiight

DaddyLongStroke: Aiight, I'm back

ILoveSweetCum: Oh, okay. I almost thought you forgot about me

DaddyLongStroke: Never that. So when u tryna wet this dick?

ILoveSweetCum: Call me. 973-555-3303

DaddyLongStroke: Aiight. I'ma hit u up lata

DaddyLongStroke: I'm back

ThicknDaHips: Geesh. Took you long enough. Musta been one helluva piss

DaddyLongStroke: Well, I gotta long dick so it takes me longer to piss

ThicknDaHips: LMAO. U stupid

I take a deep breath. All this back 'n forth IM'in' is startin' to give a muhfucka a damn headache.

DaddylongStroke: Nah, baby, ain't nuthin' stupid 'bout me stickin' this Mandingo cock up in ya

ThicknDaHips: Then let's have at it

DaddyLongStroke: U talk a good one, baby

Another IM screen pops up. I shake my head. On some real shit, I can't tell you the first thing 'bout any of these bitches, other than the fact they gotta pussy. And wanna fuck. I hear the garage door open, I log off the computer, abruptly cuttin' all them cock-hungry hoes off.

My cell rings. I shake my head, glancin' at the screen. It's Candy; another one of them chunky-monkey bitches. She's one of those tight-pussied chicks who borders between ugly and beasty, dependin' on how the light shines on her. Her long, fake eyelashes and wide, pudgy nose makes her look like a chocolate Miss Piggy. Actually, the bitch kinda reminds me of a much thicker and wider version of that funny-lookn' chick, Tiffany sumthin'. You know, the one who played New York on that busted-ass reality show, *I Love New York*. Anyway, ugly and fat or not—wit' the lights out, she's a damn good lay, a greedy cock sucka, and she knows howta lace a nigga.

"Yo, what's good?"

"Hey, baby. You know it's almost that time, so what you want for your birthday?" she asks. *Damn, when did I tell her my birthday was?* Shit, I have so many of 'em I forget which ho I done told which date to.

"My birthday?"

"Yeah, fool. Isn't your birthday on the eighteenth of next month?"

"Right, right," I say, chucklin'. "I got so much shit on my mind I almost forgot."

She laughs. "You need to lay off the trees, baby. They got you forgetting your own birthday."

Shut ya Samoan ass up wit' that dumb shit! I think, sparkin' a blunt. She's been givin' me a birthday fuck, along wit' a few gifts, for the last four years. I haveta laugh 'cause chick really thinks she's doin' me a favor and givin' me sumthin' special. But, I let her fat ass think it's the nicest shit anyone's ever done for me. It makes her feel good that she's makin' a muhfucka feel special, so who am I to steal her joy. Besides, once a year is 'bout as much as I can stomach from her linebacker ass.

"Well, you know I 'preciate you always rememberin'. I can always count on you to come through to make a muhfucka like me feel special. That means a lot."

"Awww, that's so sweet."

"Not as sweet as you and that tight pussy," I tell her. Yeah, it's a small lie, but it makes her feel good, and gets me what I want. "You need to let me come through so I can stretch that shit out for ya, now."

She laughs. "You stay tryna fuck somebody."

"And?"

"And, nothing; I'm just saying."

"Well, what you sayin'? Can I beat that shit up, or what?"

"Yeah..."

"Oh, aiight. That's wassup. Tonight?"

"No," she says, suckin' her teeth, "on ya birthday when I see you, like we always do."

"Yeah, yeah, yeah...I know. You can't knock a nigga for tryna get some pre-birthday sex."

She laughs. "Whatever. I know you got enough bitches keeping your dick wet the rest of the year. But as long as I'm the one fucking that big-ass dick on ya birthday, it's all good."

I laugh wit' her. "I feel you, baby. Yo, you votin'?"

"Are you kidding? Hell yeah, I'm voting. I'ma be at the polls bright and early. Me, my mother, grandmother and three sisters."

"Oh, aiight. That's wassup. 'Cause if you weren't, I was gonna haveta cancel this dick on you."

She laughs again. "Well, that's not about to happen, so I'll see you on ya birthday."

"No doubt," I tell her, hangin' up.

21

I'm layin' 'cross my bed playin' wit' my dick. A nigga's in the mood for some hot, nasty phone sex. But I don't really have anyone I can hit up 'cause most of these bitches wanna fuck after 'bout a minute of me talkin' this good shit to 'em. And all I wanna do is beat my dick, bust this nut and chill today. I grab the baby oil, wet my dick up wit' it, then close my eyes. I long stroke it, usin' my other hand to grab my balls, creatin' a scenario of voices in my head.

Yeah, baby, you like this big dick, don't you?…

Oh, yes…

You a nasty lil' bitch.

I'm your nasty bitch, nigga…fuck my pussy.

Yeah, you want daddy to bang up that tight pussy; don't you, you slutty bitch?

Yeah, nigga…fuck me with that long-ass dick. You nasty, black muh-fucka.

Damn, you wettin' a nigga up, baby. Hmm…this pussy's good…let me take this dick out and slap it across them big-ass, slutty-dick suckas…

Oooh, yes, slap my lips with that heavy-ass dick, muhfucka. You gonna let me suck all over that thick-ass dick, nigga?

Yeah, I'ma let you suck ya pussy juice all off this dick…you gonna let me spit in ya mouth, then run this dick down in ya throat?

Nigga, if you spit in my mouth, I'ma smack the shit outta you.

I got both hands on my dick now, double strokin' it.

Yeah, bitch, that shit turns me on…smack me, slut…I wanna bust this nut in ya hot-ass pussy. You gonna let me creampie you, then suck that shit outta ya?

Mmmmm…oooh, you a nasty, freaky muthafucka…I want you to slap ya dick on my ass, then fuck me deep in it…

I quicken my strokes, "Uh…uh…aaah, shit," I moan, splatterin' my nut all over my chest and stomach. I lie still for a moment, steady my breathin', then wipe my nut offa me wit' one of my cum rags—old washcloths I strictly use for jackin'. "Damn, that shit was good." I rub my balls, pinchin' my left nipple. I wanna nut again.

My cell rings, disruptin' my private moment. I reach for it off the the nightstand and glance at the screen. It's my nigga, Short Stacks…damn, I mean Glenn. We're not as tight as I am wit' Red, Mike, and Gee, but we still cool. We actually went to the same high school, played varsity basketball together and ended up at the same college. Of course he graduated, and you already know what it was wit' me. If you ran into 'im on the streets at night, you'd think he was just another saggy-pants-wearin', tree-blazin' hood nigga, but dude actually got his shit together. By day, he's a proper-talkin', suit-'n-tie-type nigga down on Wall Street makin' moves. But the minute he comes 'round his boys, he flips—like many of us—right back into hood mode, blazin', drinkin' and talkin' mad shit.

"Yo, my nig, sound like ya ass's already blitzed."

"Nah, not really; just a little sumthin'. Me and Gee had a few shots of Cuervo."

I laugh. "Aaaah, shit. And I bet that tequila got ya ass feelin' right."

"No, doubt, son. You already know."

"Yeah, I know, nigga. I know ya ugly, black ass is a damn lush."

"Nigga, fuck outta here. Ya ass's blacker than me."

We both laugh. "Yeah, and I gotta longer dick. But what that got to do wit' ya ass bein' a damn drunk?"

"Shit. But I pull more bitches than you."

"Yeah, okay. But, ya ass's short strokin' 'em, so it don't matter how many hoes you mackin'. At the end of the night, you just an appetizer to 'em, muhfucka."

"Fuck you, nigga," he says, laughin', "appetize on these nuts."

"Yeah, aiiight, muhfucka. That's the same shit I told ya moms after I finished nuttin' in her mouth."

He continues laughin'. "Awww, damn. Why you gotta go there? That's some real foul shit, nigga."

"Well, watch ya mouth then, muhfucka. Don't hate on me 'cause ya stroke game is whack."

"Yeah, yeah, yeah. Whatever, nigga," he snaps, soundin' offended. I laugh at his ass. 'Cause he knows I'm keepin' shit real. No homo. But, after all the trains 'n shit we done pulled on bitches growin' up, and the group epps we done swung wit' chicks, he knows I know what it is. Not to put him on blast or nuthin', but there's a reason they call 'im Short Stacks. 'Cause the nigga's shit is thick as hell, but most bitches be snappin' on his ass for not knowin' how to keep his dick in 'em. My thing is, if ya dick is constantly slippin' outta a bitch's hole, then maybe you need to change up ya stroke, feel me? But this nigga here ain't get the memo. Or he just too stuck on retarded to understand that a short-dick muhfucka can't long stroke no pussy.

"So, what's good, muhfucka?" he asks, bringin' me back to the conversation. "You tryna roll out wit' us or what?"

"Where ya'll niggas goin'?"

"The Rhum Lounge."

The Rhum Lounge is located on the lower level of this slick lil'

Jamaican restaurant called Negril in the Village. The food is bangin' and the in-house DJ spins reggae, calypso, soca, hip-hop and R & B joints while you sit back, chill, and get ya eat and drink on. I think for a minute. Try to decide if I really wanna fuck wit' 'em tonight like that. I mean, these my niggas 'n shit, but sometimes they go overboard wit' the drinkin' and start poppin' a buncha shit, especially Gee's dumb-ass.

"Listen, muhfucka, I ain't beat for no drama tonight, word up. Ya'll muhfuckas be on some extra shit sometimes. If you gonna be mixin' ya drinks 'n shit, throwin' up all over the place, let me know now." He laughs. "Ain't shit funny, nigga. The last time, you fucked 'round and threw up all in my muthafuckin' whip. Had my shit all fucked up. And ya black ass still owe me for the detailin'."

"Nigga, stop whinin'. I got you. Besides, I'm drivin' my own shit tonight."

"Yeah, whatever, muhfucka. Just have me my money."

"Nigga, fuck that shit you talkin'. You hangin' or not?"

"What time ya'll muhfuckas tryna roll?" I ask, glancin' at my watch: 7:25 p.m.

"'Bout nine."

"Oh, aiight. That'll work."

"Bet. You just need to scoop Ron up."

"Ron? I thought that nigga was on ya side of town?"

"Not tonight he's not. He's at his sister's."

I shake my head. Not to kick dudes back in. But when it comes to women, he's 'bout as dumb and pussywhipped as they come. "I take it he done got his dumb-ass put out, again." He laughs. Asks me what time I'ma swing through and scoop 'im up. "Which sister's spot is he at?"

"Lynn's," he tells me.

Lynn's his younger sister; a cutie wit' a juicy bootie. She's also a real hot-box. And, of course, I thrashed it a few times on the low. I dicked her upside down and inside out; gave her pussy a beatdown she'd never experienced before. Not once, not twice, but at least a dozen times before her dumb ass started actin' like she wanted to chain a muhfucka down. So she got dismissed. But she got mad props for keepin' her cum-guzzler shut 'bout our epps.

"Yo," I say to Glenn, "let that nigga know I'ma be through 'round nine-fifteen."

"Aiight, bet. See you cats later."

"One."

At nine-thirty I text Ron to let 'im know I'm 'round the corner and to be at the door ready to roll. The minute I turn onto his sister's street, a bright-ass porch light flips on, and I see him comin' out the door. He's rockin' a slick brown leather blazer over a brown pullover wit' his signature platinum and diamond fist danglin' from a platinum chain. The nigga's neck is practically glowin' from the lights hittin' hit. And he has his brown Negro Leagues fitted cap cocked to the side. I pull up to the curb, unlockin' the door. As soon as he opens the door, I can smell the combination of leather and cologne way before he gets his ass in the car. He smells like he practically washed himself in a whole bottle of Dolce & Gabbana.

The minute he shuts the door, I say, "Damn, muhfucka. What'd you do, bathe in that shit?"

"Nah," he says, fastenin' his seatbelt. He reaches over and gives me a brotherly pound. "What's good?"

"Shit," I say, pullin' off, makin' my way toward I-280 East. I crack the front windows before the muhfucka suffocates me wit' all them smells goin' on. "What's been up wit' you?"

He sighs, placin' his head back on the headrest. "Not much

man. Same shit, different day. Or should I say, same shit, different broad."

"I hear you, man. You 'n ya peoples at it again."

"Man, listen. E'ery week it's some shit wit' her ass." I nod knowin'ly; but don't say shit 'cause I know he's gonna fill me in. "She started spazzin' the fuck out last night over some dumb shit, and poured bleach all over my shit. Shoes, boots, sneakers, clothes, you name it. She straight housed my shit."

"Get the fuck outta here! You for real?"

"I'm dead-ass. She fucked up all my shit, man. Jewelry, watches, you name it—trashed! The only shit I have is what's on my back. And then she took all my fuckin' money outta the bank. I had to borrow money from my sister, so I could at least have some clean muthafuckin' drawers 'n shit to put on."

See, this is the kinda shit I'm talkin' 'bout. And it's exactly another reason why I don't be fuckin' beat to be in a relationship. Bitches always wanna fuck a muhfucka's shit up when her ass starts feelin' some kinda way 'bout shit. Then after she done finished fuckin' up all ya wears 'n shit, she puts ya dumb ass out. But I'm not surprised. Like I said earlier, he fucks wit' a buncha unstable bitches. It's like he has a magnet for emotionally unbalanced broads. I listen to him go on and on 'bout he's gettin' tired of her shit, blah, blah, blah. Then he sits here and tells me *she* locked him outta a spot that *he* pays the rent to, but the shits in *her* name. I look at dude like he's crazy. I feel like sayin', "You stupid bitch-ass nigga! What the fuck you doin' havin' a muthafuckin' joint bank account wit' a ho you ain't even married to?" But I'ma leave it alone 'cause there ain't shit he can say that's gonna make an ounce of sense to a muhfucka like me. All I can say is: I wish the fuck I would! What a retard! I'm startin' to think this nigga likes bein' abused 'n shit. I shake my head.

"So whatchu do this time?"

"Man, nuthin'. She be on her bullshit, listenin' to them fuckin' crab-ass bitches she fucks wit', lettin' that shit they put in her ear go to her head."

"What kinda shit?" I ask, already knowin' this nigga stays caught up in craziness.

"All kinda dumb shit. Them bitches all up on my dick instead of havin' their busted asses somewhere gettin' fucked. Hell, if they had some dick in their lives they wouldn't have so much time worryin' 'bout what the fuck I'm doin' wit' mine."

I impatiently drum my fingers on the steerin' wheel. "Muhfucka, what the hell you do?"

"I was at this spot in Paramus winin' 'n dinin' this shorty, and one of ole girl's nosey-ass friends saw me and ratted me out."

"Nah, nigga, that ain't enough for a bitch to house ya shit. I know you. What'd you do? Keep it gee."

"I stayed out all night…"

"And you didn't answer ya phone," I finish for him.

"Yeah, somethin' like that."

"Nigga, you dumb as hell. You know you livin' wit' ole girl, so how the hell you gonna stay out *all* night and not answer ya cell?"

"Actually, it was two nights."

"*Two nights*? *And* you didn't answer ya shit. Oh yeah, muhfucka, you knew you had it comin'. Then you probably stumbled up in there smellin' like pussy. Nigga, you was askin' for shit to pop off."

"I ain't beat. She'll get over it."

I laugh. "Yeah, and in the meantime, ya dumb ass walkin' 'round homeless and bare-assed 'cause ya girl done did you dirty."

"Never that, dawg," he says, soundin' offended. "I'ma always have me a spot to lay my head. And she'll be blowin' up my ringer tryna get me to come back."

"Whatever, nigga," I say, grippin' the steerin' wheel wit' my left hand, and leanin' my right arm on the armrest. "Ya retarded-ass gonna be right back there gettin' ya ass dragged for tryna fuck her over."

"Maybe."

I laugh harder. "Nigga, *maybe* my ass. Ya simple-ass will."

"Yeah, whatever." He pauses, thinkin', I'm sure. Hell, I'm thinkin' for his ass. I'm thinkin', why the fuck is he so goddamn stupid? And when the fuck is he gonna stop doin' dumb shit? I'm won-derin', why the hell a bitch will fuck up all your shit, then say she blacked out and started wildin'? But when you look 'round the room, your shit is the only shit fucked up. Nuthin' else is touched. How the hell you call ya'self blackin' out and not tearin' the whole house up? What a buncha bullshit!

I hit the button for the CD player. Go to disc four; track four. Wait for Erykah Badu's "I Want You" to rip through the speakers, then spark a blunt. "Yo, nigga, ain't no need sittin' over there stressin' 'bout shit you can't do nuthin' 'bout. It is what it is. Hell, you brought the shit on ya'self. So ain't no need to be bitchin' up. You might as well take a hit off some of this good shit, and let Erykah help ya get ya mind right." I take two deep pulls, then pass the blunt to 'im.

He takes it to the head. "Yo, good lookin' out. This is exactly what I needed." We let silence in. Bob to the beats, passin' the blunt back 'n forth. A haze of thick smoke starts to fill the car. I crack the back windows, and the sunroof. As much as I love to blaze, I hate the smell of that shit in my clothes. And by the time we get into the city, and I make a left onto Beach Street, we've burned two blunts and are feelin' right. Then outta the blue, this muhfucka hits me wit', "Yo, can I squat at ya spot for a few days?"

I cut my eye over at him, blowin' smoke out. "What the fuck just happen to 'I'ma always have me a spot to lay my head,' nigga?"

He sighs. "Man, listen, both of my side pieces beefin' with me, too."

"And why can't you stay at Lynn's or ya other two sisters' spots?"

"I can. But then I gotta hear them bitchin' 'bout shit. I ain't beat."

I shift my focus back to the road, bearin' onto West Broadway, shakin' my head. "You'se a dumb muhfucka."

"Yeah, whatever. So can I crash at ya spot or not?"

I glance back over at him, almost chokin' on blunt smoke. This nigga and I are cool, but we ain't *that* cool where I'ma let 'im rest at my crib. And on top of that, dude's smashin' three chicks and they all muthafuckin' crazy. His ass is on foot now, thanks to one of them nut jobs bustin' out all his windows and tossin' red paint up on the hood of his 2008 Lexus. And another one of them hoes he's fuckin' was responsible for settin' his apartment on fire. Yeah, he says it was an accident; that the curtains caught fire by a candle she knocked over. I'm like, "yeah whatever, nigga." I know better. The bitch caught him in bed wit' another ho and went Fire Marshall Bill on his ass. Fuck what ya heard. This muhfucka's attached to too much damn drama for me. Besides, what the fuck I look like havin' another muhfucka walkin' 'round in his boxers, scratchin' his nuts up in my shit? Not gonna happen.

"Hell no, muhfucka. Ya ass got too much shit goin' on, word up. You betta stay right where you at 'til you can take ya ass back home."

"Damn, that's fucked up. I thought we were boys."

Boys? This nigga done banged his damn head. "Fucked up, hell. I'm keepin' shit real. And that's why I'm not lettin' your triflin' ass rest at my spot, or bring drama up in my space, fuckin' up our friendship. He looks at me kinda funny, but I don't put too much energy into tryna figure out what the look's for. 'Cause bottom line, I don't give a fuck!

He sucks his teeth, sighin'. "Pass me the blunt, muhfucka."

I take another pull, then hand it to 'im.

He takes a deep pull, holds the smoke in his lungs, then says, "That's still fucked up, man."

I make a left onto West Third Street. "Nah, nigga, what's fucked up is you gettin' ya shit housed and not havin' a place to lay ya dumb-ass head."

"Fuck you."

I laugh. "Yeah, aiight, muhfucka. The only one bein' fucked is *you*." I drive 'round the block lookin' for parkin' while thinkin', *what a loser!*

∽22∾

On some real shit, the whole month's been one big-ass blur to me. It seems like the days and weeks flew right past me. I mean like, damn...where the hell did the summer go? It's all good, though. It's already the first week of October. Before you know it, we'll be celebratin' Obama's victory 'cause he's really 'bout to bring it straight to them crackers' heads, for real. Watch what I tell ya. Anyway, I'm chillin' at my spot gettin' ready to tear into this bangin'-ass Philadelphia burger—a thick angus burger topped wit' provolone cheese, grilled onions and hot peppers—and sweet potato fries I picked up at Bobby's Burger Palace when my cell rings. I glance at the screen. It's a 770 area code. I lower the sound to the stereo.

"Yo," I answer.

"Hello, Alley Cat?"

"Yeah, who's this?" I ask, tryna figure out the voice.

"It's Kanika."

"Who?"

"Kanika," she repeats, chucklin'. "You forgot who I am that quick. You called me a couple of months ago, and left a message. We were on the same flight to Atlanta."

"Oh yeah," I reply, surprised to hear from her. *Took ya fine-ass long 'nough to hit a muhfucka back.* "What's good, baby girl?"

My stomach growls. As bad as I wanna fuck this burger up, I don't wanna start smackin' up in her ear 'cause this shit right here calls for usin' two hands, then gettin' down 'n dirty. I dip a few fries into some honey mustard sauce, then shove 'em into my mouth, chewin'.

"Sorry for not calling you sooner. The minute I got back, I had to hit the ground running. It's been nonstop."

"It's all good, baby," I say, swallowin', then takin' a sip of grape juice. "Yo, sorry 'bout that. You caught me in the middle of gettin' ready to eat."

"Oh, don't let me disrupt your meal. I can call you back later."

"Nah, you good. So what's good wit' you?"

"Nothing much; just working a lot. This is actually the first time in weeks I've had a real moment to sit and chill. So I figured now would be a good time to finally return your call."

"I can dig it. I thought I was gonna haveta ring all the doorbells in Stone Mountain to get at ya sexy-ass."

She laughs. "Annnnywaaay, before this conversation goes any further, please let the record state that I will not be added to your little fan club list."

"Dig, you don't have to be. I got a special spot reserved 'specially for you, pretty baby—real talk."

"Oh, is that so?"

"No doubt. So, dig, baby, you gotta man?"

"No, not at the moment," she answers. "What about you?"

"Hell muthafuckin' no, I ain't got no man," I snap, laughin'. "I *am* the man, baby. All six-feet-four, two-hundred-and-fifteen pounds of me. I ain't wit' that dick-grindin' shit."

She laughs wit' me. "You're a mess. I wasn't asking if *you* had a man. I would hope not. But I'm glad you cleared that up. Then again, you never know these—"

"'Then again' nuthin'. I'm strictly 'bout the clit 'n tits attached to a beautiful chick wit' a sweet, wet kitty. So, to answer ya question, I'm solo, baby, but I got a buncha friends."

"Mmmph. I bet you do."

I get up from the sofa and go upstairs to my bedroom. I remove my T-shirt and boxers, then stand in the mirror, flexin' my chest muscles. I pull at my dick and make a note to hit the gym—after I get some pussy today.

"Mmmmm. So, tell me, Mr. Single Man with a Bunch of Friends, what is your belief about relationships and monogamy?"

Shit! That relationships are overrated and monogamy is practically extinct. I pull a half-smoked blunt from outta the ashtray on my nightstand, light it, then take a deep pull, slowly blowin' it out. "Why, you tryna marry me, or sumthin'?"

"Not hardly," she replies, laughin'. "I'm asking to see where your head is, that's all."

I'm hopin' between ya pretty-ass legs—big head, lil' head; either one makes me no never mind. "Oh, I feel you, baby," I say, pausin'. I wanna keep shit real wit' her, but I know if I tell her what I really feel 'bout relationships—that they require too much fuckin' work, that they come wit' too much stress and aggravation for a muh-fucka like me—it'll most likely ruin any chance of me pushin' this dick all the way into the back of her pussy. And I already know if I tell her that I'll take whoremongerin' over monogamy on any given day, hands down, it's a wrap. I take another pull from my blunt.

"Are you smoking?"

"Yeah," I answer, blowin' a cloud of smoke out. "Why, you gotta problem wit' that?"

"Depends on what you're smoking," she says.

"Trees," I tell her. There's a moment of silence, then she starts firin' off a buncha muthafuckin' questions, like she's doin' research for the American Council on Weed Control—not that that shit exists, but hell, it might as well the way she's comin' at my neck. She asks: How often you smoke? *Whenever the fuck I feel like it.*

How long you been smoking? *'Bout as long as I been fuckin'.* Why you smoke? *Uh, duh…I like smokin' the shit. Why you so mutha-fuckin' nosey?* Do you think you're addicted to it? *Hell no! The only thing I'm addicted to is good pussy and wet head.* But, on some real shit, I'ma probably keep burnin' trees 'til the day I die. Fuck what ya heard. You ain't never heard of a muhfucka catchin' lung can-cer from blazin', or a muhfucka dyin' from an overdose. Have you? Exactly!

I keep my answers to myself, changin' the subject. "So, what's good? Can a cat holla or what?"

"Mmmph. Well, if you're trying to see *me*, then I suggest you answer my question."

"Which one? You done hit me wit' so many. You know I smoke. My memory's all jacked up."

She chuckles. "Oh, puhleeze. How convenient. I bet you remem-ber what you wanna remember. I asked you about relationships and monogamy."

I laugh. "Oh, that one." I spark another blunt. "On some real shit, I think relationships only work when two people want them to work. Both parties gotta be on the same page; otherwise, you just askin' for heartache, feel me? And as far as monogamy goes, well…umm, listen. Let me get back to you on that."

"Just what I thought," she says, laughin'. "You probably can't even spell it."

I join in her laughter. I'm diggin' her style. I already know she ain't gonna be no easy lay, and I'm wonderin' if I really wanna put in the work. I mean, I wanna taste them drawers—but, on some real shit, a muhfucka ain't really that pressed. We go back 'n forth for another twenty minutes. She shares some basic shit 'bout herself. And I share some 'bout me. I learn she's twenty-six. That she's an ATL transplant by way of L.A. That she moved to

Atlanta three years ago for a change of scenery and to be closer to her older sister. That she doesn't have any children. That she's a professional model, and travels a lot. But what I really wanna know is: Is she fuckin'?

"So can a brotha spend some time wit' you or what?"

"Maybe. When will you be in town again?"

Now you already know I didn't have plans to be in Atlanta any-time soon, but to get a chance to get up in them hips, a muhfucka gonna make it happen. "I'ma hit you up to let you know."

"Do that," she says, chucklin'. "I'm getting ready to pencil you in right now."

"Nah, baby, wrong answer," I say. "Ink me in. Better yet, I want you to use a bright-red Magic Marker to mark me in."

"And what should it say?"

"It should say, 'Big daddy's comin' through.'" We both laugh, then talk a few minutes more before I say, "Have a good night, pretty baby. I'ma hit you up one day next week."

"Should I hold my breath?"

"Only if you believe." We hang up. I slip my hands back down into my underwear, then cup and massage my balls, smilin'.

Ten a.m., Wednesday mornin' my cell rings, wakin' me the fuck up. I start to let it go into voicemail, but reach over and grab it off the nightstand. I peep the caller ID, then answer. "What's good?"

"Hey, baaaaaaby," Vita screeches into the phone. I roll my eyes up in my head. Between her notes on BlackPlanet, her IM's and these calls, I'm thinkin' this lil' bitch has the potential to become another stalker if her ass wasn't so afraid of gettin' on a plane and leavin' her lil' box of a world. I guess it's a good thing the ho doesn't travel anywhere farther north than North Carolina. Otherwise, she'd be tryna hunt me down e'ery chance she got. "How you been? Did you get my messages? I've left you like four and sent you a few notes on BP."

I yawn and stretch. Although I'm not beat to fuck wit' her ass, today I decide to indulge her. I'm tryna get at Kanika's fine ass, and I want her to sponsor my trip. "I'm good, baby," I say, iggin' all the other questions. "I've been thinkin' 'bout you."

"For real?" she asks, soundin' surprised 'n excited.

"No doubt, baby."

"Then why haven't I heard from you? I was starting to get worried about you since you haven't returned any of my calls or responded to any of my emails. I didn't know what to think. Is everything okay?"

"Yeah, baby, e'erything's good. I've just been real stressed out 'n shit. But it's nuthin' for you to worry ya pretty lil'"—*Pumkin*, I think—"head over. I'ma be aiight."

"What's wrong?" she asks, soundin' concerned for a muhfucka. "Why are you stressed?"

"This job shit," I lie, "has me 'bout ready to snap on a muhfucka. A nigga can't seem to get a break. I been out beatin' the pavement puttin' in mad applications, and these muhfuckas ain't bitin'. And the ones who are ain't tryna pay a nigga shit. Or, as soon as they know I gotta record, they get on some other shit, like 'we'll get back to you,' knowin' damn well they gonna toss my app in the trash. Baby, I'm tellin' you, it's real hard out here for a muhfucka wit' a record."

"A record?" she asks, soundin' surprised. "What kind of record?" *Duh, a criminal record, what else?* I sigh, then give her a bullshit-ass story 'bout hustlin' drugs, then gettin' bagged 'cause some jealous, bitch-ass niggas snitched on me. "OhmyGod, that's messed up. How long were you locked up?"

"Five years," I tell her. I figure since I'm already on a roll with the lies, I might as well stretch the shit out as far as it can go.

"Five years? Wow. How long have you been out?"

"I've been home for three years, and been off parole for two. I swear, baby, I don't wanna go back to the streets. But these muh-fuckas gonna have a nigga hittin' up the block, if sumthin' doesn't pop off soon."

"You gotta be patient, and not give up," she offers. "You gotta keep the faith, and know something greater is coming to you. Selling drugs is only a temporary fix. Sure, it'll put fast money in your pockets, but what happens if you get locked up again?"

I roll my eyes up in my head. I know she means well, but I don't need no preachy-ass ho tryna give me no sermon. The only thing I wanna hear is how much money she's gonna peel off to a muhfucka.

"Well, I say," sighin', "at this point, I'll take my chances. A nigga needs some paper in his pockets, you smell me? It's got me feelin' low 'n shit. That's why I haven't called you..." I pause, smilin', givin' her biscuit-head time to sort out what I've told her. I decide to go in for the kill. "...You got my head all fucked up, baby. I've been thinkin' 'bout you, and missin' you, and wantin' to see you 'n shit. I wanna hold you in my arms real bad, but a nigga can't even afford to buy a muthafuckin' plane ticket. That's how broke I am. And it's got my head all fucked up right now."

"OhmyGod, for reeeeeeaaaaaal? You don't know how that makes me feel. I wanna see you, too. You have no idea how much I've been missing you. All I've been doing is thinking about you, and how much I enjoyed being with you. The last thing you need to do is be thinking about selling drugs again. Why don't you come out here and stay for awhile? Who knows, you might have better luck finding a job here."

I grin. "Baby, where am I gonna stay?"

"With me," she replies, soundin' all excited to have some dick in her life, "where else? My home is your home, baby. And you can stay here for as long as you need to, until you can get on your feet."

I slide my hand down in my pants, play wit' my dick, grinnin'. I'm tellin' you. Fuck a weak-minded or emotionally starved broad right, and she'll do whatever you want wit' little to no coercion.

I don't say shit; let her think the phone went dead.

"Hello, Alex? You still there?"

I lower my voice, sniffle a bit. "Yeah, baby. I'm here."

"What's wrong?"

"I'm thinkin', that's all. I can't believe you wanna do all this for me."

"I know this might sound crazy because we don't really know each other, but I feel like I love you, Alley Cat."

Umm, med check...please, I think, sparkin' a blunt. *Looks like we gotta looney on the loose.* I thought I already warned her once not to catch feelin's. I decide to give her a gentle reminder. "Listen, boo, on some real shit, I really 'preciate you havin' my back and all, but a muhfucka ain't wit' all that love shit, right now."

"I know, I know. You already told me that. And I respect that. Still, you can't stop me from feeling what I feel, whether you ever feel the same or not."

I sigh, shakin' my head. She's been warned.

"I'll call you in a few days with your flight info, okay, baby?"

"I'll be waitin'," I tell her, disconnectin' the call.

23

Three days later, Vita hits me up on my cell. "Yo, what's good, pretty baby?"

"Hey, sexy man," she says, soundin' like she's grinnin' from ear to ear. I can practically see this thirsty bitch droolin'. "I've been thinking about you. You miss me? I know I miss you, bad."

What the fuck?! Hell no, I don't miss ya weeble-wobblin' ass. "I've been thinkin' 'bout you, too. Hearin' ya voice really put a smile on a nigga's face. What's good?"

"You," she tells me, like I don't already know this. "I made your flight reservations. I'm gonna text you the information." I roll my eyes. *Why the fuck didn't you just text the shit in the first place?*

"Oh, aiight. That's wassup. Good lookin' out, baby." Eight seconds later, the text comes through wit' all the flight info. She got me leavin' out next Wednesday on Delta. *What the fuck? I don't fly no muthafukin' Delta! All my frequent flier miles are wit' Continental.* I look at the text again, then frown. "Ya text came through. But, uh, where's the return info?"

"Oh, I got you a one-way ticket."

No shit, bitch! I take a deep breath, shakin' my head. "Why?"

"I thought you were gonna stay for a while so you can check out the jobs here. Whenever you're ready to go back, I'll just book you a return flight."

What a dumb ass. "Oh, aiight. And you still gonna hook a nigga up wit' some wheels while I'm out there, right?"

"It's all taken care of."

I smirk. "That's wassup."

"I told you I was gonna take care of everything."

"True that. Good lookin' out, babe. I hope you know how much this means to me."

She giggles, then whispers. "I can't wait for you to get here, so you can show me just how much gratitude and appreciation you have. I got something real tight waiting for you."

"Is it wet?"

"Yep. And real slippery."

I lower my voice. "Stop that, baby. You makin' my dick hard."

"Oooooh, squeeze it for me."

I roll my eyes up in my head. "I'ma let you squeeze it when I see you, aiight?"

She giggles again. "That's even better."

For some reason, imaginin' Vita bent over a tool bench wit' her pudgy-lil' feet stuffed in a pair of red stilettos, while poppin' her puffy ass wit' a wooden paddle, makes my dick pulse. "What kinda panties you got on?" I ask her, pullin' my dick outta the slit of my boxers.

She whispers into the phone, "Pink lace."

"Thong, g-string, French-cut; what type?"

"Thong," she says.

"Oh, aiight. That's wassup. Listen, baby, you got a muhfucka wantin' to nut, so I'ma bounce so I can pop one off, aiight?"

"Mmmm, I wish I was there to watch."

"Yeah, me too, so you could lick all 'round these big-ass balls for me."

"Mmmm, daddy. I...can...not...wait to see you."

I shake my head. "Look, boo, I done warned you 'bout gettin' too caught up in a muhfucka like me; just let shit flow."

"I know, I know. But, still…I miss you. And my pussy misses you even more."

It's obvious she's the type who has to learn the hard way. I shake my head. So I guess it'll be my fault when this ho falls outta her cuckoo's nest, and starts losin' it, right? Yeah, whatever!

"Damn, I wanna get up between them legs and slow fuck the shit outta you."

She moans into the phone. "You make me so horny when you talk like that. Shoot, I gotta go, though, 'cause I'm still at work." She sucks her teeth.

"Oh, aiight. Enjoy the rest of your day."

"You, too, big daddy."

"Hit me up later, aiight, baby?"

"Are you gonna pick up? Seems like whenever I call you, you don't answer my calls."

Maybe, I think to tell her. But I say, "No doubt," instead.

The minute we disconnect, I hit Kanika up. She doesn't answer, but I leave her a message lettin' her know when I'ma be in town.

I want my dick wet, I think, scrollin' through my address book. I decide to hit up Shalonda—this lil' brown-skinned shortie I fuck wit' e'ery now and then over in Bloomfield. We met last summer on a chatline. The bitch is broke, but she sucks a mean dick. And she swallows. So that's basically all she's good for. She answers on the third ring.

"Hey, stranger, long time, no hear."

"What's good, baby?"

"You," she tells me.

"That's wassup." I pause, decidin' to get straight to the point. "Yo, you still suckin' dick?"

"Yeah, why?"

I suck my teeth. "'Cause I want my dick sucked, you stupid

bitch!" I hear myself sayin' in my head. Instead I say, "You should come through and hit me wit' some of that bomb-ass lip service."

"We fuckin'?"

"Nah, baby, I just want my dick sucked, feel me? No convo. No fuckin'. Just suck and muthafuckin' go. So, you wit' it or what?"

She sighs. "If I'm comin' out, I wanna ride down on some dick."

"Look, I told you I ain't checkin' for no pussy right now; just some slow, sloppy, wet dick suckin'."

"Damn, that's real fucked up. You comin' at me like I'm some real live dick washer."

Stupid bitch, you are! "Yo, it is what it is. I'm keepin' shit real wit' you. You either suckin' this dick, or you not. What's it gonna be? 'Cause I ain't 'bout to be on this phone all day goin' back 'n forth wit' you."

"I'm not," she says.

"Then that's what it is. I'm out." *Click.* I bang on her retarded ass, then call Keisha. She picks up all eager 'n shit on the first ring.

"Hello?"

"What's good, baby?"

"You."

"Oh, word? It's like that?"

"You already know," she says. I can tell the ho is smilin' from ear to ear. Another call is comin' through. I peep the number. It's Sholanda's dumb-ass callin' back. I guess her trick ass has a change of heart and is ready to get her throat stretched. I ignore the bitch and keep on talkin'.

"That's wassup. You feel like swabbin' some dick?"

"I don't know. It all depends on whose dick it is. Why?"

Why the fuck these silly-ass hoes gotta play? "I'm tryna get this nut off, that's why."

She sucks her teeth, sighin'. "Well, you gonna have to come to me 'cause I don't feel like driving."

I smile. "I'm on my way."

Twenty minutes later, I'm showered, dressed and headed toward the parkway. Foxy Brown's old joint "Hot Spot" is pumpin'. I got the windows down, and my left arm draped outta the driver's side, chillin'. It's nice as fuck out, and a nigga's pissed that I'm posted up in this muthafuckin' hooptie, instead of flossin' in my shiny whip. But it is what it is. Like I said before, I'll be damned if I let another ho fuck my shit up again. I shake my head, thinkin' 'bout Racquel's smutty-ass smearin' dog shit on my muthafuckin' windows, talkin' 'bout the dog shit was for bein' such a lyin', no-good dog. Go figure! What kinda bitch would scoop up animal shit and smear it on a muhfucka's windshield? A *craaaaazy*-ass one would!

I'll never forget the night that it happened. I was at this club in Newark chillin' 'n flossin' wit' my boys and poppin' mad shit to a buncha bitches. At three a.m. we comin' outta the club, and as I get to the spot where my whip is parked, I see my muthafuckin' shit is sittin' kinda low. I'm like, "What the fuck?" I walk up on my shit, and all four tires are slaughtered. Somebody had flat-bedded me! A muhfucka was heated. Muhfuckas were out there clownin' me, word up. And I wasn't diggin' it. Then to add insult to injury, someone had smeared shit all over my windows. I was out there spazzin' for real, tryna figure out who the fuck did me in. Then all of a sudden, a dark car slowly drove by and I spotted *her*. She yelled outta her window, "Hey, Alley Cat! I hope you like the smell of that dog shit, nigga, 'cause that's just what the fuck you are; you black bastard!" She sped off, laughin'. Yo, you shoulda seen me. I started chasin' the car like a madman, but the bitch ran a red light and left me in the dust. Man, listen...that night, if I'd had a brick, I woulda thrown it straight at her dome.

I sigh, shakin' my head. *Crazy-ass bitches! If they weren't good for suckin' dick and givin' up the pussy, I wouldn't fuck wit' 'em. I'd beat my dick and keep it movin'.* I pull up in front of Keisha's spot and park. I text her, lettin' her know I'm outside and to be on her knees ready to take this hard, horny dick in her mouth. She texts back: The doors already unlocked. I'll be on my knees waitin'. Have ya dick out and I'll take care of the rest. I grin, walkin' up to her door, unfastenin' my belt and unzippin' my jeans.

Yeah, it's broad daylight, and? If ya ass ain't seen a muhfucka's dick before, then I guess you 'bout to catch more than an eyeful. I open her door, holdin' my dick in my hand, closin' it behind me wit' my foot. I smile. She's on her knees blindfolded and naked wit' her mouth wide open, ready and waitin'. I walk over to her, then slowly slide the head of my dick in between her wet dick suckas. I pump her skull 'til a thick cream coats her throat. Then I pull out and jack the rest of my nut all over her face, smearin' the last few drops 'round her lips.

24

"Yo, baby girl, what's poppin' wit' that threesome? Or were you just runnin' ya dick sucka?" I ask as soon as Falani picks up. I get outta bed, stretchin'. I was 'posed to get at her weeks ago 'bout settin' this ep up. She probably thought I forgot. I yawn, glancin' over at the clock: 9:24 A.M.

I spark a blunt. Take two puffs, holdin' the smoke in my lungs, then head to the bathroom to drain the snake.

"Well, damn. It's taken you long enough to finally get back to me. But no, I wasn't fronting. It's a go. All you gotta do is get here. My girl was asking me the other day if I had heard from you. She's definitely with it. After I told her about you, that's all she's been talking about." I exhale. "We're waiting on you."

When I'm done pissin', I wash my hands, starin' at myself in the mirror. *You'se a sexy, black muhfucka*, I think, dryin' my hands. "Oh, aiight. That's what it is. What's the chick's name, again?" I walk back into the bedroom. I throw on a pair of sweats and a hoodie, then sit on the edge of the bed to slip on my Nikes.

"Lydia."

I grab my car keys and head downstairs, walkin' into the kitchen. "Oh, aiight. She look good?"

"Yeah, she's decent-looking." I frown. When a chick says another chick is only decent-lookin', that means one of two things for me: She's either fly as hell and bein' hated on, or she's related to a damn gorilla.

"Don't have me layin' up wit' nobody lookin' like Shrek, or some wildebeest 'n shit."

She laughs. "She's far from either, trust me."

"Oh, aiight. Just makin' sure. So when we makin' it pop?"

"You tell me. You're the one who seems to have the busy schedule."

"Next Friday," I tell her, lookin' at the mini calendar on the 'fridge door. I open it and take out a bottle of Dasani water, open it, then guzzle it down.

"Okay, perfect. I'll let her know."

"Bet. You gonna eat that ho's pussy while I fuck you from the back, right?"

She laughs. "I don't know about all that. I might let her eat mine, but I don't think I can stomach licking another woman's pussy. And why she gotta be a ho?"

'Cause that's what the fuck she is. I suck my teeth, iggin' the question. "Yo, go 'head wit' that corny shit. Talkin' 'bout you ain't eatin' no pussy. Fuck outta here."

She huffs. "OhmyGod...how is that being corny? Would you be down to suck a nigga's dick, if I wanted a threesome with you and another dude?

Is this cum-breath ho fuckin' serious, askin' me some dumb shit like that? She knows damn well no real nigga suckin' another nigga's joint, period! "You musta bumped ya damn head. Hell muthafuckin' no! I ain't on that homo shit."

"Hmmm...but, you think I am."

"Yo, ain't nuthin' homo 'bout two freaky broads gettin' it in," I tell her, lockin' up Pops' spot and then gettin' in my ride. "I think that shit's sexy as fuck, watchin' a fly-ass chick munchin' another bitch's snapper while throwin' her fatty up on this big-ass dick. It's time you take ya friendship to the next level. Step outta ya box, baby, and let it do what it do. Slurp ya girl up while I stretch ya back out. I'm tellin' ya; it'll make y'all's bond tighter." I spark a blunt, then take two pulls, slowly blowin' it outta the side of my mouth. Fuck the dumb shit she talkin'. I already know what it is. Wit' a few drinks and the right mood, this freak bitch'll be lappin' at the clit.

"Yeah, whatever." She laughs. "That's what your mouth says."

"Nah, baby…it's what I'm tryna get ya mouth to do, but you wanna be on some extra-dumb shit."

"I can't believe you're serious."

"Hell muthafuckin' yeah, I'm serious. Oh, so what you thought; I was gonna lay back and let both of you suck my dick, then fuck you both one at a time and that was gonna be aiight wit' me?" I ask, slowin' down to pay the toll. *Crook-ass muhfuckas*, I think, handin' the attendant a twenty. *A fuckin' dolla to ride the muthafuckin' highway. That's some real bullshit.* I take my change, then pull off.

"I told you, she can eat me. Other than that, I'm not making any promises."

"Nah, baby, I ain't that kinda dude. I need a lil' more than that. Seein' two chicks freak is what bricks my dick. I wanna see you sixty-ninin' that shit."

"Hmmm…and what am I getting out the deal?"

"The best of both worlds," I say, laughin'.

"Yo, what the fuck, asshole?!" I snap on this dumb-ass cracker bitch who keeps ridin' his brakes in front of me. "Oh, my bad," I say, gettin' into the next lane. "This dumb fuck in front of me, tryna cause a damn accident out here." I drive up alongside the car, ready to ice-grill whoever it is. But, I shake my head when I see it's an old-ass woman wit' her seat way up to the steerin' wheel. The dumb bitch is practically sittin' up on the dashboard. "So, you tryna let a nigga taste ya girl's pussy on ya lips or what?"

She finally says maybe; that she'll think about it.

I grin, finishin' up my blunt, then tossin' it out the window. "Yeah, baby, you do that. I'ma see what's really good when I come up next week."

"Cool."

"Yo, I'ma need a few dollas, though. You got me?"

She sighs, pausin'. "Listen, I'm not really into making it a habit of giving a man money, especially one I'm not dealing with."

"Oh, aiight, I feel you. It is what it is," I say, knowin' she's talkin' that shit for now. But just like I had her peelin' off paper the last time, she'll be doin' it again—real soon. Believe that. In the meantime, where one won't, two more will. So it's all good. "Look, baby, let me get up off this line. I'll get at ya next week."

The week flies by and a muhfucka's been real low key for the most part of it, chillin' here at my own spot. Hittin' the gym hard, and not really fuckin' much; just straight chillin'. Oh, and gettin' brain a few nights here and there, but nuthin' major. And believe it or not, I turned my cell off for two days, so I didn't have to be bothered wit' anyone. When I finally turned the shit back on, my mailbox was full. Most of the calls were from Vita, Akina, Maleeka, Shalonda, and Tamera's smutty ass. You already know I ain't hittin' her back. And the rest of 'em can wait 'til a muhfucka's beat to fuck wit' 'em.

My cell rings. I peep the caller ID, and smile. It's Cherry.

"What it do, pretty baby?"

"It bangs my pussy up until it whistles, and fucks a horny woman like me into a coma."

"Damn, you tryna get shit poppin', I see. You ready for this dick, huh?"

"I've been ready. And I'm long overdue. Speaking of which, I bought your ticket. And I wired you a few dollars to hold you over until you get here. The money is already there waiting for you."

I grin. See, this is what I like 'bout Cherry. She hooks a muhfucka up wit'out me havin' to go through a whole buncha extras. No questions asked, she makes shit happen. And she doesn't stress a muhfucka out tryna keep tabs on 'im. "Oh, word? Good lookin' out. You know I really 'preciate you, baby."

"Well, hopefully you'll give me at least two weeks to show me how much."

Two weeks? What the fuck?! "Damn, baby…you know I can't leave my moms home alone that long. I told you she's in a wheelchair." Yeah, yeah, yeah, I know it's fucked up sayin' shit like that 'bout Moms and all, but hey…it is what it is.

"Oooh, big daaaaddy," she coos into the phone, "don't do me like that. I need you."

"Oh, word?"

"Mmmm, you have no idea how bad. Besides all the shopping we'll do, imagine two weeks of you fucking me deep in my tight ass, my wet pussy and down in my throat anywhere, anytime, as many times as you want."

I almost laugh. This bitch knows damn well she ain't ready to have me punchin' up her tonsils. "Damn, baby, you tryna get my dick hard."

She laughs. "Is it the shopping, or the idea of fucking that's doing it?"

"Both," I tell her, laughin'. "And right now, my shit's on brick."

"Mmmmph, just how I like it. Give me two weeks with you, baby. I promise you I'll make it well worth your while."

"Damn, baby, you makin' this hard for me to say no to. But…"

"No, 'buts,'" she says, cuttin' me off. "Before you say anything else about leaving your mother alone unattended, you need to know I've wired you enough money for you to hire someone to stay with her while you're gone. So please. No excuses. I wanna see you. And I want you all to myself for two whole weeks."

She tells me she's hit a nigga up wit' five gees, and will keep my pockets lined while I'm there. Even though two weeks is a bit extra, you already know a muhfucka like me ain't tryna pass up on an opportunity to fuck and shop, then fuck and shop some more. And still come off wit' some paper. So a muhfucka's gonna do what he's gotta do.

"I'm all yours, baby," I finally tell her. "I'm all yours."

25

Friday night rolls 'round, and shit's 'bout to get poppin' up in this piece. I fucked Falani down real good, earlier today; served her this dick nice 'n slow. Although I wanted to beat that shit up, I didn't wanna have her insides burnin' and her walls swollen. So I went easy on her. And since she had her beaver shaved this time, I gave her an extra treat. I ran a few laps 'round her fat clit wit' my tongue, held her pussy in my mouth and tongue fucked her, before drivin' this dick deep in her. I slow stroked her hole, while suckin' on her titties 'til she cried.

Now here I am stretched out 'cross her sofa in a pair of red silk boxers, waitin' for the freak show to begin. Oh, and just to let ya know. The ho came up offa some paper like I said she would. Talkin' that dumb shit 'bout not makin' it a habit givin' a nigga money. Fuck outta here. That shit might apply to them duck-ass niggas she's used to fuckin', but unless I'm straight charity-fuckin' a broad, she can say whatever she wants. But if I push this dick up in her guts, eventually, she's gonna come up offa that fetti. And that's what it is. I glance over at the clock on her glass and wood end table: 8:27 p.m. She's already twenty-seven minutes late. *I hope this bitch don't front.*

Five minutes later, the doorbell rings. Falani goes to the door and opens it. I hear her greetin' someone, and as soon as her peoples walks through the door, I do a double-take. The first thing I see is a set of long, shapely legs in a pair of stilettos. I slowly lift my eyes over her as she closes the door behind her. She's a fine, thick, milk-chocolate chick wit' a long black ponytail—*a muthafuckin' clip-on, I bet*—big doe-shaped eyes, long lashes, and beautiful thick, dick-suckas. I immediately imagine 'em wrapped 'round this dick, deep throatin' it 'til I coat her throat and tongue wit' this hot custard. Falani greets her wit' a hug, then walks her into where I'm sittin' and introduces her.

"Lydia, this is Alley, uh…Alex. Alex, Lydia."

I slowly lick my lips, standin' up. "Yo, what's good, baby," I say, eyein' her as she steps outta her black three-quarter trench. She's wearin' some kinda red spandex-type dress that clings to her curves. I lick my lips, again.

She smiles. "OhmyGod, giiiirl, you didn't tell me he was *this* fine."

"Oh, whatever," Falani says, rollin' her eyes. "I did, too."

"No, what you said was he looked aiight. Not that he was a deep dish of delicious, dark chocolate."

I laugh. "Thanks, baby. And she told me you were decent-lookin'."

"Typical Falani," she replies, cuttin' her eyes over at her, laughin' wit' me while walkin' over and extendin' her manicured hand. "Always hatin'. Nice to finally meet you."

I step into her space. "I wanna hug," I tell her, pullin' her into my muscular arms. "Nice to meet you, too." Her light, airy scent is intoxicatin'. "Damn, baby, you smell good and feel good."

"Thanks. You don't smell too bad yourself."

"I'm gonna leave the two of you to get better acquainted while I get things ready," Falani says, goin' toward the bedroom.

"Yeah, you do that," Lydia says, runnin' her hands along my chest, then squeezin' my arms. "Oooh, and a rock-hard body to go with all that sexiness. Your pictures do you no justice."

"Aaah, baby, you tryna make me blush." *I knew Falani was hatin' on this broad*, I think, still holdin' onto her toned, tight body. I press my cock up into her stomach, let her feel what she's 'bout to get, then let go. She takes a seat on the sofa and I sit in the chair 'cross from her. I decide to get right to the point. "So how often you get into threesomes 'n shit?"

"Not that often. I've only been in three, maybe four, over the last five years. Last year was the last time."

"Mmm, that's wassup. So, what you like gettin' into?"

She sits back in her seat and crosses her legs, revealin' her smooth, silky thighs. "I like it all."

I smile. Ask her to elaborate and she does. She tells me how she likes eatin' pussy, suckin' dick, eatin' ass, takin' dick in her ass and deep in her pussy; that she likes strappin' on dildoes and fuckin' other chicks—and niggas. I keep a straight face when she says that shit. But I'm thinkin', "what the fuck?"

"I see you a real freaky chick."

"Just very open-minded. And you?"

"I can rock wit' the best of 'em, baby. I'm pretty much down for whateva, 'cept fuckin' and suckin' another muhfucka or gettin' dicked in the ass. So if you got any ideas 'bout runnin' that rubber dick up in a muhfucka, you can cancel that. You got the wrong one."

She sucks her teeth, diggin' in her bag. "Damn," she says, pullin' out a long-ass pink dildo. "Not even the head?" She laughs. I don't.

"Damn straight," I say, eyein' her. "Unless you tryna get ya jaw broke, don't even think it."

Falani walks back into the room wearin' a dark-pink lace bra and crotchless panty set, carryin' a tray wit' two drinks—one for her, the other for Lydia—and a bottle of water, for me. She looks sexy as hell. I lick my lips and grin, rememberin' how she bounced her fluffy ass up on this dick earlier.

"I brought ya'll something to drink," she says, handin' Lydia a glass, then walkin' over and handin' me mine.

"Thanks, babe."

"So, have the two of you gotten acquainted?" The question is for the both of us, but she looks over at me as she takes a seat on the sofa.

I smile. "Oh, no doubt. I'm diggin' her style."

Lydia uncrosses her legs, shifts in her seat, then crosses her right leg over her left. "And I'm diggin' yours." She looks at Falani, takin' a sip of her drink. "Giiiirrrl, this is delicious. What is it?"

She grins. "Oh, just a little something I whipped up with pineapple and cranberry juice, Ketel One and a splash of Patrón to help us get the party started. After three rounds of drinks and thirty minutes into all this meet-'n-greet shit, a muhfucka is startin' to get restless. I'm not beat for all this back-'n-forth chitter-chat. I'm ready to put work in."

"Yo, ya'll need to come up outta all them clothes," I say, standin' up and pullin' off my boxers. "I'm ready to see and feel some wet pussy." Lydia's mouth drops and her eyes widen as she takes in my body and gazes down at my dick. I take it in both hands and start strokin' it.

"OhmyGod, you gotta beautiful body," she tells me, tossin' her head back and gulpin' down her drink, "and a scrumptious-looking dick."

Falani smiles, standin' up. "Well, I guess it's time we take this party into the bedroom."

"No, not yet," I tell her. "I want ya'll to sit next to each other on the sofa and watch me stroke this dick while both of you play in ya pussies." I shake my dick, then stroke it backward and forward in deep slow movements 'til it starts to thicken. They both spread open their legs. Falani throws her left leg up over Lydia's right leg. Lydia leans in, slips her hand between Falani's legs and begins massagin' her pussy. Falani does the same. They both start to moan, tryna make the other nut. "Yeah, get them pussies wet."

The two of them go at it for about 'nother twenty minutes, kissin' and suckin' on each other's tits, before they finally bust off all over the other's fingers and hands. When they finish nuttin', I tell 'em to lick their fingers, then kiss. They do. I stroke my dick deeper, harder and faster. And as I'm about to nut, I order them both to get on their knees to catch this milk. Interestin'ly, Lydia's real nasty 'n greedy wit' it. She wants the dick in her mouth, wants to taste this nut instead of havin' it splattered on her face. The bitch doesn't wanna share any of it wit' Falani, either. And it's aiight by me. I allow her to guzzle it all down. When she finishes, she leans over and grabs Falani by the back of the head, then shoves her tongue down into her mouth. They are swappin' spit and cum back 'n forth. I grin. Say what the fuck you want, but I already know what it is. Falani's freak, nasty-ass is a lyin'-ass bitch. She's played in this scene before.

Ten minutes later, we are in the bedroom. Falani is lyin' back on the bed wit' her legs open. She starts rubbin' her clit and pussy, while Lydia crawls between her legs, kisses the inside of her thighs, then shifts her body into the sixty-nine position. Her pussy hovers over Falani's face and I'm watchin' to see what the fuck she's gonna do. Lydia starts suckin' her pussy and Falani lets out a moan.

"Yo, eat that shit, baby," I urge Falani as I stroke my hard dick. After a lil' more coaxin', she finally does what she's told. Lickin' 'n lappin' and moanin'. "Yeah, there you go. You talkin' 'bout you wouldn't eat no pussy. You tearin' that shit up, baby. That's right; tongue-fuck her pussy."

I watch the two of them gettin' it in, munchin' on each other's pussies, moanin' and buckin' their hips as I roll a condom down on my dick. I grin at Falani, thinkin', *This bitch eats pussy better than me*. My dick hovers over her head. She peeps what's 'bout to go down—as I slide my dick into the back of Lydia's wet, slippery hole—and reaches up and rubs the back of my balls. Lydia's ass is big, soft and fluffy as cotton, and her pussy's tight and hot.

"Gotdamn, you got some wet pussy," I say, slowly pushin' my dick in her. She moans. But the ho doesn't flinch as I keep pushin' more of my dick up in her. When I finally get all of it up in her, I stand still and let her bounce her ass back up on it. Falani is still beneath us. She cups my balls, then lifts her head up and starts lickin' 'em as they smack up against the back of Lydia's pussy. Man, listen...havin' my balls rubbed and squeezed and licked while diggin' out some pussy has me goin'.

I groan. "Aaah, shit..."

I pull open Lydia's ass, spit into her hole, then stick my middle finger into her asshole. She moans, rotatin' her hips, and greedily eatin' Falani's pussy, causin' her to shake. Both of these hoes are moanin' loudly. I'm thrashin' the shit outta Lydia, feedin' the back of her pussy wit' this dick. She starts nuttin' and wettin' my dick, splashin' pussy juice all over. I squeeze her hips and continue assaultin' her slippery walls. "Uh...ooooh, aaah...ooh, ya dick feels so good..."

After 'bout ten minutes of Lydia eatin' Falani out, she climbs off of her. And Falani lifts and spreads open her legs, waitin' for me to slide up into her eager hole. I hover over her, then push my dick in as she wraps her legs 'round my waist.

She moans. I grab and squeeze her titties, then slip her left nipple into my mouth. While I'm long-strokin' Falani, Lydia gets behind me and starts playin' wit' my ass. She pulls it open. I tighten, then relax my ass muscles as I feel her tongue brush against my hole. She sticks her tongue in it. A muhfucka moans—loud, and my already bricked dick goes straight to steel, causin' me to stretch Falani's insides more. She screams, diggin' her nails into my back. Lydia starts bitin' on my ass, then lickin' and kissin' up my spine. Lickin' and kissin' my shoulders, then kissin' and nibblin' on my neck. I crane my head toward her and allow her to slip her tongue into my mouth. The mixture of Falani's pussy and the smell of my scent on Lydia's tongue got a nigga feelin' extra horny. We slob each other down while I'm beatin' Falani's pussy up.

I continue slow-strokin' Falani, while Lydia leans in and starts flickin' her tongue against Falani's clit, 'causin' her to arch her back. Lydia reaches up and pinches and tweaks Falani's left nipple. I lift her legs and push 'em toward her chest so I can stroke the front, back and center of her pussy. I give it to her deep. She continues moanin' and beggin', bitin' down on her bottom lip. Her face twists up from the combination of pleasure and sweet pain that I'm servin' her.

"Yeah, baby, nut for daddy," I urge, stickin' a finger into her asshole.

All of a sudden Lydia starts grindin' down on Falani's face, moanin'. Then starts talkin' real slick-like. And the shit was turnin' a muhfucka on. "Oh, yes…oh, yes…suck my pussy, bitch. Yeah, you fine, black muthafucker, eat that bitch's pussy…make her pussy nut, you sexy nigga…I'ma bust my nut all in this pretty bitch's mouth…" Falani moans. She moans. And don't ask me why a muhfucka starts moanin', too. But I do. Then I shock the shit outta myself. I stop tongue-fuckin' Falani and tell Lydia to go put on her strap-on. I want her to fuck Falani while I fuck her from the back. I go back to eatin' Falani 'til she comes back wit' her rubber dick swingin' from its harness. I back outta the way and let her slide up in and start strokin' Falani's walls. Falani gasps. I get behind Lydia, pull open her ass cheeks, then start eatin' her pussy and asshole.

Both of these freaky bitches are moanin', which is only turnin' a muhfucka on more. I stick two fingers into the back of Lydia's pussy, twist and probe her walls. When I find her spot, I massage it, causin' her to scream and slam her rubber cock deeper into Falani.

"Suck my titties, you sexy bitch," Lydia orders Falani, thrustin' a mile a minute in and outta her. I can hear the swishin' of her juices as Lydia beats her pussy up.

Falani moans.

"Yeah, you freaky bitch," I chime in, slappin' Lydia's ass, "fuck her pussy…"—I reach over and stroke Falani's clit—"You like how she's fuckin' you, don't you, baby?"

Falani moans again. Then Lydia moans.

I stand up, dip at the knees, then slide my dick into the back of her pussy. She gasps, sucks in a buncha air. And braces herself as her legs start to shake. I slow-grind into her. Give her a chance to get used to this dick. She catches her breath. I grind. She grinds. I'm fuckin' her. She's fuckin' Falani. And together we find a rhythm that causes us all to moan. I can't front, they both got some good pussy, but Lydia's takes the prize. She's deep and wide, and knows howta pull my dick into her. The bitch almost has Maleeka beat in takin' this dick.

I slam my dick into Lydia. She slams hers into Falani. All three of us start moanin' and groanin and pantin' and gruntin' like wolves in heat. We fuck, suck 'n lick each other 'til almost three A.M., then fall asleep wrapped up in each other's arms—sweaty, funky and exhausted.

26

This bitch can't suck dick worth shit! I think while I'm stretched out in the middle of Cherry's king-sized California bed. I caught the 6:50 A.M. flight into L.A. this mornin'. The flight got into LAX at 9:54. We got to her spot at 10:40, and was butt-ass naked by 10:43. Now it's 11:38 and she's on her knees beside me bobbin' her head up 'n down, scrapin' my shit wit' her teeth. "Yo, ma, go easy down there. It should be more lip 'n tongue and no teeth." She wants to learn to suck this dick bad. But she's failin' miserably! I told her ass the last time I was here that she needs to throat train on a five- or six-inch-dick muhfucka, or practice on one of her dildoes—first. Shit. To teach a bitch howta suck dick requires a buncha patience that I don't have. I wanna ho to already know howta throat a muhfucka, feel me?

"Hol' up," I say, raisin' up on my left forearm. "Give me ya hand"—I take her right hand, and place it midway on my shaft—"now take ya tongue and lick the tip of my dick like you would a lollipop or an ice-cream cone." She does. But her tongue service is dry as hell. "C'mon, baby, put some spit up on that dick. Wet that shit up." I slide two fingers into her wet pussy. Jab 'n twist 'em in 'n outta her hole. She moans. Although I 'preciate her attempt to wet this dick, she's gonna need a whole lotta practice, or end up gettin' her teeth knocked the fuck out. Goddamn! If I don't stop her now, I'ma end up screamin' on her ass, or punchin' her in the back of her muthafuckin' head. I close my eyes, take a deep breath, then slap her on the ass. "Yo, baby, 'nough of this half-ass dick-suckin'." I reach for her. Pull my dick from outta her grip. "Let me eat this sweet-ass pussy from the back, then stroke ya guts up." She reluctantly stops what she's doin' and gets on all fours. I get behind her and put this tongue to work. She starts moanin', groanin, beggin' and clutchin' the sheets 'til she nuts. Then I slide my dick in her, slowly stirrin' it in and out, then thrustin' deep 'til I'm ready to spit this milk. I pull out. Yank off the condom. "Here it comes, baby," I say, pumpin' my dick in and outta my hand. She quickly turns to face me, opens her mouth and holds her titties in her hands, eagerly waitin' for me to paint her lips wit' my nut. I grunt, deepen my strokes, then pop a thick, hot nut all on her face, in her mouth and over her titties. She licks her lips, then sucks the nut off her titties. "Yeah, baby, you daddy's lil' cumslut, huh?" She moans. Reaches for my still-hard dick, and slips it into her mouth, suckin' the last drops of my nut out.

When she finishes, we lay on top of the covers. I kiss her, stickin' my tongue deep into her mouth. Then plant soft kisses on her forehead. No words are said between us. I hold her in my arms, allow her to rest her head on my chest, and wait for her to drift off to sleep before slippin' outta bed and steppin' out onto her terrace, takin' in the view of Los Angeles. I try to wrap my mind 'round payin' close to a million dollars to live up in this piece. Yeah, it's a slick spot wit' its bamboo wood floors and floor-to-ceilin' windows and panaromic views of the mountains and all of downtown located in the South Park district. But, man, listen…eight-hundred thousand dollars for a two-bedroom, three-bath upscale apartment? *Un*fuckin' believable!

I think 'bout havin' her slumped over the railin', slidin' this dick in and outta her. I grab my shit and stroke it. Get it slightly hard. Yeah, I'm out here nude, and? I'm on the thirty-first floor. So it is what it is. I try to imagine livin' out here on the West Coast. Try to visualize bein' thousands of miles away from Jersey and New York. Funny thing, I can't. I dig L.A. wit' all of its palm trees, glitz and beautiful weather, but it lacks the kinda fast-paced swagger I'm used to. Although I know I could bag a slew of hoes out here, a muhfucka like me would become bored and homesick real fast.

On the way here from the airport, Cherry was beatin' me in the head 'bout movin' out here, talkin' 'bout she'd give me my space and let me parlay here at this spot, and she'd move back into her crib over in Santa Monica. All she wanted from me is this dick on-call. Yeah, it sounded all good—and if I was a weak-type cat, I'd probably take her up on it, but that shit would never work for a muhfucka like me. Livin' in someone else's shit and then haveta adhere to some kinda expectations and rules, nah... never that. And I'll be damned if I ever give a ho the chance to put me out on the streets. So I told her, "Thanks, but no thanks, baby. I'll fly in as needed."

I go back in to take a shower, but peek in on Cherry and change my mind. Seein' her lyin' in her nakedness bricks my dick. I climb back in bed. Spoon behind her, kiss her on the back of her neck, on her shoulders. She stirs, opens her eyes and cranes her head to face me. "Mmmm," she coos. "I've missed you."

"I've missed you, too, baby," I say, rollin' a condom on. I lift her leg, then slowly slide my dick back into her still wet pussy. I fuck her nice 'n slow. Torture her with unhurried strokes for forty-three minutes 'til we both nut, and fall off to sleep.

"C'mon, sleepyhead," Cherry says, gently shakin' me to get up. "Let's go grab a bite to eat." I stretch and yawn, lookin' 'round the room. She's hoverin' over me wit' her cell in her hand. She's already showered and dressed in a white linen wrap dress that stops to her ankles and a pair of orange strappy heels. Of course, top-of-the-line shit. Still, I'm lookin' at her like, "What the fuck?" But it dawns on me that I'm in southern California, so what she has on is what's poppin' for out here. And I can't front, she's lookin' real sexy.

"Yo, what time is it?" I ask, grabbin' and pullin' at my dick, stretchin' my legs out. She tells me it's almost five-thirty. I let out a loud groan, lyin' in bed a few more minutes before I finally sit up. Between the flight and fuckin', I'm whipped. "Damn, that pussy knocked me the hell out."

She laughs. "Yeah, and it had you snorin', too."

"Yeah, right," I say, tossin' a pillow at her. "Get the fuck outta here wit' that." She tosses the pillow back, badgerin' me to get up 'cause we have dinner reservations for seven o'clock. Her cell rings, she glances at the screen, then answers.

"'Cuse me, I gotta take this call," she says, walkin' toward the door. "It's one of my property managers."

I glance at the clock on her nightstand. "Oh, fuck," I say aloud, yawnin'. "I just wanna stay in fuckin' bed." I flop back on the pillows, pullin' the sheets up over my head. I can't front, this bed feels fuckin' good. It feels like I'm lyin' on a bed of cottonballs. And her one-thousand thread-count sheets feel good against my naked body. I yank the covers back and get outta bed before I end up fallin' back to sleep. I walk into the bathroom, take a piss, then hop in the shower. When I finally walk into the livin' room dressed in a pair of MEK jeans, a thin-fitted black knit pullover and a pair of black Prada loafers, Cherry is sittin' on a stool patiently waitin' on me. She smiles.

"You are one sexy chocolate man,' she says, gettin' up, grabbin' her oversized pocketbook and keys. "And I can't wait to get back here so I can finish fucking the shit outta you."

I grin. "You ain't said nuthin' but a word. Hell, we can order in, and let it do what it do right now. It makes me no never mind, baby. I'm loaded wit' nuts, and they all got ya name on 'em."

"And when we get back," she says, switchin' toward the door, "I want every last creamy drop." I follow behind her, shakin' my head.

Of course, Cherry doesn't tell me where we're goin' to eat. And I don't ask. Between you and me, I'm too damned jet-lagged to care. But, wherever it is, I already know it's gonna be some high-end spot that is probably extremely overpriced and not worth all the hype. But, hey, I'm not the one footin' the bill. While we're drivin', we talk some, but mostly listen to the radio. I find myself takin' in all the scenery along Rodeo Drive. She makes a turn onto Wilshire Boulevard. When we finally turn into Spago Beverly Hills, we pull up to the entrance for valet parkin' and get out, then make our way inside. It's packed as hell up in this piece. I look 'round the room. In the far right corner, I spot Angela Bassett sittin' at a table wit' two other chicks. *Damn, she looks good*, I think, catchin' Cherry starin' at me. She smiles. "She bought her last two homes from me," she says, leanin' in and lowerin' her voice. "She's a real sweetheart. Would you like to meet her?"

"Nah, I'm good," I tell her. Now had it been my girls Beyoncé or Halle—even Nia Long, I'da been like, "Hell muthafuckin' yeah!" But, Angela Bassett, umm, no thanks! Now, hol' up…I'm not sayin' I wouldn't bang her back out 'cause you already know what it is. She catches Angela's eye and waves at her.

"I'll be right back," she tells me, walkin' off. She heads over to her table. Angela stands up and the two of them hug as if they're old friends. Angela introduces her to e'eryone else at the table. They exchange a few more words, then I peep Cherry goin' into her bag pullin' out business cards and handin' them out. Then some white cat gets up from his table and greets her. He kisses her, then Angela, on the cheek. I know I've seen dude somewhere, but can't put my finger on it. They talk a few more minutes, then she follows him over to his table. He introduces her to e'eryone there. And, again, she goes into her bag and starts handin' out cards. I grin. *Get that paper, baby*, I think, pullin' out my cell. I decide to check my messages.

"You have twenty new messages." I sigh, waitin' for the first message to play. *"Hello, Alley Cat. This is Marissa. Doctor Sweet Pussy. I'm ready to meet up."* *Yeah, I bet you are. Now your ass's gonna haveta wait 'til I'm ready to feed you this dick.* I delete.

The next message is from Sherria. *"Call me."* *Bitch, you fuckin' crazy!* I delete it.

"I miss you. And I hate myself for allowing you into my life. But I hate you even more for having me feel this way, you black, selfish-ass motherfucker! I hope you die, you piece of shit!" This bullshit-ass mess is from Ramona. The last time I spoke to this ho is when she called me a while back talkin' that 'I'm pregnant' shit. And I stopped fuckin' her months before that. She needs to let go, word up. *This bitch is* really *fuckin' crazy*. I decide to save it; just in case sumthin' pops off.

"Hey, it's Falani. I thought I woulda heard from you after our three-some. Hit me up as soon as you get this."

"Alley Cat, it's ya girl, Electra. You stood me up, punk! Stop playin' games and bring ya ass to Brooklyn so I can super soak that dick. Get at me when you can." I grin, pressin' "seven" to save.

"Hey, sexy man, it's Lydia. I'm hopin' to get some private time with you real soon. You know Falani's feelin' some kinda way that you haven't called her since the other night, and she's been actin' kinda shady toward me"—she laughs—*"I think she knows I slid you my number. Oh, well. She'll get over it. Call me. By the way, I still would love to bend you over and fuck your tight, muscular ass with my strap-on. All you gotta*

do is say the word."—she laughs, again—"*There's nothing like turning a masculine man into my little whore-bitch, baby.*"

I crack the hell up laughin'. Yo, think what you like, but after that ep wit' her and Falani, I was tryna figure out how I could get at her wit'out straight up dissin' Falani. So, when she slid me her digits on the low, I already knew what it was. And damn straight, the minute I get a chance to, I'ma give her all the private time she needs. But the freak-nasty bitch'll never run anythin' up in my ass 'cept her muthafuckin' long-ass tongue, real talk.

"*Alley Cat, where are you? I'm at the airport waiting on you. Did something happen? Call me.*" Oh, shit, I think. *I was supposed to be in Atlanta. Damn!* I totally forgot to call Vita to let her know that I wasn't gonna be comin' out there; that there was an unexpected change of plans, resultin' in wetter pussy and deeper pockets. *Damn!* She's left eleven more messages, each one soundin' more frantic. The last one sent thirty minutes ago sounded like she had been drinkin' 'cause the bitch was straight wildin'. "*Goddamn you, you black motherfucker! You didn't have to dis me like that. Why the fuck did you have me pay for a goddamn plane ticket and you weren't gonna use it?! The least you coulda done was called me, you thoughtless bastard! You ain't shit, motherfucker! You're just like the rest of these sorry-ass niggas.*" Click.

I should be on some "fuck her"-type shit, but I won't 'cause it was foul on my part to do her like that. And she's right, I shoulda at least hit her up and told her what it was. I decide not to do her dirty and call—*tomorrow*. I delete the messages.

"*Alex, it's your mother. You know. The one who gave birth to you; the one you forget to call.*" I smile, shakin' my head. I delete the message, makin' a mental note to hit her up later, if it's not too late.

"*Yo, what's good, son? It's Gee, nigga. Hit me up when you get this.*" I finish listenin' to my other messages, watchin' Cherry as she makes her way back over to me. She apologizes for leavin' me hangin'. But I'm cool wit' it. I ask her who that white dude was and she says all nonchalant, "Oh, that was Leonardo DiCaprio."

"Oh shit, dude who played in *Blood Diamond*." She nods. "I knew he looked familiar." Now a muhfucka ain't never been starstruck, but I can't front. I was impressed. I knew Cherry was out here doin' it big, but I had no idea she was fuckin' wit' the celebrities like this. Most of the time when I'm here, we don't go out; we're layed up fuckin' for three days, then I bounce.

After 'bout fifteen minutes of waitin', we're finally seated out on the patio, which is kinda cool 'cause the tables aren't as bunched together like the rest of the tables in here. Man, listen, I can't stand eatin' somewhere feelin' like the muhfucka next to me can reach over into my plate. When the maitre d' comes to our table, Cherry orders a seven-hundred-dollar bottle of Bordeaux. She's the only one drinkin', so why the fuck she didn't just order a glass of wine instead of a whole damn bottle is beyond me. I keep my mouth shut. Let her do her. While she's lookin' over the menu, I glance 'round the room, takin' in the decor. Now I ain't a Martha Stewart-type cat, but this spot needs a serious makeover. All the shit up in here seems outdated, like they're scared to let go of the nineties or sumthin'.

Outta the corner of my eye, I peep this beauty breeze by our table, but outta respect for Cherry I don't turn to see who it is or how that ass is shakin'. Besides, at the moment, it doesn't really matter. *I need a damn blunt.* Cherry knows I blaze, but she ain't havin' that shit 'round her, which is probably why I only stay no more than two days a pop when I come out here. How the hell I'ma go two weeks wit'out sparkin' an L, is beyond me. Not that I can't do it. I don't want to. Big difference, feel me?

I bring my attention to Cherry. Stare at her. I can't front, she's one classy-type chick. She fucks good, looks good, gotta bangin' body, and makes major moves. And if she didn't have so much damn forehead, wasn't stuck on wearin' weaves 'n shit, and knew howta suck dick, she'd be a ten, hands down.

"Is everything okay?" she asks, lookin' up from her menu

"I'm good, baby; just checkin' things out." I wink at her.

She smiles. "And do you like what you see?"

"Oh, no doubt," I tell her.

"Good. So do you know what you want to eat?"

"Nah, what do you suggest?" She recommends the lobster and spinach raviolinis in a cream sauce. What the fuck?! I frown, shakin' my head. She chuckles, then suggests I try one of the pork, chicken or fish dishes.

"I gotta use the bathroom," I say, gettin' up, "You order for me; make it sumthin' simple. No pork or beef, though." She tells me she'll order me the halibut and seasoned vegetables. "Oh, aiight, cool."

When I get to the bathroom, I do what I gotta do, then wash my hands. I glance at my watch and decide to hit mom dukes up real quick. I call her on the house phone, and she answers on the third ring.

"Glad you remembered my number," she says sarcastically. "I wasn't sure if you needed me to leave it for you or not."

"Ma, go 'head wit' that," I say, chucklin'. "You my number one girl. You know I know how to get at you. Is e'erything aiight? You good?"

"Humph, that's what you say. Actions speak louder than words, though. But to answer your question, I'm good. I'm just making sure you are."

"Oh, no doubt. I'm chillin'," I tell her while checkin' myself out in the mirror. Although I usually keep my face smooth-shaven,

I'm kinda diggin' the five-o'-clock-shadow thing I got goin' on. *Damn, you'se a fine, chocolate muhfucka!* Hell, yeah, I'm in love wit' myself. Why the fuck shouldn't I be? What, you think I'm 'posed to stand 'round wit' my dick in my hand, waitin' for someone else to love me? Yeah, right. Picture that shit! If I don't love me, then how the hell can someone else? That's the problem wit' some of these dumb-ass muhfuckas and hoes out here. They always lookin' and expectin' love from someone else. Then they wonder why they end up in fucked-up situations, and don't know howta get the fuck outta 'em.

"Well, when three or more days go by, and I don't hear from you or see you, I start to worry." I smile, knowin' if I tell her not to worry it's only gonna go in one ear and out the other 'cause that's what she's gonna do. I tell her I'll try to call more, then let her know I'm outta town for a few days. "Humph, I shoulda known. Out whorin', I'm sure."

I laugh. "Actually, I'm workin'."

"And I'm a three-legged, one-eyed fool." I continue laughin'. We talk for a few more minutes before hangin' up. As I'm walkin' outta the bathroom, I'm so busy goin' through my text messages that I'm not payin' attention to where I'm goin' and end up bumpin' into someone, almost knockin' 'em down.

"Oh, damn. My…" Our eyes lock and I almost pass the fuck out. "Oh, shit, baby. I must be in heaven. What are *you* doin' out here?" It's Kanika.

She smiles, seemin' surprised to see me as well. "This is home for me. So what's your excuse? This is a long way from Jersey. Oh, let me guess, a *friend*?"

I grin. Gotdamn, she is finer than a muhfucka! Her fuckin' skin is glowin'. And her beautifully painted lips are sexy as hell. I feel my dick stirrin' inside of my boxers. "Sumthin' like that. So, dig, how long you gonna be out here?" She tells me she's here for the L.A. Fashion Week events and will be here 'til the end of next week.

As bad as I wanna stand here and keep this thing goin' wit' her, I know I gotta get my ass back over to my table before Cherry puts out an APB on me. "Dig, baby, I gotta get back to my table. But how 'bout I hit you up tomorrow? Maybe we can meet up and you can show me L.A."

She smirks. "And will you be bringing your *friend* along?"

"Nah, baby, I'ma be dolo." She rolls her eyes. Tells me to call her, then excuses herself to go to the bathroom. I stare at her ass. Watch the way her hips sway, then head back to the table, tryna figure out how the hell I'm gonna ditch Cherry for a few hours so I can get at that Stone Mountain beauty. I don't know how I'ma do it, but the one thing I am certain of: Come hell or high water, a muhfucka's gonna make it do what it do. Believe that!

27

I wish she would take her ass out somewhere. That's what I'm thinkin' lyin' here in bed. Man, listen, five days of bein' confined and a muhfucka's startin' to get antsy. Cherry has been up underneath me, bouncin' up and down on this dick practically e'ery damn three hours. Don't get me wrong; keepin' this cock coated is all good. But, damn…can a nigga get out and breathe a lil', feel me? I know I told her I was gonna be all hers while I'm out here, but gotdamn! I need a fuckin' break from her ass. Wakin' up to the same broad for more than three days is not the norm for me, and I'm already startin' to look at her ass some kinda way; 'specially after seein' her droolin' in her sleep. I gotta keep remindin' myself that she's cool peeps, and that the paper I'ma walk up outta here wit' will be worth all the extras I'm puttin' up wit'. See, if I had me a bag of Get-Right, I could roll a fat-ass blunt, take it to the head, then zone the fuck out. Then a muhfucka could handle her bein' all up under me. She musta read my mind 'cause when she steps outta the bathroom dressed in a bad-ass, cream-colored business suit and a pair of brown Gucci heels, I know it's 'bout to be on and poppin' today.

"Good morning, baby," she says, standin' in front of the full-length mirror, puttin' in her five-carat diamond studs. She looks at me through the mirror. "I hate to leave you all by yourself, but I have to go out to Santa Monica to show some houses this mornin', then I have a lunch meeting in Malibu this afternoon. I tried to get out of it, but—"

I sit up in bed, tryna keep from smilin'. But inside I'm screamin', "*Muthafuckin' YES!*" "Oh, it's all good, babe," I say, cuttin' her off. "Get that paper. I understand."

"I feel bad, though." I get outta bed, walk up behind her, then kiss her on top of her weave-covered head, lettin' her know there's no need to feel any kinda way 'bout it. When she tells me she's gonna leave me the keys to her convertible Jag, I press my bare dick up in her back. Decide to fuck her down real good, then send her on her merry way wit' a smile on her face. I grind into her. "Unh-uh, don't," she says, tryna step outta my embrace, "start tryna get the kitty all cranked up. I don't have time. I'm gonna have to fight traffic as it is, or I'll end up being late. So you're gonna have to wait until I get back."

I grab her by the waist and pull her into me. At first she tries to resist. But I am persistent, so she doesn't put up much of a fight for too long. "C'mon, baby, let me get a lil' dose of that sweet 'n sticky. Five minutes, boo." She rolls her eyes, knowin' I'm lyin' outta my black ass 'bout nuttin' that quick. I grin, strokin' my dick. She looks down at it as it starts to thicken. She licks her lips. I already know she gets wet just thinkin' 'bout this dick up in her, so seein' it got her juices bubblin'. "What you gonna do, baby? You gonna let this dick wait for you? Or are you gonna milk this nut up outta it real quick?"

She glimpses at her watch. "Damn you," she says, pullin' out her BlackBerry. She makes a call, tells whoever answered to push her first appointment back 'cause she's gonna be an hour late. She disconnects, unbuttonin' her jacket.

I stop her. "I got this," I say, grabbin' her by the hand. She sits down at the foot of the bed. I remove her jacket, then her blouse. I remove her bra and unleash her beautiful titties. She stands up, allows me to unfasten her skirt. It drops 'round her ankles and she steps outta it. I tell her to sit back down. Then kneel down in front of her, slip off her shoes, and caress the bottom of her feet. *Damn, she got some pretty-ass feet*, I think, kissin' the balls of her feet, lickin' them, then slippin' her left big toe into my mouth. I slowly suck on it before pullin' two more of her toes into my mouth. I slip my tongue in between her toes, then lick the bottom of her feet. She tosses her head back, and moans. I slide my hand up the inner part of her thigh, reach for her wet pussy, then slip two fingers in.

"Oh, yes, baby. See how wet you got my pussy?"

"Yeah, you ready for some dick, ain't you?"

"Mmmm...oh, yes..."

I pull my fingers outta her sticky snatch. Tell her to lie on her stomach. I lick my lips. I run into the bathroom, then come back out wit' a bottle of baby oil. When I pour it onto her back, she flinches, then relaxes when I slowly start massagin' her neck and shoulders and back, then her juicy ass. I'm kneadin' the kinks outta her body so good that I got her purrin'.

She whispers, "Aaaaah, this feels so good, baby." My hands slide down to her calves, then back up to her thighs, lightly brushin' her pussy. She spreads her legs, hikes her ass up in the air.

"Yeah, you want daddy to long stroke this wet pussy, don't you." She moans. I run my hand along the back slit of her hole, take two fingers and press on its opening, then slide them into her.

"Mmmm-hmmm..." She bucks her hips. "Stop teasing me. And fuck me." I eat her from the back, then reach for a condom, slidin' it on. I plunge deep into her. She gasps. "Ohhh, shiiiiit..." Her pussy clenches my dick, milks it. My shaft strokes her clit as I lift up on my arms and pump in and outta her. I reach in front of her and grab her titties and start squeezin' on 'em. I dick her down slow 'n deep at first, then pick up the pace and start feedin' her with long, fast strokes. Pullin' all the way out, then slammin' it back into her. Ten minutes later, I pull out, flip her over onto her back, then slide back into her. Her eyes roll up in the back of her head. The bed starts to rock. She clutches the sheets. Sweat rolls down my face, then drips onto her chest. Two minutes later, she is growlin' and howlin' and creamin' all over my dick. I snatch the condom off and start jerkin' my shit off in rapid strokes. She plays wit' her clit as she watches me.

Five minutes later, my body starts to jerk. I moan, splash out a hot nut, then flop over on my back, tryna catch my breath. Cherry jumps outta bed, and hops in the shower. Fifteen minutes later, she is dressed and racin' out the door. I glance over at the clock; 8:53 A.M. It's almost noon back home. *Let me call this ho,* I think, gettin' outta bed. I pull my cell outta my pants pocket, then dial Vita's number. She doesn't pick up. I call back. Still no answer. *I know this midget bitch sees my number. She's probably still swoll.* This time, I leave a message:

"Damn, baby…I'm sorry for not makin' it out there. I had a family emergency and had to rush outta town…" I pause, then continue. *"My grandmother passed away."* Yo, hol' up…don't look at me like that. I'm not lyin'. Why the fuck would I say some shit like that if it wasn't true? She *did* pass away. Ten years ago. So technically, it ain't a lie, feel me? *"We knew she was sick, but we thought she'd still be here for at least the holidays. I'm sure you're feelin' some kinda way 'bout me not hittin' you up. But, this got us all fucked up. I really wanted to see you, and I feel bad for not makin' it down there. But this shit right here got me all fucked. The wake is today, and the funeral is tomorrow. I probably won't be home until next week sometime. I'ma hit you wit' some paper to pay for that ticket, aiight? Hit me up when you get this. Later."*

I decide to hit Kanika up. She picks up, soundin' like I woke her. The thought of bein' up in the sheets wit' her stretches my dick. I squeeze it. We talk for 'bout fifteen minutes, makin' plans to meet up 'round noon. I only have a small window of opportunity to make shit pop, so I let her know to be ready and not have me waitin'. I know I'm gonna haveta come up off of some paper today, so I'm glad Cherry left me eight bills up on the dresser. I toss my phone beside me on the bed, then roll over on my side and eventually doze off to sleep.

Twelve o'clock, I scoop up Kanika in front of her people's spot. The minute she gets in and buckles up, I speed off. It's sunny and clear skies. I let the top down and the wind is blowin' her hair all over the place, but she doesn't seem to give a fuck. I wanna reach over and run my hand through it, sumthin' I can't do wit' Cherry's weave-wearin' ass. I can't front, I was impressed when she came out as soon as I pulled up. I suggested she dress comfortable, and not wear heels. But she laughed, sayin' heels were her life. However, bein' the thoughtful cat that I am, I picked out a pair of sneakers for her. Aiight, aiight...I ain't gonna front. I ransacked Cherry's shoe closet and found a brand-new pair of white Gucci sneakers in the back of her closet that I brought wit' me. I even found a Gucci shoppin' bag to put 'em in. I just hope them shits fit. E'ery so often, I cut my eyes over at her. She has her head back on the headrest.

"So where are we headed?" she finally asks, liftin' her Prada shades up and turning her head toward me. She's lookin' fly as fuck. I feel like pullin' my dick out and lettin' it hang in my lap as I drive to give her sumthin' to look at while I'm flyin' down the 405 freeway. On some real shit, I wanna pull over on the side of the road and fuck her bad as hell. But, I'ma keep shit in check. So far, she's been actin' like a classy chick, so I'ma continue to treat her as one. But, there's a part of me that is hopin' she ends up bein' a bird, so I can pluck her tail feathers.

I smile, glancin' over at her. "You've been kidnapped, beautiful lady. Do I need to blindfold you, too?" I ask, jokin'. She play-fully hits me in the arm. I decide to drive down to Huntington Beach, which is 'bout forty miles south of L.A. It's pretty much eight miles of beachfront wit' a buncha shit to do, from hikin' to kayakin', from horseback ridin' to skateboardin' and surfin'. I've been there once 'bout three years ago, and kinda dug its vibe, so I decide to take the thirty-five-minute drive wit' this beauty sit-tin' next to me. I figure I can take her to Huntington Harbour—a part of Huntington Beach that's made up of five man-made islands wit' a buncha of channels and canals. Kinda makes you think you in Italy somewhere. That's the vibe it gives you. We can take a gondola ride, take in the view, grab a bite to eat at one of the eateries, then jet back to L.A.

Right off of Pacific Highway, I pull into Peter's Landing Marina, then park. "Aiight, pretty baby, we're here," I say, pullin' the key outta the ignition. I slip my cell under the seat. Decide I'ma give her my undivided attention, so I won't be needin' it.

"How did you know this used to be one of my favorite places?" she asks, unfastenin' her seatbelt. I tell her I know 'cause I'm psy-chic. She smiles. "Whatever. I wish you would have told me this is where you were takin' me. I would have worn something else."

In my head, I'm sayin', *"I don't know why bitches don't wanna listen. I told her ass to dress comfortably. But she wanna be on some cute shit, wearin' muthafuckin' heels."* I can tell her sexy ass is fuckin' hard-headed. I pop open the trunk. "Don't worry, baby, I got you." I pull out the Gucci bag and hand it to her. "I got these for you."

She peeks inside the bag, then looks up at me. "What's this?"

"Open it up and find out."

She pulls the box outta the bag, then opens it. "OMG, you bought these?" she asks, surprised. I nod. "That's so sweet of you. But why?"

"Because I knew you were gonna need 'em," I tell her, grinnin', "so I scooped 'em up this mornin' for you. Here, let me help you put 'em on." I walk 'round the car and open the passenger-side door. She follows behind me, then sits in the car. I squat down in front of her, then remove her heels. Word is bond, my mouth starts to water the minute I see her pretty-ass toes. I wanna suck 'em, but a muhfucka keeps his cool. I slip the sneakers on her feet.

"Wow, and they fit. How'd you know my size?"

I flash a wide smile, winkin' at her. "I told you I'm psychic, baby."

"Oh, please," she says, playfully wavin' me on. "Try another lucky guess. But I'm impressed."

"Yeah, aiight. Call it what you want, baby. Either way, I'm pretty good at sizin' up a woman."

"Is that so?" She stands up, glancin' down at her feet. I can tell she's pleased wit' my selection—compliments of Cherry, of course. I take her shoes and place 'em in the trunk of the car.

"No doubt, baby."

"I'm almost afraid to ask what else you're good at."

I grab her by the hand and lead her toward the dock. "Stick 'round, beautiful, and I'ma show you e'erything you need to know." She smiles, shakin' her head.

Two hours later, we're at Habana Cabana—a Cuban spot—waitin' for our waiter to come back wit' our food. Kanika orders jumbo shrimp, and sliced lobster tail simmered in a Cuban red creole sauce. I order a mixed salad wit' lettuce, tomatoe, avocado, cucumber and onions and the Polla a la Habana, grilled chicken breast cooked in a red sauce wit' onions and peppers and a side order of plantains.

We're both kinda sittin' here in chill mode, sorta caught up in our own thoughts. I'm thinkin' 'bout the hour gondola ride we had, and how she sat in front of me, laid back on my chest wit' my arms wrapped 'round her as we went through the channels. Then dude—the Gondolier—pulled up under a bridge and started serenadin' us in Italian. The whole vibe was sexy as hell. And on some real shit, I wanted to tongue her down, then fuck her right there on the spot wit' dude watchin'.

She reaches over and lightly touches my hand, bringin' my attention back to her. She smiles. "Everything okay?"

I return the smile, then hit her wit': "Yeah, e'erything's perfect. I was thinkin' how runnin' into you at Spago musta been fate. It's definitely a sign."

"Oh, yeah?" she asks, lookin' me dead in the eyes while cuppin' her hands underneath her chin. "A sign for what?"

"It's top secret, baby," I tell her, grinnin'. "Just know that right at this very moment, I'm enjoyin' e'ery minute wit' you."

"Awwww…how sweet. I'm enjoying the time with you as well. I have to say, you're definitely full of surprises. I had no idea you could be romantic."

"I told you, there's a lot 'bout me you don't know. I can be anything I wanna be, or whatever it is you need me to be. My only purpose today was to put a smile on ya pretty face, baby."

"And that you did," she says, smilin'. *Damn, I wanna lick and suck all over them pretty-ass lips.* As fine as she is, though, she's probably one of them pillow princesses. You know, one of them pretty bitches who thinks all she has to do is lay there and be cute and not put in any work; 'cause a muhfucka is just happy to have a chick like her in his bed. Like a muhfucka should be honored that she's breakin' him off some pussy. Fuck outta here! I hate them type of hoes, real talk. And those are the kinda broads I try to straight rip open for bein' muthafuckin', lazy-ass fucks. *Nah, fuck that! She's one of them undercover freaks.* She tilts her head, runnin' her hand through her hair. "Why are you looking at me like that?"

I place my forearms on the table and lean in. "You don't really wanna know," I tell her just as the waiter returns to the table wit' our food. He places our plates in front of us, asks if he can get us anything else, then leaves when we tell 'em we're good. She presses the issue, puttin' a forkful of shrimp into her mouth. I smile, watchin' her lick her lips and moan. "Damn, it's good like that?"

"Mmm-hmm, it's delicious. I love seafood. Now tell me what you were thinking when you were looking at me like that."

"I was thinkin' 'bout makin' love to you. Wonderin' how it would feel to be deep inside of you."

She grins.

I smile. "So is that a yes-you-can grin, or a no-nigga-you-done-banged-ya-muthafuckin'-head grin?"

She laughs. "Neither. It's an if-I-were-a-ho-I'd-probably-let-you-find-out-right-here-right-now grin. But since I'm not, I guess you're gonna have to keep wondering…"

"Damn. I guess that's too bad for me."

She sticks her fork into another shrimp, then stops before puttin' it into her mouth. "Looks that way—*for now*, anyway."

I smile. "Oh, aiight. I like the sound of that 'for now.' That's wassup."

She bites into her shrimp, then moans again, smilin'.

I shake my head. "Yo, you fuckin' wit' me. You know that, right?"

"I don't know what you're talking about," she says, laughin'. "I'm just enjoying my meal."

"Yeah, aiight. Keep it up and you're gonna end up gettin' a whole lot more to enjoy."

"Hmmm. Is that a threat or a promise?"

I grin, winkin' at her. "You take it however you want, pretty baby."

"I just might do that."

We spend the rest of the time laughin' and talkin' and flirtin' to the point where we both lose track of time. When I finally glance down at my watch, it's almost five o'clock. *Oh, shit!* I pat my pockets for my cell, then remember I left it in the car. *I gotta get the fuck up outta here. I bet Cherry's been blowin' my shit up.* As much as I would like to spend the whole damn night wit' Kanika's sexy ass, I'm not about to fuck up my paper, feel me? She and I will haveta continue this vibe when I get back out to Atlanta. In the meantime, it's time to rock 'n muthafuckin' roll out. And I already know the freeway traffic is gonna be a bitch tryna get back into L.A.

I pay the bill, and I'm impressed when she says she's got the tip. I smile. She gets mad props for that, word up. I can't stand for a ho to get a paid meal, then sit with her arms wrapped tight 'round her muthafuckin' pocketbook like she ain't tryna come up offa no paper. Lucky for me, I don't haveta deal wit' that bullshit since you already know a muhfucka like me hardly ever comes outta his pocket to buy a bitch shit. Yo, hol' up…So what if the money I spent today ain't mine. It never is.

When Kanika says she has to use the bathroom, I tell her I'ma run out and get the car, so she doesn't haveta take that walk back. She thinks it's me bein' sweet that I offer, and I don't let her know any different. But, on some real shit, it's me needin' to check my phone messages wit'out her bein' all up on my ear, if I need to make any calls.

I get to the car and immediately check my phone before pullin' off. I have seven missed calls and five new messages. Cherry hit me up only once, which is surprisin'. The other calls are from Akina, Vita, Carla, and Maleeka. I listen to the messages. Cherry says she's not gonna get in until after eight, which is a big relief for me. Now I don't haveta feel rushed. Akina wants to know why I haven't called her. Vita apologizes for goin' off, says she's sorry to hear 'bout my loss, and wants me to call her as soon as I can. Carla and Maleeka want dick, as usual. I delete all my messages, then hit Cherry up. When she doesn't pick up, I leave a message: *"Hey, baby. I got ya message. I took a ride down to Huntington Beach; should be back 'round seven. My dick's been hard all day, so you already know what it is. I'm horny as fuck, so be ready to get that pussy beat up real good tonight."* Hell, I ain't lyin'. Kanika's sexy ass got my shit on rock. But since she ain't passin' off them drawers, Cherry's gonna haveta make it pop for me.

Next I call Vita and leave a message as I'm pullin' up in front of the restaurant. Kanika's standin' outside waitin' wit' a smile. She hops in. I wait for her to put on her seatbelt, then speed off toward the freeway.

"So when am I gonna see you again, baby?" I ask, glancin' over at her.

"I don't know," she says, smirkin'. "I'll need to check my calendar to see if I can fit you in."

"Oh, it's like that, hunh?"

"Yep." She giggles. "You can't think a meal and a boat ride is gonna make it easier for you to see me again. Oh, no, Mister. You're gonna have to come harder than that."

I laugh. "Baby, you ain't said nuthin' but a word. All you gotta say is when and where, and how hard you need it…I mean, me, to *come*. And you got it."

She playfully swats at me. "You're a mess. I guess I opened myself up for that one."

"Yeah," I chuckle, "you fell right into it. So you might as well open wider and say, 'Aaaaaaah.'"

She sucks her teeth, laughin' as she digs into her pocketbook and pulls out a pack of gum. She offers me a piece, but I'm good so I tell her, "No thanks."

"Annnnnnyway, pervert...when's the next time you're gonna be in Atlanta?"

"I'm not sure. Why, you wanna see me?"

"Maybe," she says, rollin' a piece of Doublemint into her mouth, "maybe not."

"Yeah, aiight. Don't front. You know what it is."

She laughs.

My cell vibrates and the screen lights up. I take a quick glance at it sittin' up on the console, and see that it's Vita callin'. It dings when she leaves a message, then starts buzzin' again. She's callin' back.

"Do you need to get that?"

"Nope."

"You sure?"

I take my right hand off the steerin' wheel and reach over and grab her hand. "Yeah, I'm very sure. The only person I'm interested in talkin' to at this moment is sittin' right beside me."

"Good answer," she says, squeezin' my hand.

"It's the only answer, pretty baby," I reply, pullin' her hand up to my lips and gently kissin' it. On some real shit, I wanna drag my tongue along the center of her palm, but I restrain myself. She's been keepin' it classy, so I'ma respect her space and keep it gentlemanly. She smiles, pulls her shades down over her eyes, then places her head back on the headrest, holdin' my hand in hers the rest of the ride. I turn on the radio and tune into Power 106, L.A.'s hip-hop and R&B station and maneuver my way through this fucked-up traffic.

28

"I wanna talk to you about something that's been on my mind," Cherry says, lookin' up at me. She moves a wet strand of weave from her face. We finished fuckin' less than five minutes ago, and we're both sweaty and still pantin' like wild beasts. And this ho wants to flap her jaws. Why the fuck chicks wanna talk right after they finish gettin' their backs gutted is beyond me. What the fuck?! I'm in no mood for talkin'. I wanna lie here and rest in *silence*. But I know that's not 'bout to happen.

I glance at the clock. It's ten-thirty in the mornin'. My flight leaves for Jersey tonight at nine-fifty. And between you and me, a muhfucka can't wait to get the fuck home. As nice as it is to get away, there's nuthin' like chillin' up in ya own spot, in ya own damn bed, feel me?

"What's up?" I ask, proppin' up on my forearms.

"Well, you know…I really enjoy spending time with you when you come out here. And I think this thing we have works really well for the both of us. There's no pressure from either of us. I'm not looking for a relationship, or expecting anything more from you than what I already get…" *OhmyGod, I wish she get to the muthafuckin' point!*

"No doubt. So wassup?"

"Well," she says, pausin'. "I want a baby."—she puts a finger over my lips to stop me from speakin'—"Now before you say anything, hear me out first. I'm thirty-five and very successful with no prospects of having a husband anytime soon. But I want to be a mother with no strings, or stress, or baby daddy drama. I am more than capable of raising a child on my own, so I'm not looking for someone to help me raise it."

I tilt my head, tryna figure out where she's goin' wit' this. "Ohhhkay, and what does that haveta do wit' me?"

"Well, I've been seriously thinking about getting pregnant."

"Ohhhkay, again, what does that haveta do wit' me?"

"I want a baby with *you*."

My eyes almost pop outta my head. "Say whaaat?" I ask, almost knockin' her over as I sit up in bed. She repeats herself. "Oh, I heard you the first time. It just caught a muhfucka off guard. I mean, damn...you want me to paint ya insides up wit' my nuts. That's a big-ass request. I don't know if it's one one I can help you fill."

She sits up in bed. "I'm only asking you to be my sperm donor. Not marry me, or claim the child as yours. I know you and I trust you, opposed to going to a sperm bank or some online site and not really knowing who or what I'm getting. With you, I know I'm getting a sexy black man with above-average intelligence and excellent bone structure." I frown at her on that "above average" intelligence shit. Although I know it's not meant as a dis, for some reason, I don't like how the fuck it sounded, like I'm a step or two up from bein' retarded. I decide to let it go. "And aside from your weed smoking, I know that you take relatively good care of yourself. You can be in its life or not; the choice would be entirely up to you. Either way, I wouldn't ask you for any monetary support."

I scratch the side of my head. "Ummm, why not adopt?"

"I thought about that. But I want to experience the joys of motherhood being pregnant, carrying my own child."

"I don't know. I mean, that's a big request to hit a nigga wit', feel me?"

"I know. But before you flat out say no, just give it some thought, *please*."

"Umm, there's nuthin' really to think 'bout. A muhfucka like me ain't—"

"I'm willing to pay you fifty thousand dollars," she bursts out, cuttin' me off. Now that gets my attention. My dick starts to twitch.

"Yo, let me get this right. You're willin' to pay me fifty gees to knock you up?"

She nods. "Yes, half up front, then the other half once I'm pregnant."

My dick thickens.

Damn, and all I gotta do is plant this nut up in her. Now you all know I ain't the most moral muhfucka and I know I can be a bit—aiight, aiight...very—unscrupulous at times, but damn... gettin' paid to knock someone up is askin' a bit much, even for a muhfucka like me. I mean, damn...I can understand her desires to be a mother and even bein' willin' to pay to become one. But, fuck! To expect me to be aiight wit' givin' her my seed, then turnin' my back on it. Man, listen...I can't wrap my mind 'round any muhfucka willin' to walk away from a child, knowin' it's theirs. As disconnected as I can be when it comes to chicks 'n shit, I think that's one thing I'd have a hard time detachin' myself from. I think it would fuck wit' me, knowin' I had a child, a lil' man or baby girl of my own, out here. And it damn sure would have my moms spazzin' the fuck out, knowin' I deprived her of a grandchild. But, then again, for fifty grand...

"Let me think on it," I finally say.

She smiles, reachin' up on her tippy-toes, givin' me a kiss on the lips. "Thank you."

"I'm not makin' any promises."

"And I'm not askin' for any."

"Cool." I pat her on the ass, then grab and squeeze it, pressin' my dick up against her. "So, you ready for another round of dick?" She nods her head, grabbin' my joint and grinnin'. She drops down to her knees and starts lappin' my balls and lickin' the underside of my hard dick. Before she can attempt to put her mouth 'round it—'cause I ain't in the mood for her grazin' my shit wit' her muthafuckin' teeth—I pull her up and toss her up over my shoulder, walkin' her back over to the bed, then ploppin' her down on it. I push her legs back and dive into the center of her pussy wit' my tongue, lickin', lappin', kissin', slurpin' all over it, 'til she cracks a sticky nut. When she finishes buckin' her hips, I roll a condom down on my dick, then slowly push in, windin' my hips, tip drillin' her slit, e'ery so often pushin' another inch in, then pullin' back out to the head. She tosses her head from side to side, pulls in her bottom lip. Her eyes start to roll up in the back of her head. OhmyGod, this bitch got some good pussy. I lean in, whisper in her ear, let her know how hot 'n wet her pussy feels 'round my dick before dippin' my tongue in her ear and suckin' on her earlobe.

She moans.

I push this dick deep into her.

She moans again, louder.

I pull out to the head, then push back in.

"Oh, Alex…hmmmm…ooooooh, baaaaaby…you make me feel soooo good…whatever you do…please…Don't ever…stop… fuckin' me…"

I grin, lockin' my arms up under her hips. "Don't worry, baby, I'ma keep fuckin' you for as long as you want," I whisper, rockin' her box for one straight hour 'til she breaks down and cries.

The rest of the day, we lounge 'round her spot naked, fuckin' whenever the mood hits, and watchin' flicks in between. 'Round four o'clock, we head downtown to do some last-minute shoppin'. Cherry laces me wit' a few pairs of DSquared2 V-neck tees, two pair of Gucci jeans, and a slick pair of Versace shades to go along wit' the rest of the shit she's already hit me wit' durin' my stay here. I can't front, she spoils the fuck outta me. Hell, as crafty as I am, I know I probably should dismiss the rest of the hoes on my team and give her the lead spot. And who knows, maybe one day I will. But for now, I like shit the way it is between us. However, I'm thinkin' I might wanna start comin' out here e'ery other month or so to keep my pockets lined more frequently, feel me? But if I start doin' that, is she gonna try to turn this thing into some kinda relationship 'n shit? I already know you can't give a broad too much of you wit'out her catchin' feelin's and whatnot, then wantin' more from a muhfucka. Let me not think too much 'bout it—at least while I'm still here—'cause if I do, I'ma start actin' funny toward her. Don't ask me why. That's just how I do.

When we finish our shoppin' spree, we decide to stop by this Japanese spot, Octopus, downtown over on Seventh Street 'cross from the Macy's to eat before it's time for her to drop me off at the airport. She orders a large hot saki, miso soup, two crunch rolls, and two tiger rolls. I try to keep from frownin' at the thought of eatin' salmon and freshwater eel rolled together. And I'm thinkin': *This bitch won't be kissin' me unless she scrubs down her tongue, then gargles.* I order a seaweed salad and the garlic seared tuna sashimi.

Over our meal, she tells me how much she enjoyed my stay here and how she wishes I didn't have to go. I smile and tell her likewise, then tell her how much I appreciate her lookin' out for me. Then she tells me she doesn't want more than three months to go by before she sees me again. And when I come out, she wants me to stay another two weeks. I swallow the last bit of my rice, not sayin' shit. But between you and me, two weeks wit'out blazin' is a bit much for me. I'ma haveta find me a connect out here for these extended stays to work. She pulls out her BlackBerry.

"What are you doing the week of February tenth? I would like to spend Valentine's Day with you." *Valentine's Day?* What the fuck?! Here she goes tryna turn sumthin' into nuthin'. I don't celebrate that shit. I give her a look. She catches it. "Not as lovers, silly. I know what we are to each other. But I do consider you a very special man in my life. You're more than a friend with benefits to me. I care about you, Alex. And before you start trippin', don't take what I say outta context. I'm very clear on what our arrangement is."

I smile. "Oh, you know I was 'bout to go there. I don't want you catchin' feelin's for me, then wantin' more than what I'ma give you."

"Only a fool would think such, sweetie. Believe it or not, I know you better than you think. And I know you are not capable of loving anyone more than you love yourself. And I'm okay with that. So trust, I'm *not* interested in investing my heart into an emotionally unavailable man. Yes, I care about you. And I enjoy your company. But that's it. You're good for two things, baby: a good time, and a good fuck. And that's why *I* keep you around."

I choke on my drink, laughin'. "Oh shit, you funny as hell. That's some shit I'd say."

"I know. And I put that out there just in case you thought it."

Yeah, aiight. I heard this before, I think as I decide to ask her more 'bout this baby proposition she hit me wit' earlier. She sounds like she has shit in perspective, but what happens after she gets pregnant—if she can even get pregnant? I'm not sure if I'm really entertainin' the idea or not, but it does have me curious. I wanna know if I agree to it and don't want any ties to the child, what guarantees do I have that she won't try to drag me into court in the future? Or what if I wanna be involved in my child's life, then what?

"I won't put your name on the birth certificate. And I'll have legal papers drawn up to absolve you of any financial obligations. And if you wanted to stop seeing me, I'd understand since it may be an uncomfortable position for you."

Would I wanna stay in her life? My child's life? Yeah, we have a great time together. Yeah, the sex is great. Yeah, she's attractive and smart and financially well-off. Yeah, she seems emotionally stable. But, is she the kinda woman I'd want to be the mother of my child? Is she the kinda woman I'd want to be tied to for the rest of my child's life? I honestly don't know.

For some reason, I'm startin' to feel sick, and wish I wouldna brought the subject up, again. Sittin' here thinkin' 'bout this—fifty grand or not, I don't think I could go through wit' it. I'm sure she'd be a great mother, and do a great job raisin' it on her own. And I know wit'out a doubt she'd give our...I mean, her child, the best of e'erything. But would that be enough? What happens when he or she starts askin' questions and wants to know who their father is? What is she gonna tell 'em? Yo, son, ya father's dead? I don't know who the nigga is? He was some bum muhfucka who didn't wanna be in ya life? He was some good dick I paid to knock me up? Or would she end up marryin' some nigga who raises him or her as his own? Fuck that! A child should have its biological father in its life, too. I never really gave havin' a child any serious thought 'til today. Hell, I never really thought 'bout anyone other than myself. *I know you are not capable of loving anyone more than you love yourself.* Her words play in my head. I *am* capable. Or am I? Hell yeah, I am. I just haven't been willin', big difference, right? Then why does what she said have me feelin' some kinda way?

"So does this mean you're considering it?"

I shrug, takin' a deep breath. *I can't wait to get the fuck home to blaze!* That's what I need to get my mind right. "I don't know. I haveta definitely give it some major thought before I agree one way or the other. That's for sure."

"And you should."

I stare at her. "So what happens if I say no?"

"Then I guess we keep doing what we do until I work out an alternative plan, or find a suitable donor."

"I feel you. Well, I don't wanna get ya hopes up."

"Trust me, you won't. It was only an idea. Whatever you decide is fine with me. I'm giving myself five years to be pregnant, so I have more than enough time to figure it all out. Who knows, Mr. Right may find his way into my life and sweep me off my feet. In the meantime, are you available the week of February tenth, or not?"

I pause for a minute, tryna remember what day we're leavin' for All-Star. *The twelfth*, I think. "Nah, I'ma be in Phoenix that week. How 'bout the week after?"

"That works for me," she says, markin' it in her calendar. She slips it back into her bag.

I smile, pourin' myself some more green tea. I raise my cup. "To good times and good fuckin'."

She raises her cup of sake. "Exaaaaaactly."

I glance at my watch, then lick my lips and slowly pull in my bottom lip. "So dig, baby…you think we gotta 'nough time to get another round in before my flight?"

She eyes me seductively, flaggin' the waiter. "Check, please."

29

"I'm soooooo sorry to hear about your grandmother, baby. And I apologize for leaving all those nasty messages. I was wrong for that. When you weren't at the airport and then didn't pick up when I called you, I started thinking the worst. I thought you were ducking me."

I've been back from L.A. for almost three days—ten grand richer, I might add—and this is the first time I'm actually speakin' to Vita. For some reason, hearin' her voice is already startin' to get on my fuckin' nerves. I take a deep breath, slowly blowin' it out. She's been goin' on and on 'bout how fucked up she feels 'bout comin' outta her neck sideways. And of course, I make her feel even more guilty doin' it.

"Never that, baby," I tell her, rollin' my eyes. "But I'ma keep it gee. I was kinda fucked up for a minute hearin' those messages. I was like, 'oh shit, I forgot to hit Vita up.' I had so much on my mind wit' my grandmother dyin', I couldn't think straight. We were really close so…" I pause, frontin' like I'm tryna keep from breakin' down. By the time I finish givin' her my sob story of losin' my grandmother and bein' all fucked up over it, boo-hooin' 'n shit, I'ma have her offerin' to cop me another plane ticket to ATL. Listen, think what you want, but would you rather I hurt this Potato Head's feelin's and tell her that I wasn't fuckin' beat for her ass, that's why I didn't come through? Y'all muhfuckas need to get over it. I'ma do what I do, regardless.

"…Umm, listen, this's been hard on my whole family, feel me?"

"I feel you, baby. I feel so bad, though. I wish there was some-thing I could do to help you get through this."

"You understandin' and bein' here for me is more than enough," I tell her, grabbin' my keys and headin' for the door. I'm meetin' Akina at the Jersey Gardens Loews over in Elizabeth to check out that flick *Body of Lies*—wit' Leonardo DiCaprio and Russell Crowe—and if I'm lucky, I can get her to slide her hand down in my sweats and play wit' my balls durin' the show, then drop down and bob up 'n down on this dick. "I'ma hit you wit' some paper for that ticket as soon as—"

"Oh, no," she says, cuttin' me off, "that's not necessary. I called American Express and they took care of it for me. I got a full refund for the ticket. When you didn't show up at the airport, I called them right then and told them that there had been a family emergency, even though I didn't know there was."

"Oh, word? So you lied to 'em? That's wassup."

She laughs. "Well, yeah…I guess. But it ended up being the truth, so I didn't really lie." *If you say so*, I think, wonderin' how many other muhfuckas she's sponsored, then had to call her credit card company and lie to 'em when the nigga didn't come through. How many of 'em did she haveta call, screamin' for dissin' her. More than she'd like, I'm sure. "I still hope you can forgive me for going off the way I did. I know this is probably not the right time with you just getting back and all, but I really wanna see you. I've been missing you. So whenever you're ready to get away, let me know."

See. What I tell you? I smile. "Baby, I'm ready now. I really wanna see you, too. But my paper's kinda low." She cuts me off— as I knew she would, tellin' me I don't haveta worry 'bout money; that she's gonna get the ticket; that she wants her box rocked bad. "Damn, you really know howta fuck a nigga's head up, baby."

"I really care about you. And I'm always thinking about you." I shake my head. "Don't worry," she says, gigglin' like some silly-ass bimbo. "I'm not gonna ask you to marry me or anything like that."

"Yo, ma," I warn, turnin' up into the Jersey Gardens mall. "Remember what I told you. Don't get caught up. Let shit flow."

"I think it might be a little too late for that," she tells me, pausin'. "I already am."

I hear myself sayin', *"Then ya dumb ass is a fool."* But instead I say, "Listen, don't say I—"

She cuts me off. "I know, I know. But you can't stop me from feeling how I feel." I sigh, knowin' how this is gonna go down. She's gonna get way in over her head, then end up havin' a mutha-fuckin' emotional breakdown when I dismiss her ass. "I know you haven't made me any promises, but I love you, so I'm willing to take the risk. And whatever happens happens."

Bitch, you don't even fuckin' know me. I find a parkin' space, pullin' in. As I'm gettin' out the car, Akina texts me: Where are you?

"How you know it's love, and not infatuation?"

"Because I know the difference, and what I feel for you goes way beyond infatuation. Maybe I shouldn't be telling you all this, but oh, well. I feel what I feel. And I know what's in my heart for you. It's love."

"Then proceed wit' caution," I advise, makin' my way toward the movie theater. "Listen, I gotta take care of sumthin'. I'ma hit you up tomorrow, aiight?" She says okay, then tells me to have a good night. "Yeah, you too, baby," I say before disconnectin' the call. I text Akina: I'm walkin' in now.

When I walk up, Akina's standin' by the entrance wit' her hand on her hip, lookin' sexy as fuck in a black mohair sweater, a pair of black leggin's and a bangin'-ass pair of black four-inch platform Gucci boots. I peep niggas tryna check for her—hard, but she's iggin' 'em. I grin. "Yo, what it do, pretty baby?"

She rolls her eyes, suckin' her teeth. "Nigga, fuckin' with you, we 'bout to miss the damn movie."

I glance at my watch. The shit starts at seven-thirty. And it's seven-thirty, now. What the fuck she spazzin' 'bout when there's gonna be fifteen minutes of fuckin' previews? I shake my head, decidin' to let the shit go. "Yo, you tryna lose ya teeth? What I tell you 'bout ya mouth."

"Whatever," she says, tryna stomp off. I watch her juicy ass shake and bounce.

I run up behind her, grab her by the arm, then pull her into me, givin' her a tight hug. She tries to act like she ain't beat, but she doesn't pull away. "Yo, you ready to play wit' these balls?" I ask, whisperin' in her ear before lettin' her go.

"Nope," she says, pushin' a movie ticket into my chest. "Play with ya own damn balls."

I laugh, followin' her. "Yeah, right."

Four days later, Moms, Pops, and I were standin' in line to vote. The energy out there was wild, word up! Old heads, young heads, families of all shapes, sizes and colors were in line eager to be a part of change. Now we're glued in front of the TV watchin' CNN, waitin' to hear them announce Barack Obama as the next president of the United States. We've been waitin' all day, and now the time has finally come. When the announcement is finally made, the three of us are standin' in the middle of the livin' room, huggin' and shoutin' and high-fivin' each other. Moms starts wipin' tears. It's a beautiful moment watchin' Obama come out wit' his family, all holdin' hands, once it's official. Even Pops gets teary-eyed. Aiight, aiight…I ain't gonna front, I'm kinda emotional, too. I mean, damn…history's been made and I was a part of it, feel me? Hell, I'm so amped that I wanna celebrate the moment by beatin' up some pussy. I wanna slide deep up in it, then long stroke it 'til it skeets all over my dick. And that's exactly what I plan on doin'—well, after I blaze a fat-ass blunt. I give Moms and Pops hugs and tell 'em, "I'm out." It's already close to midnight, and I wanna get this dick wet before it gets too late.

As I'm gettin' in my ride, scrollin' through my address book to see who I can hit up for a quick pump 'n dump, my cell starts goin' off. It's a number I'm not familiar wit'. "Yo?"

"Alley Cat?"

The voice sounds familiar, but I can't figure out who the fuck it is. "Yeah, who's this?" I ask, startin' the engine. I light the rest of my blunt, then back outta the driveway, takin' a deep puff.

"It's Sherria."

I frown. *"Sherria?"* Unfuckin' believable! I haven't fucked wit' this broad in months. And the last time I heard from her is when she left that bullshit-ass message on my cell.

"Yeah."

"Why you callin'?"

"I was hoping we could talk. I don't like how things went down between us."

"Bitch, what the fuck we need to talk 'bout? How I rammed this dick up in ya fat ass?" I hear myself snappin'. I sigh. "Yo, check this out. You were dismissed. There's nuthin' else to talk 'bout."

"Dismissed, as you call it, without cause. I mean, damn…I thought things were going good between us. Then all of sudden, you just stop calling and returning my phone calls. I wanna know why?"

See, this is the shit I can't get wit'. I told this ho months ago that I wasn't beat to fuck wit' no chick who is always tossin' a damn bottle back. E'ery time we were together, this bitch had to have a bottle stuck down in her throat. I don't mind a chick who gets her drink on, but gotdamn…e'ery damn time I'm wit' you? That shit doesn't work for me. I confronted her once 'bout it, and she said she was gonna try to not drink as much 'round me. And for a minute, she was aiight. But, then her ass started doin' the same shit again. I'ma grown-ass man; I ain't wastin' time repeatin' myself. I'ma tell ya ass one time. If you don't take heed, then the shit's on you. I'ma dis ya ass. "You drink too damn much. That's why. And I got sick of it."

"Well, how come you didn't say something to me? I woulda cut back."

I laugh. "So instead of drinkin' seven days a week, you woulda cut back to what, six? Give me a break. What the fuck I look like sayin' sumthin' to you when I had already brought the shit to your attention from the jump? You musta banged ya damn head, if you think I'ma keep bringin' shit to someone's attention. I ain't that dude."

"Nigga, puhleeeze. You smoke weed all fucking day, but I never said shit about that. I accepted it."

I crack the windows, takin' another pull from the blunt. "And I'm smokin' now. So what does that haveta do wit' anything? You knew I smoked from the door, so if you had a problem wit' it, then you shoulda spoke on it. But you didn't, so that's on you, boo."

"And would you have stopped?"

"Hell no. I woulda fucked ya ass real good, then told you to keep it movin'. And that woulda been that."

"So basically I was somebody you could fuck, then fuck over?"

"If that's how you see it," I say, pullin' up into Pops' driveway, "then I guess that's how it was."

"Is that how *you* saw it?"

I glance at my watch, gettin' outta my whip. It's gettin' late as hell. Fuckin' 'round wit' her dumb ass I'ma end up not bein' able to get at some twat and end up beatin' my dick. I ignore the question. "Listen, I'm tryna get up in some pussy tonight, so I'm done wit' this back 'n forth wit' you. I'm tryna fuck; not waste energy on you or this phone call."

"Fuck YOU!" she screams into the phone. "You are so fucked up, nigga."

"Is that 'posed to make me feel some kinda way? 'Cause if so, I don't."

"You know what? Forget it. Where are my house keys?"

"*Your keys?* Are you fuckin' serious?" This ho is really reachin' now. She knows damn well she hasn't given those damn keys a thought. She called here on some other shit, and now all of a sudden, she wants to ask 'bout some muthafuckin' keys when she doesn't like what she's bein' told. Fuck outta here! "Dig, you had more than enough time to have ya locks changed. And if you didn't, then that shit's on you. But I tossed 'em. Now delete my number and beat it." Before she can open her dick sucka to say anthing else, I end the call. Then I text Carla: U feel like gettin' ya pussy popped?

While I wait for her to respond back, I text Maleeka: U wanna ride this dick tonight?

Whoever gets at me first gets the prize. My phone rings; it's that silly bitch callin' back. I press IGNORE. She leaves a message. I shake my head.

Carla texts back: U know I always want some of that big-ass dick. I wanna 69, 2!

I text back: I'll be there in 30 mins. Have them drawers off and that box clean 'n ready. Big daddy's cumin' through to bust that ass!

She texts back: See u when u get here.

My phone rings. It's Maleeka. "Yo, what it do, baby?"

"What time you tryna come through? I'm still doin' heads."

I start to tell her to forget it; that I already got plans, but quickly decide fuckin' two hoes in one night is a much better way to celebrate Obama's victory. "You tell me, what's good for you?"

"I should be done this last head 'round two-thirty. If you still up, swing through then."

"I gotta make a run, anyway. So that works out good. I'ma hit you up when I'm on my way."

"I don't have the kids, so you stayin' the night, right?"

"Awww, shit. You tryna get ya back dug out 'til the sun comes up. That's wassup."

She sucks her teeth. "Whatever. Just make sure you come through, so I can fuck the skin off that dick."

I laugh. "That's what ya mouth says."

"Don't front, nigga. You already know."

"Yeah, aiight," I say, takin' off my clothes. "I'll holla later." I toss the phone on the bed, goin' into the bathroom. I turn the shower on, take a piss, then hop in the shower. I grab the Tone body wash, and wash my ass, dick 'n balls extra good. Ten minutes later, I'm out the door. I hop in my hooptie, crank the engine, then back outta the driveway. *Yeah, these bitches love Daddy Long Stroke*, I think, sparkin' a blunt, makin' my way 'cross town to slay my first round of ass for the night.

30

A week later, I'm over at Pops' spot—up in my room chillin', shufflin' through mail and puffin' on a L while flippin' through TV channels tryna find sumthin' to watch. *Ain't shit on this bitch*, I think, tossin' the remote over on the other side of the bed. *Pay all this fuckin' money for a buncha hot garbage*. I turn on my laptop and wait for it to boot. I hear the doorbell ring, but don't give it much thought since I know Pops is somewhere in the house. I click on Internet Explorer, then hit up my Yahoo account. The minute I log on, it chimes, alertin' me I have new messages; eighty-seven, to be exact. As I'm goin' through 'em, a buncha IM's start poppin' up. Of course I ain't beat for any of 'em today. I don't know why I don't make myself invisible, knowin' this is the kinda shit I gotta deal wit' e'erytime I sign on. These thirsty bitches stay tryna get a taste of this chocolate stick. I ignore 'em all.

My cell rings. It's Akina. I decide she can leave a message. She calls again. I let the call roll into voicemail, again. Five minutes later, she's callin' back. I pick up. "What's good?"

"You need to check your messages," she says, soundin' tight. "Ya voicemail's full."

"Oh, aiight," I say, loggin' off Yahoo. "So what's poppin'?" I hit up my BlackPlanet page, then Myspace and Facebook pages, readin' and deletin' notes and ignorin' friend requests.

"Why is it the only time I hear from you is when you want

some pussy, ya dick sucked, or you need me to do something? Other than that, I'm the one always calling you."

"Ohhhhkay, ya point?"

"Muhfucka, the *point* is it would be nice if you took time outta your day to hit a bitch up to say, 'Hey, I was thinking about you. I don't need or want nothing; just wanted to see what's good with you.' Hell, it's not like I'm looking for you to come outta ya pockets 'cause we both know ain't shit in them bitches, except lint, any-damn-way…" This bitch tryna make it sound like I'm some bum-ass nigga. I frown, but keep my mouth shut and let her go on. "…I'm sick of feeling like I'm being used."

On some real shit, I'm kinda surprised she's comin' at me like this. Outta all the chicks I've smashed, she's been the one I kept 'round the longest 'cause she's never tried to stress a nigga. I mean. E'ery now and then she might get on some bullshit, tryna question me or some other shit, but she's never come at my neck. We had an understandin' that we do what we do and get up when we get up. At least that's what the fuck I thought. Man, listen…I don't know why the fuck bitches can't stick to the muthafuckin' script. Things would run so much smoother if they played their fuckin' positions instead of tryna turn shit into sumthin' extra. Damn, we only FUCKING!

I shake my head. "Yo, hol' up," I say, gettin' up off the bed, "you must be PMS-in' real bad to be comin' at me all sideways 'n shit. But, I'ma tell you what. Take that shit somewhere else 'cause I ain't beat for it. Not today, baby, real talk."

"You know what, Alley Cat. Kiss my motherfucking fat ass, for real, *baby*. You ain't never beat. Every time you don't like how something's being said to you, you wanna dismiss a bitch, like that shit's supposed to mean something. Fuck you, nigga! All them bitches you fucking and got sucking your dick ain't ever gonna have your black-ass back the way I've had it. But it's all good 'cause I'm done with ya dumb ass."

I sigh. "Yo, check this out. Where the fuck is all this comin' from?"

"Ask ya motherfucking boy, Ron, nigga."

"What? *Ron?* What that nigga got to do wit' how you comin' at me?"

"I saw him at Divas last night all drunk up 'n shit. That nigga was tryna press up real hard 'n shit and ride all up on a bitch." For some reason, I feel myself gettin' tight hearin' this shit. Not 'cause I got some claim on her, but 'cause that nigga knows what it is wit' me and her. And he straight disrespected that.

"Okay, so he was tryna get at you. And? You still ain't said what that got to do wit' how you talkin'."

"The nigga told me all about your stay in Atlanta. You know. The motherfucking trip I FUCKING paid for! I asked you straight out if you went there to see some other bitch on my dime, and you told me no. But come to find out, you were out there fucking some big-faced, handicapped bitch in a wheelchair or some shit. At my FUCKING expense! That shit is foul as hell. It's one thing for you to have another bitch's pussy all dried up around your funky-ass balls while I'm sucking your dick. And it's another to take my hard-earned money and go see some other bitch, then lie about it. Nigga, I don't think so!"

Ain't this some shit?! That hatin'-ass, bitch-ass nigga! I always knew he was diggin' her, but I didn't think the pussy-ass nigga would try 'n snake me to get at her. I'ma confront his ass. But, instead of goin' in his mouth, I'ma let 'im think he got that off. And the next time his girl comes at me on some slick shit, tryna wet this dick, I'ma fuck the dog shit outta her ugly, knotty-headed ass. I'ma wipe this nut all over her big-ass dick suckas. Straight disrespect her ass on the strength of how that muhfucka tried to play me, word up. I might even take a few snapshots and post 'em up on Facebook. The crazy part is I never told the nigga 'bout that ep. The only person I said anything to was Gee's dumb ass.

"I thought we already had this conversation, and I told you what it was. I also told you I'd give you your money back, but you didn't want it."

"No, nigga, I wanted the truth."

"And I gave it to you."

She sucks her teeth. "Yeah, muhfucka, your version of it."

"So you mean to tell me, after three years of us kickin' it, you gonna believe some muhfucka you don't even know over me? You gonna let some drunk-ass nigga get all up in ya head. Damn, I thought you was bigger than that."

"Muhfucka, don't go there. Ain't nobody get up in shit. If *you* was bigger than that, we wouldn't be havin' this conversation. Dude seemed to know what the hell he was talking about. Why would the nigga wanna lie on you, if he's ya boy 'n shit?"

"That nigga ain't *my* boy. He's a muhfucka I chilled wit' on the strength. Obviously, the nigga wanna smash or beat ya throat up."

"Whatever. The only thing that nigga can do is beat it. He can't do shit else for me."

"Yeah, but you believin' what the fuck comes outta his mouth. What kinda shit is that?"

"It's me thinking that maybe the nigga spoke the truth since I was kinda doubting ya lyin', sneaky ass any-damn-way. Your freak-ass probably was fuckin' some crippled bitch. Who knows what the fuck you be doing."

"Yo, get real, what the fuck a big-dick nigga like me look like fuckin' some disabled bitch in a wheelchair? That shit don't even sound right. I'd rip her fuckin' box out the frame. But since you wanna believe some crazy-ass shit like that, then go 'head. Do you."

"Muhfucka, don't try that reverse-pyschology bullshit with me. I know your kind, nigga. And I think there's some truth to what that nigga told me. So you can say what the fuck you want. As far as I'm concerned, you're real fucked up for it."

I sigh. "I see you wanna beef, so I'ma let you go."

"Yeah, nigga, you do that!"

"Peace," I say, disconnectin' the call, then tossin' the phone onto the bed. I feel a muthafuckin' headache comin' on. And I'm all outta blunts. *Fuck!* I swing open the bedroom door and head downstairs to get sumthin' to drink. All the lights are out and the house is quiet. *Pops musta dipped over to Moms',* I think, walkin' into the kitchen. I grab a glass from outta the dishwasher, then open the 'fridge and pour myself some cranberry juice. I take the bag of Cool Ranch Doritos off the counter and head back into the livin' room.

I flop on the sofa—still heated. I can't believe that crab-ass nigga told Akina that bullshit, tryna fuck up my groove. Got her comin' at my neck all crazy 'n shit, like she's 'bout to dismiss a nigga. She's straight trippin', for real. Aiight, aiight...what I did was fucked up, but that nigga had no muthafuckin' business runnin' his muthafuckin' mouth tellin' her shit. I can't front on the chick, though. Akina's always had my back. No matter what time of the day or night it is, anytime I've called her, she's always been Johnny on the spot. Not that she was sittin' 'round waitin' on me to get at her. She just seems to always make time for me when I do. But now this fake muhfucka done went and tossed salt in the game.

I grab the remote off the coffee table, turnin' the TV on. *Nigga, what in the hell you sittin' here trippin' for? She ain't ya girl. If she wanna bounce, then tell her bounce. You had a good run. The shit wasn't gonna last forever. Eventually, she was gonna be out anyway. So, fuck it!* I think, flippin' through the channels. I contemplate callin' Gee's dumb ass and blastin' 'im for runnin' his muthafuckin' mouth, but decide to get at 'im the next time I see 'im, or the next time he hits me up. I tell u, muhfuckas gotta always be on some extra shit. *I'ma give her a few days to cool off, then get at her to see where her head is.* "Hopefully, back in this lap," I mumble, chewin' on a mouthful of chips. I take a long gulp of juice to rinse 'em down. As usual, ain't shit on the television. I'm relieved to catch *Dexter* on Showtime. Yo, this dude is one sick muhfucka; a muthafuckin' serial killer workin' for the police department. That's some shit right there. Although I've missed most of the season's episodes, I make a mental note to purchase the DVD when it comes out.

Ten minutes into the show, my cell rings. I suck my teeth. It's Akina callin' back. I consider iggin' the shit, but I don't. "Where are you?" she asks the minute I answer. She doesn't sound as tight as she was earlier, but there's still a sharp edge to her tone.

"I'm at the crib, why?"

"I need to see you."

"For what?"

She huffs. "I'm on my way over. I'll get into it then." She hangs up before I can respond. I sigh, shakin' my head.

Twenty minutes later, she's at the door wit' her face all twisted up. I open it and let her in. "I hope you ain't come over here to beef 'cause if so, you coulda did that shit over the phone, word up."

She rolls her eyes, brushin' past me wearin' a brown three-quarter leather coat and a pair of knee-high boots. "Nigga, ain't nobody come here to beef with you," she says, unfastenin' her coat. "I'm here to set the record straight. And get shit out in the open, once and for all."

I stare at her shiny lips. They have me thinkin' 'bout havin' 'em wrapped 'round the head of my dick. I wanna grab my shit, pull it out, but don't. She squints her slanted eyes at me. She knows my mind is startin' to wander. Knows I'm startin' to become preoccupied wit' sexin' her. She shifts her weight from one foot to the other. She has a strand of hair swooped over her face and it makes her look sexier than she already is.

She removes her coat and wraps it over her arm. She smells good as hell. I inhale, tryna figure out what she has on. I can't front, like so many of the other broads I fuck—okay, okay...and fucked over—this bitch is bad as hell. She'd definitely be a good woman for someone, just not me. For me, she's only good for fuckin'.

"You want me to take that?" I ask, reachin' for her coat.

"Nope," she says as she walks over to the sofa. I peep the way her designer jeans wrap 'round her ass like an extra layer of skin, and feel my dick jump. She sits down. "I won't be here long."

"Oh, word? So what you gotta say to me in person that you couldn't say over the phone?"

"Look, let me be clear on something. I know what it is...I mean, what it was, between us—absolutely nothin'. The only thing we've been is fuck buddies. And I've been cool with that. But what I'm not cool with is you tryna play me as some dumb-ass chick. That does not sit well with me."

I decide to keep some distance between us and sit in the chair 'cross from her. "Yo, I don't think that."

"Yes, you do."

"Yo, how you gonna tell me what I think?"

"Well, you act like it. And it pisses me the fuck off that you would even come at me like I was. And it pisses me off even more that I've allowed you to make me feel vulnerable and used and disrespected. I know I can't be mad at you 'cause you told me what it was wit' you from the gate. And you've shown me time and time again who you really are. But I still chose to fuck with you. So I get what I get 'cause I've allowed it..." She pauses, stares at me, throws her head back, fights back tears.

"I can't keep lying to myself. I love you, nigga. I don't know when it happened. But it did. Even though I knew in my head I shoulda kept it moving; that I shoulda never let you in my head, or my heart, 'cause you're no motherfucking good, I still allowed myself to fall head over heels for you anyway. And it hurts knowing that you don't love me back. It hurts knowing that you aren't capable of loving anyone other than yourself..."

Damn, that's the same shit Cherry hit me wit'. I shift in my seat. She's right. I don't love *her*, I like her. But that doesn't mean I'm not capable of loving someone other than myself.

"...I've tried to act like you fucking other chicks doesn't bother me, but it does. You're the only nigga I'm fucking. I cut e'eryone else off, still knowing you were gonna be plowing ya dick through a buncha bitches. You get at me when you get at me, and my stupid ass sits around waiting for you to toss me the scraps them other hoes leave behind. I'm not blaming you. I blame myself. But the shit still hurts. You told me, warned me, not to get too caught up in you, but I did any-damn-way. And it's gotten way outta hand. I thought I could handle it, but I can't.

"And right now, I need for you to look me in my face and tell me the fuckin' truth. Not the lie you've turned inside-out to become the reality you've created in your fucked-up head. I want the real T-R-U-T-H. That's the only thing I wanna hear. Can you do that?"

I take a deep breath. I'm really not beat for this shit right now. But I created this shit wit' her, and listenin' to her spill her heart out to me has a muhfucka feelin' some kinda way. If she wants the truth, then I owe it to her. That's the least I can give her, feel me? "You got that," I say, leanin' forward in my seat, restin' my elbows on my knees.

"Then tell me this. Is anything that nigga Ron said true? Were you in Atlanta fuckin' some crippled-ass bitch on my dime?"

"Hell, no," I tell her, frownin'. "She was a mid…uh, I mean, little person."

She blinks, blinks again. Tilts her head as if she's tryna wrap her mind 'round what I've said. "*A little person,*" she repeats in disbelief, "like in *midget*?"

I nod. "Yeah, sumthin' like that."

"Wait. Wait one goddamn minute! You fucking dissed me to stick ya dick up in some midget?!" She stares at me in disbelief. "OhmyfuckingGod, pleeeeeeease tell me you're joking. You're actually telling me you fucking looked me in my face and lied about having a dying grandmother, so you could get out to Atlanta to FUCK some goddamn dwarf bitch?!"

I run my hands over my face, then cup the back of my head. "Yeah, I mean, no." She tilts her head, raises her eyebrow. "Yeah, I lied about my grandmother bein' sick. But chick lied to me. I didn't know she was a half-pint 'til I got there."

"And that's supposed to make the shit better? Nigga, puhleeze! That's exaaaactly what ya lying, sneaky ass gets," she says through clenched teeth. "I'm sooooooo fucking pissed right now. OhmyGod, I don't believe this shit. I really hoped what the nigga was talking was a buncha shit." She stares at me, shakes her head. "You know what? I can't even be mad at you 'cause you were only being who you are. I knew from the jump you were a dog, so I don't know what I was thinking. Niggas like you don't change 'cause you don't ever think what you're doing is wrong. And because there's bitches like me who'll keep allowing you to do the shit you do, you'll always do what you do. We always want what we can't have. And I know for a fact I will never have you. No one will. 'Cause ya black ass is too goddamn selfish!"

She breaks down and starts that cryin' shit. A part of me wants to tell her to shut the fuck up wit' all that noise; to go wipe her snotty-ass nose; to get the fuck out 'cause I told her so, but... another part of me, is feelin' kinda bad for her. Then again, why the fuck should I? She brought this shit on herself.

I get up from my seat and excuse myself while I go upstairs. A few minutes later, I come back down. She's still crying, but not howlin' like a damn wounded hyena. I hand her five bills. "Yo, here's ya money back."

Instead of her takin' the shit, she stares at my hand, then fuckin' snaps, jumpin' up swingin' off on a nigga, like she's possessed. "Nigga, I don't give a fuck about that money. You fuckin' tried to be on some slick shit. You think handin' me that paper's gonna change shit?"

"Yo, hol' up," I say, grabbin' her by the wrists.

"Get the fuck off me!" She yanks her arms, but I gotta tight grip on 'em. "Why the fuck you have to lie to me, huh, nigga? Why the fuck did you have to fucking play me?" She starts tryna kick me. We wrestle a bit 'til I get her in a bear hug. I'm really tryna keep from swingin' her ass into a wall, then straight smashin' her chin, but she's not makin' it easy for me. The whole time I'm wrestlin' wit' her ass, I'm glad Pops ain't here. And I'm hopin' like hell he doesn't walk in on this shit.

"Yo, c'mon, baby, you wildin' out, for real."

"C'mon, hell, nigga. Don't fucking 'baby' me. Get ya fucking hands off me!" She starts tryna kick my shins, and stomp down on my feet. The bitch has me shufflin' 'round tryna keep her from diggin' her six-inch heels in me. I swear I don't need this shit right now. I squeeze her tighter. Flip her ass onto the sofa, knockin' shit over. I pin her down. She's still cursin' and screamin' and tryna wriggle herself free. She's straight beastin'. And I've never seen her like this. Wild and muthafuckin' crazy. "Get the fuck off of me!"

"Not until you calm down," I say, pressin' my forearm into her neck.

"You're...choking...me..."

"Then stop tryna fight me. I don't wanna fight wit' you. I understand you're mad. But I'm not 'bout to apologize for you gettin' all caught up in ya feelin's."

"Fuck you! Get the fuck off of me!"

"You need to calm down first, for real." After 'bout ten more minutes of her thrashin' around, she finally stops movin'. I slowly let up on my grip, takin' my forearm from offa her neck. "You calm?"

"Get...off...of...ME." My gut tells me to keep her ass pinned down a lil' longer, but I don't listen to it. I let her go, and as soon as I do, she jumps up and starts hookin' off. "I hate you, you black motherfucker!" She hits me in the mouth, bustin' my lip. I try to grab her. She swings again. I block her blow. Grab her by the arm, and twist it behind her back. I don't wanna hit her. I swear I don't. But I'm startin' to think I'ma haveta knock her the fuck out, or break her goddamn arm to calm her ass down. I grab her tighter. And this bitch bites my arm. She grinds her teeth into my skin. Now she has me hollerin' and screamin' like a lil' bitch.

"Yo, what the fuck! Owww...get the fuck off.... Fuck!" I try to pry her off of my arm before she bites a chunk of my arm off. And, before I know what's come over me, I punch the bitch in her damn head. One, two, three quick blows to her dome before she finally lets go of my arm. I grab it. She grabs her head. Blood is comin' from my mouth and arm. "Fuck!"

"OhmyGod," she says, holdin' both sides of her head. "I can't fucking believe you punched me in my head like that. Ohmy-fuckingGod, you fucker! I got a big-ass knot in my head."

This ho put her hands on me, *first*. Then sunk her muthafuckin' fangs in me, busted my lip, and got me comin' outta pocket. "Bitch, you damn straight I lumped ya ass up. What you did wasn't cool, at all. Puttin' ya muthafuckin' hands on me. And right now I feel like hittin' ya ass, again. Dead in the center of your muthafuckin' forehead. So you best get ya shit, and get the fuck out before I break your muthafuckin' jaw."

I'm pacin' the room, practically foamin' out the mouth. I literally feel myself 'bout to black on her ass. Her eyes bulge. I can tell I'm scarin' her. Good! She's crossed the muthafuckin' line, feel me? I have never put my hands on a broad, but you got the game fucked up, if you think I'ma ever sit back and let a bitch hook off on me and shit's gonna be sweet. I ain't that nigga! And all I know is if she doesn't bounce the fuck up outta here in less than ten seconds, I'ma forget my vow to never put my hands on a female, and beat this bitch the fuck up tonight, word up!

✑ 31 ✑

"What happened to your lip?" Moms asks the minute I step through the door. It's still swollen from that shit wit' Akina the other night. I know Pops already told her how he walked in and found the livin' room all tossed up and Akina lookin' all wild-eyed, yellin' and screamin', runnin' outta the front door, holdin' the side of her head, almost knockin' him over. And there I was standing there with blood dripping from my arm and lip. He straight blacked on me.

"Nigga, I fuckin' told you I didn't want this motherfucking shit up in my house. I warned your black ass some bullshit like this was gonna happen. But you wanted to keep bringing these unstable broads up in here, disrespecting my goddamn house. But I tell you what. You done fucked ya last piece of ass up in here!"

"My bad," I said, pickin' pillow cushions from off the floor and puttin' them back on the sofa. Yeah, I know it was some weak shit. But what else could I say? He was right. I fucked up. I swear, I never seen dude go off the way he did walkin' up in that piece seein' his coffee table knocked over, the sofa cushions all over, pictures on the wall crooked. E'erything was outta place.

"*My bad?* Nigga, are you fucking crazy? My bad? That's all you gotta…" He stopped in midsentence, opened and closed his right fist. On some real shit, I know he wanted to swing off, but he didn't. And he woulda had a right to. But on some real shit, I don't know if I coulda stood there and let him straight duke me wit'out goin'

in on 'im, Pops or not. He bit his bottom lip, shook his head.
"Leave e'eryting where it is. Get your shit...and get the fuck out
before I forget you're my son, and fuck you the hell up."

"It's nuthin'," I tell her, kissin' her on the check. "I got into a
lil' scuffle wit' a disgruntled customer."

She smirks. "Uh-huh, 'disgruntled customer,' my ass." She shakes
her head. "You don't have to lie to me. You *know* I already know."

"I know, so why'd you ask?"

"Just to see what you were gonna say. And I heard ya father
finally put your ass out, too."

*And leave ya fucking key on the table when you leave 'cause you are
no longer welcomed to come in and outta here.* I couldn't be mad at 'im,
though. Bottom line, it's his crib. And I disrespected his space.

She shakes her head. "I told him it was only a matter of time
before you brought that mess up in there, but he didn't wanna
listen to me. The best thing he coulda did was take his house keys
from you. He shoulda did it a long time ago. Instead of complaining to me about all that fucking you had going on up in there, he
shoulda been talking to you about it. I told him ya ass was too
damn old to be still laying up over there, *and* not paying bills.
Mmmph. I love you dearly, but ya ass is a magnet for drama. And
this is only the beginning. I've tried to warn you to stop fucking
over all those women. But ya ass is hard-headed. Lord only knows
what else is about to go down. But whatever it is, I know it ain't
gonna be pretty 'cause you done fucked over too many women.
I hate to say it, but you are worse than your father ever was."

The center of my head starts poundin'. And hearin' her tryna
compare me to Pops and ramblin' on and on is only makin' it worse.
"Ma, I'm a grown-ass man. I didn't come here to be lectured,
aiight? Damn. I don't need this shit right now."

She slams her hand on her hip, stares me down. "'Scuse me?
What did you just say?"

Not thinkin', I repeat myself.

"Oh really? Well, I tell you what. You can take ya black ass on up outta here. I don't know who the fuck you think you talking to, but I am still your goddamn mother!"

Fuck! She's the last person I need to be beefin' wit', for real. "You right, Ma, my bad. I apologize."

She clucks her tongue. "Mmmph. You just oughta be. 'Cause I'm not the one. I will smack your damn face up."

"I was outta pocket, Ma," I say, walkin' up on her and givin' her a hug. "You know I'd never disrespect you." I try to kiss her on the cheek.

"Hmmph," she grunts, sidesteppin' me. "Try it and get fucked up, okay? Now, are you hungry? I made some smothered chicken and brown rice."

I smile. "You already know."

"Hmmph, I shouldn't give your black ass nothing," she says, switchin' off toward the kitchen. I follow behind, apologizin' again. I pull a chair out and sit at the table. She brings me an empty plate, then tosses it down in front of me.

"I don't know why the hell you sittin' there like I'm about to serve you. Get your spoiled ass on over there"—she points toward the stove—"and fix your own damn plate. Hazel the Maid is done servin' your fresh ass, Mister Grown-Ass Man." I get up, shakin' my head. "And when you're done, wash your motherfucking dishes. You done lost what's left of your goddamn mind talking shit to me."

I'm not sure what's set her off, but whatever it is, I'm convinced it has nuthin' to do wit' me. I keep my mouth shut, though. Let her rant 'n rave as I scoop out a big spoon of rice, cover it wit' three pieces of chicken and a buncha gravy, then stick my plate in the microwave.

Fuck!

While I'm standin' there waitin' for my food to heat up, when

I sit down to eat, up until the time I finally finish my food, the only thing she does is stare at me. Lips twisted, eyes squinted, starin' through me—in disgust. Yeah, I'm kinda pissed that she's actin' all funny-style 'n shit. But I ain't gonna sweat it. I get up from the table, wash my dishes, take out the trash, then walk over to her and kiss her on the cheek, then dip. I get into my car, spark the rest of my blunt and head the fuck back to my crib down at the shore. I glance at my watch: 8:15 p.m. *I feel like gettin' this dick sucked tonight. Maybe I'll hit up Crystal's fat ass and see if she feels like wettin' it.* "She just needs to keep her muthafuckin' socks on," I say aloud.

I dial her number. "Hey, baby," she says, "I was thinking about calling you."

"Oh, word? Wassup?"

"You left your boxer briefs here."

I frown, shakin' my head. What the fuck?! I rocked her box three weeks ago and she's tellin' me this dumb shit, now. Why didn't this bitch hit me up before? I knew I left 'em there, but I wasn't pressed. "Yo, you can toss them shits," I tell her, takin' another pull off my blunt.

"Oh, no, I'ma hold onto 'em."

Why the fuck you wanna hold onto a muhfucka's worn drawers? I think. Whatever! I let it go. "Did you wash 'em?"

"No," she says.

I frown. "Why?"

"Because I love to sniff 'em," she whispers, "while I'm playing in my pussy. I can still smell you in 'em." *What a nasty bitch*, I think, shakin' my head. *Sniffin' a nigga's crotch like a dog in heat.* When you got a bitch sniffin' yo' dirty drawers, beatin' her pussy, you already know you gotta nut on ya hands. But, I knew why she kept her nose pressed up in 'em. Sometimes, when I know I'm 'bout to lay this pipe, I mix a little Egyptian Musk with some baby oil, then rub it into my pubic hairs, underneath my balls, and the crack of my ass. Other times, I just dab coconut oil on. The way I like to fuck and get sucked, a nigga gots to keep his dick 'n balls fresh at all times. Well, that is, unless I'm leavin' a ho's cum juice dried up 'round my balls for someone else to clean off, feel me? Then it's straight musk and pussy funk.

"Listen, baby, you feel like suckin' on this dick tonight?"

"I feel like doing a whole lot more than just sucking. I wanna fuck, too."

Damn, why the fuck can't I just get a fuckin' dick suck wit'out the extras? I sigh. Decide to go the fuck home. "You know what, forget I called."

"Why?"

"I'm not checkin' for pussy tonight."

"Well, damn. Can you at least finger-pop me?"

You suck.

You swallow.

You please me 'til I'm satisfied.

You ask no questions, 'cept, "May I suck you, again?"

That's the kinda mood I'm in. "Nah, I want my dick wet, that's it. So don't sweat it. I'ma head home and watch *True Blood* instead."

"Are you fuckin' serious?"

"I sure am."

She sucks her teeth, then the phone goes dead. *Bitch musta hung up*, I think, slowin' down at the toll booth, then tossin' four quarters into the bin. I take the last pull off my blunt, then toss it outta the window.

As soon as I get in the house, I take off my clothes, then hop in the shower. I lather up my body, soap up my dick, then start strokin' it, cuppin' and yankin' my balls and dippin' at the knees. I work my nut up to the tip of my dick, then abruptly stop. I let it roll back down into my balls, then work it back up again. I repeat it three more times 'til my balls start to swell and ache, then let it blast out all over the shower walls. "Gotdamn, that shit was good," I say, steppin' outta the shower and wrappin' a towel 'round my waist, lettin' water drip all over the floor as I go into the bedroom. I oil my body, slip on a pair of boxer briefs and a wife beater, then head downstairs.

After I hit up Papa John's and order a veggie pizza, I flip on the flat-screen, spark another blunt, then wait for *True Blood* to come on. My cell rings. "Hello?"

"We need to talk."

Fuck! "Yo, I ain't fuckin' wit' you," I tell her. Akina's been hittin' me up for the last two days and I've been iggin' her. But today she got on some slick shit and called me from another number. "There's nuthin' else we need to say. You said what you had to say, then you fucked up and put ya hands on me, so it's a wrap, boo."

"Nigga, you put ya hands on me, too."

"Bitch, are you on crack or some shit? I was fuckin' tryna get you off of me. I wouldna punched the shit outta you, if you weren't tryna bite my damn arm off."

"And you grabbed me by the throat."

"Yeah, and?"

"*And?* Nigga, you coulda killed me."

Yeah, I tried to snap her muthafuckin' windpipe. Once she bit my arm up and I saw blood, it was a wrap. I've never put my hands on a chick, and I have never allowed one to put their hands on me. So why this bitch thought she was gonna be an exception is beyond me. I shake my head. These hoes kill me. They jump up in a nigga's face, hookin' off on a muhfucka, then don' think they should get the shit beat outta them. Fuck what ya heard. Don't put ya muthafuckin' hands on me, and I won't put mine on you. I'm not down wit' that shit. But, be clear. If you bring it, then all bets are off. You gonna get lumped the fuck up. And that's what it is.

"Then I guess you woulda got what ya ass deserved."

"Are you fucking serious? You think I deserved having my neck snapped?"

"You put ya muthafuckin' hands on me, hell, yeah. You lucky I didn't break ya damn face."

"Well, you shoulda never lied to me."

I shake my head. "So I lied. And?"

"And you should feel fucked up about it. I thought we were better than that. You know I woulda done anything for you. All you had to do was kept shit real. But, noooo, nigga. You had to be on some extra shit."

I sigh, rubbin' my chin. "Yo, listen. You right. I shoulda kept it real wit' you. But I didn't." She wants to know why. And on some real shit, I don't know. "Because I felt like it," I tell her. She sucks her teeth. Asks if I'm gonna at least apologize. "Listen, what I did to you mighta been fucked up, but I'm not gonna apologize for it. I did what I did 'cause I wanted to. Just like you put ya hands on me 'cause you wanted to. And that's what it is."

"So basically fuck me, right?"

"Your words, not mine," I say, endin' the call.

32

Six A.M., I wake up. My dick hard, heavy, and achin' wants release. A muhfucka's mad horny. And straight jackin' my shit ain't gonna cut it. Not at this moment. I need to stick it in sumthin'. But I ain't beat for a buncha noise. I get outta bed, go into my walk-in closet and come back out wit' my "Baby Got Back Sex Doll" wit' the wireless vibratin' pussy and ass. I lube it up, then fuck it doggie-style grabbin' its perky titties and thrustin' this naked cock up in it. This is the only time I get to fuck raw. I close my eyes and imagine I'm gettin' it in wit' Halle Berry. I'm tearin' that ass up a mile a minute, givin' her all of me. Its pussy walls vibrate along the sides of my dick. I pull out, pour more lube up in it, then slide my dick back in, pumpin' 'n gruntin'. "Aaah, shit."

Yo, hol' up, I know there's no substitute for some real, live, pussy. But e'ery now and then, a muhfucka ain't beat for all the extras. I don't use this thing often, but when I do…man, listen, I get my two-hundred-and-sixty dollars outta it. And the good thing is, I ain't gotta worry 'bout it stressin' me the hell out. I can bust all up in it, clean it up, then lock it away 'til the next time. And that's exactly what I do.

'Bout eight-thirty I head over to the gym, get in a two-hour workout, then come back home to shower. As I'm steppin' into my boxers, my cell rings. The special ring tone alerts me that it's Moms.

"So you gonna let days go by without calling?" she asks as soon as I answer.

"Nah, I been busy," I lie.

"Mmmph," she grunts. "Too busy to pick up a phone, I see."

"Sumthin' like that. But if you really want the truth, I figured I give you some space since you were spazzin' out the last time I saw you."

"Well, if you wanna live in your feelings, then you go right ahead. When you're ready to get over yourself, you know I'ma still love you. And I'ma still curse you the hell out when need be."

"Yeah, I know."

"Well, I'm calling you for two reasons. One, to let you know your father was admitted into the hospital last night."

I flop down on my bed, shocked. "Hospital? What happened to him?" She tells me that he was havin' chest pains. That his blood pressure is sky-high and they're keeping him under observation for another night. That he's at UMDNJ University Hospital in Newark. She gives me the visitin' times. And for some strange reason, I'm feelin' responsible for what happened to 'im. "Damn," I say, rubbin' my forehead, "was he havin' a heart attack or sumthin'?"

"They're not sure. Hopefully, they'll know more once all the tests are in. In the meantime, that's where he's gonna be."

"Cool. I'll be up there later on tonight. Now, what was ya other reason for callin'?"

"I met Ramona."

"Who?" I ask, frownin'. She repeats herself. "I heard you. But I'm surprised. Where'd you meet that broad at?"

"Over at your father's. She showed up there looking for you, but when your father told her you weren't there, she asked to come in to speak with him. He thought I might wanna have a chat with her as well."

"About what?" I ask, feelin' myself gettin' agitated.

"She told us she's carryin' your baby."

"Yeah, and? She's the chick I was tellin' you about."

"I figured that. Well, she says she's keeping it. She also said you told her you wanted nothing to do with her or the baby."

This fuckin' bitch! I clench my teeth. Feel the muscles in my jaw tighten. "She's right. I don't want shit to do wit' her. 'Cause that's. Not. My. Baby."

"Are you sure?"

I suck my teeth, sighin'. "Ma, of course, I'm sure. That broad's not pregnant by me. She's delusional."

"She also said you've put your hands on her, too. Is that true?"

"Say, what?!? What the fuck! I've never touched that fuckin' lyin'-ass nut."

"I hope not. But after your incident at your father's, I'm not so sure."

A muhfucka's 'bout to black. "Ma, I gotta go. I'm not gettin' into this wit' you. I'll talk to you later, aiight."

"I'm not done talking."

"Well, I am. I'll see you at the hospital." I disconnect the call before she can say sumthin' else, then immediately hit Ramona's ass up. She answers on the fifth ring. "Aye, yo, what the fuck are you doin'?"

"Ummm, whadaya mean?"

"Yo, what the fuck you mean, 'whadaya mean'? Don't fuckin' play games wit' me. You know what the fuck I'm talkin' 'bout."

"I knew I'd hear from you," she states calmly. "How you been, baby?"

"What the fuck you doin' goin' over to my Pops' spot?"

"Well I needed to get your attention some kind of way. And obviously, I have."

"Yo, you fuckin' crazy, for real, yo."

She laughs. "Nigga, you can call me crazy all you want. The fact still remains that I'm pregnant. And it's yours."

"No, the fact is you're a lyin' nut-ass."

"And I'm still pregnant."

I can tell this ho is gonna be a muthafuckin' thorn in my side. It's moments like this I wish I had a buncha sisters I could call on when I needed them to rock a ho's snotbox. "Okay, maybe you are, but for the hundredth time…It's. NOT. Mine!

"It *is* yours."

"Whatever, yo. Anytime we fucked I wrapped up."

"Well, a few times I poked holes in the condoms."

"Say what?"

"You heard me."

I blow out a buncha aggravated air. "And how the fuck you do that?"

"Easy. I'd wait until you went into the bathroom, then I'd reach over and take the condoms you'd leave on the dresser, or I'd sneak and get the ones you had in your pants pocket and poke 'em up. Of course, I didn't do it right away. I waited for the right time. Watched your moves every time you were with me before doin' anything. And voilá! I'm with child. Your child. Now what would you like to name him or her?"

On some real shit, a muhfucka can't believe what the fuck I'm hearin'. But, then again I can. This goes to show how mutha-fuckin' desperate this bottom-of-the-barrel bitch really is. Yeah, she mighta poked holes in the condoms, but a muhfucka never nutted in her. I'd always pull out and bust down in her throat, or all over her face and titties. So unless she scooped the shit up offa her nipples and lips, then planted it up in her, she's a mutha-fuckin' lie. So the joke's on her retarded ass. "I'm not namin' it shit, 'cause it ain't mine. You know it, and I know it. Now stop callin' me. And stay the fuck away from my family."

She laughs. "Or what, my baby daddy?"

I shake my head. "Yo, do us both a favor, and go jump ya dizzy-ass off a cliff." I disconnect the call, sparkin' a blunt. Fuckin' wit' her ass done gave me a splittin'-ass headache. *This psycho bitch tryna drive a muhfucka to start lacin' his shit*, I think, blowin' smoke up at the ceilin'.

By the time I get to the hospital to see Pops, it's close to six-thirty. Visitin' is over at like eight, I think. When I get to the visitor's desk, I get my visitor's pass, then make my way to the elevators. There's mad heads e'erywhere up in this piece. I shake my head, hopin' like hell I never end up in this bitch. Pops' room is up on the tenth floor. I walk toward his wing, then look for his room number. A few nurses speak and smile. I speak back, but keep it movin'.

"Hey, old man," I say, walkin' into his room. He's sittin' up in his bed readin' the *Star-Ledger* newspaper. There's a *New York Times* on the side of him. "You mean to tell me you didn't have anything better to do than get ya'self put in the hospital." I give him a pound, then a kiss on the forehead. Pops and I have always been close; not like I am wit' Moms, but still our bond is tight. On some real shit, they're all I got. If sumthin' happens to either one of 'em, I'ma be fucked up. Seein' him up in this piece gotta muhfucka feelin' some kinda way. I really fucked up.

He smiles; seems happy to see me. "I needed a break, what can I say. Glad you made it up to see me. But you coulda waited until I got home. They claim I'm being released in the morning."

I take a seat in the chair next to the bed. "Oh, word? So e'erything's aiight wit' you, man?"

"So they say. They ran a buncha stress tests. My pressure's high and they tell me my sugar's up. But other than that, they say I'm okay." I feel relieved. And fucked up for how things went down at his crib wit' Akina. I decide to apologize, again. Tell 'em I was really outta pocket for bringin' that shit up in his space like that. "Look, son, that's water under the bridge. It was bound to happen, sooner or later. Unfortunately, I had to walk in on it. I tried to warn you, but ya ass is too damn hard-headed…"

"Just like you," Moms says, walkin' into the room. I get up and give her a hug and kiss. "He's you, all over again."

Pops chuckles. "Woman, I wasn't that bad."

She grunts, shakin' her head. She hangs her coat up in Pops' closet. They go back 'n forth 'bout it. I decide to stay outta their lil' debate. Ya'll already know how I feel 'bout it. And I'ma keep sayin' it 'til I'm blue in the face: "I ain't nuthin' like him." I take the other seat 'cross the room. Let Moms sit next to Pops.

"Well, it shouldna never went down like that," Pops says. "I hope you learned ya lesson."

Yeah, I learned a lesson, aiight. I learned to only fuck wit' outta-state hoes from now on. I decide to keep that shit to myself. "I had no business bringin' that drama up in ya spot, Pops."

"You got that right," Moms adds. "And you shoulda never put your hands on that girl."

"And you right," I agree, sighin'. "But she threw her hands up, first. Then she bit me. So she got what she got. I don't feel good 'bout it, but it is what it is."

"Still doesn't make what you did right. You're lucky she hasn't filed complaints on you."

"Ma, listen. The only thing I regret is that it happened up in Pops' crib. Other than that, had she kept her hands to herself, I wouldna lumped her up."

Moms opens her mouth to say sumthin' else, but Pops reaches over and squeezes her arm. She pulls in her bottom lip. Lets it go, for now. "Tell us about this Ramona gal," Pops says, changin' the subject. "Your mother told you she stopped by the house looking for you, right?"

"Yeah, she told me earlier today. There's really nuthin' to tell. We kicked it for a minute. I sexed her down. She was too clingy. I dismissed her. That's it. And now she's claimin' to be pregnant. But it's *not* mine. Then I learn today that that desperate broad was punchin' holes in the condoms." Pops shakes his head. Moms stares at me. "I'm tellin' ya'll she's a real nutcase."

"And you did nothing to create this mess?" Moms asks, shiftin' in her seat. I can tell she's ready to get it started. It's probably givin' her flashbacks of that shit wit' Pops, too.

Yeah, I stuck my dick in the wrong bitch! "The only thing I did was cut off her cum supply. I didn't make her any promises. And I warned her over and over again to not get caught up in me. But she did. And that's on her."

"Son," Pops says, "I'm not tryna tell you what to do, but you need to slow down. Or you're gonna end up with a lot more than just a baby on your hands."

"Well, let's hope it's not his," Moms states.

"It's not," I tell 'em both, gettin' up. I've had enough of this wit' them. I know if I stay any longer, it's gonna turn into a lecture hall. I glance at my watch. I've been here thirty minutes already. "Listen, I gotta get goin'." I walk over and give Moms a kiss on the cheek, then give Pops a pound and a hug. "Take care of ya'self, old man. I'll hit you up sometime tomorrow to check in on ya."

"Aiight, talk to you then."

"Come by for dinner tomorrow night," Moms says.

"I can't," I tell her, grinnin'. "I'ma be somewere laid up."

She rolls her eyes. Pops chuckles. They both shake their heads, watchin' me dip out the door.

33

Damn, I can't believe it's December already. And on some real shit, I can't wait for this year to be fuckin' over. Man, listen, the last two-and-a-half weeks have been hectic as hell. First, Ramona's nutty-ass has been callin' me nonstop and she's gone back over to Pops, again, supposedly lookin' for me. *After* I told the bitch I no longer live there. Then she went to the police and told a muthafuckin' bold-faced lie, talkin' 'bout I threatened to throw her over a cliff, if she didn't get rid of her baby. What kinda shit is that? And them dumb muhfuckas believed her. I wouldna known shit if Pops hadn't called me tellin' me I had to go to the police station 'cause they were lookin' for me. And then when I get there, them bastards talkin' 'bout I'm bein' charged wit' terroristic threats. Terroristic threats? Can you believe that shit?! I told them muthafuckas, "I never threatened that crazy bitch!" But they still charged me wit' the shit and told me I'd haveta take it up wit' the judge. So thanks to that delusionl ho, a muhfucka had to be dragged into Union County Municipal Court; all because some bitch got her panties in a bunch 'cause a muhfucka didn't wanna keep feedin' her his dick. Do you know how embarrassin' it is to be all up in court wit' a buncha muhfuckas and havin' all of ya business aired out in the open? The shit's fucked up. Lucky for me—twenty-five hundred dollars later and almost three hours of testimony and cross-examinin'—the shit got dismissed two days ago 'cause the bitch was all over the place wit' her story.

And then fuckin' Sherria's unstable ass was harassin' me wit' her bullshit. Between textin' and callin' and leavin' a buncha messages, the bitch wouldn't let up. Talkin' 'bout she was gonna keep blowin' my line up 'til I agreed to see her. That wasn't gonna happen. I told her raggedy-ass to beat it. Instead, she kept callin' and talkin' shit. Threatened to cut off my dick and shred it in a blender. Lucky for me, I kept all of her messages and was able to use 'em in court to get a fuckin' restrainin' order against her psycho ass. Fuck what ya heard. A bitch dragged me into court, so I returned the favor and dragged one into court, too. Call it a punk move if you want, but a muhfucka ain't beat to be changin' phone numbers 'n shit. If I tell ya ass to stop callin', then gotdamn it…stop fuckin' callin'! The last thing I need is another ho tryna jam me up in court wit' some bullshit-ass lies, so I beat her to it. Got that broad banned from contactin' me or anyone else in my personal space or comin' anywhere near me. And there you have it!

I'ma tell you this much: Fuckin' wit' unstable hoes like Sherria and Ramona is a major headache, which is why you need to fuck 'em 'n dump 'em the first time you see any signs of nuttiness; especially when you know you ain't tryna wife 'em. Ain't no need in investin' a buncha time and energy into a ho you know you ain't tryna build wit', feel me? And that's how I'ma haveta do it from now on, especially when the bitch ain't comin' up offa no paper.

I stretch and yawn, gettin' my naked ass outta bed. I slide my feet into my slippers, go into the bathroom to take a long piss, then go downstairs to crank up the heat in this bitch. "It's colder than a dead whore's ass up in here," I say out loud, pickin' up my cell to hit Pops up to check in on 'im. We talk for 'bout fifteen minutes, then I call Moms. As usual, she's tryna beat me in the head 'bout shit I'm not gonna change. I glance outta the window. It looks like it's gonna snow today.

"I hope you plan on making some changes in your life for the New Year. You can't keep doing the same old stuff." I shake my head. She seems to always call me when things aren't goin' right. For some reason, I wonder if she knows 'bout all the shit I've been through the last week or so wit' Ramona and Sherria. But if she does, she doesn't let on. And I'm not gonna offer, not now anyway.

"Why can't I?"I ask, closin' the curtain. "It works for me."

She sighs. "Okay, Mr. It Works For Me, do you. I'm leaving it alone. If you're not worried, then neither am I."

I laugh, walkin' back upstairs to my bedroom. "Yeah right, Ma. How many times have I heard that?"

"I've lost count," she says. "But this time I'm really serious. I'm done. A new year is coming in and I refuse to keep worrying about you. Just like I had to do with your father, I have to accept the fact that you're not going to change until you get good and ready."

I sigh. Why she insists on comparin' me to Pops is beyond me. But I'ma leave it be. "Ma, you know I love you, right." It's more a statement than a question. My nice way of changin' the subject wit'out gettin' into any extras wit' her.

"And I love you. Now, what would you like for Christmas?"

I grin, almost forgettin' it's the season to be jolly, and for givin' and receivin'. Not that I'ma be givin' out anything other than nuts. But a muhfucka's definitely lookin' forward to doin' a buncha receivin'. "I don't need nuthin' major, Ma. You know how I do. Besides, I may be outta town for the holidays." I don't have any specific travel plans as of yet 'cause it's still early, but I tell her this, just in case sumthin' pops off. I ask her what she wants for Christmas as well, knowin' whatever it is I'ma haveta drop some major paper on it. But she's worth it. And, yeah, I spend my own shit. She's the only woman I will dip into my own pockets for. I'm not *that* fucked up.

"Well, I want a new handbag." I ask her what kind and she says she's peeped a new Louis bag she'd like to have. I tell her we can go out to Short Hills and pick it up one day next week. "And I want some sex toys. You promised me two years ago you were gonna buy me some, and I'm still waiting for 'em."

I burst out laughin', lyin' back on the bed. "Ma, you serious? I was only jokin'."

"Well, I'm not."

"I said that when I thought you was single. But you and Pops gettin' it in now, so you don't need that mess now."

"The hell if I don't. Your father may be holdin' it down, but I still want a lil' extra in the bedroom. And if he knows like I know, he'd want to sit, or lie back and watch."

Ugh. I try to shake the visual outta my head. "Ma, aiight, aiight. I don't need to hear all this. I'll just give you the money so you can go buy whatever freaky gadgets you need." My cell phone beeps. It's Cherry. "Hey, Ma, I gotta go. I have another call I gotta take. I'll hit you up later on in the week."

"Okay, go 'head. I'll talk to you later." We say our good-byes, then I click over.

"What's good, pretty baby?"

"Is there a reason why I haven't heard from your sexy ass?"

"Nah," I say, slippin' into a pair of gym shorts, then goin' back downstairs. I stretch out on the sofa. "My bad, baby. I've been meanin' to hit you up."

"I want to see you before the holidays."

"Damn, baby, I'd love to. But..."

"No 'buts.' Can you make time for me or not?"

I sigh. "When you wanna see me?"

"Now," she coos into the phone. "I need you to come to me, *right now*."

"Oh, word? You want me to come, or do you want me to *cum*?"

"Both."

"Well, I think I can handle that. Is there anything else you want?"

She bursts into song. "Santa, baby, you're all I want for Christ-maaaaaas."

I laugh. "Oh, that's wassup. So you want Santa to come ride ya sleigh?"

"I want him to ride my sleigh, slide down my chimney, and unload his gifts deep inside me."

"Oh, word? Well, dig, baby…I think he can handle that," I tell her, tuckin' my hand down into the waistband of my shorts.

"Good. Can you come this weekend?"

I slide my hand all the way down into my shorts, play wit' my balls. Damn, although I was just there a few weeks ago, I could definitely go for another dish of her hot, sweet cherry pie. I stroke my dick. "Tell me when, and I'm there."

"Perfect! I'm online as we speak booking you a flight."

"Daaaamn, baby, you wanna see big daddy bad, hunh?"

"Yes. I've been a bad, bad girl. And I need daddy to come spank this ass up, ASAP." My dick jumps. She books me on a flight for Thursday night, and has me returnin' on the Sunday night red-eye.

I grin, squeezin' my dick. "That's wassup. I'll see you Thursday night."

I go down into the kitchen, open up the 'fridge and pull out some leftover baked chicken and string beans from Boston Market, then put the plate in the microwave. I pour a glass of grape juice, then roll a blunt while I'm waitin' for the food to heat up. I spark it up, decidin' I had better roll four more for later.

I take my plate, drink and blunt out into the livin' room. I flip on the television, decidin' to check out that flick *Pathology* on DVD 'bout a buncha sick muhfuckas who work down in a morgue butcherin' up already dead bodies. Thirty minutes into the movie, my cell rings.

I glance at the screen, not sure whose number it is. "Yo?"

"Hello, Alley Cat?" The voice sounds familiar, but I can't figure out who it is.

"Yeah, who's this?"

"It's Candace. How've you been?"

This nasty freak! I roll my eyes up in my head. *What the fuck she want?* "Yo, wassup?"

"I miss talking to you," she says, soundin' overly excited. "I would really like to see you. You know, get a quick fix."

"*A quick fix* of what?" I repeat sarcastically. "Some hot piss? Or how about I throw in a bucket of shit."

"Oooooh, big daddy, let me find out you tryna get kinky wit' it now."

I shake my head. What a filthy ho. I glance at the clock, decide to fuck wit' her for a few minutes. "What you have in mind?"

"Well, I was kinda thinkin' you could come through one night after the gym, with your balls all sweaty and whatnot, and use my face and tongue as your gym towel."

What the fuck?! "Oh, word? Then what?" I ask just to see how far this smut will take it.

"I'll get on all fours and crawl over to you, then you spit on me. Slap my ass and talk real dirty to me."

"Oh, you want me to call you a dirty, filthy, nasty-ass, cum-suckin' bitch?"

"Ooooh, yes, baby…"

"How 'bout a nut-swallowin', slutty, heathen-ass cunt-box?"

"Mmmm, oh, yes. You really know how to get my pussy hot, daddy."

Whatever! "Then what?"

"Then you go into the bathroom, sit on the toilet and take a shit while I suck all over your dick. And I want you to spit in my face while I'm doing it, too. Then when you're done, you get up without wiping your ass. I step into the tub, jerk your dick off and stick my finger in your shitty asshole until you nut all over my face. Then I want you to piss all over my face and mouth, rinsing it off of me."

I frown. *This tramp-ass bitch is really outta control.*

"Yo, dig," I say, disgusted, "you take freak to a whole 'nother level, word up. You do know that, right?"

She giggles. "Freak is my first name, daddy. So are you up for freaking with me?"

"You done banged ya biscuit, baby, thinkin' I'ma ever fuck wit' ya trashy ass, again. You a dirty gutter-rat, baby."

"Excuuuuuuuse me?"

"You heard me. I said you're a nasty, trashbag ho."

"Kiss my ass!"

"Is that what you learn in Bible study? How to be a sewer whore?"

"Fuck you, motherfucker!"

"No, fuck you, baby. Oh wait, I already did," I say, laughin'. She bangs in my ear, like I give a fuck. *Nasty bitch!* I turn my phone on QUIET, then put my feet up on the coffee table, finishin' up my blunt while watchin' the rest of this movie. I lay my head back on the sofa and before I know it, I'm knocked the fuck out.

34

I'm in seventh heaven right now. Candles are lit 'round the room. Jill Scott's playin' low in the background. Cherry's on her knees, back arched, head pressed deep into the pillow, sheets wrapped 'round her hand, moanin'. And I'm in back of her, ass cheeks pulled apart, dick deep inside of her. I reach under her, play wit' her clit, then slide my fingers deep into her wetness. Fuckin' her in the ass causes her to have multiple orgasms. She clutches and unclutches my fingers wit' her walls, winds her hips. I keep still. Let her push back on this dick, then bounce on it. "Oh, yes…big daddy."—she looks back over her shoulder—"Bust this asshole open, baby. Oh God, no one fucks me *this* good."

My flight got in three hours ago, and I'm tired as fuck. But I had to feed Cherry some of this good shit before I can go to sleep. As soon as we got through the door, she was all over me; definitely missin' the kid. Again, she tried suckin' this dick, but it was a bust, so I flipped her over and started eatin' her out instead. Just as I was 'bout to slide up in it, she stopped me. Told me she wanted it in the ass tonight. And, of course, that was fine by me. I can't front, her asshole gets hot and wet like a pussy. And it feels damn good. Nah, scratch that. Better than good…muthafuckin' great!

But keepin' it real wit' you, the way she loves takin' this dick up the ass, it's only a matter of time before she starts shittin' on herself when she walks. Hell, I'm surprised shit's not stainin' her drawers already as big as her hole is. She says she has total control of her ass muscles. So far, that may the case. But in a few more years…man, listen. I hope she has a buncha stock in Depends. 'Cause if she keeps fuckin' wit' this dick, she's gonna end up needin' an ass plug just to keep e'erything in.

I grab her by the hair and yank her head back. She likes it rough; wants it hard. And I give it to her just how she wants it.

"Oh, shit…aaaah, shit…oh, yes, baby…"

"Yeah, you like this dick, don't you?"

She moans.

Of course, you do. They all do. I bang her back in for close to an hour before finally pullin' out, snatchin' off the condom and nuttin' all over her ass and back, then roll over and pull her into my arms.

She catches her breath, lays her head on my chest, then looks up at me, smilin'. "I'm so glad you came."

"Yeah, that good pussy made me cum hard."

She laughs, playfully hittin' me. "You're such a mess. I wasn't talking about that kinda *came*, silly. I meant you coming here. I'm happy you're here."

"Me, too, baby," I tell her, lightly kissin' her on the lips and pullin' her in closer to my chest. I hold her tight, then drift off to sleep.

Eight A.M., I awake to the smell of sumthin' cinnamony and sweet. I get outta bed and stretch, headin' to the bathroom to take a piss. I wash my hands, then go out into the kitchen. I'm shocked as fuck to see Cherry at the island stove, *cookin'*. I smile. All the times I've been out here, she's never lifted a pot or pan for a muhfucka. Truth be told, I thought the shit was there for decoration.

"Damn, baby," I say, walkin' up on her, "you in here doin' ya thing, I see. Daddy musta really put it on you last night." I slap her on the ass, then press up against her.

"Whatever," she says, suckin' her teeth. "Good mornin'."

"Yeah, good mornin' to you, too." She cranes her neck to look at me. I give her a quick peck on the lips. "Smells good, baby. What you got in all them pans?" She tells me she's made spinach quiche, salmon patties, cheese grits, homefries, and sweet potato biscuits. "Damn, I didn't know you can throw down like that," I say, impressed.

"I'll have you know, there are a lot of things you don't know about me, Mister." She scoots 'round me, pullin' plates down from outta the cabinet.

"What else I need to know?"

"That's for you to find out," she says playfully. "Until then, be happy with the things you already know."

"Oh, yeah? And what's that?"

"One, I make my own money. Two, I enjoy your company. Three, I love riding your dick. Four—and this is in the words of Lil' Kim—'I *take it in the butt*, what.' And five, I'm gonna learn how to deep throat your dick if it's the last thing I do, even if it kills me. Now let's eat."

I laugh, shakin' my head as I pull out a chair and take a seat. My stomach growls as she puts e'erything on servin' platters, then places each dish in the middle of the table. I wait for her to take her seat, then start diggin' in. I take a bite into a biscuit. Lick my lips, then pop the rest of it in my mouth before bitin' into another one. "Damn, baby, these fuckin' biscuits are good as hell."

She smiles. "I'm glad you like 'em. It's my grandmother's recipe."

"Is she single?" I ask, lickin' my fingers.

She laughs. "She's happy."

I grin, placin' a forkful of quiche into my mouth. I swallow.

"Let her know I got sumthin' that can make her even happier."

"Oh yeah? And what's that?"

"Me."

She flicks her hand at me, crackin' up. "You're a damn mess. Finish your food."

"Yeah, but you love this mess."

"Whatever," she says, rollin' her eyes. I laugh at her. Finish up eatin', then go for seconds. By the time I'm done, I'm so damn stuffed the only thing I wanna do is go back to bed. But, Cherry has other plans. She wants to *fuck*, then take the forty-five-minute drive out to Costa Mesa to hit up South Coast Plaza, an upscale shoppin' mall. And you already know doin' both is aiight wit' me.

After we finish rockin' the springs, Cherry jumps in the shower. She invites me in wit' her, but I ain't beat. I tell her to go do her, and stay in bed a while longer. For some reason, I'm tired as fuck. I doze off for another thirty minutes 'til Cherry comes back up in the room and starts shakin' a mufucka to get up. I shower and dress, then come out into the livin' room in a pair of MEK jeans and a burgundy Affliction thermal and a pair of tan Timbs. "It's breezy out today," she tells me, starin' at me like I'ma freeze to death. "Aren't you gonna wear a jacket?"

"Listen, baby. It's twenty-four degrees back home. This fifty-degree weather is like spring to me. If you need to be bundled up like you in the middle of the Antarctica, then do you. But, I'm cool wit' what I got on."

She smirks, grabbin' her bag and keys. "Well, alrighty then. Let's roll." I follow behind her, lockin' my eyes on her swayin' ass and hips.

When we get to the mall, I gotta say I'm impressed. The shit has two sections: the Main Plaza, which is big as hell. And Crystal Court—a much smaller mall, both connected by a bridge. We hit up the specialty spots like D & G, Chanel, Versace, Gucci, and Louis Vuitton, then make our way to over Bloomingdale's and Saks. By the time we walk up outta there and head back to the car, it's almost six o'clock. And we're loaded down wit' bags.

As soon as we get into the car, I lean over and kiss Cherry on her luscious-ass lips, softly at first, then I get forceful, pushin' my tongue deep into her mouth. All the paper she's dropped on me got a muhfucka's dick hard, hot and horny. I start grabbin' her titties. If she knew howta suck a gotdamn dick, I'd have her spin my top. Oh, well.

"I wanna fuck you, right here in this parkin' garage," I tell her, unbuttonin' her blouse, then reachin' in and playin' wit' her titties.

She moans. "You can get this pussy anywhere, anyhow, you want it."

I grin. "Oh, word? Baby, you lucky I don't have any condoms wit' me. Otherwise, I'd tear ya ass up in the backseat."

She grins, reachin' for her bag. "Hold up for a minute." She opens it, pullin' out a box of Durex condoms. "Don't you know a diva is always prepared?" I grin back at her, unzippin' my jeans and fishin' out my dick. I recline my seat as far back as it will go. She takes out a wrapper, rolls it down on my joint, hikes her skirt up over her hips, then climbs her bare ass up over me and slides down on this dick, rodeo-ridin' this cock 'til we both bust.

Thirty minutes later, she starts the engine, then backs outta the parkin' space—happily fucked. "So have you thought any more about my proposition?" she asks, glancin' over at me. *Shit, I was hopin' this wasn't gonna come up.*

I adjust my seat upright. "Nah, actually, I haven't. I know ya biological clock is tickin' and all, but right now, baby, I can't see myself plantin' a nut up in you. I'm not ready for sumthin' that major."

"Fair enough," she says, bearin' onto I-405 South. "So, let me ask you. And be honest."

I hope this bitch ain't 'bout to beat me in the head wit' no bullshit, I think, cockin' my head to the side. "Wassup?"

"If it weren't for the money and shopping sprees that I freely hit you with, would I still be the type of woman you'd spend time with?"

Fuck! If this is 'posed to be a trick question, she done failed 'cause I ain't 'bout to fuck up my paper tellin' her no dumb shit. "No doubt, baby."

"Why?"

"'Cause you got some good pussy," I say, grinnin'. She sucks her teeth, rollin' her eyes.

"Oh, so that's the only reason?"

"Keepin' shit gee, it's the biggest reason. But, it's not the *only* reason. You also got ya shit together. I dig how you stay on ya grind, makin' major moves. Baby, you're a strong, independent, beautiful woman."

"But?"

You gotta head like a damn globe. Kickin' some real shit, moon face or not, the more time I spend wit' Cherry, the more I'm startin' to dig her. "No, 'but,' baby. Whether you lacin' me or not, I'd still wanna fuck wit' you." I'm shocked at myself for sayin' this, and actually meanin' it. She smiles. "But I ain't gonna front and say you don't have a muhfucka spoiled as hell, word up. You got me rotten, baby—right down to the damn core."

She laughs.

"So, you tell me. If I wasn't packin' all this big-ass dick, would you still be fuckin' wit' a muhfucka like me?" Now on some real shit, I already know what it is. It's this dick that's got her strung 'cause it's not like a nigga's comin' to the table wit' sumthin' else, feel me? Yeah, I'ma fine, sexy, black nigga, but all I'm ever gonna offer her is good dick packed wit' hot cream and a buncha mind-blowin', toe-curlin' sex.

"As fine as you are, I probably would."

I bust out laughin'. "Stop lyin'. You know damn well if I was servin' ya ass wit' a little-ass dick, you'd be feelin' gypped. Little dick *and* broke, you'd dismiss a nigga quick, and you know it."

"That's not so," she says, tryna sound offended. Fuck outta here!

"Yeah, right," I say, smirkin'.

"No, I'm serious. Yes, it's nice being with a well-endowed man. But trust me. It isn't the most important thing. A big dick doesn't guarantee a good experience. I've dated some men who were average size, but they knew how to work what they had and it was great. It's not the dick that makes the experience. It's the man behind it. It's the connection."

"Yeah, okay; sounds good. But I know better. Ya ass'd be bored to death wit' a muhfucka short-strokin' you. Baby, be real. You know like I know, you got too much pussy for a short-stroker."

She shoots me a look. "So you tryna say I have a big pussy?"

I grin. "Nah, I'm sayin' a little dick would drown in ya deep waters."

She rolls her eyes, mergin' onto I-5 North. "Same difference, nigga."

I laugh, takin' in the scenery as she speeds down the interstate.

Whoever said it doesn't rain in Southern California is a mutha-fuckin' lie! It rained all Friday night, and all day Saturday. But today it's in the damn sixties. Cherry and I are standin' outside Roscoe's House of Chicken 'n Waffles over on Pico Boulevard, waitin' to be seated. It's packed as hell up in that bitch. Cherry's kinda tight that we're here, but this is where I wanna eat. A muhfucka was tired of hittin' up all them shi-shi, foo-foo type spots she drags me to. I wanted to get my grub on in the damn hood for a change. Not 'round a buncha pretentious-ass bitches. She complains 'bout how ghetto and rude the staff can be at times here; how the wait is too long; how she doesn't feel like dealin' wit' anyone bummin' her for change on our way out; how they put too much damn butter up on the waffles; how the chicken is too greasy; how if she has to eat Roscoe's, she'd rather go to the one over in Hollywood. I let her ass go on and on. But I feel like tellin' her to shut the fuck up. Luckily, a call comes in that keeps her ass occupied for the next twenty minutes. My flight tonight can't come soon enough. A muhfucka's ready to bounce. I watch Cherry as she walks and talks. She paces up and down the side-walk, e'ery so often stoppin' and posin' wit' her bag hangin' in the crook of her arm, and one foot lifted up on the heel of her shoe. I decide to check my voice messages while she's yappin' her jaws. There are thirteen.

"When you comin' back to Brooklyn, nigga? It's ya girl, Electra." Delete.

"Yo, son, what's good? It's Gee. Where the fuck you at, nigga? Hit me back when you get this."

"Alley Cat, it's Falani. What's up with you? I guess since you got what you wanted, you're not beat to hit a sista up. It's all good, though. I just thought you might wanna know Lydia and I want another round with you. And we might have another friend who's down. So if you're down for a foursome, give me a call." Hell muthafuckin' yeah, I am! *Save.*

"Hey, sexy man. It's Vita. Call me when you get a moment." Delete.

"Hey, Alley Cat. It's Carla. When am I gonna see you?" Delete.

"Hey there, it's Marissa. I was calling to see if you were free tonight. I have a few hours to myself and was hoping to see you. I know it's last minute. But if you can, let me know." This ho calls me from a blocked

number, so how the fuck I'ma let her know shit, when I don't have a number to call her ass back? *Delete.*

"Alley Cat, it's Akina. Call me." Delete.

There's also three messages from Maleeka, one from Moms, and two from Tamera's crazy ass, talkin' real slick. I swear she's gonna have me gag her wit' this cock. I delete 'em all. By the time Cherry walks back over to me, we're ready to be seated.

Cherry orders a breast and waffle, wit' a side order of mac 'n cheese. I order one of the house combos: mac 'n cheese, greens and corn bread wit' a breast and a side order of waffles. The waitress comes back wit' our drinks. Cherry ordered a Sun Rise, a mixture of lemonade and fruit punch; and I got the Eclipse, a mixture of lemonade, OJ, and fruit punch. The shit is bangin'.

While we wait for the waitress to return wit' our orders, we talk 'bout the holidays and what kinda plans we have. She's goin' to St. Lucia to visit her family. Says she'd love for me to go wit' her. I smile, tell her I'd love to go as well, but haveta do the family thing. She understands. Somehow the conversation shifts to relationships and her wantin' to know how many women I'm fuckin'. The question catches me off guard 'cause it's not sumthin' she's ever asked before.

"I have a few friends handlin' this dick. Why?"

"No particular reason. I mean, I know you're in hot demand and all, but I was wonderin' if you ever see yourself settling down."

I take a sip of my drink. "Not anytime soon. Maybe one day. But for now, I like keepin' my options open"—I grin, pausin'—"*wide* open, if you know what I mean?"

She takes a sip of her drink, shakin' her head. "Yeah, I bet you do." I'm glad the waitress finally comes back wit' out food so we can get the fuck off this topic. The first thing I bite into is my waffle. Man, listen, I swear these muhfuckas dip 'em in cinnamon and crack 'cause these muthafuckas right here are addictive!

We eat and talk and laugh 'bout stupid shit, like Toni Braxton bein' eliminated on *Dancing with the Stars* before Susan Lucci's old ass; to chicks writin' tell-all books 'bout who they fucked 'n sucked, or how they got done dirty by some industry cat, basically playin' themselves like real birds. Somehow we start talkin' 'bout celebrity deaths and tragedies that happened over the year, like the deaths of Isaac Hayes and Bernie Mac, and the brutal shit that went down wit' Jennifer Hudson, losin' her mother, brother and seven-year-old nephew.

"My heart goes out to all their families, especially to Jennifer and hers," Cherry says, takin' a sip of her drink. "I met Jennifer three months before it happened at an event here, and she looked so happy and in love." She shakes her head. "And now this."

"Yeah, it's fucked up." Just thinkin' 'bout that shit and tryna imagine goin' through that got me feelin' some kinda way. I glance at my watch, quickly changin' the subject. "Aye, yo, it's gettin' kinda late. I'ma haveta get to the airport in a few hours."

"Don't remind me," she says, pushin' her plate away from her. "I wish you'd pack up and come out here to live. I told you before I'd put you in contact with some people who I know would give you a job."

"And I 'preciate that. But you know I can't leave my moms like that."

"Bring her, too. I know some wonderful assisted-living facilities in the area where she can get around-the-clock care. You already have a place to live. I told you I'd let you live in the condo. It's paid for, so all you'd have to manage is the utilities."

I shake my head, knowin' Moms would snap if she knew I had this broad thinkin' she was in a wheelchair, practically an invalid. "Seems like you got it all figured out."

She smiles, gazin' at me. For a split second, a muhfucka thinks he sees love twinklin' in her eyes. I dismiss the shit, knowin' she's not crazy enough to go there. *Or is she?* "Let's just say I've given it a lot of thought."

Yeah, more thought than you should. "Dig, let's not overthink things. Let shit flow, baby. Whatever's gonna happen is gonna happen, feel me?"

She grins. "Oh, I feel you."

"You wanna get some dessert?" She nods. "Cool. What you wanna order?"

"You," she says, lickin' her lips.

I pull in my bottom lip. "Oh, word? Let's blow this joint, then." I flag the waitress over. Tell her we're ready to bounce. Then, believe it or not, I pay the check and tip. Yeah, a muhfucka came outta his pockets. But wit' another ho's paper, of course.

35

Two days before Christmas and here I am out and about at the mall wit' Moms, so she can pick up her gift. Goin' out to L.A. on some last-minute shit threw me off, but it's all good. Cherry laced a muhfucka—as usual, wit' some paper and wears. And I got some good ass and pussy to go wit' it. So I'm not complainin'. But bein' out in this muthafuckin' mall wit' all these heads is effin' madness! I thought we were gonna dip into the Louis store, cop Moms a fly bag, then be out. But, noooo! She wants to get her shop on! So here I am, four hours later, carryin' mad shoppin' bags and she's still not ready to go. When she decides to hit up Bloomingdale's, I tell her to go on in wit'out me, that I'ma be out here wit' the bags, waitin' on her. I take a seat in one of the leather chairs, takin' in the sights. A muhfucka can't front, there's some real dimepieces out here. And I'm sittin' here hopin' I don't run into any hoes I know, especially any I've had to dismiss. The last thing I need is some mall drama wit' my moms catchin' the shit firsthand.

There's a buncha bitches rockin' Juicy jumpsuits, Uggs and Louis bags. I peep a group of pampered white broads dipped in ice 'n chunky jewels, pushin' double strollers. They reek of money! I glance at my watch. It's goin' on four o'clock. My balls are heavy as hell right now. And I wanna bust a couple rounds off. I pull out my phone and scroll through my address book to see who I can set up some head wit' for later tonight. As I'm scrollin' down the list of hoes on my roster, most of these greedy bitches gonna wanna fuck, or sixty-nine. Right now, I'm on some selfish-type shit. I'm not feelin' any extras. Hell, as long as she loves to suck dick, she can be ugly as dog shit as far as I'm concerned. My eyes are gonna be closed any-fuckin'-way, so who cares what the fuck she looks like. I decide to hit up this turtle-neck broad, Nicole, I used to fuck wit' from Rahway. She's 'bout five feet, six inches; one-hunnid-and-eighteen pounds wit' this long-ass neck like a turtle, which is definitely good for throatin'. It's been a minute since I punched up her throat. Last time I was wit' her, she told a nigga he can get at her anytime he wanted; didn't make a difference who she was wit', she'd always suck down on this dick.

"Hey, stranger," she says, soundin' happy to hear from me.

"What's good wit' you?"

"Nothing much; just work and school. That's about it. What's been up with you? I haven't heard from you in almost a year; thought you forgot about me."

"Nah, baby, never that."

"Well, that's good to know. I was starting to think I did something wrong to chase you away."

I laugh. "Nah, baby, I don't run easy. You know how it is. Life 'n shit got a cat busy."

"Yeah, I know what you mean."

"Yo, you feel like swallowin' tonight?" I ask, peepin' these two young hoes checkin' for me. I can tell they real hot in the ass. I act like I don't see 'em, though. Too damn young. I watch 'em bounce 'n shake their asses as they walk, shakin' my head. "Daddy's lookin' for someone who wants to suck 'n throat this hard-ass cock tonight. Is that someone gonna be you?"

"Is head all you want?" she asks, lowerin' her voice; tryna sound sexy 'n shit.

"Wet 'n sloppy," I tell her, "wit' a buncha slurpin', gulpin' and gurglin'."

"About what time?" she asks as Moms comes strollin' over wit' three Bloomingdale's signature brown bags.

"About nine."

"Okay, cool."

"Dig, let me get back to you, baby," I tell her before disconnectin' the call. "You ready to bounce?" I ask Moms as she hands me her shoppin' bags. She got a muhfucka loaded down wit' shit, carryin' four bags in one hand, and three in the other.

"There's one more store I wanna go into," she tells me. "Well, actually two more."

I sigh. "You killin' me, Ma, for real."

She chuckles. "Whatever little plans you have, or had, you need to cancel them 'cause I'm the only woman you gonna be spending your time with today. And right now I'm not finished shopping, so get over your self."

I smile, shakin' my head. "Aiight, Ma. You got that."

"You damn right, I do." I laugh at her. Tell her I'm gonna be in the American Express Members lounge—yeah, a muhfucka gotta AMEX card. And?—while she finishes burnin' up her paper. I dip into the lounge, find me a spot in the corner and set the bags down. Then grab a cranapple drink. My cell rings. It's Mike. "Yo, what's good?"

"Chillin', son, you know how I do. What's good with you?"

"Shit, man. Out here in this packed-ass mall wit' Moms 'n shit."

He laughs. "Mom Dukes got you out in all that madness spendin' paper. That's wassup."

"Yeah, sumthin' like that."

"Dig, I got our tix for the All-Star games as well."

"Oh, word. How much them shits run?" He tells me he copped

floor-end seats for the All-Star game; that they costs six hundred and fifty apiece. He was able to get 'em through a hookup, so I'ma only haveta come outta my pocket wit' half of that, but I gotta shell out two-hundred-and-twenty-five dollars for the celebrity game tix. Then he tells me he put it on his credit card, so he's gonna need my portion of the money before the due date. In my head, I'm already tryna figure out which broad I'ma hit up to recoup my paper. "Aiight, bet. I'll get that to you."

"Aiight cool. Yo, that nigga Ron pulled out, talkin' 'bout his money bein' funny, so he ain't rollin'."

"Yo, fuck that pussy-ass nigga," I snap. "That muhfucka did some real bitch shit, so I'm glad the nigga ain't rollin'. I don't want that snake anywhere near me."

"Oh, word? What that nigga do?" I tell 'em that shit that went down wit'Akina. "Damn, yo. That's fucked up. I always heard he was a shiesty-type nigga, but I didn't know he was on it like that."

"Yeah, that nigga was straight hatin' on the kid. But it's all good."

"Yo, how he find out?"

"Gee's dumb ass," I say, peepin' these two Oriental broads as they walk into the lounge, carryin' a buncha bags. Both of 'em are rockin' stilettoes and designer bags. *I wonder if them shits are real, or knockoffs.* I bet they own a buncha weave 'n wig shops or nail salons, too. I peep the bling 'round their necks and in their lobes, grinnin'. *Damn, they right,* I think, eyein' 'em as they go over to the complimentary gift wrap station. I always heard Asian hoes—well, Akina doesn't count since she's mixed wit' black— have some nice tight pussies, and seein' these two sexy chicks got me wantin' to sample a few. I try to imagine what they gonna look like in another ten years; try to figure out why the hell most of 'em age so damn hard. I make a mental note to get at a young dish of full-blooded Sushi the first chance I get. "You know that nigga can't keep shit on the low. I don't know why I even told his gossipin' ass, any-damn-way. I feel like bitch slappin' him when I see his ass."

"So what's good wit' you and baby girl? Did that nigga fuck things up for you?"

"Man, listen. You don't even wanna know. She tried to get on some ole Mike Tyson shit, throwin' punches and bitin' up a muhfucka."

He laughs. "Daaaaaaaaaam, son, she did you like that?"

"Yeah, and I had to lump the ho up."

"You did what?"

"You heard me, nigga. I knotted her dome up."

"Damn, nigga, I can't believe you punched her in her head."

"Believe it," I tell him, shiftin' in my seat. Another call is comin' through. It's a blocked number.

"Yo, hold on a minute." I click over. "Yo?" Someone's on some dumb shit, breathin' in the phone. I click back over to Mike. We talk a few more minutes 'bout that situation, then flip back to All-Star weekend. He gives me a rundown of all the happenin's to expect. In my head, I'm thinkin', *this shit can wait*, but I let him yap. The nigga sounds all excited 'n shit 'bout it. I'm like, whatever. We decide to meet up after the holidays, then hang up. I glance at my watch, sighin'. It's six-fuckin'-thirty! *This is some straight bullshit*, I think, flippin' open my phone. "Yo, Ma, how much longer you gonna be?"

She sighs. "I'm walkin' out of Macy's now. Meet me by the entrance we came in at."

"Aiight," I say, gettin' up and scoopin' up the bags. Of course, I get to the entrance before she does. Fifteen minutes later, here she comes wit' a shitload of bags. And I know most of what she's bought is shit she doesn't even need. I smile, shakin' my head. "I thought I was gonna haveta send out the robo cops to look for you. What's in all them bags?"

She bucks her eyes at me, like I'm stuck on retarded or some shit. "Gifts, what else?"

"Aiight, Ma," I say, holdin' open the door for her. "Let's roll."

"I'm starving," she says as she walks out the door. "I need to grab something to eat."

"Oh, aiight. We can pick something up on our way home."

She stops in front of Legal Sea Foods. "Umm, no, I want to eat here."

"Aww, Ma, c'mon. You killin' me. We've been out all day. And it looks packed as hell in there."

"And your point?"

I shake my head. "Aiight, Ma, you got that. Let me go put all these bags in the car."

"Good answer," she says. "I'll go in and get our table."

I laugh to myself, decidin' she's purposely tryna keep me out. But it's all good. It gives me a chance to spend the whole day wit' the only beauty who has my heart, real talk.

"Merry Christmas, Sweetheart," Ma says. I glance at the digital clock. It's almost seven in the mornin'.

I smile. "Merry Christmas, Ma. You up mighty early."

"I'm gettin' ready to head over to your Aunt Brenda's house to help finish up cooking. Everyone's meeting over there to exchange gifts and have breakfast."

"I thought e'eryone usually got together for Christmas dinner?"

"This year we decided to have a breakfast instead of dinner, so this way everyone gets to have the rest of the day with their own families. And we won't have to worry about anyone getting drunk. 'Cause you know how your aunts and uncles get when there's booze around."

I laugh, knowin' them lushes would drink toilet water, if it'd get 'em drunk. "Ma, you know like I do, breakfast or not, they gonna come strapped wit' flasks."

She laughs. "And you're probably right. But I got something for all their asses. I'm gonna be checking bags, coats, and pocketbooks as everyone comes through the door, and confiscating anything that contains alcohol in it."

I join in her laughter. "Sounds like it's gonna be a full house."

"You got that right; close to forty. Your cousin Dana and her family are here from Hawaii. And Brian and his are in from London."

"Wow, I haven't seen them in years," I say, sittin' up in bed. Dana ran off to the army at eighteen, retired at thirty-eight and has made her home in Hawaii. She's married to a retired army captain and has four children. Her brother, Brian, is also retired from the army and has lived in London for almost ten years with his wife and six children.

Between my moms' four sisters and her three brothers, she has 'bout twenty-two nieces and ten nephews. And nine of 'em popped outta Aunt Brenda's box. Then there's like forty-seven great-nieces and nephews. Although most of 'em no longer live in Jersey, it's still too damn many of 'em; especially for a muhfucka like me who ain't used to havin' a buncha kids and noise around.

"Are you coming over? Everyone's been asking about you, and they'd love to see you."

Hell no! I ain't beat for all them muhfuckas so early in the mornin'. The last time I went to a family function, Moms' sister Ella got pissy drunk and snatched off their other sister's wig, then tossed it into the punch bowl. Man, listen…Aunt Betty was hot! She turned 'round and tossed her drink in Aunt Ella's face, then they got to cursin' each other out, airin' out each other's dirt. By the time they finished, we knew that Aunt Betty used to sneak outta the house and fuck white men on the railroad tracks for money when they were growin' up, and Aunt Ella had four abortions. And two of 'em were 'cause she was fuckin' their sister Lanette's husband for almost four years. Uncle Benny almost shitted in his drawers when she spilled the beans. And Aunt Ella's husband, Larry, jumped up and started hookin' off on Benny. They tossed Aunt Betty's crib up.

"Tell e'eryone I said hello, and that I send my love. But, I'ma haveta sit this one out."

"Boy, and you sat last year's out as well."

"Yep, I sure did," I say, laughin'. "Just make sure you pack me a plate."

"Yeah, I'll pack you a plate alright, smart ass. Are you stopping by tonight for dinner?"

"And you know it. I wouldn't miss it."

"Well, then, I'll see you later on tonight. Love you."

"I love you, too," I say, smilin'. I get outta bed, take a piss, then jump back in bed ready to go back to sleep. But the phone keeps ringin'. Falani calls, then Maleeka, then Electra, then Vita—all of 'em hittin' a muhfucka up to bring holiday cheer. By the time I get off the phone, I have invitations from all four hoes to come through for some pussy. My cell rings, again. *Fuck!* I sigh, pickin' it up off the dresser and glancin' at the screen. I accept the call.

"Merry Christmas, baby," Cherry cheerfully sings into the phone the minute I answer.

"Same to you," I say, yawnin'. "How you?"

"Horny as hell," she says. "I need another dose of that good stuff."

I laugh. "Damn, you feenin' like that?"

"Yeah, I don't know what's going on with me. Ever since you left, my kitty box has been purring for that long, chocolate bone."

"Yeah," I say, slippin' my hands down into my basketball shorts. "What kitty wanna do wit' it?"

"She wants to sit on it, ride it. Fuck it 'til she weeps and aches."

"Oh, word?"

She moans.

"Yo, stop that 'fore you get my dick hard."

She laughs. "Oh, it's not hard?"

"Nah," I lie. But the shit's rock solid. I squeeze it. "But if you keep talkin' slick, it will be."

"I'm already slick...slippery wet, thinking about all the nasty things I wanna do to you."

I shake my head, strokin' my dick. I get outta bed, strip off my shorts, then go into my closet and pull out my "My Baby Got Back" sex doll. "Yo, you feel like a phone bone?"

She moans. "Oh, yessssss. Let me grab my dildo."

"How big is it?"

"Big as you," she says, makin' slurpin' and suckin' sounds. "But not as good."

"That's wassup. What you doin'?"

"I'm suckin' all over your big, black dick, baby."

"Aaah, yeah...take it deep in ya mouth. Open wide, baby...suck on that shit...tighten ya lips 'round it..." She continues makin' dick suckin' sounds, moanin'. "Aaah, yeah...oh, shit...you wanna suck my balls?" She moans. "...Aaah, fuck, suck them big, heavy muhfuckas..."

We go back 'n forth for 'bout ten minutes of her pretendin' she's puttin' her best lip work down on this dick, but, since I already know the bitch can't wet a dick right, it's hard for a muhfucka to get into it. I squirt a large amount of Astroglide inside my sex doll's pussy, then tell Cherry to lie on her back, bend her knees and let daddy run this dick up in her. I tell her to push the tip of her dildo inside her slit as I'm pushin' the head of my dick inside the doll. "Yeah, baby, that shit is tight…" She moans. I tell her to push it all in as I push more of my dick into this doll. She moans louder. I tell how I want her to bang up her hole as I'm bangin' up the doll. I turn the vibrator feature on high, and its pussy starts to beat against my dick. "Aaaah, fuck…aaah, shit. Gotdamn, you got that motor pussy…Aaah, that shit is churnin' all over this dick…" She moans and groans and screams out, lettin' me know she's nuttin'. I feel my nut risin' up in me, too. Ram my hips up into my rubber sex mate, then grunt and groan while pumpin' out my nut. "Damn, that shit was good," I say, keepin' my dick inside the doll, slow-grindin' it. My shit's still hard.

"What are you doing after the holidays?"

I sigh, shakin' my head. I just left her two weeks ago and she's already tryna get me back out there. She's slowly tryna to turn this into sumthin' more than what it is. Although if I confront her on it, she'll say she's not. She'll say she just enjoys my company; that it's only sex for her and occasional companionship. But a muhfucka like me knows what it is. She's already fallen for a nigga. I grin. "I'ma be bringin' you your Christmas gift."

"Oooh, and what might that be?"

"Me, baby," I tell her before disconnectin' the call. I pull my dick outta my doll, flip it over, then plunge back in. Its hole is wet and gushy from all the Astroglide and nut up in it. "Aaah, shit," I moan, fuckin' it deep from the back 'til I bust another nut. "'Tis the season to be muthafuckin' jolly," I say, rollin' over on my back. I take a deep breath, close my eyes, driftin' off to sleep.

36

"I want to spend New Year's with you," Vita says.

"Damn, baby, that's wassup. But you know I'm not workin', so my paper's light."

"You know you don't have to worry about money, I got you. New Year's is next Thursday, so when do you wanna come?"

"Next Monday," I tell her. She asks how long I wanna stay. I think. Decide to stay 'til Sunday.

"That's great!" she says excitedly. "That's almost a whole week. I'll call you back with all the details."

"That's wassup. But dig, you gonna haveta chill out wit' all that coke snortin' you do. I'm not beat for that shit, feel me?"

"I thought you were cool wit' it."

"Why, 'cause I blaze?"

"Well, yeah. And besides, I asked you if you were okay with it."

"Listen, you can't compare burnin' trees to snortin' coke. I told you to do you 'cause I was up in ya spot, and I wanted some of that pussy. But, nah, I wasn't cool wit' you snortin' shit up in ya nose."

"If you woulda said something, I wouldn't have done it around you."

"Baby, you good. I'm tellin' you now. So is there a problem?"

"Not at all. I don't do it that often, anyway." *Yeah, right. Who the fuck this lyin' bitch thinks she's talkin' to?*

"Cool. You ready to give me some of that pussy?"

She giggles. "I've been ready. It's all I've been thinking about."

I shake my head. "I'ma beat that pussy up, baby. I hope you been practicing on those dildoes I told you to get." I told her ass a few weeks ago to go out and find herself a ten- and eleven-inch rubber friend to get her box in shape for the real deal. And she claims she has. We'll see. We talk for 'bout another five minutes or so before endin' the call.

The followin' week, I'm standin' outside Hartsfield-Jackson Atlanta International Airport baggage claim, waitin' for Vita to scoop me up. She blows the horn, pullin' up just as I'm pullin' out my cell to hit her up to see where the fuck she is. It's brick out this bitch. Shit. I thought I was gonna be comin' down here to some warmer weather, and it feels like I'm still in mutha-fuckin' Jersey. This hawk is cuttin' through a muhfucka's bones. I quickly open the back door, toss my bag in. I'm surprised to see this pecan-brown honey sittin' in the back on the driver's side. *I hope this pumkin-head bitch ain't tryna front wit' her peeps like I'm her muthafuckin' man*, I think, openin' the front passenger door, then gettin' in. I look at Vita. Blink, blink again. She's changed her look up. She's wearin' what looks like a damn Beyoncé wig! Long, bronze-colored ringlets cascadin' down her back! If you asks me, it's too much damn hair for her lil' ass. And to top it off, she has the nerve to have muthafuckin' earrings the size of hula hoops danglin' from her ears. Lookin' at her reminds me of a preschooler bein' dressed up for Halloween. "What's good?" I say, shuttin' the door. I can tell Vita is expectin' some tongue or sumthin' by the way she tries to lean over toward me. "I see you changed up ya look."

"Hey, sexy man," she says, grinnin'. "You like?"

I grin. "It's different."

She smiles. "Alley Cat, this is my cousin, Naomi. Naomi, this

Alley…uh, my friend Alex I was telling you about." Her people says hello.

I turn my head, lookin' back at her sexy ass. Catch her grinnin' at me. I can see she's not a midget…uh, little person, like her cousin. I lick my lips on the sly. "Wassup?"

"Nothing much," she says, shakin' her head. "I've heard a lot about you. Actually, you're all Vita talks about."

Yeah, and I bet she got ya horny ass curious, too. "Oh, word?"

"Girl, stop lying," Vita snaps, laughin'. "He is not. I talk about other things, too."

"Yeah, right. But you talk about him more. For a minute there, I thought she was making everything up."

Vita laughs. "Oooh, bitch, you wrong for that! You know I wouldn't do that. Why are you tryna hate on me any-damn-way?" I'm kinda shocked to hear how Vita is talkin'. *This bitch thinks she's a hood goddess.* I wanna bust out laughin' 'cause she sounds funny as hell. But I keep quiet. Let them go back 'n forth as if I'm not in the car. "Girl, you know I ain't ever lied to you about anything."

"Hmmph, yeah, that may be true. But, sweetie, you remember all those imaginary boyfriends you used to have growing up. Well, I really thought he was one of them." She starts laughing. I cut my eye over at Vita as she speeds down Interstate 285. She looks tight that her blood is tryna play her. I chuckle, pullin' down the sun visor and slidin' back the slider for the mirror. I act like I got sumthin' in my eye.

"Ooooh, bitch, you really tryin' it. Annnyway, Alex, Naomi is going to be here for the holidays, too." She goes into tellin' me how her peeps drove up from Houston to surprise her; how she got there today, so she didn't get a chance to give me a heads-up. "I hope you don't mind."

Again, I catch this ho in the backseat tryna check for me. *Yeah, this bitch is fuckable.* I feel my dick start to thicken. "Nah, it's all good. I don't mind; not at all. The more the merrier," I add, flippin' the visor back up. I say it in a way that lets 'em both know, if they wanna get into some three-way fuckin', I'm wit' it.

Vita shoots me a look. But I ignore her ass. Her and her peeps continue yappin' 'bout one thing or another, tryna pull me into their little bullshit-ass conversation. I ain't beat. I give 'em some rhythm, but start tunin' 'em out after 'bout ten minutes. The only thing on my mind is fuckin' the cutie in the backseat.

When we finally get to the crib, I peep a metallic Benz coupe parked in the driveway. I notice the tags and know it's her peoples' whip. The minute we get outta Vita's truck and into her spot, her peoples keeps cuttin' her eyes at me on the low, smirkin'. *Yeah, this bitch wanna fuck.* Knowin' how bitches like to run their mouths, I'd bet a week's worth of nut that Vita has told her all about my stroke game. And now she wants to get up close and personal wit' this dick. *This ho is askin' for trouble.* And if I have my way, she's gonna get a dickful of it straight up in her guts. She goes upstairs, then comes back down fifteen minutes later, completely changed in a purple sweat suit that clings to her fat ass.

"Where you on your way to?" Vita asks her.

"Downtown," she says, glancin' at me. I don't know how the fuck she and Vita are related, but she's e'erything Vita's not— thick in the hips, small in the waist, and extra fine. There's sumthin' 'bout her Southern drawl that is turnin' me on. I imagine her moanin' in my ear. Feel my dick startin' to stretch. "I'm meeting up with a few of my sorors for drinks, then I'm gonna see what kind of trouble I can get into."

I look at her, grinnin'. Vita peeps it, then asks her if she has her key to get in. Tells her to have fun. I watch as her hips sway as she walks toward the door. She looks over her shoulder and says, "You two *love*birds don't wait up." For a split second I think I see the ho smirkin' at me. *This bitch is tryna be smart,* I think, shiftin' in my seat.

Vita giggles. "Bitch, you a damn trip. Don't drink and drive. If you get too wasted, keep your ass wherever you are."

"Oh please," she says, flippin' her hand, "I'm at my best when I'm drinking." She glances over her shoulder at me as she says this before closin' the door behind her, leavin' me wit' a hard dick.

I wait 'til I think the bitch is long gone, then stand up and start takin' off my shirt. I'm ready to fuck. But Vita tryna be on some ole other shit, tellin' me 'bout this Italian spot she wants to go to downtown called Brios that has great food. I glance at my watch. It's almost seven o'clock at night. "*Brios?*"—I grab my dick and shake it at her—"You see this hard-ass dick? I wanna fuck. The only thing I'm tryna eat is what's between them thick, bowlegged thighs of yours." I take off my clothes, then lie my naked ass 'cross her leather sofa. "Take them clothes off, baby, and come straddle up over my face and let me tongue-fuck you."

"But I'm hungry," she whines. "I wanna get something to eat first." She pokes her big-ass lips out, poutin' as if that shit's 'posed to change sumthin'.

"You can eat the nut outta this dick," I tell her, grabbin' and swingin' it at her. "You walkin' 'round here lookin' all good 'n shit. That fat ass got a nigga's dick on brick. And I'm ready to make it do what it do, real talk."

She giggles; quickly changes her mind 'bout goin' out, unbuttonin' her blouse, then removin' the rest of her clothes. "Don't you wanna go upstairs?"

"Nah, I want you right here."

"But what if my cousin comes back and walks in on us?"

Then I'll fuck her, too. "Then I guess she's gonna catch me wit' a mouthful of pussy. And you wit' a handful of dick." The fact is I want her to walk in on us. Want her to see how I bang up this ho's back. "Live on the edge, baby. She ain't comin' back no time soon."

She slowly walks over to the sofa actin' all nervous 'n shit. She scoops my balls up in both her soft hands, lickin' her lips. "C'mere," I say, pullin' her up onto my lap. She nods, pullin' in her bottom lip. I run my fingers over her left nipple 'til it gets hard. I lightly pinch it. She moans. I tell her to straddle up over my face. Tell her to lower her fatty down onto my mouth. She does. And I tongue-drill her 'til she nuts. I swallow, then start eatin' her asshole out while finger-poppin' her wet box. She bucks her hips, moanin' loudly, then starts shakin'. I swing my legs 'round and sit up, holdin' Vita up by the hips. I stand up, holdin' her upside down still eatin' her pussy while walkin' her up the stairs.

We get to the bed, I sit down, then lie back, never lettin' up on her hole. She nuts again, screamin' at the top of her lungs, then slumps over onto the side of me. I grin. *Yeah, you got this bitch sprung, muhfucka.* She lays there wit' her eyes closed, tryna catch her breath. It takes her 'bout ten minutes to finally get herself together. "Whew, that was so damn good. I don't know what you're tryna do to me, but whatever it is, it's working. I have never had anyone hang me upside down and eat me out like that."

"Oh yeah," I say, pullin' her into my arms. I can't front, I feel like I'm holdin' a child in my arms. It kinda creeps me out. I gotta keep remindin' myself that this is a grown-ass woman wit' a buncha paper she needs help spendin'. I lean in and give her a deep kiss wit' a buncha tongue action. Slip two fingers into her pussy, usin' my thumb to work over her clit. She nuts, again, all over my fingers. I pull 'em out and feed 'em to her, then kiss her again.

"Alley Cat, you really know how to make me feel good, baby. I'm so glad you're here," she says, gettin' outta bed.

"I'm glad I'm here, too. Yo, where you goin'?" She tells me she'll be right back. Tells me she has a special treat for me. I watch her wobble her thick hips into the bathroom. A few seconds later, she comes back out wit' a tube of sumthin'. "Yo, what's that?"

She grins. "Chocolate body sauce."

I sit up in the bed. "Oh, word? And what you gonna do wit' it?"

"You'll see," she says, climbin' back up onto the bed. She yanks the covers back, tells me to lie back, then squirts it all over me. It coats my dick and balls. Then she squirts some on my nipples, then all over my toes. Now, I'ma keep shit gangsta. I love nuthin' more than havin' my dick sucked, but on some real shit…a bitch lickin' my nipples, then suckin' my damn toes gets a nigga hornier than a muhfucka. Have me wantin' to fuck her all damn day, real talk. And I can't believe this lil' ho is 'bout to take me there.

She twirls her tongue 'round each nipple, slowly suckin' on 'em. Glides her tongue down to my navel, dips it in, then continues down to my dick. She kisses it. Licks it. Then starts lickin' 'round my nut sac, pullin' 'em into her mouth one at a time.

I tell her to suck on 'em hard. She does. A few times I feel her teeth, and haveta tell her to watch how she's handlin' the jewels. Eventually, she gets it right.

"Mmmmm, I loooooooooooooove me some chocolate balls." She moans as she's suckin' the syrup up from 'round 'em, then starts slidin' her lips back 'n forth along the shaft of my dick. "Oooh, this big-ass dick tastes soooooooo good." She swirls her tongue 'round the head, then licks the sticky treat drippin' outta the slit.

"Yeah, that's right, baby. Lick up that precum." She wraps her mouth 'round the head and rapidly sucks, then lets it hit the back of her throat. She gags, pulls back some, then tries again. She sucks and slurps this dick like it's a fudgesickle, lickin' down and 'round the sides. I can tell she's been practicin', or maybe her ass was holdin' back on a nigga the last time I was here 'cause she's *suckin'* the hell outta this dick. "Oh, shit...suck that shit...yeah, just like that...eat ya chocolate dick up."

She licks and kisses all over my body, then goes back to suckin' on this dick. Another twenty minutes or so goes by before I finally pull my dick from outta her cock washer. I lay her on her back, lift up her legs, then start eatin' her out 'til she cums again. Today, I'm on a mission. To take her to the edge of ecstasy, then throw her the fuck over. And when I'm finished, she's gonna want my name tattooed all over her ass. I reach for a condom, then roll it down on my dick. I lift her up under her arms as if she's a rag doll, align the back of her pussy wit' my dick, then prop her ass up on the tip of my chocolate shank.

I take my time. Slow-stroke her. Get her open, then turn her around. I lift up on my hands, makin' sure not to put my weight on her. I'm tryna fuck her to death, not crush her. She whimpers, moans, and pleads.

I pull in my bottom lip, bite down. I slowly push; feel the snugness of her pussy as it opens. She yelps. "Sssh...relax. Let me stretch this hole open for you, baby." She continues squealin' and moanin'. And after 'bout another ten minutes of maneuverin', I finally get past the head in. Damn, this ho got some tight pussy. I push in one inch of this dick. "It's in, baby. Relax. All you gotta do now is let the dick do what it do." I slow-grind into her slit, pushin' in another inch.

"Oh, shit...oh, fuck...it hurts."

I take a slow, deep breath. "Sssh, baby," I whisper, lookin' her in the eyes. The bitch got fear and excitement and lust all up in 'em. She's holdin' on to my arms, tight. "I'm not gonna drop you," I reassure her, pushin' in another inch. "Trust me. Let Big Daddy make love to this sweet, tight pussy…" I give her some tongue action. She relaxes. And I push another inch inside of her.

She gasps. Tears fill her eyes.

I push in another inch, slow-stroke her. I pull out. Let my dick throb against her clit. I glance over at the nightstand. Peep an egg-shaped gadget, and know it's one of her sex toys. I grab it, lubin' her asshole with my spit, then push the bullet in. She moans, soundin' like a fuckin' owl. "Ooh…ooh…ooh…ooh…oooooooh." I got that shit on high speed, and I can feel the vibrations shootin' through her juicy ass as I work my pipe back in her. I manage to get seven inches in. Give her a chance to get used to it, before pushin' two more inches into her. She arches her back, lets out a moan.

"It's almost all in. Two more inches to go." She closes her eyes, twists her face in agony, grunts. I push another inch in. She tosses her head back. I reach up under her and press on her clit.

She gasps and moans again. Sticks a finger in her mouth, and sucks on it. I take my time. Push another inch in. Even if it's anatomically almost impossible for her to handle all this dick, I'm determined to get e'ery inch of it up in her. She screams, loud.

"Relax, baby," I whisper, slowly pullin' out, then pushin' back in, strokin' her walls. Her hole opens. Slurps and pulls in the rest of my dick. Her eyes are full of tears. I can't tell if she's cryin' 'cause it hurts, 'cause it feels good, or 'cause she knows, after tonight, her pussy will never be the same.

37

"Yo, baby, what's good?" I say, peekin' outta Vita's bedroom window, watchin' her back outta her driveway. She has to go into work a half a day today. And I'm glad. I'm naked and horny, wantin' some wet, hot pussy. The kind she ain't able to serve me.

"Hey," Kanika says, soundin' like she's still in bed.

"Yo, did I wake you?"

She yawns. "Oooh, 'scuse me. No, not really. I needed to get up, anyway. How've you been? I haven't heard from you in a while."

"Yeah, I know. I've been grindin'. Tryna make some power moves, feel me? So, what's good wit' you? You busy today?"

"Yeah, I am. I wish I wasn't though."

"Damn, you think you can squeeze me in? I'm tryna see you."

"See me? You're here in Atlanta?"

"In the flesh, baby. So what time can I come through to scoop you up?"

"When'd you get in town?"

"Last night," I tell her, playin' wit' my dick. Her soft voice got me goin' through it right now. Got my shit achin' and heavy and wantin' to spit this nut. Since seein' her in L.A., I've kept her on the brain, wantin' to smash that back in. But she's too fuckin' ladylike for me to come at her on some gutter-let-me-rip-ya-spine-out-type shit. But, fuck, I wish she would! I wish she'd come outta her neck and say, "I wanna ride down on your fat, black dick. Take my pussy, muhfucka, and fuck me like it's the end of the world. Make it nut, and scream, and burn." That's what I wanna hear; that's what I need.

"Wow. I wish you would have called me sooner. I would have tried to make some time for you. How long will you be here?"

"Only for a few days, then I'm out. So come check for me. Let's go somewhere and chill out, then have lunch downtown."

"Don't tempt me." She yawns. I imagine her lyin' in bed naked, stretchin'.

"Oh, I'm temptin' you, baby. Come on out 'n play wit' daddy, baby."

She laughs. "You're a mess. But as tempting as it sounds, I'll have to pass. I have too much to do with my family today." She tells me her parents are in town from L.A. for the holidays; that they are havin' a New Year's Eve family dinner at her sister's. She invites me to come.

I smile. Try to think how I can make it happen; how I can dip out on Vita to be wit' this beauty. *Fuck!* "Damn, baby, I would love to bring the New Year in wit' you. But I already made plans. But if I can get outta 'em, I'll definitely come through."

"Well, if you can, the invitation stands."

"Thanks, baby. I 'preciate that."

"Well, I need to get up and get my day started. So I'm gonna get up off this phone."

"Daaaamn, so you gonna leave me hangin'?"

"I'm sure you'll be fine wit'out little ole me."

"Yeah, but I could be much better wit' you," I say, turnin' away from the window. Naomi surprises me standin' in the doorway, wearin' a sheer robe, watchin' me play wit' my dick. I think, try to remember if the bedroom door was already open or closed, or if she opened it herself. At this point, who gives a fuck? I'm sure she's overheard my conversation. She keeps her eyes locked on mine, then lowers 'em to my dick. I smile. Almost forget I have Kanika on the line.

"Hello? You still there?"

"Oh, my bad. Yeah, I'm here. I got distracted. But it's all good. I think I mighta found sumthin' else to keep me occupied today."

She laughs. "I'm sure you have. Well, enjoy."

Wit' my legs spread apart, I keep my eyes on Naomi. Flex my chest muscles, while holdin' my dick. She doesn't blink, doesn't shift her eyes. "Oh, I plan to. I'll hit you up later." I end the call. "See sumthin' you want?" I ask Naomi.

"Maybe, maybe not."

"Yeah, aiight. You know like I do, you wanna wet this dick."

She rolls her eyes. "You're real cocky."

"And as you see I gotta whole lot of it, so what's good? You wanna feel it?" I keep strokin' my dick. She can try 'n front all she wants. But I already know what it is. She wants this cock.

"Does my cousin know you're here trying to make plans to see someone else?"

"Should she?" I ask, lettin' go of my rock-hard pole. Her eyes bulge. I grin. "Does she know you're standin' here lookin' at my dick?" She raises her eyebrow. "Just what I thought. But dig, if you gotta problem wit' me steppin' out on ya peeps, then I can always stay in and chill wit you, baby. Don't think I didn't catch how you were tryna check for me on the sly last night."

"Ohhhh, pleeeeeease," she says wit' attitude. "Wasn't anybody trying to check for you."

"Yeah right, don't front. You want me to get up in the hips, don't you?"

She grins, lookin' over at the crumpled sheets on the bed. "So you're willing to fuck me right here in my cousin's house?"

I stare at her thick nipples. Shrug. "Yup, right here in her bed."

"How do you think she'd feel if she found out?"

"I won't tell, if you won't. Besides, we both know you want it."

"And what makes you think that?"

"C'mon, ma, don't waste my time playin' games. Why else you standin' in the doorway in that flimsy-ass robe wit' nuthin' on underneath, starin' at this hard-ass dick aimin' at you? You like what you see, don't you?"

She gives me a blank stare, tries to act unimpressed. "I've seen better."

I grin, walkin' toward her. "Yeah, right; stop frontin'. Better or not, you want what you see. It's all in ya eyes, baby." I step up into her space. She doesn't budge. I pull her into me. Wait for her to tell me to let her go. She doesn't. "You want this dick, don't you?"

Silence.

I lean in. Kiss her on the lips while pinchin' her nipples. She lets out a moan. "What if Vita comes back?"

"You weren't worried 'bout Vita a few minutes ago when you were gettin' ya peep on and had ya eyes locked on this cock, so don't worry 'bout her now."

"She really likes you."

"That's nice," I say, slippin' my hand between her legs. She's already wet. The bitch probably lay in bed playin' in her box before prancin' her ass up in here.

"Why are you fuckin' *her*?"

Let me find out this freak's hatin'. I untie her robe, push it back and watch it fall off her shoulders. "For the same reason I'ma 'bout to fuck you. I love pussy." As I'm up on her, she kinda reminds me of this ho, Tammy, I fucked a few years ago. Same body type— thick cornbread hips, Duncan Hines booty, and juicy, ripe melon titties; same golden skin tone, but hopefully she doesn't have the same breath. 'Cause, man, listen...that bitch's breath smelled like she gulped down a bucket of hot shit. I remember her askin' me while I was fuckin' her from the back why I wouldn't kiss her. I told her, "'Cause yo' stankin' ass is a walkin' slosh bucket. And a nigga like me ain't kissin' no bitch who smells like she's been suckin' on week-old chitlin's." She tried to act like she was offended—like I gave a fuck, talkin' 'bout get off of her. So I pulled my dick outta her, then told her to take her funky ass on home and gargle wit' some bleach.

Fuckin' this bird's gonna be easier than I thought. I reach between this ho's legs. Play wit' her clit. Stir up her juices, slidin' my finger into her slit. She moans again. I lift her up into my arms and carry her over to Vita's bed. Yeah, I'ma fuck her on the same sticky sheets I fucked Vita on. That's what the fuck she gets for trustin' another ho, blood or not, in her house when there's a man around. You never leave a single, horny bitch alone wit' a muhfucka wit' a dick, 'cause nine times outta ten she's gonna fuck him. Obviously, Vita's dumb ass didn't get the memo.

"So you gonna let me get up in this fuck-box, or not?"

She grabs my dick, squeezes and strokes it. "Damn."

"You like how that shit feels, don't you?" She nods her head. I tell her to get up on the bed. She does. She lies back, spreads open her legs. Waits for me to roll a condom on, then bends at the knees.

"Don't hurt me too bad with that big-ass dick."

This scandalous bitch, I think, slappin' my dick up against her clit and hole, *is outta control.* I beat her twat up 'til it turns red, then push the head in. "Don't worry, baby. I'ma take it nice 'n slow, then beat it up just right." She gasps. Her eyes roll up in the back of her head. And then I stretch her insides 'til a muhfucka's balls are deep in her. I rock her box 'til she begs and pleads for a muhfucka to nut; 'til she screams out my name and cries out in agony mixed wit' pleasure. I flip her over on her stomach, slide my dick back in her, then ride her ass 'til she passes out. When I'm finally done guttin' that back out, her messy ass lies here for almost ten minutes, tryna get her mind right before gettin' up and limpin' her bare ass back to the guest room, closin' the door behind her. I stretch out in the middle of the bed, thinkin', *Bitches ain't shit!* Then fall off to sleep on sticky, wet sheets.

"Hey, sleephead," Vita says, shakin' me.

I open my eyes, wipe the slob from my mouth, stretchin'. "Oh, damn. What time is it?"

"It's almost one o'clock. I can't believe you're still in bed. You must have been exhausted."

"Yeah, ya little ass wore me out last night," I lie, watchin' her go over to her closet. It looks like she's limpin', too. I smile. "Yo, baby, you aiight?"

She giggles, removin' her clothes. "Mmmph, yeah, I'm okay. I'm sore, but I'm not complaining. Last night you put it on me like no other. I can't even lie. It was the best sex I've ever had. But I'm paying for it now. Mmmph. I can still feel you throbbing inside of me."

I stare at her fatty bunched up in her green panties, then down at her stumpy legs. I still can't believe I'm actually fuckin' this broad. That I had her legs pinned back plowin' this steel up in her. I should feel guilty as hell pushin' this dick up in her the way I did last night, but I don't. If it was hurtin' her, she took it like a true warrior. I gotta admit, I kinda admire the ho for that. "You know daddy tryna get you used to handlin' this dick."

She laughs. "And you're doing a good job at it." She slips into a pair of sweat pants, then pulls a white tee shirt over her head. "I see Naomi's still knocked out, too."

Her slutty ass just oughta be. I get outta bed, head toward the bathroom. "Oh, word? I didn't know she was here."

"Well, she didn't get back up in here until almost four o'clock this morning. I tell you, that girl loves to have a good time. She'd party all night, seven days a week, if she could."

"Oh, word? She likes to get it in like that?"

"Unh-uh," she says, laughin'. "That girl loves a good time."

No, what that bitch loves is good dick. "I bet she does," I say.

"Did you eat anything?"

"Nah." I tell her the last thing I ate was her.

She giggles. "Well, what else would you like to eat? We can go out if you want, or I can pick up something at the store and cook." I tell her I'd rather go out. "Okay, cool. We can go down to Atlantic Station and eat at Boneheads. It's a nice spot and they serve a lot of grilled fish and chicken dishes."

"Sounds good to me," I say as I'm brushin' my teeth. I turn on the shower. "Let me jump in the shower real quick, then we can bounce."

"Okay. I'm gonna see if Naomi wants to come, too. Do you mind?"

I smirk. "Nah, baby, it's all good. She seems like real cool peeps."

"Yeah, she is. Out of all my cousins, she's my favorite. She'll do anything for me."

Yeah, even freak a nigga you fuckin' in ya bed. Tramp ass! "Sounds like you got a lotta love for her."

She smiles wide. "I do. She's my heart."

Now what the fuck is a muhfucka 'posed to say after hearin' that shit? Not a damn thing! Who am I to bust her lil' bubble? No one, so I'ma let her keep on thinkin' that that ho in the other room is e'erything she thinks she is. *I should get this silly bitch to suck her* heart's *pussy juice from 'round my balls.*

"Ten…nine…eight…seven…six…five…four…three…two…one: Haaaaaaappy New Year!" Vita shouts, raisin' her champagne glass up in the air. She plants a juicy kiss on my lips. I part my lips and let her slip her tongue into my mouth. I squeeze her fat ass, then slip my hand up under her and start playin' 'round the outer edges of her puffy pussy while twirlin' my tongue 'round hers.

Damn, I can't believe another year has come and gone. Oh-nine is here. And, I'm ringin' it in wit' a muthafuckin' "little person." Who woulda thought? But like they say: Out wit' the old, and in wit' the new. That means, good-bye, old pussy—well, good riddance to most of it. And hello, new!

I can't wait to blow this joint. "Happy New Year to you, too, baby," I say, fnally unlockin' my lips from hers.

She smiles at me, reachin' for her flute of champagne. I watch her as she takes another sip. The bitch done drank almost the whole bottle. But she's kept her nose away from the white lines. Well, as far as a muhfucka knows. "The past year has been full of blessings," she says, wipin' the left corner of her mouth wit' her thumb. "And meeting you has been one of them. I can't begin to tell you how much I have enjoyed spending time with you and getting to know you. It has meant a lot to me…"

Cuckoo, cuckoo, cuckoo!

"Now, before you say anything, I know you don't have the same kind of feelings for me that I have for you, and I don't expect you to. But I do hope that the New Year allows you to open your mind and your heart to the idea of new possibilities."

Yeah, the possibility of you becomin' a certified pain in the ass, I think, strokin' the side of her face. "Listen, you gonna haveta ease up, baby. I keep tellin' you I'm not lookin' for anything heavy. I don't wanna see you gettin' hurt."

"I know. You've been up front with me about that from day

one." She pauses, stares at me. "You wouldn't intentionally try to hurt me, would you?" She almost looks as pitiful as she sounds askin' this.

"Nah, baby, I wouldn't intentionally try 'n drag you." *Not unless you deserve to be.* "As long as you don't get on no extra shit tryna smother a nigga, we cool." She gets up from the sofa and waddles over to the coat closet, then comes back wit' sumthin' in her hand.

"Here, this is for you," she says, handin' me a small square Gucci box.

"What's this?" I ask, takin' it.

She sits next to me. "Open it."

I open the box. Inside is a sterling silver Gucci key ring wit' a set of keys, and a small white card wit' four numbers written on it. They look like house keys, and the code to her alarm. I grin. "Yo, are these to the crib?" She nods. "Why?"

"Because I want you to be able to come and go anytime you want."

I wanna shake my head and tell this fuckin' broad she's nuts for giving a muhfucka she barely knows the keys to her spot. That she's askin' to get dragged. "Uh, listen. Givin' me a key is not gonna make me ya man, you dig? Is that what you tryna do, put claims on me?"

"No, no, not at all. I don't wanna have claims on you. I only want a part of you. I know you have other women in your life. And I'm okay with that. I only ask that you make time for me, too. And that you never disrespect my place by bringing another woman into my home while I'm at work. Can you do that?"

"Nah, I wouldn't ever disrespect ya spot and bring another chick here." *But I'll fuck one who's already here.*

"You promise?"

The way she tilts her head and looks at me, it almost makes her look pitiful. And…sound desperate. I sigh. Decide to nip this shit in the bud before it gets outta hand. I place the keys back in the box. "Listen," I say, handin' the box back to her, "I can't take these."

She looks at me surprised, confused. And on some real shit, I'm shocked my damn self that I'm givin' her her house keys back. That I'm not gonna drag her. That I'm actually feelin' sorry for her retarded ass. "Why?" she asks, sittin' next to me.

Bitch, 'cause you a muthafuckin' lost cause! "'Cause you don't know me, and I don't think havin' a key is a good idea; not now, anyway."

She pushes the box back at me. "I know enough. And I know what I feel in my heart. And giving you a set of keys to my home is what feels right for me. Whether you use them or not is entirely up to you. So take them…*please*."

I take the box back, place it on the table. "C'mere," I say, leanin' into her. I peck her on the lips. "You're really sweet, baby, I…" The front door swings open, and Naomi stumbles in. The bitch is clearly lit the fuck up.

"Oh, shit! Ya'll almost scared the shit out of me. Happy New Year to both of you."

"Yeah, same to you," I say.

"Happy New Year to you, too," Vita says, gettin' up outta her seat. She walks over and gives her peeps a hug. Naomi leans down and hugs Vita, lookin' over at me. I wink at her. She flicks her tongue at me. "Girl, it's only one o'clock. What are you doing back so early?"

She keeps her eyes locked on me. "I got bored." Vita looks out the window, asks her how she got back to her spot. "I had one of my sorors drop me off. I'll get my car in the mornin'." The minute Vita turns her back, she mouths, "I want you." Then walks toward the stairs. "Ya'll two lovebirds enjoy the rest of the night. I'm goin' to bed."

"Good night," Vita says, sittin' back next to me.

"Yeah, you have a good night," I say, eyein' her. "Sleep well."

"Oh, I intend to. *Trust* me."

Yeah, I bet you do. Before she gets her hot ass up the stairs good, I already decide that I'm gonna dick Vita down, then slip into her room and rock her box, again. I lean in, kiss Vita on the lips, then look her in the eyes. I pull in my bottom lip. "C'mon, baby, let's go upstairs. I'm ready to get up in them hips and twist up them walls."

"Ooooh, daddy," she coos, "let's." She gets up off the sofa, turnin' off the TV. As soon as she walks up on me, I scoop her up in my arms and carry her up the stairs. She giggles, squeezin' my biceps. "I love havin' a big, strong, strappin' man here. You're spoilin' me."

"I do what I can," I say, layin' her on the bed. I watch her as she takes off her clothes, then tell her to lie back and spread open her legs. I dive between her thighs and start lickin' 'n kissin' her wet spot. She moans. I lick her clit, then suck on it.

"Ooooh …oh, yes…I love it when you do me like this."

I lift my head, grinnin'. "You like that?"

"Oh, yes…your tongue feels so good on my pussy."

"I'ma fuck you to sleep, baby…"

She moans, again.

And then I'ma be fuckin' the shit outta ya slutty-ass cousin.

38

Just as the BET Honors Awards show comes on, my cell rings. I start to ignore the shit, but I wanna get my dick wet. And I already know it's a ho in need of some dick before I even reach over to grab it offa the end table. I glance at the number. It's a private caller. "Yeah?"

Silence, then breathin'.

"Yo ,who the fuck is on the other end?" No one says shit. I end the call. My cell rings, again. This time it's Cherry.

"I got your plane ticket," she tells me. "You're leaving out on Wednesday night, and coming back the following Monday."

"Cool. I can't wait," I tell her. And I say that shit truthfully. It's cold as fuck here! And, although I was just out there, a muhfucka could use some sunshine, and some more of that Cherry pie. Yo, on some real shit, a nigga's really feelin' her. She's so unbothered by shit; doesn't sweat the small stuff. And she's always eager to please me. Hol' up now, that still doesn't mean she's someone I'd wanna wife. But I gotta admit, Cherry holds a nigga down in and outta the bedroom. And she's definitely who I'm considerin' to bump up to the number one cock-ridin' slot. The ho who gets this dick on demand—first, no questions asked.

"Me either. Are you all ready for your All-Star trip?"

"Yeah, I guess," I say, takin' a deep pull from my blunt. I exhale. She asks when I'm leavin'. "Next Thursday."

"How many boxes of condoms are you bringing with you?"

"Two," I tell her.

She laughs. "I should have known."

"You know how I do, baby. Gotta keep my man wrapped."

"I know that's right," she says, gigglin'. "Speaking of which, do you use them all the time?"

"No doubt. I don't play that naked dick shit. You should know that by now. Wrap it up, and tap it up; that's how I do mine, baby."

"That's good to know. But wouldn't it be nice to be able to go raw in someone?"

I think, try to remember the last time I gave a ho this dick naked. My mind drifts back to the days down in my boy Red's basement and all the bitches we fucked raw and how good that shit was. Then LaTonya's nasty, skank-ass flashes in my head and a nigga frowns. She was the last bitch to get it naked, and the first—and last—bitch to give me an STD. "Nah, I'm good," I say. "Broads can't be trusted; when that pussy gets hot, they'll get straight nasty wit' it to make that thing pop."

"That's not true. All women aren't like that. At least I'm not."

"Well, okay, most of 'em, then."

"Don't you ever think about being with one woman?"

I sigh. *Didn't we already go over this the last time I was out there? What the fuck?!* See. This is the shit I don't like 'bout bitches. They wanna ask a muhfucka the same muthafuckin' questions they done already asked, like the fuckin' answer's gonna change. "Nah, I don't. Why?"

"I'm curious; that's all. I asked you before, but you never gave me a straight answer."

"I didn't give you a straight answer 'bout what?"

"About how many women you're sleeping with."

I roll my eyes, shakin' my head. "I thought I did."

"I'm sure in your mind you thought you did."

"I told you I had a few friends wettin' this dick. How was that not answerin' ya question?"

"Hmmph, okay. Well, now I want to know how many women did you sleep with last year?"

I frown. *What the fuck is up wit' her today? How the fuck I know? I don' keep count.* "I don't know; a few."

"A few like in three, or in five?"

I see she's not gonna let this shit go 'til I give her what she wants. I take another long pull off my blunt. Hold it in my lungs, then slowly blow it out. For some reason, I close my eyes and start countin' in my head. *Cherry, one...Ramona, two...Electra, three... Akina, four...Falani, five...Lydia, six...Sherria, seven...Maleeka, eight...Crystal, nine...Vita, ten...Stephanie, eleven...Keisha, twelve... Lahney, thirteen...Tameka, fourteen...Ramona, fifteen...Nicole, sixteen... Carla, seventeen...Naomi...eighteen...Shalonda, nineteen...* Damn, only nineteen. Fuck! I need to do better in oh-nine.

"If I told you fifty, would that change anything?"

"No, not at all. Like I said, I'm only curious."

"Oh, aiight."

"Well?"

"Well, what?"

She sucks her teeth. "Did you sleep with fifty women last year, or not?"

"Not."

"Well, how many then?"

"Let's just say over ten," I tell her, decidin' she doesn't need to know the exact number.

"And out of all of those you've slept with, were there any who you considered being exclusive with?" I tell her no. Ask her why. "Do you think you might be addicted to sex?"

"Hell no, baby," I say, laughin'. "Sex is addicted to *me*. It won't leave me the fuck alone. E'ery time I turn 'round, it's yankin' my damn dick."

She laughs. "OhmyGod, you're a hot mess. But seriously, do you think you might be?"

"Nah, I'm not. Pussy isn't the only thing I think 'bout. It's one of the things, but not the only thing."

"Okay, then answer me this. What's the longest you've gone without having sex? And that includes getting head."

Damn! Is this broad serious? Okay, okay, she got me. I love to fuck and be sucked. Does that make me some kinda addict? Hell no. I ain't consumed by the shit, feel me? I try to remember the longest I've gone wit'out gettin' this dick wet. "Does masturbation count?" I ask.

"Yes," she says.

"What about usin' sex dolls?"

She laughs. "No sex, silly, means no sex. No fucking, no sucking, no cumming. Nothing."

"Well, shit, if that's the case, I plead the Fifth," I say, laughin' wit' her.

"Exactly what I thought."

Since she wants to play Twenty Questions, I decide to flip the script and ask her the same shit. "What 'bout you? How many dicks you ride down on last year?"

"One," she answers.

"One other besides mine?"

"No. One as in only yours."

"Oh, word? Why?"

"Because sexually, you've been all the man I've needed. Besides, it's too risky out here. God forbid, I ever catch something. I need to know exactly *who* I need to confront. I don't want to be running around trying to figure out or guess who gave me shit. My body, my pussy, I have to be responsible for. Not you or anyone else. But it would be nice to one day be able to give myself to a man without using condoms; to be able to feel him cum deep inside of me and him feel my warm wetness all over him. Sometimes I fantasize about that someone being you, but then I laugh, knowin' that's the craziest shit to entertain."

"Why you say that? Anything's possible."

She laughs. "Alley Cat, please. I might be many things, but I will never be delusional. You know like I do that you're the type of man who is always going to want, maybe need, multiple partners. And unfortunately, there's not going to be too many women who are going to accept that for what it is. At some point, they are going to want more from you. And get frustrated when they can't have it."

That's their problem, not mine, I think, chucklin'. "Damn, you got a muhfucka all figured out, huh? Are you speakin' for ya'self?"

"Not at all. I know there will never be a shortage of pussy for you. And I'm not bothered or concerned about it."

I ask, jokin'ly, "So tell me, pretty baby. Are you addicted to the sex or to *me?*"

"Neither," she says, laughin'

I laugh wit' her. "Yeah, right, don't front."

"Let's just say you're my guilty pleasure. I'm very clear on our arrangement. Like I told you before, it works for me because it's what *I* want for now. Everything I do for you, and with you, is because I *want* to. Not because I *need* to. The minute this thing we got goin' on no longer works for me, then I will walk away. And you can do the same. No hard feelings."

Outta nowhere I say, "Not if you have my baby." I'm not sure if the trees got me talkin' sideways, or if it's the fact that I've been kinda thinkin' 'bout her proposition; sorta wonderin' what my seed would look like; tryna imagine what kinda father I'd be. I never really gave havin' kids much thought 'til she asked me to give her one.

"Excuse me? OhmyGod, did you say what I think you said?"

Silence. *Damn, nigga, what the fuck you thinkin'? Ya ass is buggin', for real. I knew I shouldna bought my smoke from that nigga, Storm. He probably got my shit dusted out; got a muhfucka talkin' crazy 'n shit.*

"Alley Cat?"

"Yeah, wassup?"

"Repeat what you just said to me."

"I'm sayin', yo…there's no way you gonna bounce, if we have a child together."

"So does that mean you're considering it?"

"It means I've been givin' it some thought. We can talk more 'bout it when I get out there."

"That works for me. Listen, I gotta get ready to drive out to Santa Monica to meet with a client. Have a great time in Phoenix. And try not to give out too much of that good stuff while you're out."

"Thanks, babe. Don't worry. I'ma have enough nut for you when I get back."

"Mmmmm, you promise?"

"No doubt. You know this dick comes fully loaded, baby." Wit'out thinkin', I slide my hand down into my boxer briefs and start playin' wit' my shit. E'ery time I talk to her, she bricks this dick.

"And I can't wait for you to get here to unload it all over my pussy, ass and face."

"I got you, baby," I tell her, strokin' my dick 'til it thickens. She got me wantin' to bust a nut. "Yo, keep that pussy tight for me."

"Always, baby."

I smile. "What's my name?"

She sucks her teeth, laughin'. "Daddy Long Stroke."

I deepen my strokes. "Say that shit like you mean it, Cherry."

She moans. "Daaaaaaaddy Loooooooong Strrrrrrrrrrrroke."

"Yeah, that's what I'm talkin' 'bout. Don't forget that shit either."

"Bye, Alley Cat."

"Bye, baby. You be safe out there."

"You, too," she says. "Call me when you get back."

"No doubt." We disconnect. I set my cell up on the counter. Spit in my hand, then yank a hot one out right here in the middle of my kitchen floor.

When I'm done spittin' my nut, I walk over to the kitchen sink and wash my hands. I take the paper towel I use to dry my hands and wipe up the floor, then toss it in the garbage. *The weed and poppin' that nut got a muhfucka hungry as hell*, I think, openin' the 'fridge and pullin' out a pack of four veggie patties. I place 'em in a pan wit' some olive oil, then let 'em brown. I pick up my cell and decide to hit Pops up. "Hey, old man," I say the minute he answers. "How you?"

"Good," he says. "Where you been? I haven't seen you in a while."

"I've been kinda layin' low, feel me?"

He chuckles. "Woman drama, hunh?"

"Never that. I don't entertain that mess. Why you say that, though?"

"You haven't been around, so I kinda figured that's what it was. On top of the fact you got these gals coming here looking for you."

"Man, them broads are crazy."

"They're only as crazy as you make 'em. And it looks like you done drove a few of 'em over the edge."

"Man, they were already there. All I did was stop givin' 'em their dose of dick."

"Shit," he says, laughin'. "And now they got you ducking 'em. There was a time I couldn't get rid of you; now I hardly see you."

I laugh. "Hey. You threw me out, remember?"

"Yeah, fool, but I didn't tell ya ass to stop coming by."

"You right, man." He tells me 'bout Akina comin' to the house twice lookin' for me and how she apologized to him. "Yeah, she told me that."

"That gal seems to really care about you."

I huff, flippin' my patties over. "Well, she had a fine way of showin' it."

"Look, son, you know I try to stay outta ya business. And you know I'm not gonna take sides, but she told me what happened. And she was hurt by what you did. I'm not sayin' she was right for what she did, but you gotta take some of that blame, too. Ya'll both were wrong."

I bite my bottom lip. Think before I speak to keep from snappin'. "Yo, that shit's over wit', man. It is what it is. I ain't beat for her. I told her to stop comin' by there. Speakin' of which, that nut Sherria hasn't been by there, has she?"

"No. But that other gal has."

"Who?"

"The one who claims you knocked her up."

I suck my teeth, sighin'. "What'd you tell that nut?"

"I told her I'd let you know she was looking for you when I spoke to you, and for her to stop coming over here."

I shake my head, thinkin' I'm haveta take out a restrainin' order on her ass, too. "Yo, that chick is real extra wit' hers. Let me get off this phone. I'ma try to come through to check you out before I leave for Phoenix in a few days, aiight?"

"Phoenix? What's out there?"

"All-Star Weekend," I tell him, puttin' my patties on a plate, then sittin' at the counter. I dig in.

"Oh, that's right. How long you gonna be out there?"

"'Bout a week."

"Oh, aiight. Well, you be safe out there."

"Always," I tell him before endin' the call. I scroll through my address book, then hit Ramona's ass up. Her shit's disconnected. *I'm not 'bout to let these crazy bitches stress a muhfucka out*, I think, sparkin' another blunt. I hit up Maleeka. "Yo, what's good, baby?" I ask the minute she answers.

"Shit. Chillin'. What's up with you?"

"Tryna fuck, baby. You feel like wettin' this dick?"

"When?"

"Now," I tell her, puffin'.

"You smokin', nigga?"

"You already know."

"I shoulda known, with ya fiend ass."

"Yeah, aiight. I gotta fiend for that ass, aiight."

"Then bring it on, nigga."

"See you in an hour," I say, laughin'. I finish up my blunt, then head upstairs to hit the shower. The minute I step under the showerhead, I hear Cherry's voice. *Are you addicted to sex?* "Hell, no," I say out loud. "Like I said, sex is addicted to me!"

39

The 2009 All-Star Weekend in Phoenix is aiiight this year; nuthin' major, like how it was in Vegas. I haven't gone to an All-Star yet that compares to that one. Anyway, it is what it is. The weather's great. The W in Scottsdale is tight. My room overlooks Camelback Mountain, and I dig the floor-to-ceilin' windows. Last night I had them shits slid open to let that fresh desert air in while I was butt-ass naked underneath the comforter. I slept good as hell. I swear I didn't wanna get up. All I needed was some pussy to knock down into the featherbed, and I woulda been good to go. But most of the bitches I've been seein' here so far are fuckin' mediocre! So when these muhfuckas woke me up this mornin', talkin' 'bout goin' to the Phoenix Suns forward Amare Stoudemire's All-Star Brunch, I wasn't really feelin' it.

For one, we didn't get in 'til almost three in the mornin' from the comedy show down at the Orpheum Theatre last night. That muthafuckin' Joe Torry is funny as shit, word up. The rest of them comedian cats were aiiight. Then we headed to the after-party down at club PHX. And that shit was whack! Yeah, I popped shit to a few broads up in there, and did a two-step here 'n there wit' a few of 'em, but that was it. There wasn't one bitch in that spot that made my dick jump, or that I would consider lettin' gargle my balls. Hell, lickin' my ass, for that matter. Maybe if they were comin' up offa some paper, but to straight fuck, nah…none of them hoes were worthy of this cock 'n cum—for *free!*

Second, this brunch shit was from nine to eleven, which meant

I had to get up early as hell. I'm like, *what the fuck?!* Yeah, it's all gravy that Amare and his crew are hostin' the shit to benefit the Ronald McDonald House and some kinda Each 1, Teach 1 Foundation. But for a buck-twenty-five…man, listen, I ain't feelin' it. But I'm up 'n dressed and downstairs in the hotel lobby wit' Mike, waitin' on Gee and Glenn to get down here. Mike looks like shit. His eyes are red and puffy. The nigga is definitely hung the fuck over.

"Man, you look like shit," I say, glancin' at my watch. It's eight-thirty. "Looks like you been up all night."

"I have," he says, stretchin' out his six-four frame. "And I feel like shit, too."

"Yeah, and you smell like it, too," I joke.

He laughs. "Muhfucka, go 'head wit' that."

"What ya'll niggas get into after I dipped?"

"I'm not sure what Gee's drunk ass did. But Glenn and I ended up hittin' the casino. Man, them slots weren't doin' shit. They were rapin' muhfuckas."

"Oh, word…what they get you for?"

"Like eight hunnid; somethin' light. You know a muhfucka like me knows when to get the fuck up. But Glenn's dumb ass let 'em drag his whole wallet, then the muhfucka gonna ask me to spot his ass."

I shake my head. "Did you?"

"Yeah, I hit that nigga wit' a couple of hunnid."

I laugh. "What a loser."

"I told that muhfucka I want my shit back, too."

"Good luck. You know that nigga don't like payin' up."

He shakes his head. "Nah, I ain't tryna hear that shit, man. That's my boy and all, but let 'im fuck around and don't pay me my money. I'ma end up goin' in his mouth, real talk."

I shake my head, checkin' out these two honeys standin' at the concierge desk 'cross the lobby. I squint as they turn 'round and make their way toward us. "Gotdaaaaaaaaaaaaaaaamn, them bitches are bad," I say, practically droolin'. They the hottest and baddest hoes I've seen this whole trip.

Mike agrees. "Word up, but I bet they some stuck-up ho-types."

They both look mixed. One of 'em is light-skinned wit' long, thick wavy hair pulled back into a ponytail; the other is the color of cinnamon wit' bone-straight, shoulder-length hair, lookin' like an Egyptian goddess. They fine as fuck, and I'd dick 'em both. But the one who stands out the most is the one wit' the chinky eyes. She looks exotic. And she has the kinda swagger that lets a muhfucka know she's 'bout her business. She catches me starin' at her. And I swear I think I see her lick her lips at me. Her hips sway, hard. And I'm convinced she's throwin' me the twat. *That bitch got some good-ass pussy, I bet.* My mouth waters.

"Yo, what's good?" I ask the minute they walk past.

No response.

No, these bitches didn't disregard me like I'm some crab-ass nigga. Mike looks at me, smirkin'. I frown. "Aye, pretty ladies," I say, gettin' up and followin' behind 'em.

The Egyptian goddess tosses her hand up in the air, not botherin' to look back at me. "Beat it," she says.

I hear Mike laughin'. "I told you, man," he says. But I ain't the one to be dismissed or easily deterred when I see sumthin' I wanna get at. I get up behind them in the revolvin' door. "Oh, word. It's like that? A muhfucka speaks to two beauties and he can't even get a simple hello?"

"What, nigga, you want some pussy?" the light-skinned broad snaps, cuttin' her eyes at me.

I smile, flashin' my pearly whites. "Now we're gettin' somewhere. Yeah, as a matter of fact, I do. But for now, a simple hello will do."

She stops, smacks her lips, pullin' her Louis V shades up over her head. The Egyptian goddess walks off as if I don't exist, bouncin' her hips toward the parkin' lot. I try to keep from starin' at her ass shakin' 'n bouncin'. The beauty in front of me, stares me down. Although she's not who I have my sights on, I decide if I can break the ice wit' her, eventually, I might be able to get at her peeps. "What's good?" she says wit' much attitude, eyein' me.

"There you go,' I say, grinnin'. Shit, she's sexy as hell. *Stay focused, nigga.* "Was that hard? Where ya'll from?"

"Brooklyn," she says, shiftin' her Dolce & Gabbana bag from one arm to the other.

I laugh.

She raises her brow, ice-grills me. "I say sumthin' funny?"

"Nah, baby, I'm laughin' 'cause wit' all that attitude ya'll got goin' on, I shoulda known."

She smirks. "Whatever."

"So, sexy lady from Brooklyn, you gotta name?"

"Chanel," she says as her peeps pulls up, pushin' a shiny bronze CLK550.

"And ya peeps, she gotta name?"

"That's for her to tell you. And from the looks of things, she ain't interested."

"Damn, it's like that?"

The Egyptian beauty rolls down her window, and yells. "Bitch, will you come on? That nigga's all dick, and no dollars. And he smells like trouble. Let's roll."

"See," Chanel says, smirkin', "told you."

I laugh, watchin' her sashay her juicy ass over toward the passenger side. "Damn, baby," I say, throwin' my arms open. "You done sized me up all wrong. Now, what's up wit' that? I ain't no killer, baby."

"Yeah, well, I am," she says, rollin' up her window, then peelin' off. And for some strange reason, my dick starts to stretch down the right side of my leg.

Four hours later, we're at Scottsdale Fashion Square mall down at the food court chillin 'n shit, people watchin' while we eat. I'm killin' a vegetarian sandwich on multigrain bread and two bangin' cream cheese brownies from Paradise Bakery & Café. There's muhfuckas and hoes e'erywhere.

"Man," Mike says, pointin' up to the second level, "look at Akon's dumb-ass wit' all them muhfuckas walkin' 'round wit' him." Dude is here walkin' 'round and goin' into stores 'n whatnot, but wasn't buyin' shit. And he had 'bout fifteen to twenty heads rollin' wit' 'im. Then when peeps try to snap flicks of 'im, he's tryna act like he ain't beat to stop and pose up wit' 'em. "That's the corniest shit I've seen today; you up in the mall, walkin' 'round just to be seen." He shakes his head. "That nigga just want some attention."

Gee adds, "Yo, that's some clown shit, for real."

"Yo, whatever," I say. "Let that nigga do him. I don't listen to the cat's music, so who gives a fuck."

The rapper Young Buck swaggers by all iced-out and whatnot on some solo-type shit. If he had a crew wit' him, they weren't all up on him. I watch a buncha white kids run up to him, hittin' him up for his autograph. They couldna been no more than eleven, maybe tweleve, but they knew who he was.

Two local chicks grab a table next to us. I overhear one of 'em say she's never seen so many fine black men in one place before. The other agrees, then says how Phoenix isn't used to all this excitement; that they're probably scared to death of so many blacks in one place. They laugh. I chuckle to myself, lookin' 'round. *And we spendin' major paper up in this muhfucka, too!* Yeah, they

mighta not been used to us bein' here, but I bet they're sure glad
we came through this bitch to boot up the economy.

"Aye, yo," Mike says, tappin' me on the arm, "there go them
fine-ass hoes from the hotel."

"Where?" I ask, tryin' not to sound all thirsty 'n shit.

He points straight ahead over in their direction. "Right there,
gettin' ready to go up the escalator."

All eyes follow where he's pointin', zoomin' in on the view. And
there they are, fine as ever, carryin' a shitload of shoppin' bags.
Gee says, "Gottttttttdamn, they fine."

Glenn agrees.

Mike laughs. "And they stuck up as hell. Yo, this nigga here"—
he points at me—"tried to holla at 'em this mornin' when we were
waiting for ya'lls dumb asses, and they played the shit outta him.
The one bitch threw her hand up at him like he wasn't shit." This
nigga is crackin' up.

"Yo, whatever, muhfucka."

He's still laughin'. "Yo, dawg, am I lyin', though? Keep it gee,
nigga. That ho played you, son."

Gee and Glenn shake their heads, laughin' wit' his dumb ass.

"Now the light-skinned one," Mike continues, "seemed like she
was a little more approachable 'cause she did stop and give you
some rhythm. But that other one, whew...man, listen. That ho is
a problem." Instead of him deadin' it, this muhfucka keeps the
shit goin'. "Yo, ya'll shoulda seen how she played him like a real
crab."

"Damn, yo, she did you like that?" Gee asks, surprised.

"Yeah," I say nonchalantly, "she was on some funny-style shit.
But it's all good."

"Yo, the shit was funny as hell. And instead of this nigga leavin'
it alone, he gets up and follows 'em out the hotel. They was probably thinkin' ya ass was a real nut, yo."

"Damn, yo, get up off my dick," I snap. Listenin' to him talk 'bout it got me feelin' some kinda way. I don't usually get straight igged like that. But her evil ass made my dick bulge earlier wit' her slick talk. And a muhfucka ain't gonna be satisfied 'til I can get at her. Fuck what ya heard. I don't give up easily. I keep my eye on 'em, watch which direction they walk in.

He laughs louder. "Damn, son, let me find out you bein' all sensitive 'n shit."

I laugh it off. "Fuck outta here. I'm just sayin'. Give it a rest, damn. Ya'll niggas come out here to shop or bullshit?"

"Both," Gee says, crackin' up. I see these muhfuckas wanna be on some extra shit. I get up and toss my trash into the garbage can, then bounce.

"Peace, I'm out," I say, throwin' up two fingers. "I'ma get at you niggas later."

"Aye, yo. Where you goin'?"

"I got sum shoppin' to do."

They all start laughin'. "Yeah, right, muhfucka. The only thing you tryna do is get ya feelin's hurt."

"Whatever, yo," I say, headin' toward the escalator. "Hit me up when ya'll niggas ready to bounce."

When I get to the top of the escalator, I turn in the direction the two Brooklyn beauties went, then slowly walk past stores 'til I spot 'em. After 'bout nine stores, I still don't see 'em so decide to head down to the first level. I stroll by a few stores, and still no sign of 'em. *Nigga, what the fuck are you doin'? Ya ass is buggin' for real, yo. Chasin' behind a piece of ass. Nigga, you better get ya mind right.*

"Fuck them hoes," I mumble, dippin' into the 7 For All Mankind store. I browse 'round, try on two pair of jeans, and then six hundred dollars later, I walk up outta there.

Right as I'm 'bout to hit up my niggas to let 'em know I'm ready to bounce, I spot the two Brooklyn beauties comin' outta a store and walkin' in my direction. The light-skinned one sees me and says sumthin' to her peoples, then starts laughin'. As soon as I get up on 'em, I grin, stoppin' in front of 'er peoples, blockin' her path.

"Chanel, right?" I say, lookin' at her. She gives me a phony smile and nod. *Is this bitch bipolar, or what? This mornin', the bitch spoke. Now she's actin' brand-new.* I turn my attention to her girl. "Why you so mean?"

"Why you all in my face?"

Her girl snickers, shakin' her head.

"I'm tryna get ya name."

"Why? You tryna stalk a bitch or sumthin'?"

"Nah, I ain't on it like that, baby."

"I can't tell," she snaps.

"Kat, will you please give this fool some rhythm so he can be on his way?"

"Kat? Damn...I like that."

She cuts her eyes at her girl, suckin' her teeth. "Ugh, bitch, you make me sick."

"Whatever. The nigga's fine and you know it. So stop frontin' and let's be done wit' it. I'ma be over in the Aveda store." She grins, shootin' me a look, walkin' off. The beauty in front of me stares me down. I grin.

"What the fuck's so funny?"

I shake my head, still smilin'. "You're too damn fine to be so damn evil, baby. All a cat's tryna do is get ya name, but you actin' like I'm the muhfucka who broke ya heart."

She shifts her weight from one foot to the other, lets her Dior bag hang in the crook of her arm. "I'ma tell you this only once, so get it right or get got. First, I'm not ya baby. So, don't call me that shit. Second, I don't give a nigga the chance to break my heart, trust. And, third, whatever it is you sellin', a bitch like me ain't fuckin' buyin', so step." She brushes past me, but I ain't havin' it. This bitch is too damn bad for a muhfucka to let get away that easy.

I walk up alongside of her. "Yo, check this out. I'ma follow you all 'round this muhfucka 'til you talk to me. And if I gotta stand outside ya door at the hotel, I'ma do that, too. But you not gonna just dismiss me like I'm some bum-ass nigga."

She stops, raises her eyebrow, then grins. "Nigga, you wanna talk, then let's."

I flash her a wide smile. "See, baby, that's all I'm askin'."

"Nigga, you already fucked up. I told you, *once*, I'm not ya baby, so don't call me that. And you do the shit, anyway. Obviously, you don't listen."

"I can't help myself, boo," I tease.

"I ain't ya fuckin' boo, either."

"Well, maybe I wanna make you both."

She shakes her head. "Nigga, you can't *make* me nuthin'. I know ya kind. And it ain't what I'm lookin' for."

"Oh, yeah…and what's that?"

"A nigga I would haveta put a bullet in."

I laugh. "Yo, ma, you funny as hell wit' that."

She ice-grills me. "Nigga, I ain't laughin'." I keep my smile plastered on my face, but on some real shit, a muhfucka almost believes her. The tone in her voice, the look in her eyes, tells me this sexy-ass bitch is a loose muthafuckin' cannon. But a nigga like me likes livin' on the edge. I feel my dick gettin' hard.

"I'll take my chances," I say, grinnin'.

"Then ya ass is dumber than I thought."

I laugh. "Nah, I'm just a sucker for a beautiful woman."

She smirks, licks her lips, steps up in my space, lowers her voice and tells me to lean down, so she can whisper sumthin' in my ear.

"And I bet you a sucker for good pussy, and a bitch who can suck down ya dick and lap at ya balls, too…" I grin, noddin'. I let her keep talkin'. "…Well, guess what, muhfucka? I'm *that* bitch, be clear. Fine, fly, fabulous and freaky wit' a pussy 'n throat game, so ill it'll make a nigga sick. But, guess what, muhfucka?"

I can't front, this bitch talkin' all slick 'n greasy, got my shit on brick. "Wassup?"

She steps back, stares me up and down, locks her eyes on mine, then back down to the bulge in my pants. She steps back up in my space. "You all dick and no dollars."

"Oh, word? You think?"

"I *know*. And like I said, I *ain't* the one. So do ya'self a favor and beat it."

"So what, you a gold digger?"

"No, boo-boo, don't get it twisted. I got my own paper. I don't need a nigga for shit. But I know what wets my clit. And a broke nigga ain't it."

"Good, then we on the same page 'cause I don't need a nigga for shit either. And I don't have a clit."

She smiles, shakin' her head.

"Damn, underneath all that meanness, you gotta pretty smile."

"Flattery will get you nowhere wit' me."

"Will it at least get me ya number?"

"For what? It's not like you gettin' some pussy."

Damn, I wanna snap her muthafuckin' back in. "Yo, ma, check this shit out. I'm standin' here tryna rap to you 'cause you fine as fuck, but don't get shit twisted. I ain't pressed for no ass. I get that wit' no effort, so don't get it fucked up. But what I *want* to do is get to know you. Maybe take ya sexy ass out to dinner, then, maybe, to a show. But you on some extra stuck-up shit."

She glances at her frosted timepiece. "It's been real," she says, as her girl approaches us, "but ya time's up."

I laugh. "Yo, it's all good, ma. But know this. I'ma be at ya door tonight."

She sucks her teeth. "Bitch, let's go," she says to her peoples. "This nigga right here is crazy."

I laugh. "Ya'll be easy."

"Whatever," Kat says, walkin' off. Her girl smirks at me, shakin' her head, followin' behind. I watch as they get lost in the sea of shoppers, pullin' out my cell. I see I have six missed calls and five voice messages. I hit Mike up and tell him I'm ready to bounce, then head toward the other end of the mall to meet up wit' 'im. I listen to my messages as I'm walkin'.

The first one is from Lydia. *"Hey, sexy man, I got everything set up with two of my girls. They're both sexy bombshells, so you'll be pleased. Hit me back when you can, so we can get this thing going. I'm horny. It's going to be a night full of whips and chains and swings. I can't wait."* I can't front the ho had me 'til she brought up whips and chains and swings 'n shit. *What the fuck kinda shit is she in to? All I asked for is three chicks to wet up this dick, and she's addin' extra shit.* I delete the message.

The next message is from Akina. *"Alex, it's a new year, we really need to sit down and talk. Hit me up when you can."* Delete. "Bitch, after that stunt you pulled, you are officially invisible to me," I say, goin'to the next message.

"Alley Cat, what's good, nigga? It's ya boy Red. I did it. I proposed to my girl. We set the date for Saturday, October thirty-first. It's on Halloween night. Don't laugh nigga. But my girl wants it to be a costume-style weddin'. I told her she's buggin', but hey, it's what she wants. So, yeah, ya ass is gonna haveta come in costume, nigga." He laughs. *"Holla back."* *What kinda shit is that? Who the fuck ever heard of a muhfucka gettin' married on Halloween night?* I think, savin' the message.

The fourth message is from Maleeka. *"Hey, Alley Cat, this is ya girl, Maleeka. Hit me back. You already know what it is. Don't have me waitin' too long, nigga." Delete.*

The last message makes me bust out laughin'. It's from Vita, soundin' skeed the fuck up. *"Alley Cat, call me as soon as you get this. Me and Naomi were here drinking and out of nowhere she tells me you tried to sneak in her room while I was at work. I told her she was lying. But she swears by it. I don't wanna believe her, but she's never lied to me before. And she really doesn't have any reason to start now. So call me 'cause I need to know if it's true." Hell no, I didn't* try *to sneak in her room; I did. And I fucked her down into the mattress.* Mighty interestin' the bitch didn't say shit 'bout gettin' fucked in Vita's bed, but she tries to play me out. *Delete.* She wants the truth; then that's the fuck what she's gonna get it.

My cell rings. It's Vita. *Yo, what the fuck?!* "Yo?"

"Did you get my message?" she asks, soundin' tight.

"What message?"

"The one I left 'bout two hours ago."

I lie. "Nah, I didn't get it. What was the message?"

"Did you try to sneak in my cousin's room while I was at work?"

"Yo, you want the truth?"

"Yes."

"Aiight, then. No, I didn't try 'n sneak in ya peoples' room while you were at work."

She sighs. "I knew you wouldn't do me like that. I knew that drunk bitch was lying."

"Yeah, she definitely was. But did she tell you how she came up in your room when you left for work in a skimpy-ass robe watchin' a muhfucka playin' with his dick?"

"She did whaaat?"

I repeat myself. "And then she let me fuck her. Right in ya bed. Instead of her sayin' no, she asked me why I was fuckin' a bitch like you. Did she tell you that?"

Silence.

"You want the truth, baby. The truth is ya girl is a slut. The truth is, you told her how good I was servin' you this dick and she wanted to see for herself. And I bust that ass down. Why you think she was still knocked the fuck out when you came in from work? Why you think she was limpin'?"

"OhmyGod, ohmyGod, ohmyGod...I don't believe this shit. You're lying."

Silence.

"What the fuck I gotta lie for? Let her show you that lil' black butterfly she has up over her shaved pussy. Let her show you her pierced clit."

She starts cryin'. "OhmyGod, why would you hurt me like this?"

"You should be askin' ya peoples that. She opened up that can of worms tryna snake me. I woulda kept the shit on the low, so you wouldn't get hurt. But since you came at me wantin' truth, I'm givin' it to you. And the truth is, I fucked ya cousin in ya house. Not once, but twice. And both times *she* wanted it."

"How could you?"

"Easy. She spread her pussy open, and I slid my dick in it."

"Of all the bitches to fuck, you had to go and fuck my cousin. The one person I love so deeply."

"Look, babe, that's between you and her. You asked for the truth and you got it. She betrayed ya trust." I see Mike and 'em talkin' to a group of chicks sittin' on one of the benches.

"Both of you did. You are so fucked up."

I sigh. Decide not to rip into her. But the truth of the matter is this dumb little bitch invited a muhfucka she met online into her home, fucked and sucked him, then put her trust in him. The bitch knows nuthin' 'bout me, but was quick to give up her pussy, her money, the muthafuckin' keys to her crib, and tellin' a muh-fucka she loves him—in less than four months. "Yeah, you right.

I'm fucked up, baby. So you wanna keep fuckin', or do you wanna dead this shit?"

The ho is still cryin' and snifflin'. "I don't know."

I shake my head. "Yo, I tell you what. Hit me up when you know. 'Cause right now I ain't beat for all that cryin' in my ear. I'm out." I end the call, walkin' up on Mike 'n 'em. "Ya'll niggas ready to bounce?"

"Yeah, muhfucka," Mike says, grinnin'. "We been ready."

"Then let's roll, punk," I say, laughin'.

40

"Yo, fuckin' 'round wit' you dumb-ass niggas, we 'bout to miss our flight," I say, racin' through the terminal to get to the gate. These niggas decided to go to some party hosted by some industry chick last night in Phoenix and got fucked up. I had to drive us back to the hotel, and we didn't get up in that bitch 'til almost three in the mornin'. And now we're tryna catch this plane 'fore we end up bein' stuck out this bitch. And there's no way I'm tryna be out here another damn day. Five days wit' no pussy, and no trees, hell muthafuckin' no. A muh-fucka's tryna get home. I don't know why the fuck he made our reservations so early any-damn-way—6:50 in the muthafuckin' mornin'! And I bet the shit's packed!

"Yo, shut ya bitchin' ass up," Mike says, tryna catch his breath. "We gonna make the damn flight."

"Whatever, nigga. Punk-ass muhfucka," I say, laughin'. "That's why ya outta-shape ass is all outta breath 'n shit."

"Fuck outta here," he says, slowin' down as we get to our gate. "I'm in the best shape of my life. It's all them damn shots of Henny that got me all fucked up." He wipes his forehead.

I keep laughin'. "Whatever, yo. I knew I shoulda rolled out wit' Gee 'n 'em instead of fuckin' 'round wit' ya ass."

"Yeah, whatever."

"This is the final boarding call for all passengers for Continental flight fourteen-thirty-four nonstop to Newark Liberty International Airport," the attendant announces. We barely make it, handin' her our tickets. "Enjoy your flight," she says, smilin'. Mike walks up in front of me while I'm fumblin' wit' my shit, tryna keep my iPod and *Black Enterprise* magazine from fallin' outta my hand.

As soon as I step on the plane, I shake my head. I can already tell the bitch is packed. *Five muthafuckin' hours packed on a damn plane. I'm glad I got an aisle seat*, I think, not payin' attention to any of the faces in first class. As I'm walkin' by a seat on my left, I hear, "There goes that fine-ass nigga."

I look in their direction and grin. "Aye, yo, what's good?" Chanel hits me wit' another one of them phoney-ass grins. Her peoples sucks her teeth, turnin' her head back toward the window. I laugh. "I'ma get at you."

I hear her say, "Not sittin' back there in coach, muhfucka."

When I get to my seat, Gee says, "Damn, nigga, I didn't think ya'll was gonna make it."

"Man, listen," I say, tryna stuff my carry-on in the overhead compartment. "I didn't think so either. The muhfuckas at the car rental spot was tryna give us a hard time 'bout some scratch that was already on the shit." An impatient attendant sees me strugglin' to get my bag in and comes over to help. She shifts a few things 'round, then gets it in. She slams it shut, walkin' off. *Bitch!* I take my seat and buckle up. Twenty minutes later, we're up in the air. And Mike's already over in the seat on the right of me wit' his head pressed up against the window, snorin'. And Gee's next to me soundin' like a damn grizzly. I elbow him, then reach over and tap Glenn on his arm. "Yo, shake that nigga."

I know if I don't wanna hear that shit the whole flight, no one else does. I put in my earplugs, turn on my iPod, then recline my seat back, closin' my eyes. I don't know when I fell off to sleep, but when I woke up, we were an hour from Newark. I look 'round the cabin. Gee and the rest of them niggas are still knocked out, growlin'. Glenn's mouth is half-open and he is droolin'. I shake my head.

The minute we land, muhfuckas are up scramblin' tryna gather their shit up. Sounds of cell phones and BlackBerrys bein' turned on can be heard, includin' mine. "Yo, ya'll muhfuckas sounded like a pack of hogs," I say over to Glenn.

"Man, listen, I was tired as hell. I can't wait to get home and get up in my bed."

"Yo, dawg, I'm with you on that," Mike says. I glance at my watch, standin' up. It's almost two-thirty in the afternoon.

"Yo, muhfucka, you were over here snorin', too," Gee says, laughin'.

"Fuck outta here. You know damn well that wasn't me. Not the kid."

"Yeah, okay. If you say so."

As soon as the cabin door opens, e'eryone rushes toward the front of the cabin, tryna get the fuck to their next destination. We exit the plane and make our way toward baggage claim. I have my cell up to my ear, listenin' to my four messages. *"Call me. This is Vita."* Delete.

"Hey, sexy. This is Cherry. Hope you had a safe flight back. Can't wait to see you this week. Hit me up when you can." Shit, I forgot I was goin' out there in a few days. Hell, I might as well not even unpack. *Thursday I'll be right back on a plane again.* We stop in front of the restrooms. Gee, Mike and Glenn's asses gotta piss. They ask me to watch their bags. "Yo, I don't know why you muhfuckas didn't piss on the plane." They ig me, walkin' off.

I listen to my third message. *"Alley Cat, what's good, nigga? It's ya girl Electra. Holla back, baby."* And just as I'm deletin' it, Chanel and her peoples come walkin' outta the women's bathroom. I grin. Chanel shakes her head, grabbin' her girl by the arm, yankin' her over toward me. She yanks her arm back.

"Bitch, don't be pullin' on my arm like that."

"Whatever, ho. You need some dick in ya life and this mutha-fucka is fine as hell, so stop frontin'," Chanel says loudly. They step up in my space. "Okay, it's obvious you checkin' for my girl, so what's ya name?"

"Alley Cat," I say, starin' at her peoples. Gotdaaamn, this bitch is fine! Her slanted hazel eyes can hypnotize a muhfucka. I've fucked some bad bitches in my day, but this one right here is in a class all by herself.

"Alley Cat, this is Katrina, Kat for short." She pushes her girl closer toward me. "Kat, Alley Cat. Now ya'll make nice and ex-change numbers. Geesh."

I smile, watchin' her girl walk off. "So, you ready to drop them digits?"

She huffs, pullin' out her iPhone. "Nigga, give me ya damn number." Gee and 'em come walkin' outta the bathroom as she is programmin' my number into her cell. She dials the number, lets it ring, then disconnects the call.

I grin. "So when we goin' out?"

"When you ready to drop some paper on a bitch," she says, switchin' off toward her girl.

"I got you, ma."

She looks over her shoulder, peeps us all startin' at her ass. "And don't be blowin' my shit up either."

I laugh. "I'ma hit you up tonight." She igs me, poppin' her hips.

Mike shakes his head, grabbin' his bag. "I see you finally got her to drop them digits."

"Yeah, man."

"Yo, I'm tellin' you, son. Leave that ho alone. She's fine as fuck. But, man listen, that bitch look like she ain't to be fucked wit'."

"Yeah, and that's the shit that's got my dick hard. I'ma see what's good wit' her ass real soon." Gee finally brings his ass outta the bathroom. "'Bout damn time," I say, handin' him his backpack.

"Yo, I had to take a shit."

I frown. "You sat ya ass down on them nasty toilet seats?"

"Nah, muhfucka, I squatted over it."

"Whatever," I say, walkin' off. By the time we get to baggage claim, our bags are already on the carousel. I snatch mine up, then wait for the rest of 'em to get theirs. We give each other dap, and hugs, then go our separate ways.

I can't even front, a muhfucka's exhausted. The minute I get in the crib, I drop my bags, put my phone on QUIET, then take off my clothes. I grab a sheet and blanket from outta the closet, then stretch the fuck out 'cross the sofa. I close my eyes. And before I know it, I'm knocked the fuck out.

Thursday mornin' I'm speedin' back up the parkway to the airport to catch my eight-thirty flight out to L.A. The last two days I didn't really do too much of nuthin'. I went up the way to check out Pops, and had dinner wit' Moms. Other than that, I basically chilled. Blazed and nutted, that's 'bout it. My cell rings. I glance at the screen. It's Cherry. *Damn, she's up mighty late*, I think, peepin' the time. It's two-thirty in the mornin' there.

"What's good, pretty baby?"

"I was calling to make sure you were up, and on your way to the airport."

"Yeah, I'm on my way there now."

"Good. How's the weather there?"

"It's brick as hell out here," I say, veerin' over to get onto the turnpike. "They talkin' 'bout more snow out this bitch. I'm glad to be gettin' the fuck up outta here."

"Well, it should be nice here today. I think in the upper seventies."

"That's wassup." I stop at the ticket booth, grab my ticket, then speed off. "Yo, I'm seriously thinkin' 'bout stayin' out there 'til this cold-ass weather breaks. I hate this shit."

"Mmmm, I'd love that. You know you can stay here for as long as you like. Hell, you don't ever have to go back. Speaking of which, I was going to wait until you got here to ask, but since we're talking now, I might as well ask you now."

"Wassup?"

"I have to go back out to St. Lucia next week for my brother's wedding, and since you're already going to be out here, I was hoping you'd go with me. It'll be like vacation within a vacation. You'll get to see the beautiful island I was raised on and meet my family, too. It'll be fun."

"Oh, you want me to meet ya peeps? You sure you want that?"

"Of course I do, I wouldn't be asking."

"You not tryna get ya peeps to approve me for marriage, are you?"

"Oh, please. Not hardly. I want you as my date. That's it. And besides, it'll be nice to get fucked deep on the beach. We have a villa down on the beach. You could make love to me under the stars. Fuck me in my ass in the blue water."

"Aaah, shit," I say, laughin'. "Let me find out, you tryna get all romantic on a nigga."

She sucks her teeth. "Will you go?"

I smile, shakin' my head. St. Lucia has always been one of them Caribbean spots I've wanted to check out. Only a muthafuckin' fool would turn down a free trip. "How long you gonna be out there?" A week, she says. "Oh, aiight, no doubt," I tell her, veerin' onto the airport exit ramp. When I get down the ramp, I pay the toll, then follow the signs for the airport toward long-term parkin'.

"Listen, I'm almost at the airport. I'll see you in a few hours, aiight?"

"See you when you get here. I'll pick you up outside of baggage claim."

"Cool." As soon as I disconnect the call, Vita calls. "Yo?"

"Did I catch you at a bad time?"

"I'm on my way to the airport. Wassup?"

"I was hoping you could come down here for a few days."

"Oh, so what you sayin', you still tryna fuck wit' a nigga?"

"I want to see you. I'm still hurt by what happened. But I know I don't want to stop seeing you, either."

This broad! I swear she better be glad I feel sorry for her retarded ass. Otherwise, I'd drag her ass for e'erything she's worth. "Well, check this out, ma. I'm on my way out to L.A. for a few weeks, so I'ma haveta hit you back when I get back to Jersey. I'll let you know then if I'm still interested in givin' you this dick."

"Excuse me?"

"Yo, you heard me. I fucked ya peoples in ya house. Gutted her all up on ya sheets; on the same bed I rocked ya box in, and you still wanna fuck wit' a muhfucka. Baby, that's some sad shit. You a cool chick, Vita, real talk, but you got some self-esteem issues you need to work on. Muhfuckas are gonna always use you and take you for granted 'til you get ya mind right, baby. Real talk. And the only reason I'm kickin' this shit to you is 'cause I really don't wanna see you get hurt. A muhfucka like me will run you ragged, baby, 'cause I know you lonely and weak. You deserve better, so I'm tryna give you the opportunity to bow out gracefully 'fore you end up more fucked up than you already are."

"OhmyGod, I can't believe you."

"Believe it or not, I'm tellin' you some real shit."

"You are so fucking arrogant and selfish!"

"I know," I tell her, pullin' up to the parkin' lot gate. I roll my window down and press the button for my ticket. "It is what it is. I enjoyed fuckin' you, baby. But this dick comes wit' an expiration date on it, and your time for gettin' it is up."

"Fuck you," she snaps. "One day you're gonna fuck over the wrong bitch. And I hope I'm there to see you get everything you got coming."

I drive 'round the parkin' area, tryna find a damn parkin' space. It's packed out this bitch. After drivin' 'round for almost ten minutes, I find a spot. "Well,'til then, I'ma keep fuckin', baby. So whatever happens happens."

"You're such an asshole."

I laugh, grabbin' my shit outta the car, then runnin' over to catch the airport bus. "I know. And I fucked you all up in yours, didn't I?" I hop on, tell the driver which airlines I'm flyin' on, then take a seat in the back. "Do ya'self a favor, boo. Delete my number. And stay far away from any muhfucka who ain't tryna treat you wit' respect, ya heard?"

She sighs. "I guess I should be thanking you. But I'm too mad at you right now."

"No thanks needed, baby. You'll get over it. Would you have rather I lied to you and kept playin' you out?"

"No."

"Aiight then. Take what I'm tellin' you as a gift. The next muhfucka might not be so generous." I end the call. Far as I'm concerned, there's no sense in goin' back 'n forth. I done told her all she needs to know. What she does wit' the shit is up to her. I got bigger and better things to do than to be tryna counsel some lost cause.

The shuttle drops me off in front of Continental. I grab my shit, hop off and head through the glass doors. Forty minutes later I'm boardin' my flight to L.A. I take my seat, and buckle up, then shut down my cell. I'm sittin' here thinkin' L.A. might not be a bad spot to make my winter hangout. I could spend three months away from this cold-ass weather, then come back to Jersey in the spring, and chill 'til the winter comes through again. It'd definitely break up doin' the same ole same ole. Not that I've been lookin', but it'll be nice to have a few West Coast beauties to fuck on those days I'm not beat to fuck wit' Cherry's ass.

LAX Airport, as usual, is busy. I peep a few bitches wit' potential, but don't really put out any energy to speak. Right now my mind's been on that sexy-ass ho Kat. I had her on the brain practically the whole flight out here, imaginin' fuckin' her all night. The shit had my dick hard as concrete. I'ma definitely get at her when I touch Jersey again.

Soon as I get to the baggage claim area to get my bag, my cell rings. PRIVATE NUMBER flashes up on the screen. I shake my head. Muhfuckas crack me the fuck up me wit' blockin' their numbers. My thing is, if you callin' me and you don't want me to know ya number, then you must already be a muhfucka I ain't fuckin' wit' any damn way. So I don't give a fuck 'bout not havin' ya digits. "Yo?"

"You might have gotten off on them charges, but…"

"Oh, so it's you who's been callin' and not sayin' shit on the phone?"

"You don't know that. Maybe it's another fool you fucked over."

I sigh. "Ramona, why the fuck are you callin' me?"

"Because I'm not done with you."

"Well, I'm done wit' you."

"You think you can fuck me, get me knocked up, then dismiss me like I ain't shit, and I'm supposed to go away quietly? Wrong answer. I am about to become your worst fucking nightmare."

"Bitch, you're fuckin' crazy, for real, yo."

She laughs. "That's already been established, nigga. And you fucked over the wrong bitch in the process."

I can't believe this ho is fuckin' threatenin' me, like that's 'posed to mean sumthin' to me. This bitch needs to let the shit go, for real. I hear Moms' voice; *You're playing a very dangerous game messing over these women the way you do...A scorned woman can become a very dangerous woman...It's only a matter of time before you find yourself lying up in a hospital bed...*

"Check this out, you fuckin' nutcase, nobody forced ya dumb ass to do anything you didn't wanna do, so if you feel fucked over, you did it to ya'self. So save all ya theatrics for a muhfucka who gives a fuck. 'Cause, bitch, I don't."

"I swear to fucking God, you won't know when or where, but I promise you—for every woman you've ever fucked over, I'm going to make you pay, if it's the last motherfucking thing I do."

"Yo, that shit you talkin' don't rattle me. Do what you gotta do and stop fuckin' callin' me."

"I hate you!"

I laugh. "*That's* already been established. But you hate ya'self even more. You hate the fact that you miss a muhfucka like me; that you can't let the fuck go, and move on wit' ya miserable-ass life. Yeah, baby, you hate me, aiight..."

"You don't know what the fuck you're talking about. I hate you 'cause your no-good, black ass ain't shit! I hate you 'cause you're a motherfucking user."

"Yeah, whatever you say. Admit it, boo. You hate it even more that a no-good, black ass muhfucka like me shut off ya cock supply; that I dismissed ya ass wit'out blinkin' an eye. Well, guess what? Get the fuck over it. Chalk it up as a lesson learned and move the fuck on."

"Until you've paid for what you've done to me, I'm not moving on."

I sigh. "Yo, do you hear how retarded you sound, right now? What you need to do is look in the muthafuckin' mirror, and deal wit' the *real* problem, baby—you, instead of tryna blame me for ya shit." She starts yappin' off at the mouth 'bout what she's never gonna go through again, 'bout how she's never gonna trust another nigga again, blah, blah, blah. The bitch is doin' all this talkin', but ain't sayin' a muthafuckin' thing that makes sense. I end the call wit' her still flappin' her jaws, shakin' my head. This shit is really gettin' outta hand. I decide to get my number changed the minute I get back to Jersey. I need to shut down all access these nut-ass bitches have to me.

Bitches kill me. Who the fuck they think they foolin'? All that dumb shit most of 'em be poppin' 'bout what they not gonna do for a nigga. That's a buncha bullshit, for real; 'specially when it comes to a muhfucka like me. I know I got good dick. And I know how to use e'ery muthafuckin' inch of it. This long black dick is a ho's blessing and her curse. It's what they all want. It's what they all obsess over. The size of a nigga's dick; how low he's hangin'; how much he's packin'. It's what they crave. And I've seen what a bitch will do to get at it. I've had bitches fall in love wit' this dick; bitches who've stalked this dick; bitches who'd run down their own mamas to taste this dick in the back of their throats. Even when they know the nigga attached to it ain't ever gonna be theirs. Even when they know the muhfucka pipin' out their insides is gonna be the same muhfucka who disses their asses. Yet, they still wanna fuck; still wanna keep gettin' this dick. So you tell me. Who the fuck is the real problem, them or me?

I peep my bag comin' outta the chute, then grab it when it comes down toward me. I head outside. Damn, it's gorgeous out this bitch. I smile, breathin' in all the smog. Bottom line, there's always gonna be a buncha horny-ass bitches out here who wanna fuck, be fucked, and suck down on this nut. I ain't braggin'. I'm keepin' shit real. And the real shit is, there's always gonna be a ho out here who's gonna always keep a nigga like me piped out and laced up. There's always gonna be a buncha lonely, low-self-esteem-havin', lovesick hoes out here who are gonna do whatever they can to have a muhfucka like me in their beds, even if it means they gotta beg, borrow, or steal. Even if it means they gotta keep lookin' in the mirror e'ery damn day, lyin' to themselves that a nigga like me is gonna one day love 'em back.

Like I told ya'll goin' into this shit, fuck wit' a muhfucka like me at ya own risk. I'm ya sweetest most dangerous addiction—that dark, chocolate nigga who's gonna melt in ya mouth and all up in guts. Have you feenin' for ya next taste. I told you if you want it rough, you want it rugged. I'ma slay ya muthafuckin' ass 'til ya shit-hole starts to smoke. No joke. You want it slow, you want it gentle. I'ma rock ya box 'til ya eyes cross, and that's what it is. A muhfucka like me ain't lookin' for love, and I ain't askin' for none in return. There are only two things I seek. The first is pussy, and lots of it—deep, wet and gushy. The second is a long throat: a bitch who knows howta suck, gulp and swallow down a dick. And that's it. All that extra shit, save it for the next muhfucka.

Cherry pulls up to the curb in her Jag. The top's down, and she's lookin' like a million bucks. I toss my bag in the backseat, openin' the door. I get in, then lean in and kiss her on the lips. Slide her some tongue.

"What's good, pretty baby?"

"You," she says, grinnin'. She's wearin' a short denim skirt, showin' her smooth thighs. "It's good to see you."

"It's good seein' you, too. You got on panties?"

"Nope," she says, pullin' off.

I lean over, kissin' her on the neck as I slide my hand between her thighs and start caressin' her clit. She moans. "OhmyGod, you're gonna make me have an accident."

"Relax, baby. I got this. You just keep ya eyes on the road and drive." She relaxes, lets her legs open wider, moanin' as I slip my fingers into her pussy. "Yeah, baby. I'ma get this pussy nice 'n wet."

"Oooh…aaah, shit," she moans, swervin' on the otherside of the highway, "you're gonna make me cum."

"Yeah, baby…nut all over my fingers. You want me to put this hard-ass dick in you."

She swerves again. "Aaah, aaah…yes…"

"What's my name, baby?"

She presses her foot down on the accelerator. She's hittin' ninety. "Aaaaaaah…aaah…I'm cummin'…"

"What's my name?" I ask, pumpin' two fingers into her wetness while usin' my thumb to flick her clit.

She starts to shake, clutchin' the steerin' wheel. She's doin' a hunnid. "Aaaah…Daddy Long Stroke…aaah, shit…I'm cummin'."

She screams and zigzags her whip in and outta traffic as she nuts. I pull out my hand, bring my sticky fingers to my lips, smell her cunt juice, then slip 'em into my mouth. "Damn, baby, you taste good," I say, slurpin' her syrup up. I grab my hard dick. "Fuck! I can't wait to get you back to the crib, so I can beat that ass up wit' this heavy-ass dick."

She smiles, reachin' over and rubbin' my bulge. "And this is exactly what I need, baby."

Yo, ya'll can look at me any kinda way you want. But be clear. Don't hate the player, baby. I didn't make the game. I made the rules, *my* rules. To serve a ho this dick and rock her box 'til she stutters and forgets her name; to run this tongue all up in her pussy and ass 'til she tosses me the keys to her whip, begs me to move in, lines a nigga's pockets wit' paper, and the list goes on— one stroke, one slurp, at a muthafuckin' time. And if a bitch gets all caught up, then that shit's on her; she gets what she gets. But no matter what, I'ma do me. Still fuckin', still nuttin', still makin' the bitches hot and the pussies pop 'cause I'm Daddy Long Stroke, muhfuckas…don't forget it!

ABOUT THE AUTHOR

Cairo is the author of *The Manhandler* and *The Kat Trap*. He resides in New Jersey, where he is working on his next literary creation, *Deep Throat Diva*. His travels to Egypt are what inspired his pen name. You can email him at: cairo2u@verizon.net. Or visit him at www.myspace.com/cairo2u, www.facebook.com/CairoBlack, or www.blackplanet.com/cairo2u

THOUGHT "DADDY LONG STROKE" WAS HOT?
CHECK OUT THIS SNEAK PREVIEW OF

"Deep Throat Diva"

BY CAIRO

COMING MARCH 2011 FROM STREBOR BOOKS

ONE

You ready to cum? Imagine this: A pretty bitch down on her knees with a pair of soft, full lips wrapped around the head of your dick. A hot, wet tongue twirling all over it, then gliding up and down your shaft, wetting that joint up real slippery-like, then lapping at your balls; lightly licking your asshole. Mmmm, I'm using my tongue in places that will get you dizzy, urging you to give me your hot, creamy, nut. Mmmmm, baby…you think you ready? If so, sit back, lie back, relax and let the Deep Throat Diva rock your cock, gargle your balls, and suck you straight to heaven.

I reread the ad, make sure it conveys exactly what I want, need, it to say, then press the PUBLISH tab. "There," I say aloud, glancing around my bedroom, then looking down at my left hand. "Let's see how many responses I get, this time."

Ummm, wait…before I say anything else. I already know some of you uptight bitches are already shaking your heads and rolling your eyes. So I know that what I'm about to tell ya'll is going to make some of you disgusted, and that's fine by me. It is what it is. And I know there's also going to be a bunch of you closeted, freaky bitches who are going to turn your noses up and twist up your lips, but secretly race to get home 'cause you just as nasty as I am. Hell, some of you are probably down on your knees as I speak, or maybe finishing up pulling a dick from out of your throats, or removing strands of pubic hair from in between your teeth. And that's fine by me as well. Do you, boo. But, let me say this: Don't any of you self-righteous hoes judge me.

So here goes. See. I have a man—dark chocolate, dreamy-eyed, sculpted and every woman's dream—who's been in incarcerated for four years, and he's releasing from prison in less than nine months. And, *yes*, I'm excited and nervous and almost scared to death—you'll know why in a minute. Annnywaaaay, not only is he a sexy-ass motherfucker, he knows how to grind, and stack paper. And he is a splendid lover. My God! His dick and tongue game can make a woman forget her name. And all the chicks who know him either want him, or want him back. And they'll do anything they can to try to disrupt my flow. Hating-ass hoes!

Nevertheless, he's coming home to *me*. The collect calls, the long drives, the endless nights of sexless sleep have taken a toll on me, and will all be over very soon. Between the letters, visits and keeping money on his books, I've been holding him down, faithfully. And I've kept my promise to him to not fuck any other niggas. I've kept this pussy tight for him. And it's been hard, *really* hard—no, no, hard isn't an accurate description of the agony I've had to bear not being fucked for over four years. It's been excruciating!

But I love Jasper, so I've made the sacrifice. For him, for us!

Still, I have missed him immensely. And I need him so bad. My pussy needs him, aches for the width of his nine-inch, veiny dick thrusting in and out of it. It misses the long, deep strokes of his thick tongue caressing my clit and its lower lips. I miss lying in his arms, of being held and caressed. But I have held out; denied any other niggas the privilege—*and* pleasure—of fucking this sweet, wet hole.

The problem is: Though I haven't been riding down on anything stiff, I've been doing a little anonymous dick sucking on the side from time-to-time—and, every now and then, getting my pussy ate—to take the edge off. Okay, okay, I'm lying. I've been sucking a lot of dick. But it wasn't supposed to be this way. I wasn't supposed to become hooked on the shit as if it were crack. But, I have. And I am.

Truth be told. It started out as inquisitiveness. I was bored. I was lonely. I was fucking horny. And tired of sucking and fucking dildos, pretending they were Jasper's dick. So I went on Nastyfreaks4u.com, a new website that's been around for about two years or so. About a year ago, I had overheard one of the regulars who gets her hair done down at my salon talking about a site where men and women post amateur sex videos, similar to that on Xtube, and also place sex ads. So out of curiosity, I went onto their site, browsed around on it for almost a week before deciding to become a member and place my very own personal ad. I honestly wasn't expecting anything to come of it. And a part of me had hoped nothing would. But, lo and behold, my email became flooded with requests. And I responded back. I told myself that I'd do it one time, only. But once turned into twice, then twice became three more times, and now—a year-and-a-half later, I'm logged on *again*—still telling myself that *this* time will be the last time.

I stare at my ring finger. Take in the sparkling four-carat

engagement ring. It's a nagging reminder of what I have; of what I could potentially end up losing. My reputation for one—as a successful, no-nonsense hairstylist and business owner of one the most upscale hair salons in the tri-state area; winner of two Bronner Brothers hair show competitions; numerous features in *Hype Hair* magazine, one of the leading hairstyle magazines for African-American women; and winner of the 2008 Global Salon Business Award, a prestigious award presented every two years to recognize excellence in the industry—could be tarnished. Everything I've worked so hard to achieve could be ruined in the blink of an eye.

My man, for another, could…will, walk out of my life. After he beats my ass, or worse—kills me. And I wouldn't blame him, not one damn bit. I know better than anyone that as passionate a lover Jasper is, he can be just as ruthless if crossed. He has no problem punching a nigga's lights out, smacking up a chick—or breaking her jaw, so I already know what the outcome will be if he ever finds out about my indiscretions. Yet I still choose to dance with deception, regardless of the outcome.

As hypocritical and deceitful as I've been, I can't ever forget it was Jasper who helped me get to where I am today. He's been the biggest part of my success, and I love him for that. Nappy No More wouldn't exist if it weren't for him believing in me, in my visions, and investing thousands of dollars into my salon eight years ago. Granted, I've paid him back and then some. And, yes, it's true. I put up with all the shit that comes with loving a man who's been caught up in the game. From his hustling and incarcerations to his fucking around on me in the early part of our relationship, I stood by him; loved him, no matter what. And I know more than anyone else that I've benefited from it. So as far as I'm concerned, I believe I owe him. He's put all of his trust in me, has given me his heart, and has always been damn good to me. And, yes, *this* is how I've been showing my gratitude—by creeping on the internet.

He won't find out, I think, sighing as I remove my diamond ring from my hand, placing it in my jewelry case, then locking it in the safe with the rest of my valuables. Jasper had given me this engagement ring and proposed to me a month before he got sentenced while he was still out on bail. He wanted me to marry him before he got locked up, but I wanted to wait until he got released. Having a half-assed wedding was not an option. But, they'll be no wedding if I don't get my mind right and stop this shit, soon! *I'll stop all this craziness once he gets home.* This is what I tell myself; this is what I want to believe.

How many dicks have I sucked over the last year? Ummm, honestly, I wish I could tell you. Truth is I try not to give it much thought. Thinking about it would make me feel guiltier than I already do. Every time I walk back up in this spot and crawl back up into bed with thoughts of Jasper, every time he calls me and tells me how much he misses me and loves me and can't wait to get home to me, every time I sit in front of him at a visit, or when he looks into my eyes and he kisses me—it fucks with me. It eats away at my conscience. But, is it enough to make me stop? It should be. I swear I had hoped, wished, it would be. But it hasn't. Something keeps luring me right back on my knees sucking down another nigga's dick.

I sigh, remembering a time when I used to be so obsessed with being a good dick sucker that I used to practice sucking on a dildo. I had bought myself a nice black, seven-inch dildo at an adult bookstore when I was barely twenty. At first, it was a little uncomfortable. My eyes would water and I'd gag as the head hit the back of my throat. But, I didn't give up. I was determined to become a dick-swallowing pro. Diligently, I kept practicing every night before I went to bed until I was finally able to deep throat that rubber cock balls deep. Then I purchased an eight-inch, and practiced religiously until I was able to swallow it too. Before long, I was able to move up to a nine inch, then ten. And once I had them mastered, it was then, that I knew for certain I was ready to move on to the real thing. And I've been sucking dick ever since.

Funny thing, I've always prided myself on being a phenomenal head giver; on knowing how to take care of a man's dick—to not only suck it, but to make love to it. To slob it because I love it; because I adore it. There's something about slobbering all over a dick, twirling my tongue all over it—its slit slick with sweet precum, gliding my lips and mouth up and down its length, engulfing it—that makes my pussy wet.

The only difference is, back then I only sucked my boyfriends, men I loved; men who I wanted to be with. But now…now, I'm sucking a bunch of faceless, nameless men; men who I care nothing about. Men I have no emotional connection to. And that within itself makes what I'm doing that more dirty. I know this. Still—as filthy and as raunchy and trifling as it is, it excites me. It entices me. And it keeps me wanting more.

As crazy as this will sound, when I'm down on my knees, or leaned over in a nigga's lap with a mouthful of dick while he's driving—it's not him I'm sucking, it's not his balls I'm wetting. It's Jasper's dick. It's Jasper's balls. It's Jasper's moans I hear. It's Jasper's hands I feel wrapped in my hair, holding the back of my neck. It's Jasper stretching my neck. Not any other nigga. I close my eyes, and pretend. I make believe them other niggas don't exist.

The *dinging* alerts me I have new Yahoo messages. I sit back in front of my screen, take a deep breath. Eight emails. I click on the first one:

Great ad! Good looking married man here: 42, 5'9", 7 cut, medium thick. Looking for a discreet, kinky woman who likes to eat and play with nice, big sweaty balls, lick in my musty crotch, and chew on my foreskin while I kick back. Can't host.

I frown, disgusted. *What the fuck?!* I think, clicking DELETE.

I go onto the second email:

Hey baby, looking for a generous woman who likes to suck and get fucked in the back of her throat. I'm seven-inches cut, and I like the feel of a tight-ass throat gripping my dick when I nut. I'm 5'9, about 168lbs, average build, dark-skinned. I'm a dominate brotha so I would like to meet a submissive woman. I'm disease free and HIV negative. Hope you are, too. Hit me back.

Generous? Submissive? "Nigga, puhleeze," I sigh aloud, rolling my eyes. *Delete.*

I open the next three, and want to vomit. They are mostly crude, or ridiculous; particularly this one:

Hi. I'm a clean, cool, horny, married Italian guy. I'm also well hung 'n thick. I'd love to put on my wife's g-string, maybe even her thigh-highs, and let you suck me off through her panties, then pull out my thick, hot cock and give me good oral. I'm 6'2", 180lbs, good shape. Don't worry. I'm a straight man, but behind closed doors I love wearing my wife's panties and getting oral. I hope this interests you.

I suck my teeth. "No motherfucker, it doesn't!" *Delete.* What the fuck I look like sucking a nigga who wears woman's panties? *Straight man, my ass!* Bitch, *you a Miss Honey!* I think, opening up the sixth email.

Yo, lookin' for a bitch who enjoys suckin' all kinds of cock. Hood nigga here, lookin' to tear a throat up. Not beat to hear whinin' 'bout achin' jaws and not wantin' a muhfucka to nut in her mouth. I'm lookin' to unzip, fuck a throat, then nut 'n bounce. If u wit' it, holla back. Delete.

Ugh! The one downside of putting out sex ads on the internet, you never know what you're going to get. It's hit or miss. Sometimes you luck up and get exactly what you're looking for. But most times you get shit even a dog wouldn't want. Truth be told, there's a bunch of nasty-ass kooks online. And judging by these emails, I'm already convinced tonight's going to be a bust. Try to convince myself that it's a sign that it's not meant to be, not tonight anyway; maybe not ever again.

Then again, who am I fooling? I am a dick-sucking, freaky-ass bitch. Dick sucking has become my weakness. Long dick, short dick, it makes me no never mind. As long as it's thick, and cut, and loaded with warm, gooey cream, I want it. I crave it. I love swallowing hot cum and licking a dick clean. And the fucked up thing is that as hard as I have tried to get my urges under control, there are times when it overwhelms me, when it creeps up on me and lures me into its clutches and I have to sneak out and make a cock run.

My computer *dings* again. I have three new emails. My mind tells me to delete them without opening them; to log off and shut down my PC. But, of course, I don't. I open the first email:

5'11", 255lbs, trim beard, stache, stocky build, moderately hairy, and aggressive. Always in need to have my dick sucked to the extreme! I love a woman who is into my cum. Show it to me in your mouth and all over your tongue, then go back down on my dick and try to suck out another load.

That's right up my alley, I think, deleting the note, *but not with you. Your ass is too damn fat!* I move onto the next email:

6'3", 190lbs, 6"cut. Black hair, brown eyes. Here's a pic of my dick. If you like, hit me back. Before I even open his attachment, I'm already shaking my head, thinking, "no thank you" because of his stats. Don't get me wrong. I'm by no means a size whore, but let's face it…a nigga standing at six-three with only a six-inch dick. Hmmph. He better have a ripped body, a thick dick, and be extra damn fine! I click on the attachment, anyway. When it opens, I blink, blink again. Bring my face closer to the screen and squint. I sigh. His dick is as thin as a No. 2 pencil. Poor thing! I feel myself getting depressed for him. *Delete!* I click on the third email:

Do u really suck a good dick? If so, come over and wrap your lips around my 8 inch dick until I bust off on your face or down in your throat. 29, 6'1, decent build here. Horny as fuck for some mind blowing head.

I smile. Maybe there's hope after all, I think, responding back. I type: *No, baby, I'm not a good dick sucker. I'm a great one! Send me a pic of your body and dick so that I know your stats are what you say they are. And if I like what I see, maybe you can find out for yourself.* Two minutes later, he replies back with an attachment. I open it, letting out a sigh of relief as I type. *Beautiful cock! Now when, where, and how can I get at it?*

I know, I know, aside from being risky and dangerous, I am aware that what I am doing is dead wrong. No, it's fucked up! However, I can't help myself. Okay, damn…maybe I can. But the selfish bitch in me doesn't want to. I mean I do try. I'll go two or three days, even a week—sometimes, two—and I'll think I'm good; that I've kicked this nasty habit. But, then, it's like something comes over me. It's like the minute the clock strikes midnight— the bewitching hour, I become possessed. I turn into a filthy cumslut. In a local park, dark alley, parking lot, public restroom, deserted street in the back of a truck—I want to drop down low and lick, taste, swallow, a thick, creamy nut. Either sucked out or jacked out; drink it from a used condom or a shot glass—I want it to coat my tonsils, and slide down into my throat. Not that I've gone to those extremes. Well, not to *all* those extras. But, I've come close enough.

And tonight is no different. Here it is almost one A.M. and I should have my ass in bed. Instead, once again, I'm looking to give some good-ass, sloppy, wet head; lick and suck on some balls; deep throat some dick, gag on it. And maybe swallow a nut. Yes, tonight I'm looking for someone who knows how to throat fuck a greedy, dick-sucking bitch like me. I'm looking for someone who knows how to fuck my mouth as if they were fucking my pussy, deep-stroking that pipe down into my gullet until my eyes start to water.

See. Being a seasoned dick sucker, I can swallow any length or width without gagging, or puking. I relax, breathe through my nose, extend my tongue all the way out, then swallow one inch at a time until I have the dick all the way down in my throat. Then I start swallowing while it to give a nigga a nice, slow dick massage. The shit is bananas! And it drives a nigga crazy.

Ding! He replies back: *You can get this cock, now! No games, no BS, just a hot nut going down in your throat. I'm at the Sheraton in Edison. Room 238.*

I respond, practically drooling: *I'm on my way. Be there in 30 mins.*

I get up from my computer desk, slip out of my silk robe, tossing it over onto my American Drew California-king sleigh bed. Standing naked in front of my full-length mirror, I like...no, love, what I see: full, luscious lips; perky, C-cup tits; small, tight waist; firm, plump ass; and smooth, shapely legs. I slip into a hot pink Juicy Couture tracksuit, then grab my black and pink Air Max's. I pin my hair up, before placing a black Juicy fitted on my head, pulling it down over my face and flipping up the hood of my jacket. I grab my bag and keys, then head down the stairs and out the door to suck down on some cock. I glance at my watch. Its 2:24 A.M. *Hope this nigga's dick is worth the trip.*